Foreplay on WORDS

E.L. KOSLO

Proofing: Brittni Van - The Romance Doctor – @the_romance_doc
Cover: Designed by E.L. Koslo
Depositphotos: marzacz, Forewer, qerest, Kwangmoo, Sanychs, antart

Envato Elements licensed fonts: Barcelony and Baskerville BT
Interior Formatting: E.L. Koslo
Artwork by @irdeinfierno
Depositphotos: huhulin, floral_set, sanneberg
Shutterstock: Serg Zastavkin

Table of Contents

Spice Index

CHAPTERS THAT TURN UP THE HEAT

Dedication

This book is dedicated to all the readers who encouraged me to embrace the characters who live inside my head and finally share them with the world.
.
It means more than you know that all of you have stuck with me on the wild ride this series has been on.
.
You are the Chase to my Evan.

All content warnings are on my website at ELKoslo.com/words-series

Chase Rodgers

OCCUPATION: ROMANCE NOVELIST

PEN NAME:

Chastity Rose

ONE

CHASE

BOSTON

My eyes were unfocused as I stared at the edge of the desk in front of me, still trying to process exactly what was being asked of me. I'd heard Isobel's request, but there was no way I interpreted it correctly. I had a deadline. There was no way she was asking me to do her a favor of this magnitude when the clock was already counting down.

While my life may have looked chaotic from the outside, I dropped into focus mode with blinders on once that release date was set and preorders were scheduled. I became the characters—ate, slept, and breathed their journey—until the last two magical words were typed into the first draft.

I didn't have time for a special assignment. I certainly didn't have time to understand the motivations of characters that weren't mine. An author's methods were sacred, and I wasn't keen on sharing mine with someone who couldn't get their novel on track.

"Oh, come on. You can't expect me to hold some rookie writer's hand," I complained as I sat stiffly in the chair across from my editor in her office at the Boston offices for my publisher.

We'd worked together for the past several years, having met shortly after I'd signed with my current publisher.

"I can, and I do."

"No. Not happening. I don't have time to walk some amateur through developing a sex scene," I adamantly refused.

With one perfectly groomed, arched eyebrow in response, I knew I was fighting a losing battle. "He's not an amateur. He's already published quite a bit, actually." The way she said it piqued my interest, but I remained skeptical of being roped into a project when I didn't have extra time to spare.

"Then what do you need me for?" The first book in my newest series was already in motion, and I didn't have time to take on some charity case for Isobel, no matter how much I enjoyed our working relationship.

"You're our highest-grossing romance novelist right now."

"And?" I'd worked my ass off to get where I was, and I wasn't derailing my career for someone I didn't even know. Her words weren't meant to inflate my ego, they were facts. It still didn't work to convince me of my value in this situation. I was a novelist, not a writing consultant. There were dozens of people in this building with advanced degrees in English that would be a million times more suited to doing something like this.

"He's currently got two books on the Times bestseller list." My eyes narrowed at her smirk, and I suddenly felt myself sit up straight in my chair. Exactly who did she want me to work with?

"Cut the shit, Is. Why do you need me to hold this guy's hand?" I was irritated, but had to admit the idea sounded intriguing with her last tidbit of information. This wasn't some rookie writer; this was a pro. I'd yet to clear the top 1000. So how did I fit into this equation?

"He's having some trouble with character development in his new novel." The nonchalance in her shoulder shrug kept her body language casual, yet her voice had an edge. She needed me on board with this.

"I have a deadline. I don't have time for this. Can't you throw a junior editor at him?"

"The higher-ups were thinking more about collaboration," she responded casually, as if she hadn't just told me I not only had to work with this guy, but I also had to share the credit when he was the one who needed me.

Oh, hell no. I was not tying my brand to some other author and then practically writing their book for them. I was halfway through book one on a three-book contract and still needed to do some research to flesh out the male lead. I'd gotten more comfortable writing from the male perspective in my career, but I always wanted to ensure it didn't come off as forced or too over the top.

"He could probably help you with your book," Isobel hinted, as she gave me an imploring look.

My hackles rose as I clenched my fists. "I don't need help. I need my editor to not drop a babysitting gig in my lap right now."

"I promise you'll like this one," she smirked as she tossed a hardback book across her desk and pulled open the cover to show me the inside of the book jacket. "Meet Evan—"

"You mean Stone Evans? What does a mystery writer's new book have to do with this conversation?" I interrupted.

"God, Chase," she sighed loudly, "quit being a royal pain in my ass and let me get through a sentence."

"Go on." I motioned as I slumped in my chair and crossed my arms.

"Stone Evans is a pen name. His real name is Evan Stineman," she explained as I continued to look at the black-and-white picture. "He's writing a new thriller, and one of the main characters is a call girl."

"I do NOT write porn," I stressed as I stared at her, unimpressed.

Isobel smirked at me from across the desk. "You write erotic fiction."

"There is a difference between a book with a romantic plot leaning heavily toward the spicy side and writing about a prostitute."

"Is there?" she asked, clearly amused. "Is there really?"

"I'm leaving," I huffed as she burst into laughter and threw a pen at me. I'd dealt with a lot of bullshit stereotypes in my day and thought she had more tact than this. The quickest way to get under a romance novelist's skin was to demean their work as something tawdry.

"Sit down. You know I'm just joking."

"Why me?" I failed to keep the whine out of my voice as she laughed. "It's not like pretty boy Evan needs help reeling in the chicks. I'm sure he could find a lady of the night to help him with his *research*."

"He is pretty, but..." she trailed off, clenching her teeth.

"Oooh, is he gay? I mean, that's totally cool and would explain why he's having trouble if he doesn't understand lady parts—"

"No!" she practically shouted at me from across the desk. "For the love of God, Chase, stop talking."

"But how...?"

"He doesn't get out much."

"What does that mean?" This was starting to sound suspicious again. Even with the black-and-white photo, it was clear that Evan had piercing, light-colored eyes framed by long dark lashes and a chiseled jawline dusted with a light layer of facial hair. If I ran into him on the street, I'd do a double-take at that face.

"He doesn't have contractual appearances. I don't think he really dates either," she said casually, avoiding eye contact. She was keeping something from me.

"Is he a..." I leaned in close, making sure no one would overhear me if they walked by, and whispered to her across the desk. "Virgin?"

Isobel lost it again and slapped her hand down, inadvertently pushing Evan's book off the edge of her desk. I caught it before it hit the floor and propped it up on my lap to study his picture again.

"I don't think he is, but maybe."

"How old is he?"

"Twenty-seven," she replied. So only a few years younger than my thirty-one. At least he wasn't too much younger. I think I'd feel dirty consulting with him otherwise.

"There's no way. But he's so..."

"So..." she coaxed with a curious smile.

"Cute?" Her smile grew as my voice rose. He was more than cute; I think we both knew that, but I wasn't going to tell her anything about the visceral reaction I had to simply seeing his picture.

"So, you'll meet him?" she asked, glancing down at her phone on the desk.

"Why are you so desperate for this?" I was wondering how Isobel had gotten dragged into this too. I knew Evan wasn't one of her authors, so there had to be a reason besides my acumen for romance that was drawing the both of us into this project.

"His new series is assigned to Adrian. He sent me some pages. It's..."

Being one of Adrian's authors was explanation enough. "The scenes are too rough?" I filled in when she didn't finish her thoughts right away. Most men who didn't know how to write a passionate scene used aggressive male archetypes to make it seem sexier.

As a romance novelist who'd written hundreds of drafts of sex scenes over the last ten years, it physically hurt to read male writers who forced sex scenes. Unless you were into specific kinds of dark romance, consent was sexy to the reader.

"Not exactly. More like too awkward." She handed me a page from a manuscript. As I scanned the dialogue and the interaction between the two characters, I had difficulty believing a bestselling author had written this. It was choppy and the actions didn't flow. I felt myself cringing more than getting turned on.

"Is he in a slump? Surely his books have had sex scenes in them before." Suspense writers often had tumultuous affairs between characters to build up some relationships in their plots.

"Not really. He's always written very well-researched mystery novels. The plots haven't lent to romantic storylines."

"None? Not even a hot scene with the protagonist nailing someone out of frustration or because they were in danger?" That seemed to be popular in more than one mystery or suspense book. *When in danger, fuck a stranger.*

She shook her head, and I was a little taken aback. Sex was a prerequisite in my genre, but others drew on sexual encounters, too. There was a reason the phrase "sex sells" existed.

"What exactly am I supposed to be helping him with? Surely Adrian can give him some pointers on structure and flow."

"He needs someone who's used to writing something more graphic that draws the reader in," she explained. "The plot is there, but he needs help getting the passion on paper. And we know if Adrian handled the rewrites, the character's voice wouldn't resonate the same way."

"Does he know you're pulling in a consultant on his book?" I didn't want to be put into an awkward situation if I wasn't wanted. "Isn't he going to be pissed at Adrian?" Everyone was pissed at Adrian at one point or another...but still.

"He does." She nodded with a sly grin. "He asked for you."

"Adrian asked for me?" He was another editor in the publishing house's mystery/action/suspense/thriller (MAST) department. He was not a fan of mine, but he did have a huge crush on Isobel.

"No," her smile grew. "Evan asked for you."

"Me?" I clarified, confused. "Has he even read my work?"

"He has. Adrian said he wasn't willing to meet with anyone else."

"Have I met him before? You'd think I'd remember that face, but I know sometimes the book jacket doesn't match up to the person."

Even in black and white, I could see how his light eyes sparkled with hidden mystery. It seemed fitting that the mystery writer would have an allure to his appearance. His hair was curled slightly, and he had an open expression that wasn't quite a smile. He was an incredibly attractive man, but there was something more...

"He doesn't do industry events."

"Writer's conferences?" I had no idea how he would know who I was if we didn't run in the same circles. Being the talent for the same publisher didn't mean that authors knew one another. Sometimes there were hundreds of authors simply in your genre.

"Nope."

"And you're sure he requested me?" I repeated, a little baffled.

"Positive."

Something wasn't adding up. Why would a successful mystery novelist be familiar with my work? I didn't always read in the genre I wrote, but if he was a spice-writing virgin, chances were he hadn't read any of my open-door romances.

"Evan wants to meet you the day after tomorrow. He's got some specific scenes drafted he wants you to work with him on," she told me, easily dropping back into business mode while I tried to figure this situation out.

"So, coffee shop? Park? Where does he write?" I liked to sit in a quiet corner of the library or a park if the weather was nice.

"Well..."

"Spit it out, Is," I urged.

"He needs you to come to his house." It seemed like a simple enough request, but the way she said it made it sound like it wasn't something I would readily agree to.

"And that's bad?"

She sighed as she avoided eye contact. "Not exactly, no."

"Is there something wrong with his house? What neighborhood does he live in?"

She opened her mouth to respond, but her eyes widened as she glanced over my shoulder toward her door.

"Hey, Is?"

I turned my head as a knock sounded, and Adrian stepped into the doorway. I would have thought he was handsome if I didn't know what an egotistical jerk he was. His athletic frame filled the space inside the doorway, with broad shoulders and an impeccably fitted suit clinging to the obvious muscles in his arms.

"Yes?" she responded, and I glanced between them. There was always tension in the air whenever they were in the same room. Part of me knew my imagination liked to create romantic scenarios where they didn't exist, but the looks Adrian sent Isobel's way weren't subtle.

"Oh, hey, Chase. Did Is talk to you about the consult..." he started to ask as he stepped into her office and sat in the chair next to mine.

He was classically handsome—tall, full head of slightly wavy dark hair and gorgeous dark blue eyes—it was a shame he was such an asshat. Isobel said it was a trait only I seemed to bring out in him, but I was skeptical. He seemed to hate most romance writers based on genre alone.

"Evan? Yes." I nodded as he straightened and turned to face me.

"And?"

"Well, she said—" Isobel interrupted. I held up my hand to cut her off and turned back to Adrian.

"She said, what is the benefit of doing this favor for your author?"

"You really need to ask that?" he asked, looking at me like I was crazy. "You'd be getting byline credit for consulting on a Stone Evans book. He blows his nose, and it hits the Times list."

"I'm not exactly struggling to get my name out there." I bristled at his tone, arching an eyebrow in his direction. He didn't need to know I'd already agreed to hold Evan's hand.

"Yeah, but your demographic is slightly different than his," he laughed. *Jackass*.

"What's that supposed to mean?" Isobel inquired as she shot daggers at him with her narrowed eyes.

"Um." He cleared his throat, and his cheeks colored as he looked at her. "Just that the female nineteen to thirty-five demo is a little bit less selective than the twenty to sixty, male-female that Evan pulls in. His draw is bigger."

"It may be a larger pool to pull readers from, but there are a lot of female readers ages nineteen to fifty-five. I don't only pull the NA demo."

"I know you don't, but his books have a wider reach. This collaboration could be good for you. Get your name out there to a new potential audience." The arrogance was back in his voice. Now I was starting to second guess my decision because it meant working indirectly with Adrian.

"Because I obviously have an issue with my hundreds of thousands of readers."

This was why I didn't get along with Adrian. He was a literary snob. He had his head so far up the asses of his writers that he couldn't see romance as a legitimate genre. It didn't escape me that most of his MAST writers were male. All waving their tiny dicks around. He saw me as some vapid bodice-ripper-writing airhead.

"Okay, kids, simmer down," Isobel interjected. I think she could tell I was about to lay into him. "Chase already agreed to meet your precious Evan. She only needs an address."

Our banter always amused Isobel. She thought it was hilarious that I could so easily wind Adrian up with a few well-placed barbs. It took all my self-control not to reveal that he could do the same to me.

"Oh, she did?" he asked, studying me with a knowing smile. He knew I could never say no to Isobel, no matter how much I despised her ability to get me to bend to her will. I was good at writing sex scenes; she was good at subtly manipulating all the little pawns in her life. Adrian and I were merely pieces on a chessboard to her.

"Don't look so smug. Someone needs to throw that poor kid a bone. Those pages were just awful," I replied with faux sympathy.

"Hey, he's got more bestselling books under his belt than you have notches on your bedpost."

"Hey! Break it up before I get the hose." Isobel's voice rose, and we both looked in her direction. "Chase, stop riling him up." She pointed a finger at him with a raised eyebrow. He'd gone too far this time.

"Adrian quit slut-shaming and get out of my office before I stab you with my letter opener," she picked up said letter opener and replaced her finger with her little metallic weapon. "1950 called, they want their misogynistic bullshit back. This isn't an episode of *Mad Men*."

The laughter burst out of me as he turned to her with a look of shock mixed with what I was sure was arousal. Gross.

"You need us. Don't be a dick. Email Chase the address and a time, and she'll be there."

Adrian let himself out of the office quietly, and I turned back toward Isobel before she could avoid my question again.

"So, what is so bad about Evan's house?"

"It's not the house that's the problem." She laughed at the face I made because I still didn't get the joke. "It's the fact that he rarely leaves it."

"Ever?"

"Pretty much." She couldn't hide the cringe, and I felt a stab of apprehension climb up my spine.

Shit. What did I get myself into?

Evan Stineman

OCCUPATION: MYSTERY NOVELIST

PEN NAME:
Stone Evans

TWO

EVAN

CONNECTICUT

"WHY AM I SO terrible at this?" I growled as I pushed my laptop off my legs and onto the cushion next to me.

Swinging them off the side of the couch, I leaned forward with my elbows on my knees, scrubbing my hands across my face.

I was stuck. Writer's block had never been an issue for me before. The words had always appeared. Half the time, I didn't consciously formulate the plot in my head; it simply flowed onto the paper. My editor, Adrian, called me his ringer. Whenever he had trouble with another author, he relied on me to knock one out of the park.

"Speak of the devil," I muttered as my phone buzzed on the coffee table.

He was hounding me for pages. I had the whole book drafted—I knew it needed work, but he'd basically told me that my sex scenes were shit. And for once in his life, Adrian was right.

"Yes?" I swiped the screen to connect the call as my eyelids drifted closed.

"Any word on when you'll have new pages in my inbox?"

"I'm working on it," I sighed, glaring at the laptop beside me.

"So, you're still hung up on the first edits I sent you?"

"No," I lied.

Yes. How could I not be? The last time we'd spoken, he'd basically insinuated I needed to get laid to finish my book.

"Man, you gotta snap out of this. I get that you're not a fan of people, but you're a good-lookin' guy," Adrian coaxed.

Oh shit, not this again.

"If you need a wingman, I can drive out this weekend," he laughed. "We can stop at that little pub down the road from your house, talk to some ladies...or guys, whatever gets the creative juices flowing."

The thought of going in there made my palms sweat. There was a reason I lived in a small town in rural Connecticut. No crowds, no subways or trains, no people if I didn't want to see them. I needed to derail this train of thought. I preferred my privacy and could only take so much of Adrian's bravado in person.

"I'm in the research phase. I've got it handled."

Literally. With my hand.

I may have had a slew of incognito tabs open on my tablet with Redtube videos I'd marked for reference. I kept telling myself it was *research*, but it didn't seem to be doing anything other than making my wrist hurt.

"So, Sloane floated an idea by me—it's not bad, but you might not be a fan," he said evenly. She was the head of publishing, so I was in deep shit if she was involved.

Missing your initial deadline was such a headache. The editors were on your ass, and their bosses were on their asses. It was a giant clusterfuck.

My outline and chapters were way ahead of schedule, but they wanted a polished excerpt to put in the next run of my last book. I was the dumbass who decided to use a prostitute as the main character. Of course, I couldn't avoid using the trappings of literary sex. It sold—it sold big—and I had avoided anything sexually graphic in my last eight books.

Fade to black in a mystery novel wasn't uncommon, and often readers were there for the plot and not the word porn. But there hadn't been anything fade to black in my previous books, thus my total inexperience in writing a sex scene.

"Our portfolio also includes some pretty solid romance writers. We thought with help you could push through this."

"You think I need a writing consultant?"

Fuck, it was worse than I thought.

"You'd benefit from someone to bounce ideas off of, work with on structure and flow," he explained.

"I'm not letting a ghostwriter take over my book," I told him. I'd worked too hard to let someone come in and rewrite everything.

"She won't. She'll be there to point you in the right direction."

"Do you have someone in mind?" I still didn't trust his judgment, but I'd run out of options.

"We have a few candidates. I overnighted a box. I know you like to flag references, so I thought hard copies might be easier."

"You sent me a box of erotic novels?" I asked dryly.

"They're not all erotic—okay, some of them are. But it'll give you an idea of the material they write."

"What if I don't like any of them?" I hadn't had time to read for recreation in years. I wasn't sure I had the attention span to sit through a whole box of books. I always had too many characters itching to get written to focus on reading.

"Those chapters need total rewrites. You need help or to get some hands-on experience to draw from," he huffed. I knew I was becoming a source of frustration for him.

"I'm not going to go have rough sex with a random stranger."

His deep laugh resonated through the speaker, and I was so glad he got amusement out of my situation. "Any sex with a stranger would probably help."

"Dick," I muttered.

"Yes, you supposedly have one. Go use it," he laughed.

"How you are considered a grown professional is beyond me."

"You love me," he teased.

"No, I really don't."

"The package will be there later today. Put down the laptop and get reading. I need a name sooner rather than later."

"Fine," I sighed heavily.

"Good."

"I'm hanging up on you now," I threatened as my finger hovered over my phone screen.

"Have fun with your research!"

I pressed the little red button and pushed my phone across the table, eying the tablet next to it. A distraction was needed until the UPS man came in a few hours. That box was like an ax hanging over my head. I did not want help with this, but I obviously needed it. It had been a while, but it's not like I was totally inexperienced. I had girlfriends in high school and college. And after... But trying to derive anything sexy from my last relationship would bring back too much trauma I'd tried to forget.

Although my younger self had been more confident and self-assured—with the help of alcohol. Before I second-guessed every other word out of my mouth.

On paper was easier than interacting with people. I could let my fingers fly, and eloquent words would fill the paper—or the screen. The things that came out of my mouth, not so much. I could be charming on paper when I was pretending to be someone else.

Switching out of incognito mode, I opened a new Chrome tab on my tablet to attempt to guess which authors he'd be sending me books from.

Vivid Publishing's website had author bios listed by genre in a very easily accessible format. I clicked on the romance link and was overwhelmed by the listing of authors. There were a lot of them who wrote under pen names.

I had my own, but the romance writers had some flowery ones. One caught my eye, although it wasn't so much the name as the picture thumbnail beside it.

Now I was aware of the makeup artists, stylists, and flattering lighting that went into taking a photo for a book jacket, but she was stunning. Chastity Rose. Hmm. The thoughts her image inspired were anything but chaste. The smirk on her full lips and the subtly concealed curves drew me in, and I knew I needed to investigate this reaction to her. For all I knew, she could be a horrible writer with a pretty face.

I tapped the link to see her books, and heat surged through me as the thumbnails of her book covers popped up.

'Candace was still reeling from her divorce when her friends signed her up for an online dating website. Will young Marc help her get back out there?'

Looks like it from the cover. It showed a barely clothed, very muscular man embracing a woman who looked like she was in her forties. Damn.

'Retired rodeo cowboy Luke settles down on a dude ranch as a horse trainer to escape after a devastating injury. Will the ranch owner's daughter help him with his recovery?'

"Doesn't seem too injured to me," I muttered. This cover featured a shirtless cowboy bending a young woman in a cowboy hat backward over his arm.

'Rival CEOs Carson and Melody hate each other with a passion. Will things heat up when a merger throws them together?'

Love-hate, classic setup. Another hot cover with a barely clad woman in a sexy pencil skirt peeling a dress shirt off a man sitting on the edge of a desk.

'Coffee shop owner Blake is too focused on work to find love. When a clumsy barista falls over the threshold of his café, will they be able to create the perfect blend?'

The notes said the book was written entirely in Blake's POV, an interesting choice for a female author. A woman wearing a man's shirt with the sleeves rolled up to her elbows was sitting on a countertop with a shirtless man's face buried in her neck.

The last thumbnail didn't load, so I clicked on it, making sure my tablet wasn't glitching. I nearly swallowed my tongue when the image finally loaded.

'Kayla has never had a problem with confidence, but she's never felt fully satisfied. Will an incorrect address on a catering gig lead her to find someone who's able to finally put her in her place? Caution: Mature Themes and BDSM'

Fuck. There it was. She wrote a book about BDSM.

Since I needed someone to fine-tune rough sex scenes, this might be the author to help me. The scenes didn't need flowery dialogue and loving exchanges, they needed power struggles and all-out fucking. Things I lacked first-hand experience with.

Blowing out a heavy breath and adjusting my now tighter lounge pants, I hesitated before I clicked on the extended excerpt link.

A dialogue box popped up warning that this content was for mature readers and a little drop-down menu to input your birthdate appeared.

I scrolled through to find my birthdate and braced myself as the page viewer app loaded.

My pulse was already racing as I devoured the words on the screen with wide eyes.

Kayla could feel the atmosphere in the room change, her skin blossoming with goosebumps as she anticipated his next move.

She'd known that Michael enjoyed exuding power in his professional life, but she never anticipated how deep-seated his need for control was.

The blindfold shifted slightly as she breathed and tried to remain still. Her whole body was aware of every little sound his bare feet made on the floor across the room.

He was making her wait—building up the tension—to see if he could get her to shift out of her position.

It took control and patience to kneel—hands bound behind her back—with silk-lined leather handcuffs pulling her arms into a position that thrust her bare chest forward. She was thankful for all the 6:00 am gym sessions she'd attended over the last two years as her muscles flexed slightly to maintain her posture.

Michael had been extremely specific. Her knees shoulder width apart, tops of her feet flat on the floor, her head relaxed forward but not drooping, her shoulders back, arms extended, wrists resting over the small of her back and chest, and shoulders raised to the sky.

"You've done well, my pet." His deep voice rasped as she felt something soft touch her shoulder.

He traced across her shoulder blades and down her arms—stopping briefly on the cuffs before it lifted from her skin. It was soft, smooth, and flexible. She found herself running images through her mind of the things she'd seen laid out in the open drawer as she'd walked into the room earlier in the evening.

"Very well..."

She could hear the floor creak as he slowly circled her in his appraisal.

"Uhhh," she moaned as she felt the crack of the leather riding crop bite at the sensitive skin on the side of her breast.

"Ah, ah, ah. Quiet now, pet. You wouldn't want me to stop." His feet stopped pacing, and she felt the soft leather kiss the skin on her chin as he pushed up lightly. "Should I stop?"

"No," she breathed out as her whole body was pulled taut. She was throbbing as she waited for his next move.

"Is that how you address me?"

The swift smack to her nipple caused her chest to jerk, and she bounced in place before she caught herself.

"Nnn-no, Sir."

"Should I leave you here to think about your behavior?"

Kayla shook her head slightly before she was able to find her voice again.

"No, Sir."

> *"Speak freely, pet. What do you need?" he instructed.*
> *"You."*
> *Her chest started to heave as the soft leather caressed the waistband of her silk panties. Back and forth, back and forth. Occasionally stopping but never striking.*
> *"What do you need from me, pet?" he asked in a low, sultry voice.*
> *Her mouth dropped open as she tried to formulate a confident answer. He was going to wait her out. Driving her half mad with desire as he stood completely still.*
> *She could imagine his cool blue eyes looking down on her, that passive look on his face as he patiently let her figure out what she needed. He'd told her she could take what she needed from him; she only had to ask.*
> *"Your cock, Sir. I need your cock."*

Holy fucking shit.

Placing my tablet down, I closed my eyes for a moment before I picked it back up and tapped the screen a few times, going back into my incognito tabs. I should feel guilty for what I was about to do, but there was something about the tension in the writing and the raw sexual energy that flowed through the character while she was deprived of her sense of sight.

My hand was shaking as I shifted the waistband of my lounge pants down. Reaching into the little pocket in the front of my boxer briefs, I pulled myself out and ran my hand down the hardening flesh. My other hand pressed play, and I closed my eyes, imagining Chastity's intriguing eyes and light hair as moans filled the air around me. I tried to immerse myself in the scene, taking on the character as if I was living out the scene. While I wasn't bound, a woman, or at the mercy of a slightly sadistic Dominant, the sensation of stroking myself felt enhanced as I spread the wetness that'd built while I was reading down my shaft.

"Fuck yes," I moaned, my hips involuntarily shifting into the rhythm of my hand as my wrist moved faster.

The guttural female moans on the tablet intensified the sensation as I felt myself getting closer. Images of blonde hair covered by the strap of a blindfold danced behind my eyelids as my whole body tensed, and I let go in streams across my hand and bare chest.

My heart was hammering as I opened my eyes and grabbed the tablet. I pressed stop and threw it on the coffee table as I picked up my cell phone and opened the texts.

Evan: Chastity Rose

Adrian: Done. That was quick.

You have no idea, Adrian, no fucking idea.

Chapter
THREE

CHASE

BOSTON

LAPTOP, CHECK.

"Where is that damn cord?" I rummaged around in the bottom of my messenger bag. I was constantly losing charging cords. For everything. My phone...laptop...tablet. If it had a cord, I could lose it. I had an abundance of extra battery packs dispersed around my condo, but the cords that plugged into the wall—gone.

Isobel hated how disorganized my condo was, but it was ordered to me. Sort of. The clutter didn't bother me. Most days, I was too absorbed in my characters to put away laundry or sort through things I needed to donate. It was clean; it was just a mess—kind of like my social life.

My friends all thought I had some spectacular sex life, given that they thought I wrote lady porn—in reality, it'd been a while.

"Ah-ha!" I exclaimed as I pulled on the little C connector that I could barely see sticking out from under the couch cushion. For some reason, I thought storing a laptop cord under a couch cushion was a good idea, but I wasn't always the most logical person.

My phone started to ring, and my eyes scanned all the flat surfaces in my apartment for the hot pink case before I felt the vibration against my leg.

Whoever invented yoga pants with pockets was a freaking genius. It kept me from losing my phone most of the time. When I remembered it was in said little pocket.

"Is?" I asked as I wrapped up the cord and shoved it into my messenger bag.

"Did you find it?" Her voice was amused, but I didn't remember telling her I was looking for something.

"Find what?"

"Whatever it is that is making you late? You should have left forty minutes ago. And since I can't hear road noise and your speaker phone voice, I'm gathering you haven't gotten in the car yet."

Shit. I looked at the tiny clock in the corner of the cell phone before I held it back to my ear. I'd thought I was doing well on time, but obviously, I was not. She hated it when I went off her little itineraries.

At least it was simply meeting another author, not a book signing. My head would be on a pike if I were ever late for one of those again.

"I don't know what you're talking about. I always know where my things are." She laughed so loudly you'd think it was the funniest thing she'd heard all year. "Yeah, yeah. I'm hilarious. Laugh it up."

"Hilarious—delusional—either one," Is said in her usual dismissive tone.

"Was there a reason you're bothering me?" Other than to point out how hopeless I was.

"Just wanted to confirm that you'd gotten the PDFs with the scenes Adrian pulled for you."

They'd come through last night. To say that I was underwhelmed was being generous. Even the very first awkward sex scenes I'd written as a university student were not this bad. Romance Writing 101. If you've never done it in real life, then don't try to bravado your way through it. Research on the Internet could only get you so far—sometimes, you needed to experience it.

"I got them," I sighed, shaking my head. Evan needed more help than she'd originally led me to believe.

"You're too quiet. I thought you'd have all kinds of things to say about those pages."

The character he'd developed had already gotten under my skin. She was strong, which I'd guess you'd need to live as she did, but she also had this intense sense of loneliness that resonated with me.

It made me think about the man behind the story. Was he as lonely as this girl? What had happened to him?

She'd aged out of the foster system and done what she needed to survive. Kallie had been dealt a shit hand, but what was Evan's story?

I wasn't proud of myself, but I'd tried Facebook-stalking him. Besides an author page clearly managed by Adrian and a couple of fan groups, I came up empty.

He was a ghost. I knew he'd been a soccer player his first year at Stanford from a Google search, but he'd disappeared after that. It also coincided with the publication of his first novel.

Was that the reason for his seclusion?

Given the Connecticut address, he'd obviously relocated to the East Coast from California, but his story was a puzzle I wanted to put together.

"You're hooked, aren't you?" Isobel sounded amused. She knew I liked to figure out how people worked.

"Huh? What? No." I cringed as my voice took on that squeaky tone that I hated.

"You are! You've got a crush on the mystery writer!"

"I haven't even met him. How would I already have a crush on him?" I denied—weakly.

"So, if I went through your search history, I wouldn't find anything about Evan?" Goddammit. Was I that transparent? She knew I was a sucker for the tortured artist type.

"No."

"Liar! Get your shit together, Chase. You need to get in, do your thing, and get out," she warned.

"Do my what?"

"Get in there, show him how to make his characters angry fuck and get back to the city." I could see her rolling her eyes at me from her desk.

"You make it sound so easy. You're not the one that needs to teach a guy how to channel sexuality as a woman."

She started laughing again—my pain amused her to no end. I had no idea what I was walking into. Fame did all kinds of weird things to writers. He could be a pompous asshole for all I knew. Add in the fact that he was antisocial and there was a whole other level of shit. I'd agreed to two weeks. Who knew how long it'd really take?

"You'll be fine," she coaxed. "I've yet to see you intimidated by any man."

Despite it being an industry of mostly female writers, my first editor was a man. Now *he* was a pompous asshole. Why he'd been assigned to edit romance novels was a mystery.

He was in his late forties, divorced twice, and thought he was a literary God. He did have an excellent grasp of the written word, but interpersonal relationships were outside his wheelhouse.

As soon as I'd met Isobel at a book release for another author, I'd begged for a transfer.

"Finish getting your mess packed and get on the road. You'll end up sleeping in your car if you miss your check-in."

There hadn't been any major chain hotels within ten miles of Evan's address. He really was taking the writing in seclusion a little too seriously.

There also didn't seem to be any chain stores of any type within the same radius of his little town. How that existed a few hours outside of three major cities astounded me, but maybe leaving the metropolis of Boston for a while would be good for me.

"I know, I'm going. I found my laptop cord. My suitcase has been packed for hours."

"Looking forward to getting updates, have a safe drive," she sang like she hadn't been making fun of me.

"Thanks, Is. I'll text you when I get there."

After she hung up, I looked around my apartment to ensure I hadn't forgotten anything else. Living alone was nice, and my building didn't allow pets, but it was also a little sad that nothing would change between now and whenever I returned.

Despite living in a major city and having the modern world at my disposal, I was just as alone as Evan.

THE DRIVE WAS QUITE pleasant once I got out of the city traffic. Both Massachusetts and Connecticut had some stunning scenery.

I wasn't sure exactly what I was getting myself into as I ventured further into the increasingly rural countryside. It was only a few hours' drive, but it was like being on another planet. I was used to modern and historic blending seamlessly in an urban environment.

There was nothing modern about Ashford. It was a quaint little town with many historical markers, a few summer camps, and only four thousand or so residents. If you wanted to be left alone, this was the place to do it.

The bed and breakfast Isobel had booked for me was exactly what you'd expect from the pictures. An old colonial farmhouse that'd been restored to cater to the tourist traffic they got during the fall. It was gorgeous, and I was already getting the itch to start writing. Something about the picturesque scenery inspired me.

The owner was extremely sweet and was happy to take me on a tour of her lovely home and surrounding acreage, explaining the history of the three-hundred-year-old property. She told me about several pubs and restaurants available within a twenty-minute drive and left me in my room with a promise to see me at breakfast.

I knew Isobel was waiting to hear I'd checked in, so I quickly texted her before I forgot.

Chase: I've arrived. It's lovely.

She didn't respond immediately, so I put my phone down on the bed and pulled out the packet of information that Adrian had sent me. It had a post-it note on the top with Evan's cell phone number listed, as well as his address.

Evan knew I was driving in today, but we hadn't communicated directly yet. Isobel and Adrian had been our go-betweens. I'd been too nervous to contact him, not knowing exactly where I stood. Writers could be very possessive of their work, and I knew I needed to tread carefully.

"You're a big girl, Chase. You can do this," I reminded myself.

I picked up my phone and opened a new text screen. Carefully typing in the numbers on the paper, I tried to compose a message in my head before my fingers started moving.

> *Chase: Hi, Evan. I'm here.*

No, too vague. He might not even have my number in his phone. I deleted the message and bit my lip before I typed in a new one.

> *Chase: Evan, this is Chase. I'm at my hotel now.*

No, it sounded like an invitation. Ugh. Shit. Had Adrian even told him my real name? I had no idea.

I closed his text screen and opened Isobel's.

> *Chase: Does he know my real name?*

I saw the little dots show up and then disappear. She'd seen the message but wasn't responding.

> *Adrian: 4 pm, the address I gave you. Don't be late, he's expecting you.*

Was Isobel with Adrian? Why wasn't she responding?

I didn't even know if he knew who I was.

"Shit, shit, shit. Why am I being so ridiculous about this?" I moaned.

I knew why. I was nervous.

Something about the look on his face in that picture intimidated me. I already wanted to know more about him, and that was dangerous. That wasn't why I was here.

It was a bit after three. The maps on my phone said it took about fifteen minutes to get to his house from here which meant I had about twenty minutes to get myself ready to leave. It was also in a rural area that backed up to a state park, so I didn't want to get lost.

What did one wear to meet a colleague? A dress? I obviously couldn't wear my yoga pants, tank top, and a slouchy sweater.

I finally settled on a loose-fitting denim shirt dress and ankle boots. It was dressier than my normal writing attire, yet still casual.

The maps on my phone were useless ten minutes into the drive, and I was glad Adrian had included turn-by-turn directions to Evan's house. I would die out here if I were left to rely on modern technology.

The last turn wasn't paved and had a gravel road that cut a narrow path through the trees. I couldn't even see any other houses nearby.

It said to follow the road for 1.4 miles until it stopped. I was literally on a road to nowhere.

His house wasn't what I'd expected. Not by a long shot. The trees started to thin just over a mile in, and then it appeared—totally out of place with its surroundings.

A small lake was situated behind it; the trees open to the water. I'd been expecting something like a rustic log cabin, but I guess when you sell enough books, you can afford to build yourself a nice modern farmhouse in the middle of the forest.

The lights were on; clearly, he was home. With all those windows, he was probably watching me—wondering why I hadn't gotten out of the car yet.

Grabbing my messenger bag from the backseat. I began the walk toward his front door.

It was so quiet. No industrial noise, no cars, only the sounds of nature. I was so used to the background noise of city life that it was a little unsettling.

My palms were sweating as I approached the door, and my heart pounded. Quickly glancing at my watch, I noticed it was 3:58 pm, and I mentally patted myself on the back for being a few minutes early. Isobel would be so proud.

I wiped my hand on my dress and knocked on the door before I psyched myself out.

Footsteps echoed through the door, and I tried to remain calm as I waited. They stopped, and I stared at the doorknob as it started to turn. My eyes snapped up as the door swung open.

Shit. Don't drool, Chase.

He really was as attractive as his photo. This was not good. He was wearing a pair of loose-fitting athletic shorts with a fitted gray shirt. He'd obviously been doing something strenuous as I noticed a bead of sweat make its way down the side of his neck. My mind immediately jumped into the gutter, thinking of stepping forward to catch it with my tongue.

His hair was a shade of medium brown—almost blonde—slightly wavy with little highlights of a lighter hue. His skin had a golden glow; he obviously spent a lot of time outdoors. Deep blue eyes with a lighter ring around his pupil peered back at me. Just like in the book jacket photo, they had a certain edge of vulnerability. A soft-looking layer of scruff covered his chiseled jawline, framing full, pink lips.

"Hey." His voice was slightly strained as he took an earbud out and opened the door wider.

"Hi, uh, am I early?"

He stood there, chest heaving as he looked at me for a moment. "Oh...no. Sorry. Shit." I held back laughter as he started to look a little flustered. "No, I lost track of time." He looked at his wrist, and his eyes widened as he checked the time.

"I can come back." I offered, motioning over my shoulder toward my car.

"No! No. That's okay. I was nervous, so I went for a run. I guess I didn't realize how long I'd been on the treadmill."

His rambling was adorable. Most men who looked like him would never admit they were nervous.

I shifted the strap of my bag on my shoulder as we continued to stare at each other. His whole body was blocking the door, and I didn't want to invite myself into his home.

"So...?"

"What?" He pulled the other earbud out and moved to the side. "Shit, sorry. I'm sorry, Chastity. Come in." He stepped back further as I crossed the threshold and took several steps inside.

"Chase."

His brow furrowed as he looked at me, confusion marring his handsome features.

"My name."

He continued to stare at me blankly.

"Chase. My name is Chase."

"Oh God, I'm sorry. I guess I just got so used to seeing Chastity Rose on all your books..." He trailed off as his cheeks darkened with a rosy flush.

"All my books, huh?"

He scratched the back of his neck and averted his eyes.

"Exactly how many of my books have you read?"

It somehow seemed natural to tease him. And it secretly thrilled me that he'd read my work—and more than one book by the sound of it.

"A few." He cleared his throat and looked into my eyes. "I wouldn't be a good writer if I didn't do my research. And I enjoyed researching you...I mean your work."

And then it was my turn to blush. *Check and mate, Evan Stineman.*

FOUR

EVAN

CONNECTICUT

I COULDN'T BELIEVE I lost track of time. I had so much nervous energy pent up that I knew I needed to run it off. Adrian would kill me if my first impression was a panic attack at the front door.

Chastity—*correction, Chase*—had been the only thing on my mind the whole day. And subsequently, I'd spent the entire day on the verge of panic. It was either run it off or turn into a gasping mess on my shower floor.

When the box from Adrian had arrived only days ago, I'd plowed through the two books of hers that he'd included. I didn't even look at the other half dozen books in there by other authors because I'd already made up my mind.

After I was done with those, I'd spent the next day on my tablet, buying the rest of her books one after the other on Kindle. I couldn't stop.

I'd saved the book with Michael and Kayla for last and finished it in hours. I couldn't put it down. Well——that wasn't entirely true. I'd put it down a few times when I was so hard I couldn't focus anymore and had taken matters into my own hand.

Oh God, don't think about masturbation while she's standing two feet in front of me. These shorts hid nothing.

Fuck. I was all sweaty. I probably smelled. Such a great first impression, you moron.

"Research is always good," she smirked, a dimple appearing on her right cheek. As I continued to stare at her, trying not to be a total creep, I realized her pictures didn't do her justice. She was stunning. Her long blonde hair fell past her shoulders in soft waves. Long dark eyelashes framed bright blue eyes. She was tall, but still a good six inches shorter than me.

Shit. I was staring for too long.

"Um. You can sit in the living room or out on the back patio if you want. I should probably take a shower."

She smiled and nodded as her gaze slowly traced down my torso—my body responding as if her fingers were doing the same. I'd started to sweat through my shirt, and it was stuck to my chest in a few places, making me want to pull it off, but she'd likely flee back where she came from if I randomly started stripping. When her eyes lingered on my waistband, I knew I needed to get out of here before I rose to the occasion.

"Make yourself at home while I, uh...get dirty, I mean cleaned up," I stuttered nervously.

"Okay. I might go check out the lake. Your property is really gorgeous."

No, *you* are really gorgeous.

"That way?" she asked as she pointed to the door that led to the sunroom. I blinked a few times as I tried to process her question and will my mouth to move.

Shit. I was staring again.

"Uh. No."

She looked at me expectantly, and I felt my cheeks heat up again. "Over there. The double doors lead to the patio. You can walk down the hill to the dock from there."

There. Talking didn't have to be this hard.

Stop thinking about hard things.

"Got it."

We both smiled at each other again, and I shook my head as she giggled.

"Well, I'll uh...just go then."

"See you soon," she nodded with an indulgent smile.

Walking backward toward the hallway that led to my bedroom, only bumping into the corner of the kitchen island once, I couldn't manage to keep my eyes off her, eliciting that giggle from her again. I pivoted and turned away once she was out of sight, taking a few long strides toward my bedroom door. I needed to regroup.

"Fuck," I cursed under my breath. This was exactly why I hid from people. I always managed to say or do something completely mortifying.

Chase was out there waiting for me, probably wondering why she'd been sent out into the woods to babysit an imbecile.

Stop. Just relax. I was a good writer. I knew that. I wasn't questioning my ability to weave a well-planned out plot. I was entirely questioning my ability to interact with women. Simone had really done a number on my self-esteem, and I was still beating myself up over it three years later.

"You can do this." And now I was talking to myself again. My psychiatrist would be having a field day with my inability to function today.

Walking into my bathroom, I toed off my shoes, stripped off my shirt and shorts, and threw my sweaty clothes into the hamper.

It'd be easy to become a slob living hidden out here by myself, but I'd always respected order.

That was probably why writing always came easily to me. It was second nature to outline my stories. I had numerous diagrams, outlines, and character summaries filling folders on my laptop. I always knew exactly where the plot was going before I typed the first line of text.

Maybe that was why I was having such a hard time with these sex scenes. I could outline them and move the characters how I wanted them to, but my words only skimmed the surface.

It was mechanical, choreographed. I needed help making it seem spontaneous or passionate. Probably because I'd never had spontaneous or passionate anything, definitely not the kind of affair I was trying to convey in my novel.

The sex scenes that Chastity—Chase—wrote were a different matter. They drew you in, pulled you in to observe like a voyeur, and then made you feel what the characters were experiencing in a sensual way.

I could feel a stirring in my briefs as I imagined the scene in Michael's playroom where he had Kayla suspended mid-air with her hands bound and attached to a hoist while he fucked her from behind, ramming himself inside her as he held onto her hips.

How did she even come up with that? I knew you could research things on the internet, watch videos on YouTube—and other sites—and try to immerse yourself into the experience, but the way she wrote it made me feel like she'd experienced it.

Was Chase into bondage? Did she do more in-depth research into the lifestyle?

"Stop it," I growled at myself in the mirror. Thinking about it was making things harder. *Much harder.*

If she weren't here, in my home, I would take care of it in the shower, but that would be weird right now. When I hadn't met her yet, she was simply another sexy woman on the internet. Now she was a living, breathing person inside my house that I needed to work with for the foreseeable future. I needed to get a grip, and not on my cock. Especially not to thoughts of her.

Turning the faucet to barely warmer than room temperature, I hopped in and lathered myself up. Practicing my breathing techniques under the tepid blast helped calm me down.

It also meant I'd taken the fastest damn shower I'd had in a while.

WHERE DID SHE GO?

I stood in my kitchen, looking out the windows that lined the back wall of my house, wondering where my guest had disappeared. Surely I hadn't scared her off already.

She wasn't in the living room, and the patio was empty. I could only see the very end of the dock from the windows, so she must be somewhere down the hill.

"Chase?"

The sun was barely starting to skim the tree line, although I knew it'd be pitch black in a matter of hours. I didn't really know what to plan for our meeting, but I could offer to feed her. The market in Ashford was small and quiet, so I made a weekly trip in and stocked up on groceries since I lived so far out of town.

The soft, dulcet tones of feminine humming caught my attention as I walked down the grass-covered hill that led to the water. It was technically a pond but resembled a small lake. I knew when I toured the acreage that this was where I wanted to build my house.

"Chase?"

She was seated with her legs outstretched, about halfway down the grassy hill. Her phone was lying beside her, earbuds visible in her ears, and an old school composition notebook was on her lap.

I watched her for a moment, her pencil flying across the page. Obviously, this place inspired her as much as it did me. There was a fire pit closer to the water where I did most of my writing when the weather cooperated.

Not wanting to startle her, I stepped closer, hesitating to call her name again. But she'd probably be more frightened of me standing a few feet behind her, staring like a creeper. She had to think I was a little strange since I had used such stellar conversational skills on her earlier. Talking to people had never been my favorite thing, but around women—especially beautiful, sexually attractive women—I got flustered.

Taking a few hesitant steps down the hill, I could see the moment she noticed me. Her hand halted, and the pencil slipped on the page. Her head shot in my direction, and she yanked her earbuds out with a nervous smile.

"Sorry." She smiled as she squinted in my direction. "How long have you been standing there? I didn't mean to stay out here this long, but I couldn't help myself."

"Not long." My voice was rough with nerves. Watching her work intrigued me.

She nodded as she tossed her notebook into the grass and pushed herself up from the ground.

"It's one of my favorite places to write, too," I confessed quietly, clearing my throat.

I tried not to stare at her ass as she bent over to pick up her things, but it was right there. I couldn't look away.

She was different than I expected—curvier—her dress molded to her full hips in a way that made my mouth water. I hated it when women were afraid to enjoy eating what they wanted. Good food brought people pleasure. Why deny yourself to wear a smaller size? I'd never had issues with overindulgence, and my compulsive need to run to clear my head helped keep me in shape, but I still had a love affair with cooking.

I shoved my hands in the pockets of my jeans to resist the urge to run my hands down the curve of her hips and averted my eyes as she straightened out and turned to face me.

"So..." She smiled as her white teeth sunk into the pink flesh of her bottom lip.

"So..." I was so lame.

"I'm sorry, I'm not usually this awkward," she laughed a little and rolled her eyes.

"I am." It was the goddamn truth.

A grin pulled at my lips as her laughter rang out. She had a nice laugh. It'd been years since something I said made a woman who wasn't related to me laugh. Hearing it hit me in a way that I hadn't experienced before. I craved to hear it again.

"Shall we go inside? I can make us something to eat."

"A man who cooks and writes. You're a dangerous one, Evan," she teased, and I felt heat rise in my cheeks.

"I don't know about that," I laughed as she smiled at me. "Cooking for yourself kind of becomes necessary when you live in the middle of nowhere."

"I'd be in trouble then." She smiled, and the dimple in her cheek deepened.

"You can't cook?" I asked curiously.

"No, I can. I choose not to most of the time. Some people excel at cooking elaborate meals with farm fresh ingredients; I excel at cooking microwaveable macaroni and cheese."

I could understand that. She didn't seem like the type to spend her evenings on domestic chores.

"The Chinese food delivery person told me he uses my weekly delivery to remember what day of the week it is," she confessed with a guilty smile.

"I don't think I was ever that bad. Although the girl at the coffee shop near my last apartment did have my order ready when I walked in the door each day, and my name was spelled correctly on the cup each time," I recalled from when I still lived in the city. It felt like a literal lifetime ago.

"That probably wasn't because of a routine." Her laughter rang out again as I stared at her. "If I could look at you each morning, I'd make sure your coffee was ready when you walked in the door too."

I looked away and scratched the back of my head. It sounded like she was flirting with me, but I didn't want to read too much into it. I wasn't always the best at picking up the signals.

"I'm sorry. I didn't mean to make you feel uncomfortable," she said quietly, tilting her head to look into my downturned eyes. "My brain-to-mouth filter wasn't installed correctly at birth."

"You didn't."

"Okay." She didn't look so certain, a small frown flickering across her lips.

"I'm not the best at this."

"What 'this' are you referring to?" Her voice sounded equal parts amused and curious.

"This," I said, gesturing my hand between the two of us.

"Talking? You seem to be doing fine to me."

"Not talking exactly. Banter, witty conversation. I usually end up saying something embarrassing." Or staring and not saying anything at all, then berating myself for being so damn awkward.

"I thought I had the market cornered on that one," she giggled. "Remember that nonexistent filter?"

I liked talking to her. She didn't seem to have an agenda. It also helped that she was a little self-deprecating. I could relate to that.

Turning toward the house, I started walking, Chase falling into step a few feet to my side.

"So, what are we having?"

I shrugged, my mind trying to concentrate on the vegetables in my refrigerator, not the sexy woman following me back into my house that suddenly felt too small. "What are you in the mood for tonight? Anything in particular you like? What are you craving? Is there something that'd make your mouth water?"

She arched an eyebrow, tilting her head to the side as she responded. "You ask loaded questions. I don't think you're ready to hear my answers."

"I'm just talking about food, Chase. Although I think your overactive imagination may be reading into my words," I teased back. "I was only asking what kind of food you'd want to eat. I think you're trying to insert subtext into my very simple questions."

"Are you sure about that? Your voice dropped an octave, and your eyes dilated. For someone who claims to be so awkward and incapable of depicting sexual attraction, you don't seem to have a problem conveying it."

"You think I'm attracted to you?" I was, but I was trying not to be obvious.

"Maybe avert your eyes the next time you're watching a woman stand up. Staring with your mouth open is flattering, but doesn't hide your attention. Not that I minded being the object of your very intense perusal. I was glad I didn't accidentally flash my underwear, although then you really would have had a reason to stare."

So she *was* flirting with me. I wasn't sure how I felt about that. Was she like this with everyone? It seemed like she was the type that enjoyed getting people wound up. And I was an easy target with my awkward behavior.

"Chicken?" I needed to change the subject before she realized how much of a doofus I was. And how much I wanted to know what color those panties were.

She laughed and stopped as we reached the back patio. "It's not nice to call me names. We just met."

"For dinner," I turned and rolled my eyes dramatically, glad she let me off the hook. "Would you like chicken?"

"If you're cooking, make what you'd like. I'm easy," she shrugged.

"Is that so?" *Oh my God*. Did I pull off flirting back with her?

"I'd put almost anything in my mouth right now. I haven't eaten since I woke up this morning."

She's not talking about your dick, idiot.

My mouth went dry as I looked at her lips. She bit the bottom one and looked into my eyes, and my hand froze on the knob of the back door.

"Well, we can't have that," I cleared my throat and glanced away briefly before my eyes were drawn back to hers.

Her stomach growling broke the trance, and I looked away as she laughed again. "Told you I was hungry."

I pushed the door open and led her into the open living space. "Take a seat. Would you like something to drink?"

She continued to follow me and sat down on a stool at the kitchen island instead of staying in the living room.

"Water?"

"Is that all you want?" I asked curiously. She seemed like the type that liked to curl up with a book and a glass of wine.

"What are you offering?"

"I could open some wine," I nodded to my small countertop rack that displayed several bottles.

"Maybe another night? I have to drive back."

I smiled at the implication that she intended to be here for another meal. I liked the sound of that. Eating alone for months on end was mildly depressing.

"How far do you have to drive?" I didn't even know where she was staying. I only got a text yesterday from Adrian telling me she'd be here at 4:00 today.

He knew I had a routine I liked to keep in the morning, and I usually wrote for a while after lunch. My days were all the same.

"Not far. Only about fifteen minutes. But I'm not sure how well I'll navigate out of here in the dark." Her voice had a slight tinge of worry. It was intimidating to drive out here, where there were lots of places to get turned around.

"No streetlamps to guide you," I murmured and then cleared my throat. "I'm sorry. Maybe we should have met at your hotel."

While we talked, I started to pull ingredients out of the fridge. It was nice to have someone here with me. Chase was surprisingly easy to talk with.

"No, it's okay. The bed and breakfast Isobel reserved for me is very quaint."

"I still feel bad that I'm the reason you had to come out here, and you have to do all the work," I sighed.

"It's all being written off as a corporate expense," she shrugged before she leaned forward on her elbows, propping her chin on her hands as she watched me. "I really don't mind it. The quiet out here in and of itself is nice. I'm so used to the sound of traffic I'd forgotten what true quiet was."

I glanced back at her with a smile. It made me happy that she enjoyed being out here. Not many city dwellers could appreciate a slower life. It had been a challenge, but I wasn't willing to stay in the city after everything that had happened. It was easier to escape.

"It was hard for me to adjust to at first, but now I'm not sure I could sleep without the quiet." I confessed.

"Where did you live before you moved here?" she asked curiously, focusing squarely on me. Normally, I would have started stuttering by now, but I liked her watching me—and turnabout was fair play.

"Chicago, California. Boston for a little while, but I needed to get away from the city."

"It can be a bit of a pain sometimes, but everything is so accessible," she smiled.

We continued talking about places we'd lived and places she'd traveled as I chopped vegetables and sautéed the chicken.

I liked listening to the inflections in her voice. She had an interesting way of describing things; I could see how she'd translated that ability into her books.

We ate at the island, side by side, our knees and elbows occasionally brushing. I found myself eating slower, trying to prolong my time with her. As soon as this meal was over, she'd probably be leaving. The sun was already starting to set, and a sense of unease filled me unexpectedly. I'd enjoyed her company, warm smiles, and ability to get me to open up, even if it was about something mundane.

"Well," she yawned as she stretched and swiveled her stool to face me. "That was amazing. You've officially spoiled me. You'll have to teach me some tricks while I'm here."

My pants started to feel a little snug as I thought about tricks being taught in my kitchen. My kitchen island was the perfect height to...

"Are you still with me?"

"Hmm?" I hummed. "Oh, sorry." I must have been quiet too long while I was fantasizing about bending her over the counter. Or lifting her on the counter and dropping to my knees...

"I should probably get going. Have to get some sleep before I come back tomorrow to whip you into shape." She laughed as I felt my cheeks turn pink at the images her words conjured in my head. My mind strayed to a graphic scene she'd written between Michael and Kayla involving a flogger.

"Hopefully, you'll take mercy on me," I chuckled as I looked over at her playful smile.

"Oh, don't you worry, I'll be gentle."

I hoped she wouldn't.

She started to gather our dishes to carry them to the sink. A surge of something electric raced up my palm as I laid my hand on top of hers to stop her.

"I've got the dishes. You should probably go before it gets much darker."

"Are you sure?" she asked quietly. "You cooked. The least I can do is get my hands a little wet."

"Positive."

"Okay. So, what time do you want me?"

All the time.

"Tomorrow morning?"

I must have been staring again.

"Oh. I get up between six and six-thirty. Any time after that should be fine," I told her, and she shook her head.

"Well, I'm not getting up that early, but I could probably make it here after eight."

"That works for me. I'll be here."

Waiting impatiently.

"It was nice to meet you," she said softly, her lips quirking to the side in a grin.

I smiled back as we reached the door, trying to come up with something witty to say. She paused in the threshold and looked toward me. "I wasn't sure what to expect, but this has been nice. I'm sorry if I made things weird before by pointing out how you..."

"You didn't. Clearly, I underestimated your observational skills." I couldn't imagine anyone else here in her place, and she would keep me on my toes. "I'm glad I picked you."

"Me too." She threw a little wave over her shoulder as she turned toward her car.

I stood in the doorway as she drove away, wishing it was morning already. I didn't think I'd be getting much sleep tonight, knowing she'd be back here tomorrow.

FIVE

CHASE

CONNECTICUT

DESPITE BEING TOTALLY FLUSTERED as I drove away from Evan's house, I returned to the B&B without crashing into a ditch. It was so dark. I'd never realized how much light pollution big cities had. It got dark at night, but this was the next level of darkness.

The house was quiet as I walked up the private entrance to my suite. Normally, I'd be excited to jump in a big comfy bed and pass out for hours, but I was a little keyed up.

Maybe Isobel was right. My being here and interacting with Evan might help my new book. As I'd waited for him to get cleaned up earlier—and tried fruitlessly not to think about what he looked like naked in that shower—I'd written several pages of dialogue.

It was like the character's voices needed my head to be quiet to start pouring out of me.

Tomorrow was going to be hard—no pun intended.

Evan and I had gotten along well, not having too many moments of awkward quietness. He was easy to talk to and didn't seem offended by my teasing. I found flirtatious things coming out of my mouth without even trying. I probably should have tried to be more professional, but I couldn't stop.

He was attractive. Okay, that may have been an understatement. He was fucking gorgeous, and I'd had a hard time keeping drool from sliding out the corner of my mouth when he opened the door, sweaty and out of breath.

How was I going to survive this?

Writing about sex had never bothered me. Even when I was new to having it, it'd never embarrassed me to talk or think about it. My parents were still disgustingly in love after thirty-six years and they never made me feel like sex was shameful.

They'd been an open book—sometimes too honest—and answered questions for me without pretense or agenda. That was probably why I'd been a little bit of a late bloomer with the actual act. Add the fact I had two fiercely protective older brothers who would have preferred to see me placed in a nunnery rather than a regular high school...and I left high school with little experience.

I'd done my fair share of over-the-clothes fumbling in the back seats of cars and parents' basements, but my parents taught me to respect myself enough to set my own timeline. My high school dates had only been interested in one thing, and I'd taken great satisfaction from being the one girl they couldn't manipulate or pressure into doing something I wasn't ready for.

The ultimate honor had gone to my second college boyfriend, who had quite a few repeat performances, and I'd still give a standing ovation if his wife wouldn't murder me. He was happy to let me explore his body—learning what he liked—and he was always up for trying new positions.

He was older and had scored a single room in the dorm next to mine. We'd had plenty of privacy for our anatomy study sessions. He was also the first guy to blindfold and spank me. I wasn't fully into doing everything I'd researched and written in my fifth book, but limited sensory deprivation and corporal punishment excited me.

Working with a real-life Dominant was also a fun challenge. I was able to learn a lot about the Dom/sub roles first hand. Once, he'd even tied me up and suspended me from the ceiling of his playroom. No sexual contact was involved, yet it was still thrilling.

A startling thought occurred to me. *Oh, God. What if Evan read that book?*

No wonder he had a hard time making eye contact with me. My mother had difficulty making eye contact with me after that book was released.

Changing into pajamas, I curled up in bed with my laptop and notebook. I started transferring dialogue into a new text document and tweaking it to fit my current characters. It would be interesting to see if I could keep writing like this once I started to help Evan.

I had a feeling that Kallie, his female main character, was going to invade my brain once we started working on her POV.

After I'd finished transferring my writing onto the computer, I dug around in my suitcase for melatonin spray. I would never sleep with all the conflicting voices running through my brain.

Anyone else who said that would need to be medicated, but authors always understood what it meant to have voices in your head that were not your own. Some louder than others.

THE NEXT MORNING, I woke feeling rested. Sometimes I had trouble sleeping, and I was worried it'd continue while sleeping in a strange bed.

What time was it? I blindly reached behind me to the nightstand for my phone. I probably should have set an alarm to ensure I didn't sleep the morning away, but I was so anxious it hadn't occurred to me last night. Did I mention that authors also commonly spoke to themselves inside their heads?

It was still early—7:18 am. That had to be a record, but my growling stomach distracted me from the early hour.

The owner told me the previous day that she served a home-cooked breakfast each morning, and I was enjoying having other people cook for me on this trip.

Unsure of what to wear today, I finally settled on a pair of skinny jeans paired with a white button-down shirt tied at the waist. Evan would have to get used to me wearing clothes that weren't dresses. My usual writing attire was leggings and a baggy sweater, so this was dressy for me.

I could already smell something delicious as I came down the main staircase. The dining room was set up with several smaller tables, neatly set and waiting for diners.

"Hello?"

"In here!" I heard a shout from the room adjacent to the dining room. I assumed that was where the kitchen was located.

"Good morning," I greeted Marian, the owner of the inn. She stood over a gas range, turning a sizzling piece of thick-cut bacon over as a pot with poached eggs simmered on another burner.

"Morning dear, you're up earlier than I expected."

"I was a little surprised, too," I laughed as I watched her move around the kitchen effortlessly.

"I hope you're not a vegetarian."

"Nope, I'm a big fan of meat."

She laughed and smiled at me over her shoulder.

"It'll be done in a few minutes. You're welcome to chat with me for a few moments, or you can sit in the dining room, and I'll bring it out to you."

"If I'm not in the way, I can wait in here." Sitting alone in the other room, I'd feel weird waiting for her to serve me.

"Just sit on one of the stools, and you can tell me why you're here." She nodded to the side of the kitchen island.

"Well, I'm a writer," I started. It was still awkward for me to out myself to people.

"Hmm. Anything I may have read?"

"Maybe?" I shrugged. "I write under a pen name."

"And...?"

"It's, um, Chastity Rose," I mumbled. I wasn't ashamed of my writing, but I never knew how people would take it.

"Oh, you write some racy stuff! That last one was quite the page-turner."

I blushed and bit my lip. That book was usually the one people remembered. My other books had been steamy, but the last book's whips and chains had gotten people's attention.

"Thank you?"

"Are you working on a new book?" she asked without pause, and I let out the breath I'd been holding. Living up to others' expectations of my writing was always difficult for me.

"Yes, but that's not why I'm here. I was sent to help another author fine-tune his next novel."

"Ah, the mystery writer," she replied knowingly.

"You've met him?" I stared at her curiously. Despite Is's warnings about his reclusive nature, he seemed normal.

"Not technically. I've seen him in town, and he's occasionally bought produce from the farmer next door. He keeps to himself."

"I've heard," I confirmed. It seemed Evan's reclusive nature was common knowledge.

"Did you meet him yet?" The little smile she aimed in my direction was more than curious. It seemed Marian thrived on gossip.

"Last night. I spent a little time at his house. It's really beautiful out there. I can see why he's so inspired to write with that scenery surrounding him."

"And? Is he as mysterious and intriguing as the young ladies in this town seem to think he is?"

I thought about how uncomfortable it'd probably make him to have people imagining that he was some puzzle to be solved, like in his novels. "He is still a bit of a mystery to me, but he seemed normal. Quiet. He likes things to be orderly." Blushes when you call him out for staring at your ass.

"I think the fact that he never talks to anyone and only shows his face a few times a month makes them all endlessly fascinated."

"His land and house are amazing," I sighed, mentally recalling the peaceful scenery I'd enjoyed the previous day.

"He backs up to a state park. I was surprised when I found out he was building a house out there. They had to run fiber optic cable to his property just so he'd have Internet."

"Yeah, I don't think most of us could survive without the Internet nowadays," I laughed.

"I could do without it," she shrugged, "but I have to cater to the clientele." She pointed to a wireless router mounted above one of the cabinets.

"Us spoiled, tech-obsessed city folk."

"Something like that," she chuckled as she drizzled a thick, creamy, light-yellow sauce over the meal she'd assembled on the counter. "Do you want to eat inside or out? Are you a coffee drinker?"

"Outside would be amazing. And yes. One hundred thousand percent, yes," I laughed. The thought that people could survive without extra caffeination was appalling.

"I have a travel mug you can borrow while you're here. No Starbucks for miles." Marian chuckled at the way my eyes widened.

"That would be amazing. Coffee is my favorite food group."

The food she served me was phenomenal—a rich, hearty interpretation of Eggs Benedict with crispy bacon, cooked to perfection. I wanted to live here. This was already the best work-related trip ever.

By eight, I was stuffed; my laptop was in the car, my travel mug of caffeinated liquid gold was in my hand, and I was ready to go.

"Here I come, Evan. I hope you're ready for me."

"Hey," I smiled as he met me at his front door.

"Hey."

Damn, he's beautiful.

We stood in his open front door and momentarily stared at each other. This seemed to be a thing we did now. I wasn't opposed to it, but we wouldn't get any work done standing in the doorway.

"So, you ready to get down to it?" I laughed as I rubbed my palms together.

"Hmm? Oh, yes. Sorry. I'm doing it again. Come in." He stepped to the side and waved me into the house. "I'm not sure where you want to start. Adrian sent you some pages?"

"Yup," I nodded. "Where do you want me?"

His eyebrow arched as his gaze slowly drifted lower. "Inside or outside?"

Oh God, he kept dropping the bait. Be good, Chase, don't pick it up.

"Where does the magic happen?"

Let's see how he likes it.

His eyes drifted down the hallway toward what I assumed led to his bedroom.

Not that kind of magic, sweetheart.

"Um, uh. Outside?" he stuttered, looking away from me and scratching his head.

"Exhibitionist, nice," I teased.

A nervous laugh escaped him before he scratched the back of his neck again, clearing his throat. "It's nice out. I usually sit down in the lounger at the firepit."

"Cozy. Lead the way." I gestured for him to go ahead of me. Mostly so I could take in the scenery provided by his snug pants. If he could stare at me, I wasn't about to deny myself the same.

He stopped to put on some shoes and grabbed his laptop and a folder full of papers off the table.

I took a deep breath and slowly exhaled as I followed him. I could see why he loved being out here.

"Um, there's only one seat down here. Do you want me to grab a chair off the patio, or...?"

"I'm a big girl. I can share," I assured him. "Are you good at sharing, Evan?"

A quick nod was all I got before he walked over and set his laptop down on the edge of the unlit firepit.

"Where would you like to begin?"

"I don't know. Do you want to explain to me how it all happens?" His voice was sharper today, more nervous. This really took him out of his comfort zone.

"Well...when a boy and a girl decide the other one is attractive, they take off all their clothes, but not always *all* of them. And sometimes it's a boy and a boy, or a girl and a girl, or multiple people, and then..."

"Stop," he looked up at me with mild panic, waving his hand. "No. Geez. I know how that works."

"Which scene do you want to start with? Your writing process is probably different than mine, so what works for me may not be useful for you." I decided that maybe I'd give him a little slack, although I loved teasing him, especially as he was so jumpy.

"The scene with the detective is the pivotal point in their relationship, but it's toward the middle of the book."

"So, start there?" I asked quietly, watching his face for any indication of where he wanted to go.

"That one has more emotions involved. The ones at the beginning of the book are with her..." he trailed off, his cheeks reddening a little.

"Clients? Johns? Hole fillers?" I bit my bottom lip, waiting for the blush to go nuclear.

There it is.

"Clients. We can call them clients." He was fighting not to laugh, but I could tell he wanted to. Hopefully, my bawdy attempts at humor would get him to relax.

"Okay, do you want me to be completely honest with my impression of these, or do you want me to hold your hand?" I pulled the stack of papers from my bag and put them on my lap. There were multiple colors of post-it flags hanging from the sides, and red pen pretty much covering the pages.

"That bad?" he cringed, looking down at my notes.

"It could be worse?" I trailed off. It could be, but not much. I felt like I was an English teacher telling someone they failed an essay that was worth half their grade.

"Shit. Might as well rip me a new one." He shook his head with his eyes closed. As he pinched the bridge of his nose, I felt a pang of sympathy.

"I promised you I'd be gentle," I coaxed, hoping I didn't break his spirit on day two.

SIX

EVAN

CONNECTICUT

"OKAY, LIKE THIS PART here. You might have just as well typed 'insert tab A into slot B'." Chase frowned at the paragraphs describing their interaction. "Does the word insert sound the least bit sexy to you?"

"I guess not. Are you going to pull out your porno thesaurus and give me a better synonym?" If she was going to continue to tease me, I could give it right back.

"As a matter of fact." She picked up her phone and started typing something quickly before she held it up for me to see.

"Urban Thesaurus. What is that?" I frowned. Urban Dictionary was a little wild; I couldn't even imagine what the thesaurus would hold.

"It's a dirty thesaurus," she grinned as she typed something into the search field.

There was a listing of random words—some overtly sexual—underneath where she had typed the word *missionary* into the search field.

"What does an angry orangutan have to do with sex?" I asked. I was way out of touch.

"Click on it," she giggled and then bit her lip, holding back an amused smile.

Well, that was not what I was expecting.

"Oh, my God. Do you actually use this stuff to write?" My voice was a little astonished but mostly appalled.

"No," she shook her head, her light curls bouncing around her shoulders. "Usually, I consult it when I want a laugh. People are into some interesting things."

I couldn't help but laugh at her assessment. Some people were into *different* things, but it wasn't my place to judge.

"Clinical-sounding words like 'insert' need to be the first things to go," she told me as she pointed back to the marked-up pages in her lap, getting us back on track.

"And what do I use in its place?"

She didn't even hesitate as she started listing off words. "Glide, slide, slip, push, thrust, drive. Depends on the context."

"You *are* like a walking thesaurus," I marveled. Those verbs were not even in my toolbox of words to describe sexual interactions.

"It's one of my many talents." Her wink threw me a little off guard, but I could only imagine what other talents might lie in that curvaceous body of hers.

"So, what else?" I asked, clearing my throat and forcing myself to stay on topic. She was here to help me, not be objectified.

"The whole goal of a scene like this is to draw the reader in and capture their attention. If their heart doesn't start beating faster as they read it, it's not hot enough."

I watched her eyes dilate as she looked up at me, and I wanted to be the reason her heart started beating faster.

"What makes it hot?" I felt like I was completely clueless.

"Using provocative words, describing a sensation—you want them to be picturing the act as it unfolds." Her voice was breathy, and I pictured some things I wanted to unfold with her.

The writer's best friend was the human imagination. If you could paint a picture vivid enough for the reader, they could truly immerse themselves in the story.

"Run your finger down the side of your face slowly," she instructed as she turned to face me and tucked one leg underneath her.

"Why am I doing this?" I asked as I watched her skeptically.

"Just humor me." I tried not to laugh as she made an impatient huff. "Now, close your eyes. Take a deep breath. Do it again and tell me what you feel."

I did what she told me to and tried to think of the sensation I was feeling.

"A finger on my face?"

"Alright, smartass."

My eyes were still closed, but I could tell she was rolling her eyes at me.

"Fine," she huffed, and I jumped, feeling a tickling sensation along my sideburn and over the stubbly hair on my cheek.

"Tell me what you feel," she said in a low, sultry voice. Or maybe I imagined it was sultry.

"Warmth...it's soft...makes my breath catch in my chest."

"Good. Keep thinking of how the touch makes you feel," she urged. I wasn't sure where she was going with this, but I was strangely enjoying it.

Her finger traced across my lips, and I felt the hairs on the back of my neck rise in response. It slowly trailed to my jaw and behind my ear. Her fingers cupped the back of my neck, and my mouth went dry. I felt a stirring in my groin as her thumb slowly trailed up and down, tickling the hair above my collar.

"Do you get it now?" The sultry voice was back.

My head slowly nodded up and down as she continued to caress my skin. I was fighting the urge to open my eyes. I wanted to see if her touch was affecting her as much as it was me. My pulse jumped as I felt her put a little pressure on the back of my neck.

I leaned in and felt her hair graze my cheek, her hot breath caressing my face.

"You described the mechanics of their interaction. That was the physical action. You want to describe to the reader the sensations the actions cause and the feelings they invoke." Her voice was low, and I felt my heartbeat pick up further in response to the warmth of her breath against my ear.

My entire body was fully aware of her proximity. She smelled like fresh flowers and summer heat, her hair was soft, and the thumb on my neck felt like it had a direct line to my cock. The slow motions from her tracing the hairs on my neck was creating a chain of sensations I could feel in my whole body.

"I uh..." My voice was much deeper than normal, and I had to lick my lips before I tried to talk again. "I think I understand what you mean."

"Good boy."

Her hand disappeared, and when I opened my eyes, she sat perfectly upright next to me, like she hadn't been whispering in my ear and stroking my skin.

"So, do we want to work through this blow by blow, or would you like to try to adjust it and then have me critique it?"

The already precarious situation in my pants throbbed as she said the word *blow*. My eyes were immediately drawn to her soft pink lips. I certainly needed to adjust *something*.

I meant the writing, of course.

"Can I try to see if I can fix it?" Once she explained it to me, I started to see where I'd disconnected from the scene.

"It's your book," she laughed with a shrug.

"I know, but if it got published today, the critics would eat me alive."

"That's why you've got reinforcements," she smiled. "We'll pop this cherry and make a man of you yet."

I shook my head, laughing as I pulled my computer onto my lap and propped it up by placing my feet up on the bricks.

"My erotic literary virginity is delicate, and you promised to be gentle."

I loved listening to her laugh. She made me feel funny, charming in a way I hadn't felt in a long time. It was easy to tell her what I was thinking without worrying about filtering it.

"That I did," she promised, her lip curling into an amused smile. "Have to pop that cherry slowly so I don't frighten you off."

"Quit distracting me." I mock-glared in her direction.

"Touchy. All you virgins are the same." I loved her sarcasm. It helped keep me from overthinking things.

"Shhh," I scolded.

She stuck her tongue out at me and pulled out her pencil and composition notebook. I could respect a writer who drafted on paper. All my initial outlines were on paper. You never knew when a story idea would hit you, so writing it down quickly was key to remembering things.

When I looked at the scene again, I immediately went in and changed the vocabulary for several sections. She'd told me to be provocative. Then I broke down the actions and tried to add more descriptive words.

The feeling of the rough upholstery of the couch against the front of her thighs.
The way her back arched when he grabbed ahold of her hair.

Once I knew what to remedy, the scene flowed better and became less choppy.

"That's probably as good as it's going to get on a first try," I confessed as I saved the document.

"You're done?" she asked distractedly as she finished writing and closed her notebook.

"Take a look." I passed the laptop over, and she settled it on her thighs, tucking her pencil behind her ear before she adjusted the screen. Waiting for her feedback was making me antsy.

"Do you want a drink?" I asked quickly, hating the anticipation of her approval...or disapproval. The usual sense of unease that accompanied a panic attack started to creep its way into the periphery of my brain.

"Hmm?" She was really focused on the screen. I wasn't sure if that was a good thing. A little line appeared between her eyebrows as she concentrated.

"I'm going to run up and grab water from the fridge. Can I get you one?" I asked again, knowing I'd send myself into a spiral and freak her out if I didn't try to walk it off.

"Sure," she answered absentmindedly.

I rose from the lounger and quickly walked up the stone path to the hill, glancing back to look at her before leaving. The line was still there. But I pushed it out of my mind and concentrated on grounding myself with my surroundings.

When I returned with our waters a few minutes later—noticeably calmer—she had a new notebook with a bright red cover open on the arm of the chair.

"I'm jotting a few notes," she told me as her pencil flew across the page.

"Take your time," I sighed, but I think she could hear the residual nerves in my voice.

"It actually wasn't bad," she mused, glancing up briefly with a small smile.

"I assume it's not good if you're writing me notes." I nodded at the notebook.

"These are more suggestions on places to dive deeper into. I feel like now it's bouncing around instead of sliding along the surface."

"Better or worse?" I cringed.

"Better, much better. They seem like real people now and not sex robots." Her smile wasn't merely indulgent; I think she was pleased that I'd not been completely hopeless with her tutoring.

"That's a whole other book," I laughed, and she shook her head,

"Oh, diving into sci-fi next, are we?"

"What? You're the only one who gets to play with other genres?" I shot back without even thinking.

Her eyebrow rose as she looked up at me.

"You get leather and blindfolds. Why can't I have robots?"

The way her eyes widened after I said that almost made me feel guilty, but the way her pupils dilated as she looked at my lips afterward made it worth it.

"So, you read it?"

"I couldn't put it down." It was the truth, her words had sucked me in, and I couldn't stop turning the pages on my tablet. It was the quickest I'd devoured a book in years. I usually got so distracted by my characters I couldn't finish books written by other writers. "If you hadn't shown up yesterday, I probably would have stewed in my book hangover for days."

She was quiet for a moment before standing up next to me. "Will you show me something?"

Images of her on my bed flitted through my mind as I watched the light breeze dance with her hair.

"Sure."

"Take me on a walk," she requested quietly. "You have to have explored this place. It's so pretty it seems like a waste to spend all day working."

"I've cleared some trails around the pond," I told her as I pointed to a break in the trees.

"Let's take a break," she urged as she put the notebooks aside.

"You sure we shouldn't keep going? We just got started." I was confused at her sudden need to explore my property.

"I'm here for two weeks, and you're not as hopeless as I thought. We've got time. Come on." She started to walk toward the water's edge.

It really was amazing how clear the water stayed. I'd spent a lot of time looking over it, trying to make sense of the words in my head.

I nodded toward a break in the trees, and she followed me.

"How long have you lived here?" Her voice was quiet but curious.

"Three years."

"Why here?" I don't know if anyone ever asked me that question. Adrian hadn't cared. He'd only been upset I wasn't as accessible outside of the city.

"I was taking some grad-level courses at UConn and fell in love with the area. When I decided I wanted to build, this property was the first one my agent showed me."

"I thought you lived in Boston before you moved here?" It thrilled me that she listened when I talked.

"I did," I confirmed, intentionally leaving out the details of my time there.

"Why did you come to UConn? You couldn't have gone to Boston College?"

"I could have. But I didn't want to stay in the city anymore." It was too toxic for me to stay there.

"Because you wanted a quieter life?" she asked as she glanced over at me.

Not exactly.

"I didn't want to have to find a new apartment." I knew I was being cryptic, but I hated that part of my life.

"So, you moved to Connecticut?" She narrowed her eyes and studied my face. "It seems like there's a story there to move several hours away. Especially since your family is in Chicago."

"There is." A story I had no interest in telling her.

"And?" I should have been annoyed that she was prying into parts of my life I didn't like thinking about, much less talking about, but I had a hard time being irritated with her.

"Ex-girlfriend wanted the apartment. I wanted to get away from her."

"That's all I get?" she laughed.

"What about you? How long have you been in Boston?" I changed the subject.

"Since college." Her coy smile indicated she knew I was avoiding.

"Creative writing?" I guessed.

"Am I that obvious?" She rolled her eyes.

"Nah, most of the writers I know who went to Boston College majored in creative writing."

"What about you? Does Stanford have creative writing?" she asked with a smirk.

Ah, so she'd done her research. "Someone's been Googling."

"Oh, shut it. I can't help myself. Cyber-stalking is my superpower," she laughed, but I could tell by the pink on the high points of her cheekbones that she was embarrassed.

"So, what did you find out about me?" I was genuinely curious to see how deep she'd dug into her background search.

"Not much. Still play soccer?"

I couldn't help but laugh as we stopped where the trees opened to the water.

"I'm not sure if I should be flattered or scared?" I laughed, shooting her an amused smile.

"How have we not met before now? We were in the same place at the same time and had the same publisher," she asked as she looked over at me. "I've attended dozens of author events and I've never met you."

"I'm not sure, but maybe me being horrible at describing sex wasn't such a bad thing." If we'd met under different circumstances, I knew that my guard would have been up. I'd have never talked to her like I was doing now.

"Full disclosure. I didn't want to come here," she confessed quietly.

"Then why did you?" I knew our editors were pushing it, but they could easily have sent someone else. "Adrian confirmed you'd agreed the day after I asked for you."

"Is begged me, and..." She stopped talking abruptly, her cheeks turning pink.

"And?"

"Then she showed me your picture." The vulnerability in her voice as she came clean made my pulse jump. She'd come here for me.

"And that alone didn't frighten you off?" I teased.

"Hardly," she scoffed. We had drifted closer to each other, our shoulders touching. I could feel the plastic from the water bottle she held brushing against my knuckles. "I couldn't take my eyes off you. It sounds vain, I know, but I couldn't stop thinking about you."

"I looked you up too."

Her face turned in my direction as I whispered my confession.

"Should I be scared?" she teased.

"I wouldn't be," I laughed quietly. "Although I prefer you without all the makeup, your picture was the main reason why I was so adamant it be you."

"Did you fall down the rabbit hole too?"

"I didn't Google you, no," I shook my head. "But I may have..."

"You may have what?" Her eyes narrowed suspiciously.

"Never mind." I shook my head, suddenly nervous. She would think I was a stalker if I told her how much I'd become obsessed with her words. Or the things I'd done in response to them.

"No, tell me," she coaxed.

"Not important."

"Oh, come on. I told you that I tried to look for you on the Internet before I'd even met you. If that isn't freaking you out for being intrusive, what you did can't be bad. You can tell me." She turned those beguiling blues eyes up at me and pled in a quiet voice. "Please?"

Her eyelashes fluttered, but I had a hard time looking anywhere but her lips.

"Let's say my Amazon account took a hit earlier in the week." Her ability to get information out of me was dangerous. She was climbing past all my walls.

"Meaning?" The pleading look turned to suspicion.

"I invested in some reading materials."

"Oh, God." Her eyes widened. She stepped back and turned away from me. "Please say you didn't?"

Before I could even process the motion, I grabbed her elbow and tugged her back in my direction. The move surprised both of us; I was typically not assertive.

"I don't even want to know what you..."

"All of them," I blurted out, interrupting her. "I read all of them. Even the holiday novellas you self-published."

She was looking up at me, searching my eyes for something.

"In two days. I read all of them in two days." My pulse pounded as I waited for her reaction. It could go either way. "I barely slept, and it might have been the first time I made Ramen for dinner since college."

"Wow." Her eyes were wide and vulnerable.

My hand tightened on her elbow, pulling her closer until our chests were barely apart. At this point, I was moving on instinct.

"They were captivating. Your words...you...you're..." I hesitated.

"I'm?" Moisture glistened on her lower lip as her tongue peeked out, my eyes drawn to the motion.

"You're captivating."

Chase's eyes widened as she looked at me, her lips parting on a sigh. "Evan..."

"I'm going to kiss you," I breathed, giving her a chance to back out. After a moment of hesitation, a barely perceptible nod was my answer.

Her expressive blue eyes fluttered closed seconds before I cupped the back of her neck and captured her lips with mine, finally giving in to the feelings she had awoken in me.

SEVEN

CHASE

CONNECTICUT

THERE HAD BEEN QUITE a few first kisses in my life, but never one that felt like this one did. Drunken kisses, awkward kisses, slobbery kisses, dry-lipped kisses, some passionate kisses, but this kiss...*this kiss*...

It was by far the most unexpected, yet simultaneously most right kiss I'd ever felt. There was something about Evan that drew me in, and he had since I saw that picture in Isobel's office. Maybe it was because he wasn't trying to charm me. Perhaps it was because he was so goddamn adorable with the staring and the awkwardness.

Whatever it was, when he told me he'd read all my books and looked at me with those slightly uncertain deep blue eyes... I was lost.

My hands clutched the sides of his denim shirt as his hand slipped along the side of my face and cradled my jaw as he deepened the kiss. His lips were soft, and I gasped into his mouth when he nipped at my bottom lip.

Evan's hand tightened on my neck as he tilted my head and eased his tongue past my lips. I was almost drowning in sensation as I pressed myself against his chest.

"Fuck, you're so sexy," he panted in a raspy voice as his lips trailed across my cheek and down the column of my neck.

"Oh God, Evan," I moaned as he sucked on a particularly sensitive patch of skin near my shoulder blade.

"Which one is it? God or Evan?" His deep, rumbling laugh vibrated into my neck as he held me there, his face buried into my hair, and I arched against him.

"Maybe both?" My chest shook with unrestrained laughter. He thought he was awkward, but he was smoother than he gave himself credit for.

"Mmm, I'm okay with being compared to a God."

I giggled and pinched his side.

"Hey, don't hurt me. I'm trying to impress a woman with my godlike skills," he teased.

"You're terrible. One breathy compliment, and you've got an ego the size of Adrian's." My face was buried in his neck as he smoothed his hand down my back. "What happened to the kissing? I was enjoying that part."

He pressed his hand into my hip, pulling his face back from my hair, ghosting his lips across my cheek.

"Oh, you were?" he teased, pecking my lips once and then easing back.

"Where do you think you're going?" My hand grasped his shirt and pulled him forward again.

"Nowhere." And his lips were on mine again, hard and insistent. Heat coiled up my spine as his hand slid further and cupped my ass, pulling my hips into his.

His other hand was tangled in the hair at the base of my neck, tugging slightly as he eased his tongue back inside my mouth.

I may have only met him recently, and our chemistry was unexpected, but we were obviously attracted to each other. It would probably be too presumptuous to assume we'd be jumping into bed anytime soon. Still, if the subtle gyration of his hips against mine was any indication, we'd be compatible there too.

My heart pounded as he finally released me and stepped back, sliding one of his hands into mine. "Should we continue our walk?"

"I don't know if I *can* walk," I laughed as I tried to regain my bearings. His kisses left me beyond flustered.

He tugged me along as he continued following the trail, slowly caressing my fingers with his thumb.

"What's going on here?" I asked curiously. While I wasn't a prude, I also didn't go around making out with male coworkers I'd met a day earlier in the woods, for instance. A girl has got to have standards. "This whole situation is a little unexpected."

"I honestly have no fucking clue." He aimed an unintentionally charming grin in my direction, and my heart fluttered, as well as other parts of my body.

"Do you think we possibly crossed a line we shouldn't have? We're supposed to be working together. Aren't there codes of ethics we should be following?"

I didn't think we'd overstepped, but I wasn't sure where this put us. We were supposed to be fixing his manuscript, not making out in the woods. Plus, I lived in Boston, where I was returning in two weeks.

"Do you think we did?" He stopped and turned to face me, his hands framing my hips.

"No. I don't." My hair fell into my face as I shook my head, and he reached up to tuck it behind my ear like he'd done the same thing a hundred times.

"Good, neither do I." He pecked my lips once, gazing down at me. "I can honestly say that I probably started fantasizing about what it'd be like to kiss you the moment I saw your picture. I've never bought into instant attraction—especially with someone you've only seen a picture of—but it just intensified when you showed up here yesterday."

Damn. For someone who claimed he was so awkward, he often said things that'd make any woman swoon. Or maybe it was his earnest delivery. From anyone else that comment would have seemed aggressively forward, from him it seemed like a confession. One he wouldn't have shared without prompting.

"That's a lot for a girl to live up to." His answering smile did things to my heart. "Did I stand up to the fantasy?"

"Oh, you blew the fantasy out of the water." He pulled me into him and kissed me again. We didn't seem to be progressing much on this walk, but I didn't mind. "You're just as charming as I imagined you to be. Reading your work created quite the crush on my part."

Something warm built in my chest at his words. Knowing someone enjoyed my books was a heady sensation, but knowing *he* enjoyed my words caused a flurry of butterflies in my stomach. Which was cliché as fuck, but true nonetheless.

"We probably need to try to get some work done," he sighed heavily, and I shared his disappointment.

"This doesn't count as research?"

"You have read all the pages, right?" I nodded as I smiled up at him. "Does Kallie strike you as the type to take long walks and engage in sensual kissing?"

"Sensual, huh?" Fuck hot seemed a more apt description, but we could go with sensual. At least he was using his new vocabulary.

"You keep telling me to use provocative words," he smirked.

"Smartass."

"You seem to like my ass," he teased as he wiggled it in my direction. Playful Evan was back. I liked him.

"Whose hand was on whose ass earlier, mister?" I pretended to be affronted, but let's be honest...it was hot.

"You liked it," his voice was taunting as he narrowed his eyes at me.

"I never denied that." My shrug pulled another amused chuckle out of him.

"Come on. We keep getting sidetracked. If we finish our work, that means more time for...*other things.*" His pace was steady as he led me along the trail on the far side of the lake. I could barely make out parts of his house through the trees.

It was a nice little trail, and he'd put river rock down to keep it from being reclaimed by the forest.

"So, do you own all this? The pond and everything?"

"My property starts at the main road where you turn and stops about ten feet that way." He pointed toward the woods that ran away from his house and disappeared into the distance.

"Past that is all part of the state park," he told me. "I liked that I wouldn't have neighbors close by. The park wraps around my land."

"Your books must be selling well to afford all this."

He shrugged, flashing me an embarrassed smile. "I've been very blessed. I went to college on an athletic scholarship and wasn't sure how I would pay for room and board."

That hadn't turned up in my Google search.

"My parents helped as much as possible, but we grew up knowing we needed to work for what we wanted."

"We?" There wasn't much on his family in the things I'd read about him.

"I have a sister. She's still in Chicago."

"I have two brothers in Minnesota," I offered. He didn't ask, but I felt like he appreciated not having to drag information out of me.

"You're from Minnesota?"

I nodded. I hadn't lived there in over a decade, but it was home. "South of Minneapolis. I'm the baby. Sorry, didn't mean to sidetrack you. I'm a chronic over-sharer," I apologized, and he smiled indulgently.

"That's fine. I'm glad you're still talking to me and not running from the awkward man who forced his kisses on you in the middle of the forest."

I may have looked at him like he was crazy. If he doubted the consensual nature of our rendezvous, maybe I hadn't done it right. "There wasn't anything forced. Except maybe my hips into yours when you grabbed me. Which was hot, by the way."

"I don't have the best track record with women."

"I find that hard to believe." He was beyond charming in his own special way, and the outside package was also quite appealing. I was worried he'd think I was superficial for being so swayed by his pretty face, but our attraction seemed mutual. While I was drawn to his appearance, what was beneath the surface was the truly attractive part.

"When I get nervous, I either clam up and do that staring thing, or I just start rambling." My heart clenched at the broken look on his face. "It used to drive Simone nuts."

"Is that your ex?"

He nodded. I could tell he didn't like to talk about her.

"Anyway," he redirected, "I was a poor, ramen-eating college student. During my freshman year, I sat down and started turning a short story I'd written for an assignment into a book."

"Were you a writing major too?" I knew writers came from all backgrounds, but I wondered how he started.

"No." He shook his head. "I was actually a chemistry major."

"Then how did you come to write a short story for an assignment?" Last I checked, chemistry majors spent all their time in science labs, not computer labs.

"Core requirement. I took a writing seminar. I'd always been a fan of writing, but I also dreamed of becoming a forensic detective."

"Ah, so that's how you got into mystery novels."

He winked at me and pressed his finger to his nose.

"Why didn't you continue with forensics?" It'd be way over my head, but that sounded like a cool profession for someone with an analytical mind like Evan seemed to have.

"My roommate told me I should enter my book into a writing contest, and it got noticed," he shrugged.

"That's lucky." I'd had a pile of discarded rejected manuscripts in my closet before I'd signed my first contract deal. I'd spend years querying before anyone asked for a full manuscript sample. There had been a length of time early in my career when I wondered if I'd made a huge mistake pursuing fiction. But I could never see myself writing copy in some arbitrary company just to get a paycheck. I thrived on being creative and would've been miserable doing something like that.

"I didn't win, but one of the judges was an agent. He liked my first draft and submitted it to a publisher."

"And it got published?" Talk about luck.

"I was offered a three-book contract with another one optioned based on sales," he told me, looking slightly embarrassed.

"Holy shit. That's like the unicorn of writing contracts for a baby author." I couldn't hide my jealousy. "I was book to book for my first two." And even that took a lot of hustling on my part.

"I was shocked. But my parents encouraged it," he sighed. "With the advance from my second book, I could fast-track my degree and graduate a little early."

"You completed your studies?"

"My parents told me that I needed to follow it through. Even if my degree is now used to understand character research instead of finding real criminals."

"You've got smart parents." Mine hadn't been thrilled with my major or the rocky start to my career.

"So, my first book was published while I was still in school, and the second right after graduation."

"I didn't get published until after I'd been out for two years." I was a little envious of how his career had essentially dropped into his lap.

"But you seem to be popular. I read some of the reviews of your first book, and the critics seemed to love you," he argued, frowning.

I shrugged, hiding my face from him momentarily. "That wasn't my first book."

"You mean there's more?" He looked a little eager at this information. I wouldn't have thought a chemist who wrote mystery novels would be into romance.

"Trust me. You don't want to read them." He laughed as I shook my head.

"Oh, come on, they can't be that bad," he scoffed.

"They were before I got picked up by a bigger publisher. There's a reason I changed my pen name."

"I'll find out eventually," he told me, insinuating he was not going to let this drop.

"No, you won't. I buried them where no one can find the bodies." He'd better not enlist Adrian to dig. I'd sworn Isobel to secrecy when she'd asked to read them. The storylines might see the light of day eventually, but they needed major rewrites.

"That sounds like something I'd write," he joked. I smacked him on the arm and narrowed my eyes as he laughed at me.

A few moments later, we crossed into the clearing near the walkway to his house. I was disappointed that our walk had ended, but not what had transpired while we were on it. But as we approached the house, he started doing the shifty eyes and neck scratching again.

"Evan, are you alright?"

"Yeah, I just wish we had more time to talk. I like listening to your voice." He looked a little shy and a lot vulnerable at his admission.

"Are you kicking me out?"

He shook his head slowly.

"Then we've got plenty of time. Relax. You aren't getting rid of me anytime soon."

"Are you hungry?" He smiled as I headed toward the back door.

"What are you planning to feed me?" I asked excitedly. Getting all these amazing meals I had no hand in was a treat.

"Am I your personal chef now?" he scoffed, pretending to be offended.

"You're the one who mentioned food!"

"I did," he nodded with a little wink. "Have to keep that mouth of yours full."

"Do you have an apron? That'd make the personal chef fantasy complete," I teased.

"Oh, we're talking fantasies now?" He looked all sorts of intrigued by that topic. I was curious as well.

"No, but I think you'd look hot in an apron," I shrugged. Maybe with no pants underneath. No, definitely no pants.

"Because aprons are *so* sexy."

The exaggerated eye roll he gave made me bite my lip to contain the laughter. I stopped in the open doorway from the patio and winked at him over my shoulder.

"Who said you'd be wearing anything else."

He made a sound halfway between choking and whimpering, and I cracked up laughing as I sauntered in and took a seat at the island.

"So, is naked chef a new character I can expect from you?"

"Not in this book, but I wouldn't be opposed to starting my research early." Bantering with him was becoming my new favorite activity.

"It's a little early in the day for a striptease."

"But you'll give me one later?" I asked eagerly. "And for the record, it's never too early or too late for a striptease."

He stopped pulling ingredients out of the refrigerator and braced himself with both arms outstretched in front of him on the island. "It depends."

"On?" I was genuinely curious.

"How much work we get done today. We still have two more scenes you haven't looked at yet." Well, that was a buzzkill. All work and no play made Evan a clothed boy.

"I looked at all the pages Adrian sent me." I frowned. I'd already marked up the hard copy to let him have as a reference.

"These weren't included in that." Hmm...there was more.

"I thought the manuscript was finished."

"I felt inspired," he shrugged. "I wrote another chapter last night."

"Inspired by what?"

He winked and turned back to the fridge. "I'm sure you can figure it out. But it involves the detective pinning her to the wall in an interrogation room."

My eyes widened, and I fanned myself with my hand.

Was it getting hot in here?

EIGHT

EVAN

CONNECTICUT

WE SAT BESIDE THE firepit the rest of the day, passing the laptop back and forth. We edited most of the scenes, and I prepared a PDF for Adrian. I knew they weren't quite finished, but we wanted feedback to determine what we needed to work on next.

I was surprised at how much we were able to accomplish once the initial tension between us was broken and I didn't feel as distracted by her. It wasn't that she lost allure, but now that I knew what it felt like to kiss her, and I could kiss her when I wanted, thinking about it didn't consume me. Even though we'd only known each other for a matter of days, it felt surprisingly natural to interact with her like this.

"Back here bright and early tomorrow morning?" she asked as she packed her notebook into her laptop bag.

"I'll be up early again, so whenever you'd like to show up."

"I could probably come a little earlier, but I'm definitely not missing Marian's breakfasts." The dreamy smile that crossed her face made me a little jealous.

"Oh, I see how it is, already replacing me."

"Well, she does have a pretty fabulous apron," she teased.

"Using her for research?"

"Definitely not. I can't say I imagine what she'd look like naked." The look she gave me over her shoulder was almost predatory.

I walked around the side of the couch and grasped her hips, turning her around to face me.

"You think about me naked?" I couldn't mask the huskiness in my voice, and her eyes widened.

She ran her hands up my chest and pressed herself against me as I pulled her hips snugly against mine. There was no question that I wanted her, but I wasn't sure if all her teasing was simply that.

"More like fantasized. It's all I can think about," she whispered as she looked into my eyes. "Have you seen how hot you look?"

"You could stay tonight."

Her breath caught as her fingers gripped my shirt tighter. "I, uh..."

Shit. I'd come on too strong. This was insane. I'd only met her yesterday. Simone and I had dated for weeks before I mustered the courage to kiss her properly. "Sorry. Shit."

One of her hands gripped the back of my neck and pulled my face toward hers. My whole body shuddered as her lips gently caressed mine. Our lips met tentatively before she tugged my hair and pulled me into her.

It escalated quickly as she pushed up on her toes, then licked and bit my bottom lip. My head spun as I pressed my tongue against hers as I bent my knees, pushing my growing erection into her stomach.

I was fighting the urge to push her back onto the couch and strip her bare, but I knew that'd be going too far. We were barreling toward one-night stand territory, and I didn't want to ruin things between us for a quick release.

After a few minutes, our lips slowed, and she pulled back from me, resting her head above my galloping heart. "As much as I'd love to, maybe we should save that for another day."

I nodded and combed my fingers through her hair, willing myself to calm down. "That could be arranged."

She giggled and stepped back, picking up her bag by its strap and settling it on her shoulder.

"I should go." She pecked my lips again.

"I'll see you tomorrow." Two days, and I was already craving her presence in my life...in my home.

She stepped around me, and I followed her to the front door. Leaning against the doorframe, I watched her pull away, her taillights gradually fading as she retreated down the tree-lined drive. I wasn't sure if I'd freaked her out, but maybe I needed to step back a bit. The only problem was I didn't want to slow things down.

I obsessively checked my email for the rest of the night, waiting for a response from Adrian.

A few hours later, I gave up and went to bed. Tomorrow would hopefully give me some clarity in what was developing between Chase and me.

MY PHONE WAS PINGING long before my alarm went off.

Who the hell was texting me at 5:00 am?

Adrian: Did you get laid?

Adrian: Was it Chase?

Of course, it was Adrian.

Evan: No, and was what Chase?

Adrian: If you didn't get some, who wrote these edits?

Adrian: The scenes almost seem believable.

Evan: You're welcome?

Adrian: I thought you didn't want anyone else writing parts of your book?

Fuck off, Adrian. I am a professional.

Evan: She didn't write the edits, I did.

Asshole.

Adrian: How much porn have you been watching?

No comment.

Evan: ...

Adrian: I take it you two are playing nice?

Evan: Yes, I can be nice to people...unlike someone I know.

Adrian: You love me ;)

Evan: You keep saying that, but I really don't.

Adrian: Maybe you won't need her for the full two weeks after all.

Shit... shit... shit.

Evan: We still have a lot of material to get through.

BY THE TIME CHASE arrived some hours later, I'd scoured both marked-up files and started making the revisions they'd suggested.

The thought that maybe, at least on half of them, we'd accomplished what weeks of banging my head on my keyboard had not left me feeling a sense of accomplishment.

I felt myself behaving like an eager puppy as I answered the door, ushered her inside, urged her to sit on the couch, and made her start reading.

"These look good. Especially compared to the original drafts. It's clear something clicked into place." She leaned forward to settle the laptop onto the coffee table, but something in her expression left me unsettled.

Her sigh was almost forlorn as she leaned back and curled up, facing me on the cushion beside mine.

"Is something bothering you?" I wasn't used to this insecure, slightly sullen version of herself. She was usually so full of life and energy.

"I guess I had it built up in my head that this would take longer," she sighed.

I knew exactly how she was feeling. I was happy that we accomplished our goal in record time, but that also meant we probably didn't need to keep her here for two weeks.

"Hear me out..." A plan started formulating in my head as she looked up at me. She was either going to think I was insane or a genius.

"I'm listening." Her face had brightened a little, but she was still skeptical.

"What if we sold you staying longer as a mutually beneficial situation?"

"What are you proposing?" she frowned.

"Maybe I have some expertise that would help you with your next book." I wasn't sure what that was, but Adrian and Isobel didn't need to know that.

"Naked chef?"

I laughed as she smiled at me, reaching forward to play with my fingers as our hands rested between us.

"Not quite. How do you feel about collaboration?" I knew we were both resistant to giving up control of our work, but we'd meshed well in a matter of days. I wasn't ready to part yet.

"Like you being my consultant after I'm finished being yours?"

"No," I shook my head, "like a true collaboration. Shared byline."

"Are you saying?" She looked up at me with wide eyes.

"Write a book with me," I breathed heavily, waiting for her answer.

"Isn't what I write a little too...*soft*...for what you normally write?"

I almost felt bad for the loud laughter that burst out of me.

"Ouch." She sat up and pulled away from me, disappointment clear on her features.

"No...no!" Taking a deep breath, I calmed myself and scooted closer to her, using my finger to push a loose strand of hair behind her ear. She sighed and closed her eyes, a shy smile showcasing her dimple again. "What you wrote kept me anything but *soft*...for several days." And immersing myself in her writing helped me feel closer to her sooner than I'd anticipated. While I was awkward as fuck, I had opened up to her quicker than I had to new people in the past.

Her eyes popped open and flared with something akin to need as she scooted even closer to me.

"Is that so?" She slowly skated her fingers over my knee and thigh, causing me to shift a little.

"Mmhmm. Kind of like you're doing right now," my voice was a rough whisper as I felt all the blood pooling in my groin.

"Whatever will we do about that?" She fluttered her eyelashes at me dramatically and ran her fingernails across the fabric of my pants, dangerously close to my burgeoning erection.

"Are you trying to kill me?" I choked out as I tried to maintain the illusion of composure.

"La petite mort, maybe."

"Shouldn't we be brainstorming?" Her eyes had turned predatory again, and I was a little nervous about what was going on in that brain of hers.

"Maybe we need some *hands-on* research..." When her hand reached my zipper, I was solid and throbbing.

"Chase..." I warned as she slowly started to pull the tab down, the teeth making a steady clicking sound as they slowly disengaged.

"Shh..." she soothed as she stared down at where her hands were at work, unbuttoning and spreading the fabric apart. "Just sit back and relax."

"Kind of hard to do when a girl has her hand in your pants," I laughed nervously. A woman had not touched or seen me like this in a long, long time.

"Oh, it's hard, alright," she smiled deviously as she tugged at the waistband of my boxer briefs. I lifted my hips and helped her push my pants and briefs down my thighs.

"Are you sure about th—mfph..."

My cock throbbed as she raised herself on her knees and forcefully meshed our lips together, effectively cutting me off. Her tongue slid past my lips, and she bit at my bottom lip as her hand closed around the base of me.

I moaned into her mouth as she gripped me firmly and began to work my length. Feeling this woman's touch was unlike anything I'd felt before, desire spooling inside me until I could barely stand not touching her.

My hands slid into the hair at the back of her neck as she kissed me passionately while rhythmically pulling on my dick. The dual sensation of her hand and tongue massaging mine made me dizzy.

It'd been so long since someone had touched me intimately, I was afraid I was about to spout off like a geyser. Then she started making this move, alternating squeezing the base and twisting at the head.

"Oh my—*fuck*—slow down." I broke my mouth from hers and panted, throwing my head back against the couch.

She scooted back slightly, winking at me as she leaned down and licked around the head.

"Fuck..."

Her hand continued to tug at the base while she enveloped the tip in her mouth, sucking while she rubbed her tongue against the ridge of the head.

Holy shit, her mouth felt amazing.

My heart beat out of my chest as she brought her fingers below my shaft and gently rubbed my balls as she continued to lick and suck with enthusiasm. I was about to explode but was desperately trying to hold on to my dignity by not finishing too soon.

Rubbing my hand along her neck and back, I leaned forward to grab her ass as she continued going down on me. I was too horny to be shy with her now, simply touching her on instinct.

"Mmmm..." she moaned as she took me almost all the way in, pausing before her teeth grazed along my length on the way back up.

"I'm close," I whimpered. My voice was husky and almost breathless as I grabbed her shoulder. It was taking all my concentration to hold onto my sanity.

"Mmmm," she moaned again before taking me all the way in.

"Oh God..." I gasped as I tangled my hand in her hair and held on for dear life. Chase was trying to kill me.

I held on for as long as possible, but a man could only endure so much torture. My guttural moan cued her in, and she pressed her mouth as far as she could on my dick and sucked.

I came in a flurry of hair-grabbing, moaning, and whimpering as my hips lifted clear off the couch cushions. It was by far one of the most intense orgasms

I'd ever had. I could lie and say it was only because it'd been a long time since someone else gave me one, but it was the effect Chase had on me.

"I think you did kill me," I panted as I lazily rolled my head to the side and looked at her through hooded eyelids.

She had the biggest smile as she sat up and leaned against the cushion beside her, looking directly at me.

"But oh, what a way to go..."

NINE

CHASE

I DON'T KNOW WHAT came over me, but apparently, a hot guy asking me to write a book with him made me lose my mind. Suddenly, I needed to touch him. I hadn't intended to include a full oral happy ending, but I wanted to taste him.

"You're quite proud of yourself, aren't you?" he smirked as he looked at me.

"I guess someone doesn't want a repeat performance."

His head shot up from the couch cushion like I'd lit his hair on fire. "Definitely did not say that. You're putting words in my mouth. Sort of like you put my..."

Sticking my tongue out, I interrupted his line of commentary. I was still a little embarrassed I'd basically attacked him. While I did write racy content occasionally, I was typically a little more reserved in my real-life entanglements.

"I know where that's been," he told me, smirk firmly in place across his full lips.

"I didn't hear any complaining," I shot back.

"Only that it ended."

The teasing dynamic of our relationship clearly hadn't changed in the last twenty minutes.

"So, a book?" The prospect of teaming up with him was hard to resist. If we could channel our chemistry into a book, I had no doubt that it would sell.

"Uh-huh." He smiled and then reached out and grabbed one of my hands, slowly tracing my palm. I had to admit, I'd never considered the palm an erogenous zone, but it was starting to get me a little worked up.

"Any thoughts on content?" I was trying to let him steer me on this and not take over. He was the man with the plan.

"Something sexy." There was that little naughty glint in his eyes again. Evan wasn't quite as tame as he liked to portray.

"You finally write a decent sex scene and suddenly think you're an expert?" I couldn't resist the urge to continue ribbing him a little.

"I had a very gifted teacher."

"Charmer," I said shyly, feeling a blush rising.

"Is it working?"

"You already got yours," I accused as I tried to play off his effect on me.

"But you didn't get yours." He raised an eyebrow and nodded at my tight-fitting shirt. I was sure my nipples were trying to burrow through the fabric.

"I thought we were trying to work here," I argued, but we both knew that if he wanted to take things further, I'd jump on him in a second.

"You're the one who said we needed to 'do research.'" I'd created a monster.

"Are you going to make this hard the whole time?"

"Give me a few minutes, and I can make it plenty hard." Heat flared low in my belly as he turned the tables on me, and seductive Evan came out to play.

"I thought you were supposed to be the awkward one?" I teased as I stroked his finger suggestively.

"You bring out the best in me."

My heart melted slightly, even though his comment was a little pervy.

"Work. We're supposed to be working," I tried to change the subject. "Genre?"

"Thriller?" he offered with a shrug. That would be well within his comfort zone.

"Characters?" I was interested to see how he did the initial character development. Evan's brain was a curious place.

"Does Michael have any friends?"

My entire mouth went dry as my jaw dropped open.

Holy shit.

Evan wanted to write a sexy book with me about bondage and Domination. It's always the quiet ones.

"Are you saying...?" I wanted him to admit what he wanted.

"Maybe we write a thriller with a kinky twist," he shrugged, but I could see the tension in his eyes.

"You're full of surprises." Having read some of his older books, I knew he tended to avoid his characters being in tumultuous romantic entanglements.

"Maybe I'm ready to try something new." His readiness to jump right into this showed he was open to new possibilities, both with his writing and with me.

"More research?"

"If the right research partner comes along," he teased with a cheeky wink.

I pretended to be reluctant about his proposal, but I was so on board. "What does the job entail?"

"Lots of long...*hard*...hours." He stressed in that deep sexy voice that appeared when he was aroused. If I were a cartoon character, I would have fainted with little hearts flying around my head.

"You realize I'm not an expert, right?" I had more experience than he had in the area, but I'd only seen the parts of the lifestyle that Emory had shown me.

"You know more than I do," he nodded. "We could learn together."

The thought of Evan coming with me to train with my own Dom was amazingly hot. Instead of having Emory tying me up and simulating the scenes I was trying to write, he could be teaching Evan what to do with me. And I'd be completely at his mercy. It sounded like a dirty dream come to life. At least something—or someone—would be coming.

Is would have a field day with this. I go away for two weeks and bring back a new story pitch hotter than anything either of us had written before. Adrian was going to have kittens. He was going to think I tempted his highest-grossing author over to the dark and spicy side.

"So how are we going to spin this?" Isobel was counting on me to finish my current series. Derailing my progress for a completely new project would piss her off.

"Honestly? Let's keep them in the dark," he said, looking slightly guilty. It seemed he knew Adrian would be protesting this match-up as well.

"You mean don't tell them until it's written?"

"Bingo," he winked.

"It could take months." It typically took me a few months to draft a book. I couldn't disappear for that long without drawing suspicion.

"Can you escape for that amount of time?"

"Won't you get tired of me?" I asked warily. That was a long time to spend with someone when you were used to being alone. Especially someone you barely knew. Even if you fantasize about making her come repeatedly within the first 48 hours of meeting her. But that was just wishful thinking.

Focus, Chase.

He shrugged and then pulled me closer to him on the couch. "I honestly don't know how this is all going to turn out, but if it means I get to spend more time with you, I'm all in."

"I'm having difficulty taking you seriously with your pants still undone."

He laughed and grabbed my sides, tickling me as he raised himself over me on the couch. We crashed back into the pillows, and his mouth came down on mine in a calculated attack.

Evan's tongue and fingers were erasing every doubt and hesitation building up within me. I could feel him hot and hard pressing against my stomach, his pants still halfway down his thighs.

My hands gravitated toward his bare cheeks as he slid his fingers underneath the hem of my top, caressing the skin of my back. My breath was short as I broke the kiss and threw my head back. His fingers delved under the cups of my bra and tweaked my nipples as I bucked my hips into him.

"Oh God," I moaned as he thrust against the thin layer of my leggings, sliding one hand down my thigh to hitch it over his hip.

"Come to bed with me," he growled into my hair as I dug my fingernails into his ass, causing him to jerk his hips into me. "We don't have to..." he trailed off. "But I want to feel more of your skin against my lips. A lot more."

I nodded frantically as he began to rain biting kisses down my neck and across my collarbone. "Yes..."

Before I could anticipate the motion, he stood up, hitching his pants over his extremely erect cock—which was some seriously impressive recovery time—presumably so he could walk without tripping.

"Let's go." He held his hand out to me. Hesitating for a moment, I placed my hand in his, and he yanked me up before he crouched down, banded his arms around my legs, and hoisted me over his shoulder.

"Evan!" I shrieked as he stood back up and stalked past the kitchen and down the hallway, me laughing into the back of his shirt as he held my thigh with one hand and my ass cheek with the other.

He was a man on a mission as he kicked his bedroom door open. I saw it bounce lightly off the wall.

The world shifted as I fell backward onto his bed abruptly.

That sparked a new round of giggles as I scooted back toward the pillows. Evan stood beside the bed, kicking off his shoes before he ripped his shirt over his head.

His chest was lean and lightly muscled, with the perfect amount of hair on his pecs and abdomen.

"Is this my striptease?' I giggled as I propped myself on my elbows and watched him unabashedly.

He smirked as he shoved his pants to the carpet, stepping out of them before his socks were discarded.

"I'll turn on the music next time," he laughed as he grabbed me by the calf and yanked me toward his partially clothed body.

Before I could even lift my hips to help him, he was pulling down the waistband of my leggings. He peeled them, along with my panties, off and threw them to the floor before pushing a knee onto the bed. He climbed up until he was hovering over me.

This dominating side of him was turning me on. He wasn't going to have any problems at all with our 'research.'

Evan knelt, straddling my legs as he took possession of my mouth again, sliding his hands inside my shirt and pushing my bra up my chest. I moaned as he cupped my breasts and roughly dragged his thumbs over the nipples.

"Fuck, these are spectacular," he moaned as he pushed my shirt the rest of the way to my armpits and dropped his head to my chest. My back arched off the bed as he tugged at one of my nipples with his teeth.

"Off...off..." I insisted breathlessly as I tried to sit up and pull my shirt over my head.

He helped me discard it and released my bra clasp, throwing them both onto the pile of clothes on the floor. His eager tongue laved my nipples as his big hands framed my breasts and pushed them together.

My hips were squirming on the bed as the twin sensations of his lips and the scruff along his jaw drove me toward madness.

Grabbing his hips, I urged him to lay down, his body covering mine.

Evan panted as he looked up at me, his hard length throbbing against my thigh through the thin fabric holding it captive.

My breasts were forgotten as he slowly shifted to the side, his hand tracing a path of fire up the inside of my thigh.

"You're so wet," he growled as he dipped the tips of his fingers inside of me, and then his thumb began to slide against my clit. While his first written sex scenes may have been fumbling, he clearly knew how to locate the important parts in real life. My eyes rolled back, my back arching as I pushed my hips toward his hand, seeking friction.

"I want to make you come." His voice was rough in my ear as my eyes closed at the sensations he was stirring inside me.

One long finger slowly eased into me, and I moaned loudly as it retreated and then curled on its way back in. His cock twitched against my thigh as he added another finger and began to build up speed.

"Fuck me," I moaned as I grabbed his arm and gyrated my hips into the movements of his fingers. Getting fingered had never been this intense for me before.

"Come on, baby," he whispered, nipping along my jaw. I started to spasm against him, grabbed ahold of the hair at the base of his neck, and screamed my orgasm.

"Fuck yes." His voice was gravelly as he kissed down my stomach and settled between my legs. My eyes were screwed shut as I panted, my body completely overwhelmed with sensation.

"Chase?" he whispered as he ran his hands softly down my thighs, his eyes fixated on where I was wet and ready for him.

"Mmm…" I hummed as my eyes slipped closed. The bed shifted as Evan laid down and kissed the inside of my thigh, his tongue tracing a path inward.

The world seemed to pause as his warm breath teased me. He was hesitating. But I was borderline desperate for more of his touch at this point.

"Open your eyes, baby."

I drowsily opened them, and he smiled at me before he ran a finger down the line of my pussy. "Is this okay? If I…?"

Despite the way he'd been dominant moments ago while he coaxed an orgasm out of me with his fingers, I could see the insecurity in his eyes. He was waiting for me to tell him this was something I wanted.

Not wanting to scare him by yelling at him to start licking, I nodded, reaching down to run my fingers along his cheek. "I want you to. Please. Don't make me beg. That'd just be embarrassing."

He chuckled and nodded, blowing out a warm breath that made me squirm, and rolled his shoulders back as he settled between my legs. Part of me wanted to talk to him about why he was self-conscious, but with the first flick of his tongue and suck of his soft lips, I couldn't form coherent sentences as my back arched against his soft sheets.

Evan was a man on a mission as he thrust two fingers inside me and curled them, massaging as he teased my clit with the tip of his tongue. Whoever made him question his oral skills was an idiot. Much quicker than I thought was even possible, I was crying out and thrusting my hips into his movements, chasing down my second orgasm as my lips started to tingle and my thighs began to shake.

"Fuck," he grunted as I spasmed against him, crying out.

I must have blacked out for a moment, my ears ringing as I returned to myself. Evan stretched himself against me, massaging my breast as he rained kisses along my neck and shoulder as I clung to him, desperately trying to catch my breath. I was quite sure he was the one trying to kill me now.

Chapter
TEN

EVAN

CONNECTICUT

THERE WERE NO WORDS. For once, the characters' voices in my head were silent. I was completely present in the moment without storylines running through my brain, and it was because of one person.

Chase was curled up against my chest, fingers idly tracing the skin over my heart. I had no way to describe what had happened adequately, and for someone who got paid to craft a compelling narrative, that said something.

When I met her, I never expected to end up pleasuring her in my bed a few days later—not that I hadn't fantasized about it.

"You're thinking awfully loudly up there," her quiet voice brought me back, and I kissed the top of her thoroughly sexed-up hair.

"I don't know what you're talking about. I'm certain I've been stunned speechless." I didn't even recognize my voice.

Going down on a woman was something I'd only done a handful of times, and it'd never been as frantic as it'd been with Chase.

Once she started writhing against my face, I was determined to get her to come again. It also helped that her book heroes loved to give oral. Who knew I'd get to use some of the new skills her writing taught me on the author herself?

She smiled and kissed my chest. "What's the plan for the rest of the day?"

"I want to start drafting an outline, but I feel like the scenes with Kallie are missing something." I had a niggling feeling that we weren't quite done with them yet.

"How so?" she asked curiously.

"I know they sound believable now, but I keep thinking about what you said."

"I say lots of things," she laughed. "You're going to have to be more specific."

"I'm aware," I nodded as I ran my fingers down her bare back. "The part about if your heart doesn't start beating faster while you're reading it that it's not hot enough."

"That's good advice." I smiled at the smugness in her voice. "You don't think you accomplished that?"

"I don't know," I sighed. "I feel maybe they could be more authentic."

"You're not going to abandon me to chase down a prostitute, are you?" she teased. I doubted I could look at another woman and not compare her to Chase at this point. But it was way too early to tell her that.

"Would you want to read the whole manuscript?" I normally didn't allow anyone but the editing team to do that, but...

"You'd let me read it early?"

I'd let you do anything right now.

"If you knew the whole plotline, maybe it'd make it easier for you to help me fix it." If she was going to be my partner, I wanted her to be completely in the loop. We could start with this.

"Won't Adrian have a fit?" she asked with humor in her voice. I could tell she wasn't a fan of his. To be honest, sometimes, neither was I.

"What he doesn't know..." I trailed off.

"Okay." Her voice was quiet and guarded as she answered a few moments later.

I blew out a nervous breath and turned my face into her forehead. She snuggled further into my embrace and sighed as my lips rested on her soft skin.

"Are you sure you trust me that much?"

Positive.

"Of course, Chase. I can't think of anyone else I'd rather... How did I phrase it before?" I mused, "Rip me a new one."

She pinched my nipple before she smacked me in the chest.

"Do I need to pick up some lube on the way over tomorrow?"

"Oh, she's got more jokes," I teased, squeezing her against me.

"I've always got jokes." I could tell she was rolling her eyes at me without even looking.

"I'll show you funny," I growled as I flipped her over and nibbled on her neck and shoulder crease. She was squirming under my weight, laughing hysterically as I rubbed my stubble along her soft skin.

"Ahh. Stop!"

I eased back a little and began using my lips to kiss and suck along the same skin, eliciting a dramatically different reaction. She moaned and arched her neck as I readjusted myself to settle into the cradle of her thighs.

My barely covered cock pressed against her, and I angled my hips to grind down with a slow, deep rhythm.

"Evan." Her voice was strained as she braced her feet flat upon the mattress and gyrated against me.

The feeling of her warmth made my head swim as I adjusted and pressed my hips directly against her, pulsing them slowly until she cried out, her neck arched backward. Firmly gripping her hips, I slowly rolled myself to the side, pulling her with me. I eventually settled with my back flat on the mattress with her sitting astride my hips.

"Ride me," I urged as I bucked up from the mattress. The thought that we were dry-humping like two teenagers vaguely registered before she started to move.

Chase panted as she began to swivel her hips, grinding down onto me, my cock trapped between our bodies.

It'd never been this way for me. Watching her naked body sensually undulating in my lap was hotter than any sex I'd had in recent years, probably ever.

Things had become infrequent and stale toward the end of my last relationship, and once I caught her cheating, I was done.

Chase was a goddess, blonde hair mussed around her face and shoulders, eyes hooded, curvy breasts bouncing, cheeks flushed an enticing shade of pink. She was voluptuous—her curves filling my hands—and judging by the sultry looks she was giving me, she was entirely comfortable with her body and what she knew it could do.

Her innate sexuality turned me on immensely, and I rapidly succumbed to the sensations she was stirring within me.

"Fuck. Go faster," I urged as I chased my orgasm, my cock about to explode in my briefs.

"I'm coming again," she panted as I pressed against her, my hands holding onto her waist firmly as her movements coaxed out my orgasm, my neck straining against the pillows with the intensity of it.

She collapsed on me, her hair fanning across my face and neck. Her heartbeat pounded against my chest, the tempo almost as quick as mine.

"Shit. I can't breathe," I groaned as I panted.

"I don't think I can move," she laughed as she lay across my chest.

After a few moments, I laughed, the stickiness in my briefs gaining my attention. Chase looked up, resting her chin on my pec. "I just came in my pants like a barely pubescent teen boy."

"Well, you certainly didn't act like one..." She arched an eyebrow, running a finger down my torso. "And you certainly don't look like one."

Her fingers skated down my belly, playfully snapping the waistband against my stomach with a grimace. "But you might want to clean that up before you get stuck in these. I might want you out of them later."

"Oh really?" I laughed, liking the thought of that. I knew things were moving fast, and mixing physical intimacy with a working relationship might become complicated, but I was beyond caring.

Dragging myself out of bed, I escaped to the bathroom, pulling off my sticky boxer briefs and throwing them into the laundry basket. My reflection caught my attention as I turned toward the door, hesitating as I studied it. I looked confident for once. The tension surrounding my eyes was gone, a soft glow staining my cheeks. This woman I'd known for a few days was doing more to bring me out of my shell than years of dating the wrong women.

Chase was asleep on her side when I returned to the bed, the sheets haphazardly pooled at her waist, the curves of her full breasts almost glowing against the dark cotton. Climbing in behind her, I rolled her toward me, smiling as she sighed when her head settled on my chest. My eyes closed as our breathing and heartbeats evened out. The last thing I remembered was thinking of how comfortable we were with each other and the anticipation of having her in my arms like this again and again.

CHASE'S BODY HEAT EVENTUALLY pulled me out of sleep. My human blanket ran hot when she slept.

I didn't want to move her off me, I'd slept solidly for a few hours, but we needed to eat a late lunch and devise a game plan. I didn't want her to go back to sleep somewhere else each night. Even though I truly enjoyed my privacy, it'd be much better with her here.

I'd get to wake up to her attempts to overheat and smother me, we could write and brainstorm at our own pace, and maybe I could give her that naked chef demonstration she wanted.

Mental note: order an apron on Amazon.

"Baby..." My whisper went unanswered. She was out like a light. I wondered if she had trouble sleeping as I did sometimes.

My fingers skated down her sides, gently lifting her hips and attempting to ease her off to my side. She mumbled something and curled into the comforter as I finally freed myself. Lying on her stomach with her hair spread out around her, she looked sated.

Our chemistry—at least for me—was explosive.

I ached with the urge to climb back on the bed and slide into her from behind, but she was exhausted. And I wanted to look into her eyes the first time I was inside her.

With another person in the house, my fridge was depleting quicker than normal, so I'd need to make another trip into town this week. Maybe Chase would accompany me.

That'd get the town gossip chain going.

Feeling like I might as well do something productive, I found my laptop and worked on getting together a readable PDF of the latest re-draft of my manuscript.

My mind raced at the thought of her reading it, but I was also dying for feedback from someone other than Adrian. He was paid to be nice to me.

"Hey..."

Arms encircled my shoulders over the back of the couch as Chase kissed my ear and hugged me.

"Someone was tired," I hummed, leaning back into her embrace.

"I know. You slept forever," she yawned.

I could see what she was wearing when she walked around the edge of the couch. She'd obviously raided my closet, judging from the familiar blue plaid flannel shirt she wore. Her long legs were bare, but she also had a pair of my socks on.

"Someone is making herself at home." I was sure my smile was ridiculous.

She tucked her hair behind her ear and suddenly looked shy. I wasn't upset. She looked amazing in my shirt. It hugged her curves and hit mid-thigh, showing off a sizeable amount of bare skin.

"It looked soft," she confessed as she rubbed one of the lapels against her cheek before she settled at the other end of the couch.

"I'm never getting that back, am I?" And I was okay with that one hundred percent.

"Probably not."

This time when I stared across the space on the couch between us, it wasn't awkward or uncomfortable. My staring had to do with the fact that I couldn't and didn't want to stop looking at her, not my sometimes-intense awkward behavior. It hadn't seemed to bother her anyway.

"So, do we have a plan?" she asked as she nodded toward my computer.

"For?" I asked curiously.

"You're telling me you haven't planned the rest of the day in your head?"

I picked up the tablet from the corner of the couch and slid it into her lap. "Well, you've got some reading to do..."

"And what are you going to do?" Her soft smile warmed something inside of me.

"I skipped my run for you this morning, so I probably need to get that in."

"Are you sure I can't watch that instead?" she smirked.

"Fine," I teased as I started to tug the tablet toward myself, "if you don't want to read it then I guess I can take the tablet back."

"No! This is mine." She pulled it back and hugged it to her chest.

"I'll be on the treadmill in the sunroom," I told her as I stood up and went to find my running shoes by the front door.

"You're not going to run outside? It's such a nice day."

"I usually alternate days. I'll run outside tomorrow." I shrugged as I looked over at her. "Do you want to run with me in the morning?"

"You probably get up obnoxiously early, right?" she sighed knowingly.

"6:00 am is not that early."

She pulled a face and shuddered. "It is when you don't fall asleep till after midnight."

"Maybe you need a good night's sleep," I teased.

"The bed at the B&B is comfortable. I slept like a baby last night," she sighed.

"I'm betting my bed is nicer." Especially with both of us in it...naked.

"Meh." She shrugged her shoulders. "The mattress was kind of hard and lumpy."

"I think you meant hard and chiseled. Since you used me as a mattress," I teased, and her cheeks turned pink.

"You were warm."

"You know..." I hedged, trying to keep my voice even. "I was thinking."

"That's scary."

I ignored her and tried to keep going. "What if, in the interest of accessibility, you stayed here instead?"

"You want me to stay here because it would make me more accessible?"

Granted, it wasn't the best formulation of my argument.

"What if one of us gets inspired in the middle of the night?" I argued. "Wouldn't it be easier to write together if we could do it whenever we wanted?"

She seemed to be thinking it over.

"What's in it for me?" she teased, but I could see her lip twitch.

"You get to look at my handsome face all day." She valiantly tried to resist smiling as I batted my eyelashes at her.

"Eh. The view isn't that great." She shrugged, and I pinched her side as she laughed.

"I'll cook your food?" I offered.

"If you throw in cooking while naked, then sold," she giggled. She would not let this naked chef thing go, but the only thing I wanted to eat in the kitchen was her.

Chapter ELEVEN

CHASE

CONNECTICUT

APPARENTLY, EVAN'S ENTHUSIASM FOR my books had rubbed off on me. I couldn't put down the tablet. I'd even turned down taking a shower with his sweaty post-run self to keep reading.

Kallie's character had drawn me in, and I'd just gotten to the good part, where she met Detective Peter Raines for the first time after witnessing a murder. Of course, I wouldn't stop when it'd gotten to a good part. He should have known a lady never puts down the book in the middle of a meet-cute, even if it happens over a corpse.

After Evan had taken a shower, he'd pried the tablet out of my hands so we could leave. He thoroughly teased me on the car ride to check out and get my luggage.

I would miss my little private sanctuary, but—even though I gave him a hard time—I was looking forward to cuddling up with him each night. Things were moving ridiculously quickly between us, but I didn't want to step back either.

Even so, as we stood in the entryway of his house afterward, the enormity of what I'd agreed to hit me, and I stopped, letting the bag I was holding drop to the ground. Had I agreed to essentially move into the house of someone I'd met two days ago? Scenarios of how this could blow up in my face—and not in the fun way—started racing through my mind.

He wrapped his arms around me from behind and kissed my neck. "Are you having second thoughts already?"

The nervous edge to his voice stirred me out of my potentially destructive thoughts. "I want to be with you. I think you're right. It'll help us get into the rhythm of it if we're not limited on time." He was right. Inspiration didn't always hit during normal hours. Sometimes I woke up in the middle of the night, and pages poured out of me.

"There's another rhythm we can get into…" He teased as his hips pressed into my back and commenced a slow grind against my ass.

"You're naughty." I was enjoying this new side of him.

"You make me this way." He slowly pushed my hair off my neck and laid hot kisses along the back of my jaw. His hands roamed my front as one slid down my stomach and into the waistband of my pants while the other cupped my breast. "I don't know what I'm doing, but I also don't want to stop."

Same, dude. Same.

His fingers' slow but firm motions caused my breath to quicken—heat pulsing through my veins.

"I thought you were in a rush to start writing," I moaned as I leaned back into his chest.

"The only rush I'm in is to get you out of these clothes." The low, urgent tone of his voice turned me on even more. "And to coax another orgasm out of you. The sound of you begging does something to me."

"By all means, don't let me stop you," I panted.

He walked me toward the couch, backed up slightly, and started to pull the fabric of my pants down my legs. Kneeling behind me, he kissed the backs of my thighs as he helped me pull off my shoes and step out of my pants. The socks and panties were eased off, too, before he pressed on my back and bent me over the back edge of the couch.

Evan's strong hand traced down my heated skin and stopped, squeezing briefly. Something about how he was taking charge brought the pages I'd read earlier to mind.

A firm hand cracked down on my ass while I was spaced out, and I jumped as I moaned. "Oh, fuck."

Evan's surprised expression when I looked back almost made me laugh, but as the pleasure mixed with pain started to flow through me, I was more than down to try this.

"Again…" I moaned as he rubbed the tender skin. His large hand smacked the other side, and I grunted as my pussy clenched. I needed him inside me.

Where had this come from? He didn't seem like the type to enjoy rough sex, but I was not complaining. His actions reminded me vaguely of one of the scenes in his book, where the detective and Kallie finally gave in to their desire for each other.

"God, you look so hot…" he groaned, and I turned to look at him again. He lifted one hand and traced the place he'd struck that still stung a little bit, tickling the skin where he'd spanked me. "I don't know where that came from, but fuck, this is—"

"Hot as fuck," I chuckled, and his wary eyes met mine, something solidifying in his gaze when he realized I liked it. "Keep going. Maybe this is what you need. Use me to figure out what's missing from those scenes. You need to experience it."

"But..."

"Evan, I don't know what your middle name is, Stineman, a half-naked woman bent over your couch, is asking you to use her for inspiration to finish your novel. If you don't get inside me in the next—"

His hand cracked down again on my other side, and a strangled moan worked its way up my throat as I clenched my eyes shut momentarily, letting the pain flow through me. Rustling from behind me caught my attention, and I turned my face to watch him unbutton his pants and shove them to the floor along with his briefs. My mouth watered as I took in his bare form. He was staring at my ass with an intensity that made me wet.

"Take your time..." I teased as I wiggled my ass at him and licked my lips.

"Should we really...?" he shook his head, eyes transfixed. "Shouldn't this be more romantic?"

"Evan, we have time for you to whisper sweet nothings into my ear later. I'm safe and protected, are you?"

"Am I...?" His eyebrows were pinched as his eyes flitted between my legs and to where I was looking back at him. "Safe for what...?"

Taking pity on the fact that he was distracted by my nudity and deciding to steer this train back onto the track, I pinned him down with a look. "If you want to fuck me without a condom, it's safe. But if you don't want to, that's okay, but you'll need to find one *right now.*"

His eyes widened almost comically as he swallowed, his Adam's apple bobbing with the movement. "I'm safe too. Are you sure?"

"Then don't stop. You don't need to be gentle with me. I want this. I want you. And while I appreciate that you're a sweet guy, I need you to fuck me now."

"Fuck it," he growled as he gave up unbuttoning his shirt and grabbed me by the hips.

"That's the idea." I moaned as he rubbed the head of his cock through my opening.

"Someone is a little excited." There was no hiding the evidence of his handiwork.

He dipped the head in, pausing as I squirmed and then retreated, teasing me. I tried rocking my hips backward, but he held me firmly with both hands as he tortured me. He continued this until I was a squirming mess, gripping the couch and biting my lip as I fought the urge to yell at him. Shy, reserved Evan from before was nowhere to be found. In his place was a man determined to make me plead for more.

When I thought I couldn't take anymore and would go insane, his grip intensified on my hips, and he plunged in fast and hard.

"Fuck, this is going to be embarrassing," he moaned as I panted, trying to adjust to his size. "You okay?"

"Yes. Oh, God." I nodded as he pulled out slowly and thrust in again, harder this time. He didn't hesitate to find his rhythm, widening the stance of his legs and angling his hips to hit me in just the right place that I almost screamed from the intense pleasure. He was forcing my hips into the side of the couch with every thrust, and I was trying to hold on as my orgasm started to build.

The volume of my moans was almost obscene as he leaned over my back. His hand slipped between my hips and the rough upholstery and found my clit while he continued ramming into me from behind.

The quick circles of his fingers, the rough pulsing of his bare cock, and his hot breath on the back of my neck set me off.

"Fuck. Oh God." My voice was muffled as I moaned into the rough upholstery. His name was a filthy moan spilling from my lips as I clamped down on his cock and gripped the fabric under my hands as my muscles started spasming uncontrollably.

"Yes, fuck, come on me," he groaned as he plunged into me harder, not slowing the pace of his fingers.

I was moaning uncontrollably as he leaned back and gathered my hair into one hand, the motions of his hips never stopping. As he straightened, he lightly pulled the hair in his fist, causing my back to arch.

He moved his fist back a little more and dug his fingers into my hip with the other hand as I gasped in his hold. My body was on high alert as he manipulated me for his pleasure, and I felt another orgasm start to build. This one felt different, and as it crested, I let go of all my hesitations. No man had intrigued me like this, no man had fucked me like this, and I wasn't going to run away because I was nervous.

"Harder," I urged, and the growl he let out as he snapped his hips forward and pulled on my hair stole my breath as the orgasm rolled through me.

"Fuck," he grunted repeatedly and punctuated each exclamation by slamming me back into his hips. I was out of breath, and my entire body was tingly as he thrust once more and groaned as he held me tightly and pulsed inside me.

"Oh my God," I panted as I lay face down on the couch, thoroughly out of breath. I wanted to applaud his performance, but I couldn't move.

"Shit," he groaned as he slowly eased himself out of me and released my hair so he could rub his hand on my ass cheeks. They still stung a little bit, but I really did not mind. "Are you sure you're alright?" He asked as he let go of me, and I nearly slumped to the floor in a post-orgasmic puddle.

"Mmm. I'm good." My voice was drowsy as I closed my eyes. He laughed as I heard him rustling behind me.

I cracked one eye open, and he smiled as he watched me. His pants were pulled up again, and he casually leaned against the couch beside me as he ran his hand down my hair softly like he hadn't just wrecked me.

"How am I the only one comatose?" I wasn't sure if I could make my limbs move, as numb and tingling as I was.

He shrugged as he began to run his fingers down my back, making me squirm.

"I hate you," I mumbled as I looked at his smug face. He was a little sweaty, but he wasn't panting like me.

"Pretty sure you don't," he teased, the blue in his eyes alight with mischief. "Come on, get dressed. Don't make me spank that pretty ass of yours again," he threatened as he ran his palm over my thigh.

"What's gotten into you? I never expected to see this side of you..." I rolled to my side and stood so we were facing each other.

The content smile on his face turned more serious as he reached forward and clasped my hand.

"Hey, it's okay..." I coaxed as I watched some of the light drain out of his eyes. Gripping his hand, I led him around the couch and sat down, pulling him beside me.

He was quiet as he took a deep breath and looked down at our interlaced fingers. "I've honestly never had sex like that before."

"Really?" My eyes widened as I watched the pink stain of his blush grow on his cheeks. While he'd looked surprised after spanking me the first time, he hadn't hesitated to continue.

"I was surprised you recognized what I was doing. Trying to be my character. Be more confident when I had no idea what I was doing."

I thought back to how everything had transpired. It had been so close to how Detective Raines had bent Kallie over the arm of his couch but different enough that it hadn't mattered to me in the moment. I'd told him to put himself into the scene, and it seemed he had.

"Maybe that's what we need to do," I mused. "Act it out."

"Um, I'm pretty sure we already did that," he laughed nervously. "Or did you come so hard you forgot the last five minutes?"

"Shush," I laughed as I squeezed his hand. "We need to recreate all the scenes you've been struggling with. Put ourselves into the characters."

"Like scene for scene?" He frowned as a little line appeared between his eyes.

"Yes! Dialogue too. Like a sexy little role-play. Maybe that will give you the extra material to get them where you wanted."

"Are you sure?" He did not look convinced this was a great idea. "The only place I've seen some of this is on a screen."

My eyes widened at his little confession that he watched porn to get inspired for these scenes, but I wasn't letting him distract me. "Am I sure I want to recreate some hot, rough sex scenes with you? Hmm, let me think about it."

"They aren't exactly romantic," he cringed. "I still feel bad that our first time was..."

"Fucking mind-blowing," I interrupted as I could see him start to spiral. "Did you forget the part where you made me come twice?"

"I'm not sure if I can do everything I wrote into those scenes."

"Because you had so much trouble slapping my ass and pulling my hair?" I laughed sarcastically.

His face turned bright red as he bit his lip and stared at me.

"Hey, don't get shy on me now. You're not going to hear any complaints from me."

"Where did you come from?" he breathed out as he stared at me incredulously. "I swear it's like someone pulled you from my thoughts."

I smiled at him as I felt my cheeks heat up. "You already got in my pants; you don't need to pour on the flattery."

He shifted to face me, scooting closer and slipping his fingers behind me, tracing the bare skin along my spine.

"I'm not kidding. I've never felt like this with anyone," he whispered. "Adrian makes fun of me and doesn't understand why I won't do book signings. My ex," he hesitated. "Well, she was mean in general but..." A forlorn look crossed his face as he stopped talking. "She never made me feel comfortable when we were together."

"She sounds like a bitch."

He laughed as he leaned forward and kissed me softly. "She was, and she made me feel inadequate...sexually. That's why I never wrote sex scenes into my novels. I never felt confident in my abilities, much less so in writing a character who could please a woman. Back then, I would have never felt secure enough to do what we just did on paper or otherwise."

"But you are with me?"

He nodded, a soft smile on his lips. "I'm more relaxed with you than I've been in years. Normally, when a woman tries to flirt with me, or hell, even talks to me, I choke up and bolt."

"I'm glad you didn't bolt. Might have made it hard to finish your book." Perhaps my meeting him at his house ensured that we at least had a level playing field. Had I met him at an industry event, would he have talked to me?

"As soon as I read your books and author bio, I knew I had to get over myself and meet you."

Aw... He really was adorably perfect. Despite my best attempts not to, I found myself feeling some intense things for him.

"I don't know what to say. My words will fall short of yours today," I told him quietly.

"I wasn't looking for compliments," he shook his head as he looked over at me.

"I know, but I couldn't stop thinking about you before we met too. I wanted to know the man who wrote this incredibly strong character," I confessed quietly. "I wanted to know the person who could write so beautifully yet harbored this intense sense of loneliness. I wanted to hug him and let him know he didn't need to be lonely anymore."

His eyes searched mine as he reached up and ran a strand of my hair between his fingers.

"I'm not going to be able to let you go," he whispered, leaning forward and capturing my lips. His were soft and tentative, slowly encasing my bottom one and then retreating, only to dive right back in. He didn't try to deepen it or speed it up... He lazily kissed me until I felt dizzy.

After a few moments, he pulled back and rested his forehead against mine, closing his eyes. I cupped his jaw, running my thumb across his cheekbone. This kind but awkwardly adorable man would steal my heart if I wasn't careful. And when he finally did, I wouldn't want it back.

"Let's get cleaned up and start this outline," he whispered, and my heart burst with affection that he was opening every part of his life to me.

TWELVE

EVAN

CONNECTICUT

HAVING CHASE IN MY house 24/7 was an adjustment. She was not an early morning person. The growl she unleashed on me when I tried to get her to run on the trail with me was both adorable and terrifying.

"Go away," she groaned into the pillow she had a death grip on near her face.

"Come on. It'll wake you up. I always feel invigorated after a run."

I was wearing my athletic gear sans shoes and sitting beside her on the bed. My hand combed through her tangled bedhead as she groaned into the pillow.

"Good for you."

"Please, I'll make it worthwhile," I tried to coax.

"I hate you."

"You seem to be saying that an awful lot. I might start taking you seriously." Despite her grumpiness, I couldn't contain my smile.

"You're so annoying. Go take your morning person vibes somewhere else."

"Please," I begged. I knew she'd like it if she only got up and came with me. Even if we walked the whole time, the fresh air always inspired me.

She rolled over onto her side, facing me, and squinted her eyes open. "I was promised naked cooking if I stayed here. If you don the apron and let me smack you with a wooden spoon, I'll run with you."

What...the...fuck...

My cock didn't know what to think. The thought of her swatting me with a spoon both excited me and made me want to hide from her. She was kind of violent in the morning.

"Fine, you don't have to come this morning, but I *will* get you to go with me eventually."

She laughed into the pillow as she flipped me off. "Oh, come on, I won't hit you very hard."

"Go back to sleep." I kissed her cheek, and she closed her eyes again, pulling the comforter up to her chin.

I left her curled up in my bed and went to put on my running shoes. I especially needed to clear my head this morning. Chase had done a number on me. I don't know if it was reading all her books or writing what I'd been writing this week, but I couldn't stop thinking about sex. More specifically, I couldn't stop thinking about sex with her.

Her idea to reenact the parts of my book I felt needed work was good, but some of the things Kallie and the detective did were rougher than I was used to. He liked rough sex, and she sold her body for a living. My characters were obviously much more experienced than I was, and it gave me performance anxiety.

"Stop thinking about sex," I admonished myself. It was as if one of the characters in her books had invaded my brain.

I needed to run. Although if my line of thought continued, I wouldn't be able to with a rod in my shorts, and I would have to wake Chase up again. She'd probably growl at me, but I was sure I could persuade her with a few well-placed kisses.

"Stop it."

I could kiss her all I wanted after getting this run over. Maybe I could get her to join me in the shower. I needed to stop thinking about it. She had to be sore after last night. I'd gotten a little carried away when we returned to the house. She said she liked it, but I saw her wince when she got dressed again last night.

My feet pounded against the gravel trail, the crisp morning air permeating my lungs. I loved running. It always made me feel more alive. It was something I could do to tire out my body and clear my mind.

I completed the trail at a pace that beat my usual time. My muscles burned as I grabbed my bottle of water off the patio. I was so wound up that I could run another lap, but I wanted to shower and curl up with Chase. Hopefully, she wouldn't be as grumpy when I rejoined her.

"'I'm a Barbie girl, in a Barbie world. Life in plastic, it's fantastic.'"

What the hell? I hadn't heard Aqua's 'Barbie Girl' in years.

I crossed the threshold of my bedroom, tossing my empty water bottle onto the edge of the bed. It was empty, so apparently, Chase had decided against sleeping in. She was evidently in my bathroom, singing very loudly.

I could also hear the shower running, so she hadn't waited for me. Hopefully, I could catch her in there. As I pushed the door open, my shirt and shorts were quickly discarded in the hamper. A cloud of steam billowed out, and I wondered how long she'd been in here. I was only gone a half-hour.

I wasn't proud to know it, but when she got to the part in the song at the end where Ken chimes in, I couldn't help myself and dropped my voice as I sang the lyrics.

Chase jumped and dropped the bottle of shampoo she'd been holding as I stood in the opening of my walk-in shower. I quickly crossed to her and grabbed her by the elbow as she started to slip backward.

The last thing we needed was for me to scare her into a concussion. That wasn't the banging I wanted to get into with her.

"Holy fuck. You asshole," she laughed loudly. "You scared the shit out of me."

She continued laughing as I pulled her up against my bare chest and kissed her.

"I didn't know late 90s pop was your thing," I teased.

"It's obviously yours since you knew the lyrics!"

"I blame my sister," I shrugged.

"I blame my childhood," she snarked as she crossed her arms, which pushed her breasts together enticingly.

"You were like ten when that came out. Your parents let you listen to that?"

She giggled as she snuggled up against me and ran a hand up into the hair at the base of my neck. "No, but my brother's girlfriend did."

"Corrupting young minds, such a shame."

"I thought you liked this corrupt mind," she smiled at me.

"Oh, I do."

I was sure I more than liked it, but I was keeping that one close to the vest. She already knew I could be socially awkward. We didn't need to add 'clingy' to what she thought of me. I was serious when I told her I wasn't sure if I could let her go. I didn't want her to return to Boston.

My head knew it was inevitable for her to go home, but my heart had already made a place for her here with me. I tended to get attached to things I enjoyed, and Chase was bound to become my newest addiction.

"How was your run?"

"Fast," I laughed.

"Eager for something, are we?" she teased as she pressed against me tighter, her nipples grazing my chest.

"Nope."

Her eyes shot up to mine, and she pinched my nipple with the hand resting on my chest.

"So violent," I laughed.

"You like it," she teased softly, running her thumb over the peak. "Do I need to kiss it better?"

She was giving me a run for my money. I thought she was a tease before things became physical between us, but now, she was insatiable.

"I mean, I won't turn you kissing me down." I knew what those lips could do.

"Right answer," she said as she began to kiss and suck at my neck, working her way down my chest. Then she was nipping at the poor nipple she seemed to enjoy torturing.

"Ah, fuck," I grunted, the pain only seeming to solidify things that had started to grow when I found her wet and naked.

"Someone seems to enjoy it." Her warm, wet hand encircled my shaft, and I couldn't help but flex my hips into her ministrations.

"Fuck, you're driving me insane." But I loved every minute of it. I never expected the reaction my body had to small amounts of pain.

"Now you know how I feel," she whispered as she licked a line up to my earlobe. Her teeth tugged on it, and I moaned louder as she continued the sweet torture on my body. "I want you constantly."

My palms found the swells of her breasts and slowly caressed them until she was moaning into my neck, continuing to pleasure me. This woman was a vixen, and I couldn't think around her, much less deny her desires.

"Let me touch you," I whispered in her ear as I ran my hand down her stomach.

Chase panted as my fingers slipped between her folds and, finding her drenched with desire, slid easily against her sex.

"Be gentle," she whispered as she rocked herself against my hand, the grip of her hand on me tightening.

"I don't want to hurt you," I whispered in her ear as I slowly eased a finger inside her warmth, twisting and curling it to see if I could make her moan.

She cried out as she rose onto her tiptoes, and my finger slid in further, her legs shaking.

"Sit down, baby," I urged, turning her around and pulling her hand from me.

There was a tiled bench seat along one wall, and I helped her sit and spread her legs apart.

"Put your feet up here." I tapped on either side of where she sat. She raised her feet and settled them on either side. My hands pushed against her thighs, and I urged her legs further apart as I settled on the tile on my knees.

"Oh God!" she moaned as I leaned in and took a long, slow lick of her pussy. I paused to suck on her clit as I slipped one finger inside her, curling it slightly as I built momentum.

"Yes! Fuck yes!" she practically screamed as I felt her clit throb against my lips. I could tell she was close because she'd grabbed my hair and held it tight as I drove her to the brink. Her body responded to me in a way that made me want her all the time.

Chase shrieked as her walls clamped down on my finger and began to spasm. I pulled my finger out and kissed her clit one last time.

"That tickles a bit," she giggled, releasing my hair and stroking my cheek.

I stood up and let the water rinse my face before I leaned down and kissed her. She looked sated, slumped against the wall behind the bench with a lazy smile.

"Come here," she whispered as she reached forward and pulled on my hip, urging me close to her. "It's your turn."

"You don't..."

She shook her head and reached forward to grab my impossibly hard cock. She wet her lips with her pink tongue and then whispered the sexiest fucking thing I'd ever heard in my life.

"I want you to fuck my mouth."

My breath caught as she leaned forward and licked the head, causing it to jump between us.

Only hesitating momentarily, I braced one hand on the wall above her head and grabbed myself with the other. She opened her mouth and placed both hands on my thighs as I guided my cock into her mouth. I'd had women suck me off before, but to have her pull against my legs and encourage me to literally fuck her mouth was insanely erotic.

"Mmmm," she moaned as she dug her fingernails into my skin and began to rub her tongue on the underside with each slow thrust.

"Fuck," I groaned and slapped the tile with my hand as she grazed her teeth along the ridge at the head. My hips shot forward faster into her mouth, and she gagged. I pulled back slightly, afraid I'd choke her, but she moaned louder as she increased the suction. The water made it impossible to tell if her eyes were damp from the steam or choking on my dick, but the sight of her drove me toward the edge.

"I'm gonna come," I moaned as I closed my eyes and threw my head back. My hips were on autopilot as I plunged in and out of her mouth, chasing my release.

"Mmm." As she hummed against me again, I lost control and pushed as far as I could, hitting the back of her throat.

My hand hit the tile as I clenched and then released, pulsing in streams down her throat with a shout.

My head fell forward and rested on the cool tiles as I panted, trying to catch my breath. I slipped out of her mouth and heard her take a huge breath. "That was hot."

I cracked open my eyes and gazed down at her.

She had damp hair plastered to the side of her face, and her cheeks were pink, but she was the most beautiful thing I'd ever seen. Situations like this caused people to blurt out spontaneous declarations of love.

I wasn't going to, but I could see the appeal.

AFTER CLEANING UP IN the shower, I dressed and checked my phone. Adrian had blown it up with a flurry of text messages.

> *Adrian: Tick-tock, quit playing with your cock. I need those pages.*

> *Adrian: I know you're awake. Get your lips off Chase's ass and send me those edits.*

> *Adrian: Don't make me drive down there.*

Oh, God, no. That'd be a disaster.

> *Adrian: Isobel will harass Chase if you don't answer me.*

> *Adrian: I've never been ghosted before. I don't like it.*

Adrian was such a dumbass.

Looked like Chase and I needed to buckle down and finish some work.

Chapter
THIRTEEN

CHASE

CONNECTICUT

"THANK YOU! JUST THE package I've been waiting for," I thanked the delivery driver happily as I took the box from him. I was surprised he'd deliver out here, but Amazon Prime never shied away from frequent deliveries.

Evan would either kick me out of his house or laugh his ass off when he opened this box. I knew it was a joke—mostly, but I had ordered him a sexy apron and a wooden spoon for myself.

It featured a cartoonish illustration of a hand pointing down and the phrase, 'May I Suggest the Sausage?'

Why yes, Evan. You may suggest the sausage.

He had holed himself up in the bedroom going through more edits before he sent the manuscript back to be approved by Adrian. Apparently, I was distracting, and he needed to escape from me so he could finish. We needed to start our collaboration, and he wanted all loose ends tied up.

Speaking of tied up, I needed to contact Emory and see when he could meet with us.

I wasn't sure if Evan would be comfortable driving into Boston, but we needed expert advice on this one. Neither of us had the equipment readily available to start writing about a Dominatrix.

We'd agreed on a female lead, but I was still scared of what Emory would make me do with Evan to get into character. I didn't want to scare him away.

> Chase: Hey. Got time for another consultation soon?

Emory had been the Dom who tied me up so I could get into Kayla's head. He also loosely inspired the character of Michael. Emory liked to follow rules and enjoyed teasing his subs to build up anticipation.

He was funny, always making sarcastic comments about things when he was not in Dom mode. I'd loved working with him, and he'd only had one stipulation for offering his consultation services—he got to photograph me when he'd tied me up. He promised no pictures with my face in them, and I hadn't been fully nude, but Emory had seen quite a bit of me.

Emory: Depends. I'm looking for a model...

He was a fashion and art photographer during working hours and a secret Dominant the rest of the time. He'd been a friend of a friend, and I hadn't been able to use his real name in my book dedication.

He wanted to keep his personal life separate from his professional one. I could respect that, considering I wrote under a pen name.

Chase: Bribery. Really?

Emory: I need a fresh face.

Chase: I thought we didn't do the face.

Emory: You're walking right into this one.

Chase: Oh, shut it, you perv.

Emory: We both know that's not going to happen.

Emory: Don't make me find the paddle.

Chase: Brat.

Emory: Pretty sure you already hold that nickname.

Knowing he would react, I sent him an emoji with its tongue hanging out.

Emory: What have I told you about the tongue?

Chase: Sorry... Sir.

I laughed as I enjoyed our usual banter. Despite being a successful artist, he wasn't pretentious at all. He wouldn't engage in the fun back and forth, only when acting as a Dom in a scene.

Then he was intimidating as hell. I'd initially been a little frightened of him, but he'd been clear when we set the ground rules that my safe word put me in ultimate control.

He'd initially let me sit in on his private sessions with his current long-term sub. She was amazingly kind, yet exuded a fairly brash persona when she was outside of his studio.

I would never have taken her for the type to be submissive to anyone, but their chemistry was explosive. I had usually stepped out of the studio once they got to the final act, but her moans carried down the hallway despite the soundproofing. Maybe that's why my book was over the mildly steamy point and categorized as erotic fiction.

Emory: Revisiting Michael?

Chase: No...

Emory: Intriguing. Are you going to tell me any details?

I wasn't sure how much Evan wanted me to share with him. Evan didn't even know I planned to consult with my source again. But I knew that we needed real-life material to draw from.

Chase: I have a writing partner...

Emory: Oh! Shit just got real...

Chase: Simmer down. You can't scare him off.

Emory: Him? Even better!

And here comes the teasing.

Emory: You hitting that? Are you going to fill me in? I bet he fills you in...

Chase: ...

Emory: Oh, come on!

Emory: You know I don't like to be kept waiting.

I sat and stared at my phone for a moment and then looked down the hallway toward the door to Evan's bedroom.

Emory: Is it anyone I'm familiar with?

Chase: His name is Evan.

Emory: That's all I get?

Chase: ...

Emory: Chase!

Chase: You might recognize him by Evans...

Emory: ...

The screen was quiet momentarily, and then I saw the three little dots appear.

Emory: Fuck! You're bringing Stone Evans with you!

Chase: He's not as intimidating as I expected.

Emory: When did he get into the erotic stuff? He's usually a cockblock.

Chase: ...

Emory: Damn! Did you corrupt that poor man?

Chase: I'm not dignifying that with a response.

Emory: You totally got in his pants!

Emory: Should I be concerned I won't measure up?

Chase: I don't know! I've never seen your dick!

And Em and Talia were not seeing Evan's.

Emory: Not my fault. It's not like Talia would mind...

Chase: Keep that eggplant to yourself.

Emory: You know I like to share...

Emory: Actually, I don't :)

Chase: You've got to tone down on the flirty stuff.

Emory: Who me?

Chase: Seriously. I like him...

Emory: Aw! That's adorable. Chasey is smitten.

Chase: I can contact Nathan if you can't play nice.

Emory: Ouch. You know he'd never be as good as me. Although, he has been leaning into his switch tendencies lately. He could probably give your boy some pointers.

Chase: Who is he in a dynamic with?

Emory: Grace.

Chase: Hell no!

Grace was a Domme I'd met at one of the lifestyle showcases Em had taken me to. She was graceful, but she also carried a bullwhip and a penchant for collecting other people's pets. There was no way I was letting Evan anywhere near her. She took great joy from *breaking in* new pets.

If Em didn't scare him, Grace surely would.

Emory: Don't worry. He can be discreet. I can find another Domme to work with you if you need it.

Chase: You better.

Emory: What kind of timing are we looking at? Do I need to clear my schedule?

Chase: I need to talk to Evan. He doesn't know about you yet.

Emory: Pushing him right into the fire?

Chase: I just hope he doesn't run the other way.

Emory: He'd be an idiot if he let you go.

Emory: I've got shoots this week and next out of town. I can make myself available after that. Let me know.

Chase: I will.

Emory: Good luck! And don't forget you're mine when this is over.

Chase: I get a veto on the wardrobe.

Emory: Drama Queen.

Chase: Yeah...yeah

Emory: Behave. I'll check in later. Have fun with your new toy.

Chase: Bite me.

Emory: Maybe later.

Emory: Brat.

I put down my phone and picked up my laptop. Isabel had sent me about three emails asking for my latest pages. There were also thinly veiled threats because she was mad; I was dodging her calls, after all.

It wasn't necessarily intentional, but I didn't want to lie to her. I also didn't want to pop the bubble Evan and I were inside. We were just starting whatever this was, and I was attached to both him and the novel. Going home was honestly the last thing on my mind.

I knew he wouldn't want me moving in permanently, but I wanted to see where this went. My heart was invested, and I couldn't walk away.

Large hands covered my eyes, and I smiled as he kissed the back of my neck. "Being productive out here?"

"I'm trying. Someone told me they didn't want me getting into their head today."

I tilted my head to the side as I looked at him over the back of the couch. He kissed me softly and ran the pads of his fingers down the exposed skin on my neck.

"Now who's distracting who?" I raised an eyebrow.

"Fine. I can see where I'm not wanted." Evan started to back up from the couch, slowly turning away.

I sat up and grabbed his arm before he got too far and pulled him back to me.

"I need to talk to you about something." Might as well get this over with.

"That sounds ominous."

His hands found my hips, and he looked into my eyes before he leaned forward to kiss me softly. I hummed into his mouth as our lips languidly caressed each other.

"I promise it's not bad, but..."

"Lay it on me," he smiled.

"There's this photographer in Boston that I know. I'm trying to schedule a consultation with him."

"So, you need to go back?" He frowned, and I hated that I may have upset him. "Why a photographer? New headshots?"

"He does want to photograph me, but no. He can help us with the book."

He looked at me quizzically. "New character? How does a photographer tie in?"

"That's his day job..." I trailed off.

His eyebrows raised. "And he's a serial killer by night?"

"Well, he does like to call himself the slayer sometimes, but not because he kills people," I giggled. He looked at me like I'd lost my mind.

"I'm so confused." His face pinched up.

I took a deep breath and put it all out there.

"He has a particular set of talents that he let me document to write Michael."

The look on Evan's face was priceless. Part arousal, part pure terror.

"And...uh...you..." He was scratching the back of his neck and avoiding eye contact with me.

"Hey, what's wrong?" I grabbed his chin and forced him to make eye contact with me. "Talk to me."

"Will he touch you in front of me?" he whispered as he stared down at me. His eyes looked pained, and it startled me.

"Well, he'll need to if we want to make sure we've got the moves right." A certain amount of hands-on teaching came with being a Dominant.

He pulled my hand from his face and turned around to stalk into the kitchen. He braced his palms out in front of him with his head hung low.

Shit.

I put my laptop on the coffee table next to the box and cautiously walked up behind him.

"Hey," I whispered as I placed my hand carefully between his shoulder blades.

"Stop." His voice was low and gruff as he dipped his shoulders to shrug off my touch.

"What's going on in there?" I asked as I ran a finger across his temple.

"I guess I just thought..." The sigh he released was full of pent-up anguish.

"Thought what?"

He shook his head roughly from side to side. I could hear him taking shallow breaths, and I was getting worried. "I thought you were mine."

Oh!

He thought I'd been intimate with Emory. Shit. I hadn't been clear about my past with him. And with how things started with us, he had every right to be upset.

"Do you want me to be?" My heart was pounding in my chest as I waited for his answer.

Chapter
FOURTEEN

EVAN

CONNECTICUT

FUCK!

The thought of her letting another man touch her with me standing there made me want to punch something. I ran all those scenes with Michael back in my head, but Chase was the one on her knees instead of Kayla.

She said it was research, although I wasn't sure if this guy had touched her intimately or not. If he'd let his hands roam her bare body. It was killing me.

"Evan...?" Goddamn it. Of course, I wanted her to be mine. I didn't know how to tell her that and demand this prick not touch her at the same time.

I was constantly hard when she was near me, and if he had the same reaction to her, I would explode.

"Alright. Maybe I should go for a walk or something. Leave you alone for a bit." She sounded like she was on the verge of tears. I hated that I was making her cry. I had the words right there, but my damn mouth wouldn't work.

"Wait!" I growled as my hand shot out to grab hers.

"I don't know what exactly you think is going on, but I want you to know that Emory and I have never..."

I leaned back and turned to face her, cautiously touching her hip. I still couldn't make full eye contact with her, but I was willing to listen.

"Never?" I asked, hating that I was this insecure.

"He's never seen me fully naked." She shook her head, but the way she phrased it didn't sound completely innocent.

Fuck. So, he's seen her partially naked.

"We don't...we haven't ever..." she bit her lip as she sputtered through a response.

"Fuck, just rip off the band-aid and stop skirting around it. Who is this guy to you?"

"A friend."

"With benefits?" I deduced. Chase was an attractive woman; some scenes were downright explosive.

She laughed humorlessly and cupped my cheek, turning my face toward her.

"No! Seriously––just no." She shook her head roughly. "He was only a consultant. He tied me up a few times, but I was mostly in shorts and a sports bra."

"Mostly?" It sounded like there had been more between them, even if it was as a photography subject in the context of her literary research.

"He's a photographer. He shot our session once." She wouldn't look in my eyes as she spoke softly.

"Were you naked?"

"Not entirely, no," she whispered, "and it wasn't sexual. He only tied me up. Not every BDSM relationship is like that."

How could it not be sexual?

"He has never and will never touch me in a way that is anything other than as a friend helping me."

I scoffed.

"Stop being so stubborn and look at me," she urged, her voice strengthening.

No. If I looked into her eyes, I'd lose my resolve to be upset about this. I'd never experienced jealousy or possessiveness like this before, and I didn't like feeling this out of control.

"Evan. I don't want anyone but you," she told me vehemently.

"What if he wants you?"

She laughed, and I tried to pull away from her. "Stop. Just stop, you idiot!"

"So, now I'm an idiot. Thanks."

"For the love of..." she growled. "Shut up. Seriously. I understand jealousy, but I'm trying to talk to you."

I leaned my hip against the kitchen island and crossed my arms. My eyes finally met hers, and she looked irritated.

"Talk," I said flatly.

"Emory is a friend. I have never had sex with him. I never want to have sex with him." Her voice continued to rise with each word. "Despite being an outrageous flirt with everyone, he doesn't want to have sex with me either."

The scoff came out unintentionally this time. Who wouldn't want to have Chase?

She smacked my bicep and narrowed her eyes at me. "And you're never going to have sex with me again if you don't stop being an ass."

"I don't want him to touch you."

"Caveman much?" she asked sarcastically.

"Let me rephrase that. The thought of him touching you makes me want to punch him."

"While that's adorable, it's completely unfounded," she scoffed. "When he touches me, it will literally only be to move my body into a certain pose so I can get into the character's head."

"For you, maybe." I knew I was getting to the point where she would freak out and yell at me, but I didn't know how to process how possessive I felt over her.

"He doesn't want me like that!"

My eyes rolled, and I turned my face to look into the living room.

"You are such a jealous little ass..." she growled as she pinched my arm.

"Fine! I'll answer your damn question!" I snapped as I turned back to her. "Yes! Of course, I want you to be mine. The thought of another man ever touching you makes me want..."

"Yes?" she asked with a satisfied smirk pulling across her lips.

I growled in frustration as I looked down at her.

"Talk to me," she coaxed as she stepped forward again.

The thought of another man made me want to claim her...for real. And for good. I was pretty damn sure I loved her. I barely even knew her, but God, did I feel like I could love her already.

"I'm sorry." My whole body deflated as I tried to rein myself back in.

"I don't know what's going on in that head of yours, but you don't need to worry."

Easy for her to say. Worry was my default setting.

"I want you to be mine, too," she whispered as she looked into my eyes.

"Fuck." I closed my eyes and pulled her into my chest, cradling her head against me. "I'm sorry."

"It's alright. You were a bit of a dick, but I can understand your reaction."

"It makes me so angry to imagine..." I growled as I pulled her in a little tighter.

"Then don't imagine it. Trust what I'm telling you. I will never want Emory. I want you."

We were quiet for a few moments. She put her arms around my back and squeezed me as we stood there. My heart was still pounding. The adrenaline amping me up a little.

"You alright?" She could probably hear it thumping through my chest.

"I'm frustrated and a little bit pissed off. I'll calm down. I need a minute."

"Don't..." she breathed out quietly as she leaned back and gripped my biceps.

"Don't what?"

"Don't calm down. Channel this. The anger."

"What are you talking about?" I asked incredulously. I acted like a jealous asshole, and she wanted me to channel my anger.

"For the rough scenes, Kallie and the detective are furious with each other, right?"

Holy shit. She wanted me to push her up against a wall. My heart took off for another reason. Should we do this?

"Chase, I don't know if this…" I trailed off as I felt beads of sweat pop up along my hairline.

"Don't overthink it. Just do it," she whispered, her eyes barely concealing her excitement.

"I…" Once again, I was at a total loss for words.

She took my hand, stroking her thumb across my fingers. I searched her eyes, and I didn't see any hesitation. She was completely serious.

Our joined hands gently raised to her throat, and she moved my hand to grip it softly.

"Do I have to do the dialogue?"

She smiled at me and winked. "If that helps you."

I closed my eyes and flexed my hand on her neck as I tried to get myself into the character. The gasp she let out solidified it for me, and my cock throbbed in anticipation.

I could do this. She was suggesting this, so it had to be consensual on her part.

"Safe word?"

Her neck jerked in my hand, and she started laughing hysterically.

"Stop it. I don't want to take it too far. Please. Just give me something to work with here."

"Barbie," she smirked.

"What the—seriously?"

She never failed to entertain me.

"Okay. You're making this too hard," she rolled her eyes and held her hand on top of mine, trying to get me to concentrate.

"That's what he said!" I laughed.

"No man would ever say that." She rolled her eyes again. "Quit screwing around and fuck me."

Well, alright then…

I took several deep breaths and slowly blew them out with my eyes closed.

The scene in Kallie's apartment near the climax of the book started running through my head like a movie.

"I can't fucking believe you!"

My eyes snapped open and locked onto hers. There was excitement there and a little bit of fear. I felt myself dropping more into the character of Detective Raines and wondered if this was how actors felt.

"I don't see what the problem is. I got the information you wanted!"

I scoffed as I gripped the side of her neck firmly and pushed her back toward the wall next to the front door.

"I didn't tell you to use yourself as bait!" I shouted as I tried to channel my earlier anger.

"I was fine. I'm a big fucking girl, detective," she spat. *"I can handle myself."*

I growled as I pushed her head back into the wall. My hand moved to pull the hair at the base of her neck just hard enough that she angled her head up at me.

"He's killed people!" I yelled incredulously.

"So, have you!" she yelled back, pushing at my chest with her small hands.

"Did he touch you?"

"I'm a fucking call girl, of course he touched me!" she said defiantly.

My eyes flashed to hers, and I was surprised at the ferocity of her voice. She looked to be completely absorbed in what she was doing.

"Do you want to hear about how big his co—" she taunted.

My hand pulled harder, and her head snapped back. I waited a minute to ensure I didn't hurt her, but she winked at me.

Fuck.

"No, I don't want to hear about his damn cock. You shouldn't have even gone near it!"

I forcefully smacked the wall right next to her head, and I could see her pupils dilate.

"You knew who I was when you got involved with me. Grow the fuck up!" she spat as she narrowed her eyes at me.

"You think I like knowing that you're going out there every night and putting yourself in danger..." I leaned in and whispered angrily as I pulled her head back again, aiming it toward the wall softly. Despite the situation, I wasn't going to hurt her. *"I don't want you touching other men, and I sure as fuck don't want them touching what's mine."*

That seemed familiar.

She whimpered as she grabbed onto the front of my shirt with one hand. *"I'm not yours! You're a damn prick! My body is the only thing that's kept me alive, and I can use it how I want!"*

I pressed my hips forward forcefully, boxing her in with my body. She was shaking with what I hoped was channeled anger, which was so hot.

"If I want to fuck some guy who gives me what I want, I will. And there isn't a damn thing you can do about it!"

My cock throbbed as I pressed it into her stomach, forcing her back into the wall.

"I don't want you fucking anyone but me!" I yelled, and I watched her eyes flare with anger.

She gritted her teeth as she growled at me and grabbed hold of my dick through my pants. *"You take me as I am, or you don't get me at all!"*

"Goddamn it!" I growled.

She nodded as I leaned forward and pressed my lips to hers firmly. I gripped a fistful of her hair and pulled, eliciting a pained gasp. My eyes shot up to hers in a panic.

"I'm sorry..." I whispered, as myself this time.

"Shh. Don't break character!" Chase giggled.

I let out a nervous laugh and nodded my head.

"You're mine!" My teeth descended on the sensitive skin of her neck, biting and sucking harder than I normally would. She was going to have marks left from this. When she moaned and yanked on my shirt, ripping the bottom part of it open, I knew she was with me regardless.

"Shut the hell up!" She grabbed my cock forcefully through the denim and squeezed, causing me to hiss and slap the wall again.

I was about to burst through my zipper.

"Not until you tell me what I want..."

"Fuck you," she whispered angrily as she tried to reach for my zipper.

I grabbed her hand and pinned it to the wall, my fist tugging on her hair with the other.

"Tell me," I taunted as I pulled, and her neck arched backward.

"No!"

"Tell me, or I'm leaving!" I threatened.

"You know you can't stay away from me!" she taunted back with a dark chuckle.

I growled. Both for the character and myself. She was right.

"Fine, get yourself killed!" I yelled, and I saw her flinch a little.

"I wasn't in danger! He was so distracted by my mouth on his..."

I cringed at the thump of her head back against the wall. She let out a little huff and looked up at me.

"Come on. It's getting to the good stuff," she whispered as she slowly caressed my skin exposed by my torn shirt with the back of her fingers.

I rolled my eyes and shook my head.

"Evan, I'm fine," Chase insisted.

I took a few moments to get back into Raines' head. I didn't know how actors did this.

"The only cock I want in your mouth is mine!"

The moan she let out made my eyes widen.

It all sped up at that point.

My hand pressed down, sliding her head down the wall as she dropped to her knees. I held on tightly and stared as she unbuttoned me and yanked down the zipper. She didn't hesitate as she practically ripped my pants and forced them down my thighs with my boxers.

My dick sprang free, and she immediately engulfed it in her hot, wet mouth. She wasn't gentle as she brought both hands around to my thighs and dug in her fingernails as she bobbed her head rapidly.

I was close to losing it.

Detective Raines was supposed to yell out Kallie's name, but I didn't want to scream for another woman, not even an imaginary one.

"God. That mouth," I groaned as she started to scrape her teeth along the underside of my head.

She was really getting into character as she pulled herself forward by the backs of my legs and took me all the way down. I grabbed her by the hair again and pulled up.

She growled and released me, panting as I crouched down and picked her up by sliding my hands underneath her shoulders. Once she was standing, I yanked down her pants and underwear, flinging them across the room and ripping her shirt off over her head.

"Damn," I panted as she ripped my shirt the rest of the way open and used her foot to push my pants to the floor.

"Focus," Chase teased, and I smiled at her and nodded.

I gripped her thighs, hoisting her up, slamming her into the wall and biting her neck. She moaned as she gripped the back of my head and shoulder, digging her fingers into my skin.

"Fuck me already!"

Her moan spurred me on, so I angled my pelvis and pushed inside her in one smooth thrust. My hips had a mind of their own as I started to snap them forcefully. She grunted with each thrust and held on as I pressed her into the wall.

"Stop fucking other men," I growled into her neck, keeping up my punishing pace.

"What other men?" she moaned wantonly, gasping as she used my shoulders as leverage. She bit down on my earlobe and a groan escaped me.

"You're mine!" I shouted at Kallie—Chase—both women.

I could feel her hips falter as she whimpered in my ear.

"Say it!" I yelled as my hips kept up their punishing rhythm.

We needed to get through this last bit of dialogue, but I was about to blow.

"No!" she moaned as she avoided eye contact with me.

"Say it!" I growled as I grabbed her chin and forced her to look at me.

"Fuck you!" she yelled.

I slammed her back into the wall and adjusted my hips to an angle that made her let out an impossibly sexy moan.

"Now!" My voice was deep and forceful.

"No!" She was keening in my ear, her nails biting into my shoulders, marking me in the most primal way.

"You make me crazy!" I growled into her neck as I leaned forward. *"Stop fucking torturing me!"*

My muscles burned as I continued fucking her hard. Her muscles were pulsing around my cock, and I knew that she was close. I was waiting for it.

"Oh, God! I'm yours! I'm yours!" she moaned as she clamped down on me, milking me for all I was worth.

"Chase!"

Flashes danced in my vision as I let go in streams inside of her. My hips slowed, and I braced her gently against the wall and held her to me. I kissed her neck, and she stroked my hair as we came down from the high.

"Well, that was intense..." Her giggle jostled me inside her, and I bit my lip to keep from moaning. I was spent, but I was sure I could get it up again if I really wanted to.

"Did I hurt you?" I whispered, trying to ease my hold on her.

"A little," she winced as she looked up at me.

"Shit. I didn't mean to. We don't have to do this aga—"

"Stop it. I kind of liked it. Don't you dare feel guilty for any of that." She was deliberately trying to torture me.

"Can you let me down? My hip is sitting at a weird angle," she asked quietly.

"Sorry... I'm sorry." I shifted her, leaned back as I slipped out of her, and gently lowered her to the floor.

She arched her back to stretch and winced a little as she touched her neck. It was red from my teeth and my stubble. It didn't look like I'd bruised her anywhere, but I felt bad for irritating her skin so badly.

"I'll be right back," she told me softly. She didn't seem all that upset with me.

I groaned as she slapped my ass on her way down the hallway.

"You might want to hydrate, we've still got a lot of material to cover," she giggled as she disappeared out of sight.

Cue the instant erection.

Chapter

FIFTEEN

CHASE

CONNECTICUT

I DIDN'T THINK IT was possible, but I woke up after our novel sex marathon and didn't want to jump Evan immediately. It was probably because I was still walking like a rodeo cowboy. I'd been ridden hard and put away wet.

"Mmmm..." he hummed as his arm tightened around my waist, pulling me flush with his naked body. This had to be the best way to wake up in the morning.

His lips started trailing across the back of my neck.

"You put that away, mister," I scolded.

He laughed as he pressed his hips into me. "That's not what you were saying yesterday."

"Yesterday's Chase didn't feel like she'd been pounded."

His whole body shook with laughter behind me as he nipped at my ear.

"Yeah, she did." I loved how playful he'd gotten. But I definitely wasn't focusing on the word I'd thought about him.

"You stop it. I'm calling a ban."

He made a little noise of protest, and his hand started moving down my stomach.

"Quit it!" I whined.

"You like it," he whispered in the ear he'd been nibbling on.

"Seriously," I half moaned, half whimpered as I stopped the progress of his hand.

"I can make you feel good. I'll be gentle."

I knew he could, but my lady parts needed a break. I wasn't a machine.

"Please stop," I sighed. I wanted to, but I couldn't keep up with him today.

"Mmm," he groaned into my neck as he shifted his hips away from me.

Turning in his embrace, I snuggled against his chest. Leaving his arms was the last thing I wanted to do, but I knew we needed to get up. The fridge was almost empty, and I had plans for him.

"Let's shower," I suggested, tracing my finger across his lips.

"Now you're talking," he grinned.

"Down, boy," I teased as I felt him still hard under the sheets. This younger man thing was getting me in trouble. Despite the hiatus since his last partner, he'd built up some stamina.

He smiled at me before he leaned forward and kissed me. It started softly, but I soon found myself plunging my hands into his hair and opening my mouth to receive his tongue. My resolve was slipping, but I wanted to show him the surprise I'd been holding onto for a few days.

"Let's get wet..." I teased.

He growled, "You are such a tease," as he narrowed his eyes.

"I have a present for you. Let's go."

I rolled off the side of the bed and headed for the shower with a wink over my shoulder. I hated leaving him in the bed, but I'd need crutches at the rate we'd been going—or at least several ice packs.

"Alright, what's this present you promised me?"

"Well, it's pretty much a present for me, but it's for you to wear." I hoped that he'd indulge my sense of humor. I thought he'd enjoy it, but I wasn't sure how he felt about a little experimentation. He'd been open to it so far, but being on the receiving end was different.

His eyes shot up to mine from his seat at the kitchen island. "Where did you get this from?"

I pulled the box from behind my back and slid it across the island to him.

"Amazon. Hmmm. So probably not leather chaps," he mused, his lip twitching as he tried to keep a straight face. So far, so good.

"Those are coming tomorrow." I nodded seriously. Maybe those should be my next purchase. Evan in leather would be hot.

His head fell back with laughter as he smiled. God, he was so pretty. Dramatically, he made a show of blowing out a noisy breath and shaking his hands out.

"Just open it," I urged impatiently.

"I will." He stared at the flaps of the box warily. "I'm getting ready."

"Fine, I'll open it." I slid the box toward myself, and he slapped his hand on top of it.

"Mine," he laughed as I raised my hands and leaned against the counter behind me.

"Let's see." He cautiously peered inside the flap as I watched him. He pulled the first item out and held it up, reading the message. "Fuck! This is great."

He laughed as he stood up and held the apron to his chest. "What do you think?"

"You could probably lose the pants," I shrugged, "but I think it'll look pretty damn good."

He set it down on the counter and opened the flaps of the box wide, his eyebrows shooting up as he appraised the other item in there.

I reached inside the box, snatched it up, and held it against my chest. "This one is for me."

He swallowed heavily as I winked in response. Who knew wooden spatulas could be so much fun?

"You want me to go where?" he asked warily a few hours later.

"Oh, come on, it'll be fun," I was borderline begging, but I didn't care.

He sighed as he pressed his forehead into my shoulder. "All we need to do is run into town quickly. We need food, not locally sourced honey."

I pouted as I leaned back from him. "Please. Think of the fun sticky things we could do with that honey."

"Not the lip, put away the lip," he groaned, and his warm breath fanned over my shoulder.

"Pretty please." I was working with my best material here.

"You're lucky I..." His voice cut off abruptly as his body went still.

"You?" It could be my imagination, but it almost sounded like something else.

"Tolerate you," he sighed heavily.

I blew him a kiss as I ran to the hook by his front door to grab my purse. "Let's go, Jeeves, you're driving."

He grumbled all the way to the detached garage that was a few feet away from the house. I was bouncing on my toes as he punched the code into the keypad by the door, and it slowly started to rise.

"Nice ride," I cooed, lifting my eyebrows at him. He had an Audi sedan, a metallic sapphire blue color with shiny rims and low-profile tires.

"Chicks dig it," he nodded seriously.

I laughed at his apparent pride over his precious car while he motioned me toward the passenger door, pulling it open.

"You've had lots of chicks in your car?" I teased as I tried to play along with his bravado.

"Just one. But I know she digs it." And its owner.

He held my hand and helped guide me into the passenger seat.

"Hmmm. It's decent," I said dismissively. "But the driver's pretty hot."

Leaning inside the door, he kissed me quickly before he stepped back and closed it. I admired the view as he slowly walked to his side of the car.

"So, where exactly am I going?" he asked as he buckled into the driver's seat.

"It's in Mansfield. It can't be that hard to find." None of the towns around him were all that large.

The satellite radio kicked on as he sped down his gravel drive. Boy liked a little bit of speed. Evan laughed at me as I sang along to the music. The twenty-minute ride went quickly as I serenaded him with my mad skills. He must have been sex drunk to refrain from commenting on my off-key renditions.

When we got into Mansfield, we didn't have to look far before we ran into something.

"I thought we were going to a farmers market?" he asked quietly, looking at me with wide eyes.

The entire downtown area was full of vendors, and hundreds of people were milling around. I'd missed the memo about this not being their normal farmer's market.

"We are!" I insisted.

"Looks a little bigger than that." Evan's voice was tight, and I could see his posture stiffen the further we drove into the area of town that was crowded with people. "You owe me."

"Live a little." I blew a kiss at him and opened my door after he found a parking spot on a side street.

He crossed behind the car and slipped his hand into mine before taking a huge breath.

"Stop. Just wait a minute. Are you okay?"

He nodded quickly as he shot me a tight smile. "I don't people well."

"You don't have to talk to anyone," I insisted as I let go of his hand and pulled him toward me by the plackets of his denim jacket.

"I'm here," I told him quietly, looking up into his wary eyes. "We can always leave if it's too much."

He slipped his arms around my back and rested his forehead against mine. "I'll be fine. Or I'll give it my best shot at trying to be okay. Thanks for understanding."

He closed the distance between us and kissed me softly, humming against my lips. I knew he had some anxiety issues, so I didn't want to overwhelm him.

Pushing him out of his comfort zone would be touchy, but I meant what I told him. I was here for him.

"You ready?"

He nodded and broke the embrace, reaching out for my hand again. As we wandered through the crowd, Evan's tight grip eventually relaxed. His eyes were tracking the crowd, watching everyone move about, but they were clear.

"This isn't as scary as I built it up to be when we arrived," he let out a little laugh I wasn't expecting. "It's easier when I don't know any of these people."

"Have I led you astray so far?" This could have gone one of two ways, him pulling away from me or Evan deciding to take a chance.

He grinned at me and wiggled his eyebrows. Pulling me closer and throwing his arm over my shoulders. "You haven't led me anywhere I wasn't desperate to go."

My smile was radiant as I gazed up at him. In a little over a week, he was like a different person. Watching him come out of his shell was gratifying to see. I loved how playful and genuinely funny he was.

Who was I kidding? I loved him in general. People said you would know it right away when you found your person, and I didn't doubt that any longer.

We gathered our groceries from the different food and farm stands, returning them to the car before exploring some more.

"I TOLD YOU IT'D be fun," I giggled as I held onto Evan's arm. There may have been a local brewery that was providing drinks for the festival. And I may have drunk one or two...or four of the local brews.

"You're hammered." He shook his head as he gave me an indulgent smile.

"Oh, shush. I am not. I'm happy. Aren't I allowed to be happy? Especially since I'm on the arm of the elusive, mysterious novelist who rarely frequents town?"

He kissed the side of my head as we walked through the crowds and made our way closer to where there was a live band playing. The sun was beginning to set, and I thoroughly enjoyed being out with him.

We'd been so wrapped up in our little bubble that it was good to go out in public and do something to get away from writing. Or the naughty role-playing that had ramped up his manuscript another notch.

"Just stay here, and I'll grab some bottles of water." He'd sat me down on a bench that faced the stage. The music was upbeat, and all sorts of people were dancing. Older couples, much younger couples, and kids off spinning in their own little worlds. I admired their ability to let loose and feel the music.

"Drink this," he urged as he removed the lid and placed the bottle at my lips.

I took it from him and took several sips. His arm went around my shoulders along the back of the bench, and I scooted over until our legs touched. Evan reaffixed the lid and placed a small bag of popcorn in my hand. He took such good care of me. We'd been snacking from various vendors and restaurant booths all afternoon, but we hadn't had an official meal.

"Feeling better?" The smile hadn't left his face the whole afternoon.

I nodded as I grabbed his hand and placed it on my lap, interlacing our fingers. "Much. Thank you. You might have a hard time getting rid of me if you keep feeding me like this."

"Maybe that's been my plan all along." He smiled and kissed my temple. "Did you want to get some dinner here or head back to the house?"

All the restaurants in the area were filled to the brim, and loud laughter rang out their doors. I had a feeling that it might be too much for Evan.

"We can go home. I think you've gotten in your quota of peopling today," I replied, smiling up at him.

"I think I've met my quota for the month, but I like you referring to my house as home," he whispered into my neck before he laid a sensual kiss below my ear.

"I think the fireworks will start after dark. Let's stay for that and then go." We sat cuddled on the bench, enjoying the festive atmosphere until vibrant bursts of color filled the night sky above us.

I looked over at Evan halfway through; he wasn't looking at the fireworks. The lights were reflecting off his eyes as he gazed down at me. I couldn't describe the feeling in my altered state, but he made me feel something I didn't think I'd encountered before.

"You ready?" he asked quietly as his eyes flickered to my lips. I knew he meant to head home, but I was ready to hand over my heart as well.

I nodded my head as I felt myself leaning toward him. He met me halfway and kissed me long and deep, cradling my face with his large hands. Something had changed between us, and I wasn't sure what that would mean for the future. There were still so many things undecided.

THE ONLY NOISE IN the car was the soft music playing through the speakers. It was filled with anticipation of what would come when we returned to his house. His hand was tracing a maddening pattern on my knee as he drove.

"You tired?" he asked, holding the front door open.

"No." My voice was quiet, but I was wide awake and sobering up with the anticipation of how things were shifting between us.

He took my hand and started to pull me toward the living room.

"But I am ready for bed."

His silent stare was heated as he nodded and followed me down the hallway to his bedroom. I stopped at the foot of his bed and turned to face him.

I was nervous for the first time since we'd embarked on a physical relationship. My hand shook a little as I unbuttoned his shirt slowly. His hands found my hips and slowly rubbed circles on the bare skin above the waistband of my pants.

I could feel his heartbeat thumping against my fingertips as I worked the small buttons through the holes, one after the other. We were completely silent as we looked at each other, afraid to break the spell. When I reached the last button, he released me and slowly shrugged off his shirt and denim jacket, letting them drop to the floor.

My hands were drawn like magnets to the defined ridges on his stomach, tracing my fingers through the soft hair covering his abdomen. His breath caught as I released the button to his pants.

He gently stalled my hand when I reached for the zipper and pulled my shirt over my head. My bra was next to go as he reached around me to unclasp it, kissing my shoulder as the straps fell away.

He lowered himself to the floor, kneeling before me and gently kissing my stomach as he began to peel my leggings down my thighs. Helping me step out of them, he ran his hands slowly up my thighs as he reached for my panties.

"Ohh..." I panted as his lips followed their descent down my legs. After he'd tossed them to the side, he stood up and slowly pushed his pants and underwear to the floor.

My chest was heaving as I looked at him. He truly was a beautiful man, and my mouth went dry as his erection bobbed in between us as he stared at my exposed breasts.

Evan licked his lips and swallowed as he slowly sat down on the edge of the bed and grasped my hand. He tugged me forward and brought both hands to my waist, encouraging me to straddle his lap.

"You're so beautiful." His voice was low and sensual as he traced a single finger along my cheek, down my neck, and across the peak of my nipple. "Without the risk of sounding cliché, but what did I do to deserve you?"

"Kiss me," I whispered as I smoothed my hands across his shoulders and into the hair on the back of his head.

His lips parted slightly, and I nipped at the bottom before sliding mine to nestle with his. There was no hurry as we slowly explored each other's mouths. Slow caresses against each other's tongues and lips. My head was spinning, but the alcohol had long worn off. Evan was intoxicating me with each movement of his lips and the slow motions of his fingertips along my hips.

"Can I have you?" he asked in a whisper as he began to kiss along my jaw and toward my ear.

"Yes," I moaned as I raised onto my knees and slid onto his waiting cock. He was so unbelievably hard as I slowly settled onto his lap, his body completely encased within mine. "I'm yours."

His hands gripped my hips tightly as he led me on a slow, sensual ride. I released a breathy moan as he pulled me completely down onto him, and I rotated my hips before I rose slightly and repeated the action.

Ecstasy coursed through my veins as we looked into each other's hooded eyes. Flashes danced in my vision as my climax gradually built, a tingling sensation moving through my body. This wasn't the frantic fucking we'd been doing for days, but no less exciting. A different kind of thrill running through me as we connected in a way we hadn't before.

"Ohh..." I gasped as his fingers tightened, and he bounced me on his stiff member.

"You feel so good," he groaned before he leaned forward and captured my lips. My pace began to quicken as he kissed me, my body chasing the high I knew only he could give me.

"Yes, fuck me," he panted as I rose and fell continuously, pushing us both toward the brink.

My release crested first, and my hips faltered as I felt myself rhythmically clench him inside of me. He closed his eyes, tilted his head back, and moaned as he thrust up from beneath me, his fingers digging into my hips.

Evan groaned loudly as I felt him start to let go, pulsing inside of me.

Slowing my hips, I tucked my face into his neck, panting as he cradled the back of my neck with his hands. Our hearts pounded against each other's chests, gradually slowing as we cooled down. I didn't want to let go as I clung to him, completely overwhelmed by my feelings for him. What had started as a purely physical attraction had become something I'd never experienced before. Somehow, I felt like my writing had inadequately prepared me for this moment.

He stood with me grasping his neck, and turned around, gently laying me against his sheets.

Neither of us said anything as we settled under the covers and entangled ourselves, my head lying over his heart. My heart had his name tattooed all over it, and I was completely smitten with him. It terrified me to think about his feelings for me. I hoped his attachment was as strong as mine.

As I drifted to sleep, I could feel him kiss my forehead and whisper something, but it was too quiet to understand.

Chapter
SIXTEEN

EVAN

CONNECTICUT

I WASN'T IN THE mood to deal with Adrian. It was the same thing every time I finished a book. He wanted me to do a book tour because he thought it'd boost sales, even though he knew I wasn't interested in pimping myself out to sell copies. I hadn't been on a tour since my third book.

That was where I met my ex. She was a book blogger. I was young and thought she was attractive. She came on strong, and I'd fallen for her confidence. But she'd been uncomfortable with my going on the next one, so I'd had it written into my contract that I was not obligated to tour.

Now, I didn't want to go on a book tour for another reason. I had absolutely no desire to leave Chase. I knew I could ask her to come with me, but I wasn't sure what obligations she had with her upcoming release. Tours were often chaotic, making it hard to get any real work done.

There was also the not-so-small matter of my panic attacks. I wasn't sure I could handle the demands of being on for that many people.

MY MIND WAS ALREADY frantic with the thought that Chase might not want to return to Connecticut after our trip to Boston. She'd left yesterday to attend a meeting she couldn't skip with Isobel this morning. She wanted me to go with her, but I panicked and told her I'd like to have a car while I was there.

We hadn't talked about the night we made love at the foot of my bed. It was by far the most emotionally charged sexual experience of my life. She'd ruined me for anyone else.

I was still building the courage to tell her how I felt when she wasn't asleep. "God, I'm an idiot."

I'd proposed staying in a hotel once I joined her, but she refused and told me she'd tie me up and drag me to her condo if I didn't stay with her. While her violent tendencies were admittedly a bit of a turn-on, I knew I'd hurt her feelings with my insecurities.

The last few days had been filled with back-and-forth email conversations between Adrian and myself, trying to get my manuscript done and ready for publication.

I was disappointed that we hadn't had time to engage in her naked chef fantasy, but I was packing the apron in my bag along with the wooden spoon.

My mind was already a nervous wreck as we approached our meeting with Emory. I was completely out of my depth. I was sure we could use some levity as we continued to draft the scenes we were putting into the book.

> *Chase: I convinced Is I was taking a week-long extended staycation.*

Neither of us wanted our editors to get wind of this project before we were ready.

> *Evan: Adrian bought it too. I didn't tell him I'd be in the city, just out of touch.*

> *Chase: He doesn't run in the same circles as Emory. I'm sure we'll be fine.*

> *Chase: Have you left yet?*

> Evan: I just have to put my bag in the car, and I'm ready to go.

> Chase: I miss you…

I miss you too, sweetheart.

> Chase: I sleep better with you.

> Evan: You mean you sleep better when you have me to use as a body pillow?

> Chase: And what a body it is ;)

> Evan: Tease.

> Chase: I fully intend to follow through if you'd get in your car already.

> Evan: Kind of hard to drive with a boner.

She sent me a string of crying laughing emojis, but I was serious. It was hard—pun intended—to drive with a rod in your pants.

> Chase: Poor baby. I'm sure you'll manage. I can kiss it better once you're here.

> Evan: Not helping the situation.

> Chase: Not trying to.

> Evan: Also not turning down the offer of your lips…

> Chase: Charmer. But you'll need to be patient. We've got plans tonight.

Disappointment flowed through me as I sighed heavily. I'd been looking forward to a quiet night with her alone. It'd been years since I'd spent more than a few hours in the city, and the thought of being around that many people was already making me anxious.

> Chase: Emory is taking us on a scouting mission.

Fuck…

> Chase: Do you own any leather pants?

My palms were sweating as I hit traffic coming into the outskirts of Boston. Taking heavy breaths, I focused on the cars in front of me, not letting the panic at the edges of my brain take over.

It was the same every time I came into the city. Push myself through it with the overwhelming anxiety simmering just below the surface. The pills I kept in my center console would help, but I didn't want to rely on them alone to get through this. I'd worked with my psychiatrist on calming techniques, and together we'd developed coping methods to help me to handle moments like this.

I would handle this. The demons in my head wouldn't get the upper hand this time. I could be brave. I wanted this, and I wasn't letting anything stop me—even my own mind.

Before I left, I'd raided my closet and found something I'd hidden in the back. A gift from my sister for a Halloween costume I never wore.

Hopefully, Chase would like them because I had not considered how uncomfortable driving in them would be, especially when I was this nervous.

I'd also found some other things in my room. Her hairbrush was on the nightstand. Toothbrush next to mine in the holder on the bathroom mirror. Some dirty clothes mixed with mine in the laundry basket. It helped relieve my doubts of her deciding I wasn't worth it. I wanted her to return with me after this trip so we could finish the book—together.

It took me a while to find parking around her condo building, but I knew she had a space in the attached garage, so I'd have to ask her if she could get a guest pass.

I grabbed my duffel bag and pulled my laptop bag over my shoulder. She'd told me the code to the elevator so I could let myself up to her floor.

My heart pounded as I crossed the lobby and saw people sitting on the couches throughout the space. Her building was nice, but I felt a little self-conscious in my get-up and wanted to get inside her condo before I lost my nerve to wear these in public.

The elevator was empty when I got on, and I breathed a sigh of relief. That was the part I hated most when I lived in the city. The awkward social interactions with people in elevators, on public transportation, and going anywhere with crowds. I was not a fan.

Once I got to her door, I sent a quick text before knocking.

Leaning against the wall, I waited impatiently for her to open the door. I could hear rustling and a thump as I stood there, and then the door slowly started to pull open.

Chase's face appeared behind the security chain, and her eyes widened. She quickly closed the door, and I laughed as I watched her pull it back open and scan her eyes down my form and back up.

"I didn't think you'd take the leather pants comment seriously!"

I smiled at her reaction and then took in her outfit. Damn.

She looked hot. *So hot.*

Chase was wearing a form-fitting sparkly black minidress with long sleeves. It hugged every dip and curve and showed off her long, toned legs. Her hair was loose and full, dark eyeliner framing her luminous eyes. She was a vision, and I was not worthy.

Damn tight leather pants.

"You look—" I exhaled sharply as I released the breath I'd been holding. "Amazing. Really fucking amazing."

She blushed and grabbed me by the jacket, tugging me through her open doorway. "Get in here."

I grabbed my bags from the floor and followed behind her, my free hand finding her hip as I used my foot to close the door behind me.

"I missed you," I confessed quietly as I dropped my bags to the floor in the entryway. "I'm sorry I didn't come with you. I thought about you the entire drive up here."

She froze up and stopped, my chest brushing against her back. She took a deep breath and blew it out as my grip on her hip tightened.

"Screw it," she muttered as she turned quickly and pressed her hand in the center of my chest.

Then she pounced, pressing firmly until my back hit the door. Chase grabbed the back of my neck and practically forced her tongue between my lips. I could feel my cock stirring in its tight confines and wished I could get them off quickly to pin her to the wall again.

My arms banded around her back as I hoisted her up against me, throwing as much passion into the kiss as she was. She bit my bottom lip and groaned when I cupped her ass and squeezed her tighter.

"Mmmm." We broke apart—panting—and I was having difficulty focusing on anything other than how sexy she looked in that short dress and her sky-high heels.

"Goddamn," I groaned, adjusting myself.

"It's your fault!" she laughed.

"How was that my fault?" She's the one that told me to wear the damn pants and then jumped me as soon as I was in the door.

"You come here looking all fuckably hot with your leather pants and nervous eyes and telling me you missed me," she scoffed. "So yeah, all your fault."

"So that's all it takes? Maybe I should have dug these pants out while you were back at my house," I laughed nervously, scratching the back of my neck.

"It's not funny!" She pointed her finger at me accusingly.

"It is a little funny," I told her as I chuckled at the petulant look on her face. "Someone clearly has a leather fetish."

"We don't have time for this. The car service from Em will be here in like ten minutes, and I just finished getting ready."

I raised an eyebrow at her and pulled her back toward me. Playing with the ends of her hair as she looked up at me. "Ten minutes seems like plenty of time to me."

She narrowed her eyes at me and growled.

"Although, I don't think I'd be able to take these pants off all the way because I'd never get them back on," I mused.

"You put those away."

I laughed as she continued to scowl at me. "Put what away?"

She spread her arms apart, using her palm to gesture at my face and crotch. "Those fuck me eyes and that thing in your too-tight pants."

I started laughing harder and closed my eyes, shaking my head. "You're ridiculous."

"And you are making me want to drag you into my bedroom."

My eyebrows rose, and so did something else.

"We need to go!" she practically yelled as she glanced down at my tight pants.

"Calm down," I soothed, grasping her hand and pulling her toward me. "Why are you acting all high-strung?"

"I'm nervous."

"Shouldn't that be what I'm saying?" I thought I had the market cornered on being a nervous wreck, especially between the two of us.

"Will you promise me that no matter what happens tonight, you'll still talk to me tomorrow?" she pled in a quiet, nervous tone.

"Should I be scared? Where is he taking us?" Now her behavior was starting to unsettle me.

She sighed as she played with the collar of my jacket. "It's a Dom showcase."

"What does that even mean?"

"It's a private party where some of the local Doms can showcase the lifestyle," she explained quietly, avoiding my eyes.

"Like to the public?"

She shook her head. "No, it's invite-only. Emory belongs to a very select circle. They do these events every couple of months."

My mind was racing. Showcase implied that there would be some sort of demonstrations going on.

"Is this a sex party?" I whispered. While I'm sure it was exciting to some men, the thought of walking into a live orgy scared the shit out of me.

"Kind of, but not really. There are rules—" she trailed off as her phone vibrated on the entryway table. "Our ride is here. I'm sorry I can't explain more, but we need to go."

"Are we going straight there?"

My heart was beginning to pound. I wasn't sure this was such a good idea. She must have seen my reaction because she cupped my cheek and stepped close to me. "It'll be fine. Emory will explain more once we get to his studio. You won't be going in uninformed."

I gulped and nodded. I trusted her not to lead me into something I couldn't handle.

WALKING SLIGHTLY BEHIND CHASE, I followed along as she tugged me toward Emory's photography studio. It was located at the edge of a trendy warehouse district that appeared to be a pivotal part of the local art scene.

My palm was slipping against hers as my anxiety started amping up. I was trying to practice my breathing techniques, but it was increasingly difficult.

"Well, we're kind of going as a group. Emory, his partner, and sub, Talia; Nathan's label is a switch and his current sub."

I'd read up a little bit online about the various kinds of people involved in BDSM. Tops were Dominants, bottoms were submissive, and switch described someone who did both. But it didn't always have to be something sexual. Some subs were service subs, and others liked different fetishes. It was a lot of information to absorb at once, but I was trying.

"Like I told you before, Em flirts with everyone. He doesn't mean any of it unless it's aimed at Talia. Please don't freak out on me again. I promise it's all platonic innuendo."

I nodded, kissing the side of her head. Normally, I would tease her about the oxymoron tacked onto the end of her statement, but I wasn't sure I could talk past the lump in my throat. While I'd initially been a jealous, territorial asshole, I knew Chase wouldn't lie to me about the nature of their relationship.

"You still with me?" she asked as she looked back, smiling nervously.

"I'm trying to be," I replied honestly. This was way out of my comfort zone, but it was important to her. It was important to us.

"I know you are, baby," she smiled as she pulled the door open to the gallery on the street side of his studio. "I honestly didn't even think I'd get you out of Connecticut. So the fact you're here tonight is almost a miracle."

Following her past the empty desk and through a curtain at the back of the room, I tried to calm my breathing. I wasn't sure what I expected, but it looked like a regular studio. Lights and backdrops were set up throughout the large open space.

"We're here," Chase called out as the door closed.

A feminine squeal came through a door at the back of the studio. "Back here, Chase!"

She tugged me with her toward the door. I was imagining all kinds of things on our way across the room. Red walls, sex swings, whips, and chains. The reality was not what I was expecting. Neither were the occupants of the room.

Perched on the edge of the leather bed were a pale, lean-muscled, dark-haired man and an equally pale, petite, blonde woman. She had a leather choker and an off-the-shoulder minidress with a leather band along the top. He was dressed casually in dark wash jeans, a black T-shirt, and a black leather jacket with tattoos covering his forearms.

In the back corner was a tall, olive-skinned man with messy black hair and a neatly trimmed beard leaning against the metal grates mounted to the wall. The woman beside him had darker skin and gorgeous, shiny, dark hair pulled into a tight bun. She had on a beaded crop top and a dark skin-tight skirt. He wore a dark red suit, and his eyes lit up as Chase and I entered the room.

"Chase! I was beginning to think you'd chickened out on us," he greeted us as he stepped forward.

"Are you kidding? I love people-watching at these things. I wouldn't miss it."

How many of these had she been to?

"I told him you were probably running late, as usual," the woman to his side responded. I assumed this had to be Emory and Talia. He had a definite air of dominating energy.

"You show up late to a flogging once and you never live it down." Chase rolled her eyes as she glanced at me out of the corner of her eye.

They all laughed, and then the dark-haired man crossed the room and hugged Chase, lifting her off her feet. "It's good to see you."

He kissed her cheek and then stepped in front of me. We were about the same height, but he had broader shoulders.

"Do you want me to call you Evan or Stone?"

He held out his hand to me, and I cautiously shook it.

"Uh——I don't know. Whatever you want, I guess..." I responded nervously.

"He's adorable, Chase. Is he normally this skittish?" he asked, smiling at her.

"Yes," she laughed as she slid her arm inside my jacket and hugged me to her side.

"We're going to be in trouble with him tonight," Talia laughed. My eyebrows rose as she slowly ran her gaze from my shoes up to my head, giving me a look of scrutiny.

"Fresh meat." The blonde giggled as she winked at me.

"Don't let them scare you, man. It'll be fine," the other man said as he rolled his eyes at his three companions.

"Unless Grace gets him alone," Talia cringed.

They all laughed as Chase scowled and squeezed me tighter.

"Who is Grace?" I asked her quietly.

"The Devil incarnate," Chase muttered.

"Now, be nice. She's our host for the evening, and I'm still surprised she's letting me bring you after the last time," Emory scolded.

What happened the last time?

"I told her I wasn't a reporter like twenty times!" Chase insisted.

"You brought a hot pink composition notebook to her play party," Talia laughed.

"I didn't want to forget things!" I loved how they were teasing Chase; it made me feel a little more relaxed.

"You know better now," Emory responded as he stepped back from us. "Let's get down to business before we need to go."

Here we go...

"Grace is the host. It's at her office complex."

"Ugh," Chase huffed.

"You'll both be required to sign an NDA at the door. Standard rules apply," he continued. "No sex or nudity in the common areas. If you're not participating, always keep your red cuff visible."

He pulled something out of his pocket and tossed it to me. "Put that on. It signifies that you are an observer. You're not allowed to participate in demonstrations, and the Doms know to leave you alone."

The non-participation part was not going to be an issue. I was already freaking out a little.

"Where's mine?" Chase pouted.

"Don't get your panties in a twist," he said as he rolled his eyes.

"Who says I'm wearing any?" she shot back, and my eyes widened.

What the hell...

The woman sitting in the corner laughed hysterically as she saw me visibly react.

"Don't worry so much. This is how they are together," she told me. "You'll get used to it."

"Shit...sorry." Chase tugged on my shoulder until I leaned down, and then she whispered in my ear. "I am. That was a stupid thing to say. I'm sorry."

I blew out a shaky breath and shook my head. I wasn't used to her sassy comments being aimed at someone else.

"Anyway. Any sexual acts or demonstrations are to happen in the closed rooms," Emory told us as he continued explaining the rules. "Word to the wise. Wait until you get back home to try anything with each other. Most of the 'private' rooms have cameras, and all the demonstration sets do."

I nodded as Chase looked up at me, still looking a little wary from her earlier slip-up.

"Any questions?" he asked.

So, so many. But I couldn't find my voice. I was only going to observe tonight.

"Alright, lovelies. Let's go," he said.

"Wait! Shouldn't you introduce yourselves?" Chase stopped him.

"I'm Emory. You can call me Em," he said with a head nod.

"I'm Talia. You can call me Tal." His companion smiled.

"Mara." The petite blonde gave me a little wave.

"I'm Nathan. Nice to meet you, man. It's about time someone tried to tame Chase," the tall, dark-haired man laughed with a wink aimed at my girl.

We all piled into a black Mercedes van parked on the curb and headed to wherever they were taking me. I wasn't paying attention to anyone in the vehicle on the way, and Chase kept looking at me with concern.

"Evan, a little word of advice. Don't make eye contact with Grace. It won't go well for anyone if you do," Emory instructed quietly.

"Control freak," Chase muttered under her breath. Apparently, she didn't like Grace very much.

I clung to her hand tightly as we entered the loading dock door of a nondescript office building. Loud music could be heard coming from behind a doorway to our left. Two large security guards dressed entirely in black leather were on either side of the door.

"Hello, Gentlemen. Emory Gage," Em told them as he confidently approached the door.

They consulted a tablet and counted the number of people in our party before opening the door.

"Take deep breaths," Chase whispered as I followed closely behind her.

Easy for her to say. She wasn't the one on the verge of a panic attack.

We all signed a standard NDA and handed them to a young woman with flame-red hair wearing a leather harness and black lingerie with thigh-high patent leather boots.

I followed Em as he walked into the room, and a tall brunette immediately greeted us.

"Emory! Tal! I'm so glad you could come."

She was wearing a tight patent leather corset dress.

"Chase. Nathan." She nodded dismissively, not looking in their direction.

"Satan," Chase whispered, and I smiled at her.

"Who are these two lovely creatures?" Grace said, motioning to Mara and me.

Chase squeezed my hand and shook her head.

"Mara is Nathan's companion for the evening," Em told her in a bored tone.

"And this one?" She gave me a predatory grin, and I stared down at Chase's shoulder to avoid eye contact. This woman was intimidating.

"Is off-limits. He's an observer, like Chase." Emory's voice had changed from his jovial manner at the studio to one full of authority.

I nervously scratched my neck and swallowed heavily. I could feel her eyes narrow in on the red cuff on my wrist and was very thankful I had it on.

"Too bad," Grace sighed in a bored voice. "Anyway—I've acquired some new talent and have decided to debut him tonight."

She raised her hand in the air and snapped twice.

A man kneeling beside a lounge chair dropped to all fours and crawled across to where we were standing. Sitting up to rest on his knees as he reached her side. He never once looked up. His entire chest was covered in tattoos, and he wore a leather collar with a clip ring. His leather pants were stretched tight on his legs, and his feet were bare.

I found myself morbidly fascinated watching him move. I'd never actually seen a 'pet' before.

"Stephen is such an obedient pet," Grace cooed as she arched an eyebrow at Nathan. Obviously, there was some history there. "We'll be in my usual room. We're performing first tonight. I promise you won't be disappointed."

Terrified was more like it.

CHASE

BOSTON

EVAN WAS COMPLETELY SILENT as he clung to my hand. To his credit, he handled the whole situation well, watching our surroundings with wide eyes.

"Usually, it's standing room only with Grace's performances. Let's snag some space along the wall to keep you two out of the spotlight." Emory confidently led us down a hallway to a door that was painted bright red. Talia walked directly behind him, her hand resting on his lower back and her head bowed.

Nathan signaled to Mara with his hand, and she stepped into line with him, staggered slightly behind him off to the side. "Come."

It had always interested me to watch the dynamic of the Dom/sub relationships you saw at these things. Em and Nathan were subtle about how they expected their subs to behave. They didn't use leashes and there was no crawling across the floor. Just firm, direct commands and subtle submissive mannerisms.

I was willing to bet that was why Nathan was not here with Grace tonight. She loved humiliation and very overt displays of physical submission.

Emory gestured us over to the far corner. He and Nathan acted as a barrier between Evan, myself, and the rest of the room.

Grace worked quickly. She led Stephen into the packed room with a metal-studded leash, drawing whispers from the people surrounding us. He'd also gained a new accessory, a bright red ball gag with leather straps.

Grace made a huge production of leading him on stage, his motions cat-like. She led him over to a raised, narrow pedestal platform with short chains with leather buckled wrist cuffs attached to either side.

He slowly rose after she snapped her fingers above his head and bent himself over the platform with his arms down at his sides. She made quick work of the cuffs and scratched his scalp after she was done. He still had the leather pants on and was shirtless.

Evan gasped as Grace walked to the side of the stage and grabbed a small hand whip with a leather tail.

"You doing okay?" I asked quietly, and he nodded, eyes wide. His focus was on Grace, but he glanced down at me and squeezed my hand. Evan's grip on my hand tightened as we watched the first crack of her whip against the middle of Stephen's back.

It arched in an almost painful manner as he groaned against the ball gag in his mouth. She continued with several quicker snaps, dark pink lines forming on the exposed skin with each strike.

Stephen remained completely motionless the rest of the time she worked him over without even moaning.

We all held our breath as she stepped back and pressed her heeled boot onto the seat of his pants. This forced him over the platform's edge, his ass sticking up in the air as his arms stretched against his sides, bound to the platform by his leather cuffs.

Grace knelt behind him and released a set of snaps on the back of his leather pants, exposing a sliver of his ass. She stood back up and sauntered to a chest at the corner of the stage. She pulled a few things from inside of it and returned to her bound sub.

Evan gasped again from beside me as she uncapped a bottle of lube and squirted it over the edge of the large L-shaped phallic instrument.

"That's a pegging dildo," Emory commented.

My eyes widened as I watched her slip it under her skirt and inside herself while we all stood there. Even Talia—who had a very successful sex toy blog—looked a little stunned at Grace's performance.

The large faux appendage jutted out under her short dress, aimed directly at the exposed Stephen.

"Barbie," Evan whimpered in my ear as he pulled me against his side, pushing his face into my hair. Obviously, the thought of being the target of a large dildo was not on his list of okayed scene simulations.

As Stephen's muffled groans filled the air, I could see Evan peeking through my hair, an intense look on his face. For another five minutes, we watched Grace manipulate her new pet for her enjoyment, ending in him laying across his platform a hot, sweaty mess.

"You still with us?" Emory asked as he looked at a shell-shocked Evan.

"Yes," he answered quietly with a single nod and an exaggerated bob of his Adam's apple as he swallowed. I was happy he hadn't run out of here screaming yet. Watching a pegging your first time out was enough to traumatize any person new to the scene, much less an outside observer.

We stayed for another two hours, quietly observing demonstrations of both female Dommes and male Doms from the same back corner. Evan didn't talk. He simply quietly watched with wide eyes, never releasing my hand. He let out the occasional gasp but hadn't whispered our safe word to me again since Grace was on the stage.

She hadn't approached us after her performance, but I saw her staring intently at Evan's reactions. I could tell she was intrigued by him.

"You joining us back at the studio?" Emory asked as we prepared to leave.

I glanced at Evan, who shook his head once, making significant eye contact. "No, I think we'll catch an Uber back to my place." I pulled out my phone and requested one as we all followed Em toward the exit.

The group waited with us until our ride showed up, Talia giving us each a big hug before they retreated to their own hired car service.

Evan climbed in first and held his hand toward me, scooting across the back seat as I climbed in after him. I verified my address to the driver, and we took off across town, back to my condo building.

"Are you alright?" I asked him quietly. "You've been awfully quiet."

He took a deep breath and slowly let it out. "I'm alright. It was just a lot."

"Like *you don't want to do this anymore* a lot or *new situation* a lot?" All night, it was on my mind that this might be too much for him. I knew he'd been the one to suggest diving into the world of kink for our project, but he's never witnessed the reality first hand.

"To be honest, it scared the shit out of me, but it helped that we were there in a group," he told me quietly. "It helped that you were there."

I smiled as I scooted against his arm, leaning against his shoulder. "I wasn't sure if it was too much for you to handle."

"The only part I truly didn't like was the beginning. Please say that we will stay far away from that woman..." He was as put off by Grace as I was.

"I told you she was a lot," I laughed. He smiled and laid his head against mine.

"As long as we don't have to model our Dominatrix as quite so intimidating, I am okay with this," he sighed. "I know you trust Emory and Talia. And I trust you."

"We'll go at your pace, and Emory won't make you do anything you don't want to. That's not his style."

He nodded and kissed the side of my head. "I'm ready to curl up in bed with you."

The smile that pulled at my lips was involuntary. He was his usual honest, adorable self.

"Although, I probably need a shower after wearing these pants all night," he cringed.

"Leather isn't the most forgiving material."

We both laughed and settled back into our seats, watching the lights of the city pass by. The evening's adrenaline started to wear off, and curling up with Evan seemed like a good idea.

Emory wanted us to start with preliminary sessions tomorrow. He was going to show Evan the tools of the trade. I had to admit, the thought of him with a whip in hand was kind of hot.

"Thank you," he told the driver as we stopped at the curb.

Evan pulled his door open and helped me out of the car, tucking me under his arm as we walked into my building.

When we got to my condo, he grabbed his bags and followed me into my bedroom, slowly peeling his sweaty clothes off and neatly folding them.

He got out a pair of boxer briefs, walked around the bed—stopping where I was pulling off my jewelry—and helped me unzip my dress.

"I know I told you earlier, but you really did look beautiful tonight."

I reached my hand behind his neck and pulled him into me, humming as I kissed the side of it. Evan smelled so good despite being in a room with many semi-sweaty bodies.

"You looked pretty damn good yourself," I told him honestly. He rocked the leather pants look.

"I felt like a little boy playing dress-up," he chuckled.

"It didn't seem like that to anyone else. You looked the part, even if you didn't feel comfortable doing it. I saw more than just Grace's predatory eyes following you," I smirked. "It made me want to drag you onto one of those stages to show everyone you're mine"

"You're bad," he laughed, and I reached one hand down to grasp him through the thin cotton of his briefs. "Don't start something you can't finish."

"Oh, you'll finish," I told him as I dropped my dress and stepped free, revealing my provocative underthings. His eyes widened as he took in all the lace.

"Fuck. I did not expect you to have that on under your dress," he breathed out wide-eyed.

"Hopefully, I won't have it on too much longer," I teased as I ran a fingertip across my chest.

"You still want to shower?" His voice cracked a little as he swallowed hard.

"I may already be a little wet," I whispered in a dirty confession as he stared at me. I was afraid that tonight would make things weird between us, but his eyes still held an intense heat while he looked at me.

"Come with me." His voice was rough as he held his hand out to me. I took it and followed him into the bathroom. He flicked on the lights but then turned the one on the mirrors back off, leaving a soft glow cast by the overhead lights.

"Setting the mood?" I giggled as he arched an eyebrow at me.

"I can take one alone..." he teased as he stepped away.

"It's my shower!"

He sighed and rolled his eyes at me. "I guess you can come."

"I hope so," I told him as I bit my lip.

"So dirty," he whispered.

"You better clean me..." My voice was breathy as I looked over at him.

He laughed and reached into the shower to set the water. "Or maybe I should make you dirtier."

He pushed down his underwear and stepped into the stream of water, smoothing his hair back with both hands.

"Like that's even possible," I said under my breath.

The muscles in his back moved deliciously as he tilted his head into the spray. "You just going to stare at me?"

"Are you complaining?" I asked incredulously. "And where was all this bravado earlier?"

He shrugged his shoulders and smiled at me. Evan when we were alone, was so much different than when we'd been in public earlier. "The quicker you get your ass into this shower, the quicker we can get into bed."

"Well, when you put it like that." I reached around to unclasp my bra, letting it fall to the floor. Then I shimmied my panties down my legs and kicked them behind me.

He opened his arms when I stepped into the shower and wrapped them around me, tucking my head underneath his chin. "I'm sorry if I was quiet earlier."

"Why are you apologizing?" He had no reason to be.

"I wish I was more comfortable interacting with people. Like you are," he confessed quietly.

"Baby, you don't need to worry about that. My friends liked you. Just because I never shut up doesn't mean there's something wrong with you," I insisted. "I lo—like you the way you are."

His head dropped into the crook of my neck and squeezed me firmly. I didn't want him to feel self-conscious. He was incredible. If he gave them a chance, people would like him for who he was.

We stood there for several minutes under the warm spray of the water, breathing each other in.

Tonight was stressful, and the next week would be as well. It was nice to simply be with him.

After a while, he pulled back and reached for my body wash. He lathered it and began gently caressing my skin with his sudsy fingers. There wasn't anything overtly sexual in how he touched me, but it ignited something in me, nonetheless.

When it was my turn, I couldn't help but pay special attention to his growing erection. He sighed and quietly moaned into my neck as I stroked him, his lips latching onto it as he eventually spilled over my hands.

Once he caught his breath, he turned me around and caged me against his chest. His fingers gently spread me apart and started a slow rhythm, sliding against my clit. The combination of the steady pressure, his kissing and nipping at my neck eventually drove me over the edge, and I shuddered in his arms with my climax.

We quickly washed ourselves again, quietly watching each other. I finished rinsing off and then pulled the lever down to shut off the flow of water. Droplets of moisture were dripping from his hair and eyelashes, making his blue eyes almost glow in the dim lighting.

"Come to bed with me," I commanded quietly as I stepped out and handed him a towel. He nodded and followed me to my bedroom, quickly rubbing himself dry and dropping his towel to the floor.

We climbed into my bed, and he curled himself around me, kissing my neck and cupping my naked breasts in his hands.

I wasn't sure what tomorrow was going to bring, but I was secure in the fact that I knew he'd brave it with me.

Chapter
EIGHTEEN

BOSTON

MY INTERNAL CLOCK WAS set to wake me around the same time every morning. Chase was still dead to the world as I glanced at my phone and saw it was 6:00 am. I didn't want to be completely creepy—lying here and staring at her until she woke up—but my body was restless, and I needed to get up.

While pulling clothes out of my bag, I had an idea. Chase's fridge was bare, stocked only with condiments. I had a feeling it was like that even when she wasn't at my house.

Pulling up Google, I found the closest market and then looked around for keys to her door, seeing them on a hook inside the hall closet. She lived in a nice building, but I wasn't leaving her sleeping alone with her front door unlocked.

The weather was nice as I walked to my destination. The air had a crisp bite, but it wasn't freezing. It was just enough to wake me up. I knew I wouldn't have time to get in a proper run today with my plans.

The market was bustling; there was a little coffee shop at the back with a line growing by the second. I'd stop there last. I wasn't sure what kind of coffee maker Chase had.

I could picture myself here, shopping for ingredients to make dinner for her sometime. It seemed that every thought I'd had lately involved her with me.

My anxiety still had the hair on the back of my neck standing at how busy it was, but if it meant I could bring this fantasy to life for her, I was fine with pushing through it. Deep breaths, and don't make eye contact.

Leaning down to grab a box of pancake mix, I was startled when someone bumped into me from behind, almost throwing me off balance.

"Oh! I'm so sorry!" A slender blonde woman apologized with wide eyes.

"That's alright," I assured her, straightening back up.

She tilted her head and looked at me strangely. "Do I know you?"

"I don't think so," I shook my head. She looked vaguely familiar, but that didn't mean I knew her.

"You look really familiar..." she mused as she squinted at me.

She'd probably read my books. I occasionally ran into people who recognized me from the book jacket picture. Most of the time, I politely said hi to them and quickly escaped, but she gave me a look.

"Are you sure I don't know you?" she asked again, her brows pinched together.

"I have one of those faces." I gave her a tight smile, picked up my basket, and hurried to the next aisle.

She shook her head and continued her shopping.

We ended up in front of the eggs together at the same time, and she was clearly still trying to figure out who I was by sneaking glances at the side of my face. She was making me super nervous.

Thankfully, her phone rang, distracting her.

"Yes, I'm getting the eggs. I know. I'll be back soon."

I could hear a male voice coming from her phone, and then she laughed loudly. "Yes, I met with her yesterday. She's in the city for a week or so. I don't know what she did to your boy."

"Oh, come on, Adrian," she scoffed, and I looked at her wide-eyed. "It's not my job to babysit my writers or yours."

Fuck. This must be Isobel. Chase never told me she lived so close to her editor. I needed to get out of here fast.

"I'm sure he just needs to recharge," she responded to further mutterings from her phone. "He's been through a lot in the last few weeks, and I know Chase is hard for most people to swallow, much less someone who doesn't interact with others much."

I begged to differ. Chase was very easy to swallow and tasted fucking fantastic.

"You seriously need to lighten up," she continued, and I tried to pull my thoughts out of the gutter.

He was talking again, and I saw her cheeks start to flush.

"Oh, stop it. I'll be back soon, and then we can continue where we left off last night."

My eyes widened, and she glanced over at me with a confused look on her face.

I grabbed a carton of eggs and started moving quickly down the aisle, grabbing bacon and sausage links. Looking over my shoulder, I saw her turn around a corner going in the opposite direction.

That was entirely too close of a call.

My shopping basket was almost full, so I grabbed a few last items and made my way toward the checkout. I didn't need her to recall who I was, finally.

Adrian would want me to come into the office to discuss my next project, and I was not giving up my private time with Chase or our research.

I looked over my shoulder the whole way down the block and googled a coffee shop on the other side of Chase's condo. Running into Isobel was not on my list of things to do today and had thrown off my schedule.

My phone buzzed while waiting for my order, and I pulled it out, hoping it wasn't Chase. I wanted to surprise her.

Adrian: Where did you go? Chase is in Boston.

Evan: I know.

Adrian: Did you go back to Chicago?

Evan: No.

Adrian: Feeling talkative today, huh?

Evan: What do you want?

And why was he texting me if he was with Isobel anyway?

Adrian: Just making sure you're alive. Enjoy your fortress of solitude.

He was fishing for information, and I wouldn't be the one to leak anything to them.

The barista called out my name, and I tucked my phone back in my pocket, ignoring Adrian while I refocused on the task at hand. Adjusting the grocery bags, I grabbed the tray and nodded at her, heading for the exit.

Chase was bound to wake up soon, so I needed to hurry.

The condo was quiet as I let myself in, toeing off my shoes inside the door. I gently settled all the bags on the kitchen countertop and walked to the bedroom.

I could only see Chase's hair sticking up from underneath the comforter, her face completely covered as she cocooned herself.

My bag was still open, so I crept over, got out the apron, and set the spoon on the corner of the bed. Hopefully, she'd see it and come find me. I didn't want to make too much noise, so I returned to the kitchen, keeping my steps light.

If I stayed behind the island, no one could see what I was—or wasn't—wearing from the windows. I may have been a little paranoid of some creep with binoculars taking in the show.

"I can do this." I shook out my trembling hands and started unbuttoning my pants, pulling them off and neatly folding them onto a stool at the island.

My shirt was next, my nipples firming in the cold air. It'd be weird to stand here nude—wearing an apron—with socks on, so I pulled them off too.

The boxer briefs were the last thing to go. My dick was already semi-hard at the thought of what Chase would do when she found me. I'd never been spanked by a woman I was dating before, especially not with a wooden spoon doubling as a paddle.

If I were at my house, I would have put on music to cook, but I wasn't ready for Chase to wake up yet.

Omelets and pancakes were probably the safest bet with the ingredients I'd picked up, so I strapped on my new black apron and began exploring her cabinets.

Surprisingly, she did have anodized pans and high-quality cooking utensils. I'd need to cook the bacon first and didn't want to worry about scalding my balls with hot grease, so I was happy I'd found a package of precooked bacon in the meat aisle. The microwave would be too noisy, so I set a skillet up to crisp the bacon for a few minutes while I looked for the knives.

She had a few high-quality ceramic ones in a small knife block in one of the drawers. She sure had all the tools for someone who claimed she didn't like to cook. It'd make it easier for me to cook for her while I was here, even if I doubted they were purchases she made herself.

Keeping the noise to a minimum, I worked my way around the kitchen island, mixing the batter, dicing vegetables, and turning the bacon.

I hoped the smells from the kitchen would wake her up, but maybe I'd have to do that myself after I finished cooking. My concentration as I watched the bubbles form on the pancakes—their popping indicating it was time to flip—must have distracted me.

Thwack.

The moan that tore out of me with the impact of the wooden spoon against the back of my thigh was surprisingly loud. "Fuck!"

Chase was standing behind me when I turned with an eyebrow raised, wearing a thin satin nightgown that reached mid-thigh. "Someone is being sneaky this morning."

"Yeah, I didn't even hear you," I laughed as she tapped the wooden spoon in her palm and ran her eyes down the length of my almost nude body. The predatory look in her eyes stirred things to life behind my apron, and I had to back up a step to keep my erection from jutting into the front of the cabinets.

"You're gonna burn," she said urgently, and I narrowed my eyes, not under-standing what she was saying. "The pancakes, genius. You're gonna burn the pancakes."

"Oh, shit." I quickly refocused and flipped them over.

She stepped in behind me and ran her hands along my back, causing goose-bumps to emerge.

"I could get used to this," she cooed as her hands roamed my exposed skin.

"Me naked or the pancakes?" I asked her with a smile over my shoulder.

"You're not entirely naked..." she teased. "But pretty much the pancakes."

"Glad I could be of service," I replied sarcastically.

"Decent service would involve a drink too, just saying," she laughed.

"There's coffee on the counter." Her eyes followed as I pointed at the paper carrier on the countertop, turning back around to keep an eye on the stovetop.

"Oh, I love you..." she cooed.

Did she really...?

When I turned around, she held the caramel latte up to her face and inhaled it with her eyes closed.

Oh...she loved the coffee. Of course.

"Do I need to give you two some privacy?" I smiled as she took a big gulp and cradled the cup to her chest.

"It's fine. We don't mind an audience," she winked.

My ego was only a little bruised as I shook my head and refocused on bringing all the bowls of fillings for the omelets to the counter by the stove. "Anything you don't want in your omelet?"

"I've told you before that I'd put just about anything in my mouth."

"Cheeky," I smiled as I looked at her over my shoulder.

"No. I think you're the cheeky one," she laughed as she leaned across the counter to poke me in the butt with her long wooden paddling instrument.

"Touché," I nodded.

"It is a 'touché' as well," she laughed, pronouncing it like 'tooshie.' Obviously, she was in a playful mood today. It was probably better to start that way. It helped keep our minds off what would happen at Em's studio later.

"You're taking a page out of Adrian's book today with all the dad jokes."

"His jokes aren't dad jokes. They're just bad jokes." She gave an exaggerated eye roll.

"Obviously, there's no love lost between you two."

"He's an asshat."

I laughed as she scowled. He was a bit of a pig, but I'd gotten used to his antics over the years. Still didn't like them, but I was better at ignoring them now.

"Oh!" I gasped.

"Yes?" she asked with an indulgent smile.

"You'll never guess who I ran into at the market."

"Someone both of us know?" She looked confused.

"You could say that." I nodded.

"Alright, I give up," she shrugged as she smiled at me.

"Isobel. At least, I'm fairly sure it was her. I've only ever talked to her on the phone. And through emails."

Her eyes widened. "Did she recognize you?"

"Maybe, I kind of blew her off," I shrugged.

"Bet she loved that," she laughed.

"But it gets better," I told her eagerly.

She motioned for me to go on.

"She got an interesting phone call I overheard."

"Do tell..." Chase encouraged as she leaned forward with her elbows propped on the island, with a look of open curiosity.

"She was talking to a man, and then she mentioned his name."

"Ohh! Juicy!" Her eyes lit up.

"She told Adrian she'd be back soon to continue where they left off last night."

Her mouth dropped open. "Oh, my God! I'll have to call Kristine to get the dirt! I always knew he had a thing for her!"

Flipping the pancake onto a plate, I winked as I slid a plate across the island to her. "I've got a thing for you."

"You put that *thing* away," she laughed as she peeked over the edge of the counter.

"Fine. I see how it is." I grabbed my briefs off the stool where I'd left them. I bent over to put them on and...

"Hey! I didn't say you could put those on!" She whacked me in the fleshy part of my ass with her new toy, and I jumped forward.

"Getting into character already?" I laughed.

"Should I bring this with us this afternoon?" she giggled.

"Well..." I mused, leaning against the counter on my elbows. "You should probably break it in first. Just to make sure it works properly."

"I will..." she mumbled, her eyes lighting up despite a mouth full of sausage links. "But first, I need to eat your meat."

NINETEEN

CHASE

BOSTON

EVAN ALMOST CHOKED ON a piece of his pancakes as he cracked up laughing. I smiled as I finished chewing. Naked chef time was a fun way to wake up.

Naked boyfriend. Dirty banter. Home-cooked meal.

Holy shit! Was he my boyfriend? I knew we'd implied we would see where this went, but we'd never officially labeled anything.

My maybe boyfriend's shy grin never faltered as I ate the rest of my breakfast. It was delicious, the bacon melted in my mouth, and the scenery certainly didn't disappoint.

"Take your time," he winked as he finished and started rinsing off the dirty dishes. The muscles in his back and sides bunched and flexed as he washed the things he'd dirtied. Naked chef Evan was hot, but naked chef Evan cleaning up his mess sent my hormones into overdrive.

"Mmmm. That was yummy. I'm so full," I told him, sitting back and patting my stomach.

"Hopefully, you haven't eaten too much meat," he teased as he walked around the island and leaned against the countertop.

"Oh my..." I marveled, eyeing how the front of the black material of the apron was tented. "Is someone requesting compensation for their services this morning?"

"I'm good with providing my services for favors," he winked as he bit his lip.

"It seems like you're having a hard time with something." I nodded toward his apron, which had trouble concealing his excitement.

"Mmhmm," he nodded. "I seem to have misplaced my pants."

"They don't seem misplaced to me," I giggled as I picked up the wooden spoon and rolled it between my hands. "I can think of something that'd keep your cheeks warm."

"Oh?"

I nodded and climbed off my stool, coming around to stand behind him. Damn. Compulsive running was doing him all kinds of favors. I cupped his firm cheek, giving it a nice squeeze.

"You having fun back there?" he asked, an amused smile stretched across his lips.

"Not yet..." I reached around him, positioned his hands palm down near the edge of the counter, and stepped back.

"Hmm..." I mused as I looked at his posture. "Spread your legs shoulder-width apart."

He slowly moved into position, but it wasn't quite right.

"Straighten your shoulders, chest out. That's better," I coached as he did what he was told. "Good boy."

The look he gave me when I walked to his side to appraise his stance would've made me drop my panties if I had been wearing any.

"You remember the safe word?"

He nodded slowly as his chest heaved. His erection was rock solid as it protruded out in front of him, and my mouth salivated with the need to touch it, but that could come later. Literally.

"You ready?" I exhaled a heavy breath as I stood behind him and worked up the nerve to strike.

Before, I was swatting him as a joke. This time I would try to channel what Em had taught me. During my previous consultations, he'd shown me how to use whips, floggers, and canes. If I was going to write about flagellation, he wanted me to learn how to do it properly.

Adjusting my grip on the handle, I took a deep breath as I established solid footing within striking distance. My wrist snapped firmly, and we both jumped a little as the wood smacked the fleshy part of his ass.

"Ahh!" he breathed, a low hiss filling the air.

"Holy shit. You alright?" I questioned as I massaged the area that had already started to turn pink.

"Mmmhmm," he hummed through gritted teeth.

My heart pounded as I watched the tension drain from his shoulders.

"Again," he said quietly but firmly, flexing his arms against the counter.

I raised the spoon again, and...

Thwack.

"Fuck," he moaned as his hips flexed forward.

Cupping his shoulder, I kissed his shoulder blade. "Too much?"

He shook his head, but I could tell he was on edge. I placed the paddle down on the island and took his buttocks in both hands, slowly massaging the sting.

"Mmmm," he moaned low in his throat, the muscles in his back tensing.

"You sure you're okay?" I asked quietly.

"You hit me again, and you're going to be cleaning my cum off this cabinet."

A flash of heat ran through me at his low growl.

"Is that what you want?" I whispered, running my hand up his neck and into his hair.

He groaned and shook his head, letting it fall forward and closing his eyes.

"Evan?" Resting my forehead on his shoulder, I started to kiss along his bicep and shoulder, a low humming noise building in his chest. I didn't think I'd pushed him too far, but I was afraid to use the spoon again if he was getting all silent on me.

"Fuck it," he growled as he grabbed me by the waist and hoisted me up onto the counter in front of him.

He pushed my legs apart and slid my nightgown up my thighs, exposing my naked sex.

"Ohh!" I moaned in surprise as he leaned forward and placed one long lick along my slit, nipping at my clit.

"Mmm..." he groaned as he dove in, tonguing me like a man possessed. His firm hands pressed my legs even farther apart, forcing me to brace myself with my arms outstretched behind me.

Yes. I moaned loudly as his lips closed around my swollen bud and sucked, rubbing his tongue frantically. My hips tried to buck, but he grunted as he held me down, never letting up.

"Evan!" I moaned, feeling my muscles start to tense.

"Mmmmm," he growled into me, sliding one long finger inside, curling it, and pressing firmly on a place that made me squirm again. The fingers on his other hand dug into my thigh as he sent me spinning, my head thrown back as I let out a keening cry. My muscles clenched repeatedly as I throbbed against his lips.

"Stop, stop..." I moaned as he tried to redouble his efforts. I admired his dedication, but I wanted him inside of me.

"Please..." I panted as he stood up to his full height, his fingers slipping from my body. The look he gave me was predatory—lips glistening and chest heaving—as he reached back to untie the apron and pull it over his head, throwing it to the floor.

He hooked his palms behind my thighs and pulled me to the edge of the counter.

"You're a goddess," he panted as he pushed a sweaty lock of hair off my forehead with his fingers and grasped his hard cock in his other hand. "An absolute fucking goddess, and if I don't fuck you right now, I'm gonna lose my shit."

"Fuck me, Evan," I moaned as he positioned himself at my entrance and hesitated. He paused, locking eyes with me as he slid inside.

Mine fluttered shut as he pushed in, only to pull out and plunge back in quickly, building up a decadent rhythm. Sweat dripped down his chest and disappeared into his abs as I watched, licking my lips.

"Fuck," he groaned as he watched my breasts heave beneath the thin satin material of my nightgown. He almost seemed possessed as he fucked me, and it was wildly thrilling knowing anyone paying attention in the building across from mine could see us.

"This has to go," he growled as he pulled the straps off my shoulders, pushing it down to reveal my breasts. His soft lips descended on one breast while his hand found the other, coaxing my nipples into tight buds.

His satisfied hum as he nipped at one and then kissed his way over to the other just made me wetter as he continued to thrust.

My fingers held on tightly to the back of his head while I tried to stay upright with my other hand outstretched behind me on the cold countertop. My hand fell as he straightened and grabbed my thighs again for leverage as he started to snap his hips faster.

"Touch yourself." He nodded to where we were joined, seemingly mesmerized as he disappeared inside me. "Get yourself there so I can feel you squeeze me. You love my cock, don't you, baby?"

Nodding, my fingers drifted to my clit, starting with slow circles and rapidly increasing the pace as he pushed me closer and closer to the precipice of ecstasy.

"Can you come?" His voice was strained as his hips started to falter, his neck muscles straining as he held back.

"Yes, almost there," I moaned as I teetered near the edge.

"Fuck, you're so tight," he moaned loudly as he pulled my hips off the counter and pistoned into me with vigor. "Oh God, Chase," he groaned as he dug his fingers into the backs of my thighs.

Yes. I chanted as he came inside me, and I followed right behind him with a loud moan.

Evan's sweaty head fell to my chest as we both panted, the smell of sex overpowering the delicious breakfast he'd served me only moments before.

"I think I finally had my fill of meat this morning." My voice came out strained as I tried to catch my breath.

His chest shook as he held me tightly. "You're horrible."

"That's not what you said a few minutes ago," I giggled. "We should probably get cleaned up. Emory is expecting us at ten."

Breaking the spell of post-orgasmic bliss was the last thing I wanted to do, but we couldn't be late. My happy ass would still be wrapped up in my bed most mornings, but Evan had changed me in more than simply my sleeping habits.

I felt like he saw me. Not the sarcasm and the jokes. He saw me. And he was still here, begging for more.

"WHAT EXACTLY ARE WE walking into today?" he asked as he drove toward Emory's studio in his car.

"You're going to learn how to operate the heavy machinery."

"There's machinery?" He glanced at me out of the corner of his eye as his fingers tightened on the steering wheel.

"No," I giggled. "Emory is more of a hands-on guy. Old school equipment."

"Other than what we saw last night, I have no idea what the tools of the trade are."

"We decided we wanted her to be an old-school Domme, right? No extra machines or torture devices?" I asked. "Just good old-fashioned control?"

"Yeah, I think that'd probably be best. Anything too intense, and my readers probably wouldn't be interested," he nodded.

"I think mine will be on board with the bondage and submission, but they wouldn't expect the hard kink either. We can save that for your lessons and keep it off the page," I teased.

Thankfully he knew I was joking and laughed as he pulled into a parking space near the photography studio. "Of course, bring on the gimp suit and the ball gag."

Despite his jokes about kinkwear, we were both dressed in athletic gear. Evan wore a dark gray dry-fit shirt and a pair of loose shorts, and I had on a sports bra and black fitted shorts.

"You ready for this?"

"Nope." The smile on his face as he squeezed my hand let me know he was only partially joking.

"I would say we could turn back now, but that would just give Emory time to come up with a creative punishment to exact upon us later." Today was sure to be an eye-opener for him. I'd been exposed to this stuff before, but he was totally green. I was by no means an expert by any stretch of the imagination, but I'd been on both ends of the whip.

Em had better ease him into it slowly. Evan was way more skittish than I'd been.

"Might as well get in there," he sighed. "My ass is already sore. I don't need any spankings for tardiness."

I nodded and exited the car, waiting for him by the front bumper. "Let's not give Emory any ideas about a suitable punishment for being late."

"You're the one who took forever in the bathroom, so if anyone is getting spanked for making us late, it's you," he accused.

"Move your ass, and we won't be late," I sassed as I pinched his butt.

"Hey, hands off the merchandise. It's still a little tender from your little spoon fantasy." He threw his hips forward to escape my pinching fingers and laughed as he jogged toward the door with me hot on his heels.

"Finally, you two are here," Talia let out a relieved sigh as we walked in the door. "He's been wearing a hole in the floor in the back. You know how he is about his schedules."

"We've still got five minutes." My watch read 9:55. I'd made sure we didn't get too distracted this morning. Em hated when people wasted his time.

"Come on. We don't have all day," Emory urged as Evan, and I walked through the curtain hand in hand.

"Do you have a meeting you didn't tell me about? What crawled up your ass?" I asked before I realized my slip.

Emory arched an expressive eyebrow and cleared his throat.

"Wow. Already in that headspace, obviously," I backtracked. "Permission to speak, Sir?"

"Granted," he nodded.

"Evan, when we're back here, as this is his space," I told him quietly, "we defer to Emory for talking and commenting. If you have a question, you must ask respectfully after requesting permission to speak. While honorifics are typically a private matter between a Dominant and their sub, Emory prefers to be referred to as Sir during mentoring sessions."

Evan nodded and looked over to Emory, eyes cast to the ground.

"Oh, he's already halfway there, Chase," Emory smirked as he indicated for us to follow him back into the playroom.

"Unless I expect someone, this door will always be locked," he explained. "I don't like to share my proclivities with my photography clients, so we'll always have time scheduled in advance for these sessions so I can clear my schedule."

"May I?" I asked Em as I nodded at Evan.

He gave me a short nod and watched Evan.

"This can get a little intense sometimes. I want you to know that you can always use the safe word if something makes you uncomfortable. Emory also uses the stoplight system. If you have any hesitations, feel free to call out yellow or red and he'll explain things further until you're comfortable to continue."

He nodded and grabbed my hand, running his thumb over my knuckles.

"We don't have to stick entirely to the script either. Ask if a scene we mapped out doesn't feel right, and we can work out something different. These are just as much your characters as mine," I insisted, "and I'm open to suggestions."

Evan bit his lip and nodded again. His eyes were clear, I could tell he was anxious about this, but he wasn't worried.

"Okay, we're going to discuss wardrobe first," Emory explained. "Every Dom or Domme——male, female or otherwise——has a style. It's like with your regular wardrobe. There are things you like, and not every person will choose the same things."

"We'll start with male submissive attire," he started. "Leather is typically the material of choice, that or vinyl. It depends on if you're into a fetish style or not. Some men like to wear lace or fishnets. It totally depends on their particular kinks."

"How do you envision the submissive character, Evan?" Emory asked him, his eyes filled with curiosity.

"We aren't going to show much directly from the perspective of her male submissive. He's part of the story, but the narration really follows Frances through her journey as a Dominatrix for hire."

"Have you thought about what you want her personal style to be?"

"I hate to use this word, but *traditional*," Evan cringed. I nodded to confirm.

"So, you're thinking of a more polished look?" Em speculated.

"I think so," Evan responded quietly.

"Here, we'll look on this tablet at a selection of Fem Domme wardrobe options." He handed the tablet to Evan, and his eyes widened as he looked at it and glanced at me. We scrolled through the options, and then Evan paused the screen on one image.

"You like that one?" I asked him.

"Ye——" He cleared his throat softly. "Yes. This one."

I had to admit. It was kind of perfect for what we'd envisioned. A tightly fitted lace dress with leather accents revealed enough to be enticing, but it wasn't racy by any means.

"Order your size, Chase, and have it sent here," Emory instructed.

Evan's eyes widened as he looked at me, his cheeks a soft pink.

"Alright." I took the tablet from Evan and added it to my cart, and a few other options I thought would also fit Frances' style.

Emory motioned Evan over to start showing him some of the male options, and I bit my lip to keep from laughing at his bewildered expression.

"If she is going more traditional, chances are she'd want her sub to do the same," Emory explained, and Evan nodded. "Leather pants are always a staple, but you already have those."

Emory smirked at Evan, and his cheeks darkened.

"In most situations, those can be the go-to. Or jeans. It depends on the dynamic. But you will also need to plan for what happens in situations where spanking play or punishment come into action."

By this point, Evan's cheeks were full-on bright pink as he glanced at me—probably thinking about this morning. The little bit of heat in his eyes started my heart thrumming. His reaction to being paddled was quite a pleasant surprise.

"This is a cock cage," Emory said, holding up a little leather-strapped pouch with a ring on the front. I could see Evan visibly swallow and adjust himself in his shorts. "It's designed to confine the penis and cause discomfort if fully erect."

"Next is what I'm suggesting you wear during a scene where she punishes her sub by paddling him," Emory gave Evan a little bit of a roguish smile. I smiled as I watched Evan squirm. "It's a leather jockstrap. I'd suggest this to keep you covered while also exposing your rear. The alternative is a thong. Any opinions?"

"The jockstrap. Definitely the jockstrap," Evan tittered out nervously as he looked at me with mild panic.

I couldn't wait to get started.

Chapter TWENTY

EVAN

BOSTON

CHASE'S AMUSED GRIN SPARKED fantasies of putting her over my knee, but I knew I had to keep myself in check around Emory.

The thought of putting on that cock cage made me incredibly uncomfortable. It was not big enough. I did not need first-hand experience with that part of punishment. Just looking at the thing made me feel chastised sufficiently.

"Evan. Pay attention." Emory snapped next to my head, and I refocused on him, trying to ignore Chase. I wanted to know what else she was ordering on that tablet.

"This is a chest harness." Emory held up some leather strapping. "There are also more full-body harnesses that wrap around the groin, but this is the most common type. It's used for a few different reasons."

"It's hot," Chase whispered from behind me.

Mental note...

"Some use it because they like how it looks. It's often worn at showcases or play parties to identify that they are into kink," Emory explained. "It can also be utilized as a handle of sorts during private play. It gives the Domme something to hold onto to manipulate a male sub who is larger than her. Gives her a little bit of leverage."

"That brings a whole new level to the term 'love handle,'" Chase giggled from behind us.

Emory cleared his throat and gave her a pointed look.

"Sorry. Don't mind me. Just back here living my best life."

"Naughty girl," I whispered under my breath, and Emory's lip quirked in response.

"If you can't behave, Chase," Emory warned as he nodded at a large chair in the corner with restraints attached to the arms and legs. "We can always tie you to the chair again."

"Again?" The urge to laugh was strong, but I bit my lip to stop it.

"Anyway," he rolled his eyes. "I don't think the two of you want to dive particularly deep into hard kink."

"No," I said in a low voice, shaking my head.

He cleared his throat again and raised an eyebrow at me.

"Sir," Chase whispered from behind me.

"No, Sir." I averted my eyes and spoke quietly.

Emory nodded. "These will probably be all I need to show you. There are all kinds of torture devices for people into pain play, but you won't need to know about those."

I nodded, absolutely agreeing with that one. The crippling anxiety I felt imagining that damn cage was painful enough.

"We can always consult Grace if you decide to add anything with humiliation. She's an expert in that particular kink."

Oh, fuck no. That woman was intense, and I knew my limits. Chase clearly agreed with me by the little growl she let out.

"Let's move on to equipment." Emory led us toward the wall covered in metal racks and grates from floor to ceiling, gesturing at a few items on hooks. "These are leather wrist and ankle cuffs. They can be attached to various things. Corner restraints on a bed, each other with a clip or tie, spreader bars, wall hooks, and crosses. Cuffs are involved in most bondage acts, usually only subbed out for rope or silk ties."

"Hold out your hand," he commanded, grabbing a cuff off the clip and bringing it to my wrist. "Buckles tend to work best. You can set them tight but not cutting off circulation—only enough to hold. Never improvise and restrain someone with a material you can't control the tension on. You run the risk of permanent nerve damage. I also don't recommend metal unless it's wrapped with something softer."

He left the cuff on, and I dropped my hand, feeling its subtle weight against my skin. I knew it was there, but it wasn't uncomfortable.

"These are bondage ropes." Emory grabbed a tied bundle off the hook and held it up. "This one is what I prefer. It's a nylon rope used in boating. It can be bought at a hardware store. Don't buy it from a sex shop because you'll pay through the nose for something you can't gauge the quality on."

He nodded at Chase over my shoulder. "This is what I use for suspension."

Oh...this was probably what he used to suspend her from the ceiling grate. I shifted my feet and tried not to think about Chase suspended from the ceiling—hands bound. My shorts didn't provide much concealment, and I was sure Emory would be irritated if I developed a visible problem. We were here to learn, not as foreplay.

"It doesn't have a lot of bite to it on the skin and can't be used for elaborate things, but it's strong and comes in different ratings that determine how much weight and pressure it can hold."

"Chase?" he asked, looking in her direction. "Do you still have that book of knots I gave you?"

"Yes, Sir," she chirped over my shoulder.

Chase stepped in behind me, placing her hand at the base of my spine, her touch sending a jolt through me. She must have been done buying the Dominatrix outfits.

"Your homework for tonight is to practice tying knots with this," he instructed, handing me the bundle of rope and moving down the line to the next thing to show us.

"Chase is familiar with these," he said, gesturing to a few things sitting in brackets protruding from the frame.

"This is a small flicker whip." He flipped his wrist, and it made a soft snapping sound in the air. "Your 'Trix will probably use a heavier-duty class of whip such as a stock or bull, but you two are beginners. You need specialized training to use those effectively."

"Next session, we'll let you both try this one." Chase's fingers tightened on my shirt as she sighed softly. Obviously, she liked that idea. I wasn't sure which of us being on the tail end of the whip excited her, but I was willing to try it.

"Next, we've got a suede flogger," he picked up a dark leather-handled whip-like object with several long, wide pieces of sueded material hanging from the end.

"There are several different types of floggers. Some are for sensation play, and others are for pain play or punishment. This particular one doesn't have as much bite to it."

"Again, we'll start you with the beginner equipment. You don't need to be accidentally drawing blood." He actually broke character and winked at me.

What? The idea of drawing blood turned my stomach. Hurting Chase wasn't on my list of things to learn how to do.

"You'll be fine," he assured me as he saw my expression. "This will all be simulation play. But...there is another king-sized bed in the back of the playroom if you need some alone time after a session."

I could hear Chase snickering behind me.

"Next up is the cane." He picked up a long object from a hook that looked to be made of wood. "It's a little harder to use effectively. Plastic canes are good for beginners. They flex more and don't leave as deep of marks. These can be used for both pain play and punishment. I use a rattan cane for punishment."

He placed the long wooden cane back into its bracket and moved to the paddles hanging on the wall.

"Paddles come in a huge variety of materials and sizes depending on the use," he nodded. "I'll show Chase how to use the leather and silicone paddles. They're lower impact and cause less bruising."

"I already practiced with a wooden one," she whispered from behind me. I couldn't help the smile that pulled at my lips.

"Something you'd like to share with the class?" Emory asked with a facial expression almost approaching a smile.

"Uh," I stuttered as I looked back at Chase.

"He's already taken a wooden paddle. Might as well put that into the rotation too." She sounded amused.

"Have you two been practicing unsupervised?" My eyes widened as I took in his defensive stance, arms crossed, legs set wide, and an unamused smirk on his face.

"Uh...not practicing, per se," I whispered.

"Chase?"

"Why do I have to tell you?" she asked, sounding borderline petulant.

"Because your boy here looks like he's being led to execution. Fess up."

"Theoretically, what would happen if we played outside our sessions?" she asked.

"Well, normally, I'd punish you both, but it's the first day, and I'm assuming you don't want Evan here to flee the state."

"May I speak freely, Sir?"

Emory's eyes flashed to mine, and he nodded. "You may."

"Chase and I may have had a little fun with a wooden spoon this morning," I confessed. I didn't want to start this relationship with him on a lack of trust.

"And you were safe?" he asked as he looked between the both of us.

"I remembered what you taught me," Chase nodded.

"She corrected my stance, massaged me, and had me take a warm shower for aftercare. We acknowledged the safe word before we started," I confessed quietly.

"Then I guess you're forgiven. Please try to take this seriously—Chase—if you try to use something you aren't ready for, one of you could get hurt," he admonished.

"Yes, Sir," she replied quietly with a nod, and I echoed it.

"Of course, Sir."

"Moving on." He held up a leather riding crop, and I was happy I knew what that one was. Never a thought I'd ever expected to have. "A crop can be used for all sorts of play. Most are leather, but there are nylon ones as well."

"Last, but definitely not least, is your hand." He held up his weathered palm, and we nodded. "It can be used for any type of play. It should be established before you start what kind of spanking you're engaging in."

"There are types?" I asked curiously.

"Pain, humiliation, punishment, sensation, erotic," he listed off easily. "There are also different positions."

"Yeah, there are," Chase snickered and buried her face into my shoulder blade.

"Behave," Emory warned.

"Yes, sir," she giggled.

"Over the knee, doggy style, standing, kneeling, lying down, restrained..."

Damn...half of those were reawakening the problem I'd tried to ignore before. Chase and I had covered the doggy-style spanking, standing and bending over too. All at the same time...

"You ready to look at some toys?" Emory asked.

"Sir?"

"Yes, Chase," he nodded.

"Shouldn't you have Talia in here while you're showing off her prized possessions?"

"I'm sure I can manage," he said dryly.

Motioning to follow him, he led us to a tall chest of drawers with various-sized drawers.

"Let's start small and work our way up." He pulled a little silver capsule out of a top drawer and held it up. "This is a bullet. It is featured in hundreds of different toys. It can be used in wearables, lipstick vibes, clitoral stimulators, insertables...the list goes on. It creates a strong, consistent vibration."

He pulled out a relatively short, thin vibrator. "This is a lipstick vibe. It's compact, can be inserted or used for clitoral stimulation, anal play."

He put it back and grabbed a large phallic object. "This is a traditional dildo. I think this one is self-explanatory. They come in glass, silicone, metal, plastic..." He pulled out a vibrator that looked like a real penis, showed it to us, and laid it back down.

"This is Talia's personal favorite." He pulled out a large vibrator with a piece of silicone protruding out the side.

Was that shaped like a bunny?

"This is a rabbit. It has an adjustable speed setting for both the bunny and the shaft. The base of the rabbit has a bullet vibe inside of it. Designed to stimulate the clitoris while the shaft is used for traditional penetration."

He pressed a button, and the shaft started to rotate slowly. "This one has a rotate function too."

"That looks fun!" Chase said in an excited voice.

Holy fuck. The thought of using that on her about made me embarrass myself like a barely pubescent teen.

"Don't worry. Tal has a nice not so little bag of toys for the two of you to explore as homework tonight," he told her.

Who would have thought we'd get a swag bag while we were researching a Dominatrix?

"There are also electric stimulation devices, but I don't think you're looking for those."

When neither of us spoke up, Emory clapped and rubbed his palms together.

"Next, we move on to anal play."

My eyes widened. Obviously, I'd heard about it being done, but I had never done it, and I wasn't sure I wanted it done to me either.

"There are your standard plugs. They can be plastic or silicone. Made in various sizes to help stretch the user gradually. These can also have vibration features."

He pulled out a long L-shaped device that looked like what Grace had used on Stephen. "This is used for pegging. There are a few different kinds. We've got strap-on dildos and strap-on vibrators. This one is designed to be hands-free. It takes a bit of practice because the woman needs to be able to keep it inside using her Kegel muscles while penetrating the man."

"There are also finger extension pieces that can be used for penetration, with or without vibration."

Pegging sounded intimidating, making my asshole clench simply thinking about it.

"I think we've got one more thing that is probably relevant to your story," he said as he pulled a small ring from one of the drawers. "The cock ring."

"This can be used to delay climaxing and increase erection firmness. There are adjustable ones, silicone rings, metal rings worn at the head or base, textured cock cages like we saw before..." I shuddered at the memory.

"Some are worn at the base of the shaft; others go around the balls and teardrop ones that massage the perineum. They can also be used for partner stimulation if they have a bullet vibrator attached."

"Do you two have any questions?" he asked as he packed the items back in their homes and closed the drawers.

I wasn't even sure where to start.

"What about nipple clamps?" She had to go there. That woman sure liked to pinch my nipples.

"We can talk about sensory stimulation items. There are a few that are fairly tame." He reached into a drawer and pulled out a little metal tool with a long handle and a wheel with spikes attached to the top. "This is a Wartenberg wheel. It's used to test nerve endings in the medical field and can also be used to stimulate nerve endings under the skin during play."

"Evan, give me your hand." I held it out, and he turned my hand over, gently running the device over the soft skin on my wrist. It sent a tingling sensation up my arm and the back of my neck. He pressed a little harder, and it hurt slightly, but the feeling was amplified.

"It feels even more amazing with a blindfold on," she whispered as her hand slipped under the back of my shirt and her fingernails dragged across the bare skin of my lower back.

"Sir?" I croaked.

"Hmm?"

"Is one of those in the bag?"

He smiled and winked. "I'll make sure we put one in there."

"Now we can move on to talking about nipple clamps," Emory said as he pulled a few more things out of a drawer. "When you're starting out, they are only worn briefly. It cuts off circulation, so you don't want to cause nerve or skin damage."

"These are good for beginners," he said, holding up a leather collar with chains attached to it, small clips with a screw attached to them on the ends. "The bullnose clips have tightening screws so you can increase or reduce the amount of pressure. "

He held up a little saw-toothed clamp next. "This kind of clamp also comes without the screws and is called an alligator clamp."

"The rest of the clamp styles I wouldn't recommend for beginners. There are clothesline clamps, designed like a clothespin but with a strong spring for tight application."

"Magnetic clamps may be okay to use." He reached into the drawer and pulled out a little metal circle with two rods sticking out of either side. He used his fingers to pull the rods apart and then released one. It immediately moved to attach to the other rod.

"Subs who really enjoy nipple play can also have Thai sticks used, ones worn with weights, attached to weighted chains. The goal of all these is to stimulate endorphin release, which can make the area more sensitive and encourage stronger climaxes."

He carefully placed all the items he'd gotten out back into their drawers, closing them and then opening a cabinet at the bottom.

"This part may seem tedious, but it's a very important part of proper play and maintenance of your items," he said as he pulled out several bottles and some small towels. "We have leather cleaner and conditioner, varnish for the rattan cane, metal cleaner, and sanitizer, silicone cleaner and sanitizer. Cleaning both before and after use helps keep items in good shape, helps prevent the spread of disease if you have multiple partners, and helps prevent infection."

He spent ten minutes showing us how to clean and store multiple different types of items.

"He scare you two off yet?" Talia asked as she peeked around the door-frame to the playroom.

"Did you close up for lunch?" he asked her. She nodded and crossed the room, kissing him on the cheek and leaning her elbow on his chest. He gazed down at her like she was the only person in the room, and I could see they really cared for each other.

"Are you two staying or...?" he trailed off.

Talia pulled on his arm and spoke quietly, but Chase and I could still hear her. "Some new things came in when I ordered the items for Chase."

His face brightened, and he gave her a naughty grin. "You two can have the rest of the day off. I've suddenly got a very pressing matter to attend to."

Emory pulled her hips into his and whispered in her ear, causing a giggle as she pointed toward the door to the gallery. "There're a few paper bags behind the desk for you. You're welcome," she winked and then pulled Emory's mouth to hers.

"I think that's our cue," I said, turning around and pulling Chase's arms around me, resting my hands on the small of her back.

"I do believe we have some *research* of our own to do," she nodded as she reached up on her toes and gave me a soft kiss.

TWENTY-ONE

CHASE

BOSTON

EVAN STRUGGLED TO KEEP up as I dragged him across the studio by the hand, through the curtain, and into the gallery. Talia had left two large paper shopping bags with tissue paper tucked across the top of each.

"Grab the sex swag, and let's go," I nodded, excited to see what goodies Talia had provided. She was a bit of a sex toy connoisseur. Tal had been contracted as a reviewer for several sex toy companies as a lucrative side gig. She got all kinds of freebies and was always excited to share.

"Someone's eager," he laughed as he tapped my butt with his palm and reached around me to grab a bag.

"Can you blame me?" I bounced on my toes. "I want to know what she got us. Tal's like a regular orgasm dealer."

"Well, they both seem dedicated to us doing effective research," Evan chuckled as he lifted the bag, which seemed packed to the top.

A loud gasp, followed by a sensual moan, sounded from the direction of the playroom, and we shared a look.

"They didn't waste any time." Evan was trying to hold in a laugh as he glanced toward the curtain. The slight pink tinge on his cheeks amused me. I was immune to Talia and Emory's amorous behavior, but he hadn't seen it in action as I had.

"And we are wasting time," I scolded, motioning toward the door to the street. "Move it. There are dildos to unbox."

"I prefer dildos *in* your box," Evan snickered as he slowly walked to the front of the shop.

"I'll shove dildos up your box if you don't hurry up."

"Yes, Ma'am."

"I prefer Mistress," I giggled as I crossed the threshold of the door he held open for me.

"Of course you do," he responded with an exaggerated eye roll.

"Don't make me spank you again..." I threatened.

"You're saying it like that would be a bad thing." His eyebrows wiggled as the door closed behind him.

"Go, go, go," I laughed. We hurried to the car, and Evan helped me into my seat before opening the rear door to put the bags on the back seats.

"Hey! Why are they back there? I wanted to look," I protested.

"You'll have to be patient." I couldn't help my wide smile as he looked at me with an amused smirk.

"We both know that's not my strong suit," I pouted.

"Think of it as delayed gratification," he countered.

"Nope, don't like that either." The deep chuckle that followed my statement abated my curiosity somewhat. Evan had handled today like a pro.

The rest of the drive back to my place, we quietly listened to music, and he drove me nuts with his thumb stroking the bare skin on my thigh.

"You ready?" he asked as he parked his car in a guest spot in the garage.

"Hell, yes!"

We both knew we'd be naked within twenty minutes of entering my apartment. Screw research...literally. He carried the bags inside, and we settled on the couch with them on the cushion between us.

"Do you want to go first?" I asked as I sat up straight and held open the handles on one of the bags.

"We both know you're over there vibrating with excitement to get in there." The amused grin he was giving me showed how much he was enjoying said excitement over our new toys. I didn't even know what they were, and I was ecstatic.

"I'm not vibrating...yet," I winked as I pulled out the tissue paper and threw it to the floor.

"Blindfold." I tossed the black silk blindfold at him, and he placed it across his lap, slowly stroking the soft material.

"His and hers cuffs." The two sets of leather buckle cuffs dangled from my finger as Evan's eyes widened. One group was smaller and thinner, and the other was larger with a wider band.

"Just what every couple needs," he laughed.

"I know, right?" Or maybe only the adventurous ones as we'd apparently become.

Next was a feather tickler. I swiped it across his nose, and he grabbed the handle from me, placing it in the pile on his lap.

"Nipple clamps. Ohh. These are the magnetic kind." Gauging by how his pupils dilated when I pulled the pieces apart and let them click back together, he was also on board with trying those.

He shivered as I took out the Wartenburg wheel and ran it across the back of his hand.

"Tal must really like you," I giggled as I started pulling several different kinds of cock rings out and tossing them at him.

"Whoa. Look at this one." He opened the small box and pulled it out. Pressing the button on the end, the little toy vibrated across his palm.

"Yeah. We're definitely trying that one," I told him. He nodded as he pressed the button to turn it off.

"Giant bottle of lube," I giggled as I tossed it to him. It was twelve ounces. Apparently, Talia thought we'd be busy.

"It says it's good for anal play." He winked as he read the fine print on the side of the bottle.

"Oh, you're ready to get probed now?"

"Nope. Never mind," he said with a shake of his head and wide eyes.

I pulled out a few different lengths of chains designed to fit around the posts of your bed. Those would work well for the cuffs.

The last thing in the bag was another small bundle of rope. I'd have to look for my knot-tying book. Emory didn't mess around when he assigned you homework.

"Ready for the next one?" Evan asked as he placed the empty bag beside the couch.

"Alright. This one seems heavier." I pulled the tissue out, and my eyes widened as I looked at the boxes lined up inside the bag.

"Flicker Whip," I read off the top of the box.

"Collapsible riding crop."

My eyes widened as I looked at one box. "She gave us a rechargeable male masturbator."

"Hopefully, it's not one of those flashlight-looking ones." Evan made a sour face. "Talk about awkward. One look and people are like, 'Oh, you came in that.'"

"Nope. Much more discreet." I shook my head as I studied the box with pictures of a sleek, black, elongated toy on its side.

"Did she put your bunny in there?" he asked with interest. I thought he'd been intrigued by that one in the playroom.

"Rabbit, but yes. She hooked us up with a fancy one."

"Let me see," he said eagerly. I pulled the box out and handed it to him. It was bright pink. Both the box and the vibrator.

"Nice. I can control this with my phone," he winked at me as he read the information on the side of the box. We'd turned him into a sex-starved nymphomaniac in less than a month. It was a wireless, Bluetooth, USB rechargeable, waterproof rabbit with access to a remote-control app. It could also be hooked into remotely by the same app using a secure passcode. We didn't even have to be in the same room. Which might come in handy once I had to return home permanently, but I was refusing to think that far in the future.

"Anything else in there?"

"Oh, look. She got you a present." I held up the box and bit my lip to keep from laughing.

His eyes widened. "Are those...?"

"Beginners set of anal plugs. Aren't you lucky?" I giggled.

"Only because I get to use them on you." He thought he was so clever.

"Who knows," I mused, tapping the box with the rabbit still sitting in his lap. "Maybe after you use that one on me, I'll let you do whatever you want."

"Well, then, we better get started." He carefully started breaking the seal on the end of the box, opening it, and pulling out the pieces.

"You realize that probably needs to be charged, right?" I explained and held back a laugh at his frown.

"I'm sure we can figure out something to keep ourselves occupied until then." He moved the items from his lap onto the coffee table and back into the bags by our feet.

"Maybe we can try these out." He held up the small box with the nipple clamps in one hand and the vibrating cock ring in the other.

"Grab the lube. Let's go," I laughed as I took the vibrator and the charger out of his hands and stood up to head back to my bedroom.

"I'll grab the cuffs, too," he called out before he followed me. I liked his style.

Evan tossed the items in his hands on the bed as I walked into the bathroom and pulled my toy wash and a small towel from under the sink.

"Get the cock ring," I requested as I turned on the water to let it warm up.

"On it. One boner enlarger on its way." Evan's easy acceptance of sex toys was simultaneously arousing and amusing. He clearly understood the assignment; toys were an enhancement in the bedroom, not competition.

He took the ring out of the box and joined me at the sink, laying it on the countertop.

His arms snaked around my waist as he rested his chin on my shoulder, watching as I cleaned the cock ring and set it on the clean towel on the counter.

"Who knew washing a hot pink vibrator could be arousing," he whispered as he watched my soapy hand slide up and down the shaft.

"You have turned into a horn dog," I told him, thoroughly amused with his reaction to all this stuff. Some guys would have bailed being exposed to all the things he had in the last two days—even without any underlying anxiety issues.

"So, you've got your own toy wash?" he whispered into my neck between soft kisses.

"Yup," I nodded, tilting my head to the side. "I am over thirty and have been extremely single for the last six months."

"Should I be worried I don't measure up to the toy arsenal?" he asked quietly.

"You really want me to stroke your ego, don't you?" He tucked his nose into my neck and laughed. Judging by the size of something pressing into my hip, someone was getting aroused.

"Among other things," he said in a deep, husky voice.

"Someone thinks they're funny today."

"You can't be the only one with the jokes," he mused. "Come on, let's get that charging and go research."

He reached over to grab the USB charger, plugging it into the wall outlet. Picking up the pink toy, he turned it in a few different directions with a confused expression. "How the hell do you charge this thing?"

I took the toy from him and turned it for him to see. "Find this textured dot and press the pointy part into it."

"I know how much you like inserting the pointy part," he chuckled as he gently pressed the little cord jack in, a red light showing under the silicone when it was in all the way.

"It's completely covered since it's water-resistant," I explained. He nodded and took it from me, setting it down on the counter before pulling me toward him. He kissed me deeply, slowly pressing his tongue into my mouth.

"Hmmm. So, who gets tied up first?" he questioned after he stepped back.

"Who do you want to get tied up first?" I asked curiously. Let's see how brave he was feeling.

"I'm curious about those nipple clamps," he admitted, searching my eyes. I had to say; I was a little curious too. I'd only done solo research with some of the adjustable clamps. A partner had never been involved before.

"Let's try them. But don't worry, I'll leave your poor nipples alone for now."

Despite my attempts at levity, I was a little nervous as I walked back into the bedroom, taking off my socks and shoes. Evan followed suit and started to disrobe.

"Restraints?" He held up the bed chains and the smaller set of four cuffs.

Blowing out a short breath, I hesitated before I nodded. "Why not? Let's go for it."

He picked up the chains, and we quietly worked to attach them to all four corners of the bed, wrapping them around each post and clipping them into place. Then he picked up the set of women's cuffs, and my pulse started to race.

"Fully naked or...?" he asked as his thumb slowly traced my ribs.

My sports bra was the first thing I pulled off, enjoying how his breath caught. My shorts came off next, leaving me standing in my panties.

He attached the first cuff as I held my wrist still, slowly stroking my palm with his fingers and then raising it to his mouth to place a kiss in the center. After he attached the second one, he knelt on the floor to attach the ankle cuffs.

"You ready?" he asked quietly.

I nodded, my nerves keeping me from speaking as I carefully climbed onto the bed and lay down. Evan gently coaxed me into position as he walked around the mattress, clipping each cuff onto the corner restraints as he stretched out my limbs.

He left the room and headed toward the living room, but I wasn't sure what he was getting. Relaxing was futile as I waited for him to return, but I closed my eyes briefly and took a deep breath.

"Let's put this on," he spoke softly after he returned, holding up the silk blindfold with one hand.

I bit my lip and nodded, raising my head so he could slip it on. My heart pounded as I lay there, restrained by all four limbs, completely at his mercy. It really was always the quiet ones you had to watch out for, and I had a feeling Evan was tapping into his inner freak today.

"Still doing alright?" he whispered in my ear, startling me with his proximity. I hadn't felt the bed move, and he wasn't touching me, but he was close enough I could smell him. We'd barely started, and I was totally overwhelmed by the sensory deprivation.

"Yes," I breathed out.

The warmth of his breath disappeared, and I tried in vain to hear what he was doing. After a few moments of absolute silence, I heard a crinkling noise from the other room. The naughty boy was getting something else from the bags.

"Ahh!" I shrieked as something soft yet scratchy passed over my side and across my chest. I shifted on the bed as it disappeared and then started tracing up the inside of my thigh.

My nipples were standing erect as I waited for his next move. This entire situation was unlike anything I'd ever tried with a partner, but I trusted him. And I couldn't imagine feeling comfortable enough with anyone else in this situation.

"Shit," I laughed, and my leg reflexively jerked as something sharp but prickly passed over the sole of my foot. "You're mean."

Goosebumps formed across my chest as the same prickly sensation traveled slowly down my neck. From the sensations I'd felt, my best guess was that he'd taken out the feather tickler and the Wartenberg wheel. So much for the nipple clamps.

A sharp stinging sensation on the skin at the edge of my areola startled me. I hissed as I tried to lean away from the feeling. The bed dipped beside me as the stinging sensation traveled to my other breast. My nipples were painfully hard, making me wetter, anticipating what he'd do next.

The room was colder than I remembered it being, my skin hyper-sensitive. They always told you that your other senses would become heightened if you took one away, and being blindfolded accomplished that in spades.

As the sensations all disappeared, my head quieted, and my breathing was the only sound I could hear. The anticipation was killing me, and with the restraints, I couldn't even rub my legs together to release the tension.

The soft sound of a box being opened a few feet away was quiet, but I heard a small thump from the nightstand next to my head as he laid something down. A soft clicking noise started, and the bed dipped beside me again.

A sharp pinch to my left nipple caused me to cry out, and as the pain dissipated, a weight settled beneath it.

Clamps were intense. The blood suffusing my breasts made me squirm, and my hips rose off the bed, seeking some friction, but my restraints left me unsatisfied.

"Shh," Evan whispered as his fingertip ghosted over the part of my nipple sticking out of the clamp. He kissed the side of my neck as I felt him gently pull apart the rods on the clamp and lift it from my nipple. His hot mouth descended as the blood rushed back, and I moaned loudly as he laved his tongue against my sensitive skin, my other nipple standing painfully at attention. My hips jerked off the bed again, and he pressed his hand firmly above my pubic bone, holding me down. "Hold still. We both know you're not going anywhere. I'm not done toying with you yet. Be a good girl and lie still."

I had no idea how subs could withstand this erotic torture without making a sound and keeping still. My hips and legs thrashed against the restraints as he released my nipple and leaned back. The mattress shifted as he changed positions beside me.

"Oh fuck..." I exclaimed as he placed a clamp over the other nipple. His warm breath cascaded over the skin exposed at the tip, causing me to shift restlessly against the sheets at the sharp pain building in my skin. Something wet touched the exposed tip, and he blew a hot breath over it again.

"Shit, shit, shit," I groaned as I felt him release the pressure, the blood rushing back in. My pussy clenched as he lightly ran his finger around the engorged skin. I was close to coming, and he hadn't even touched me down there. I used to think nipple-induced orgasms were some sort of sorcery, but Evan had clearly studied his wizardry.

"Sit tight," he instructed softly as I felt his weight shift off the bed again.

"Not going anywhere," I muttered. Between the stinging in my nipples and the way I was already close to climaxing, I was in sensation overload.

The plastic cap of something being flicked open was loud as I heard him shifting at the side of the bed.

Evan's throaty moan hummed through the air, and I was deeply anticipating what caused him to make that sound.

Everything seemed to disappear for a short while, but then I heard noises in the direction of the bathroom. After a few moments, I felt the bed dip near my feet and a weight settle between my legs as Evan sat in the space between my restrained limbs.

The quiet flick of the bottle lid sounded again, and I heard something wet being spread. My hips jumped as I felt his fingers press gently into the center of my panties.

"Shit, you're so wet," he groaned as he pressed the wet lace into my center. Then his fingers gently pushed the material to the side, and I fruitlessly tried to shift into his touch again as the cool air coasted across my heated flesh. "And your nipples are so pretty. Standing up for me, but let's try to stimulate something else now."

A low buzzing sounded from where he was sitting, and I cried out as he held the vibrator gently to my clit. He tortured me as he slowly dragged the tip through my wetness, not pushing hard enough to give me relief but just enough to get me even wetter.

As he pushed the tip inside me, I moaned loudly, the gentle buzz starting to permeate through my overstimulated body.

His hand slowly rotated the toy, pushing it into me and then retreating. He built up a slow push-and-pull rhythm, my hips rising slightly with each thrust.

"Holy shit," I moaned as he sped the vibrations of the toy with a soft click. He began to fuck me in earnest—the rabbit part of the toy grazing my clit with each thrust causing me to clench as my orgasm approached rapidly. As he pressed it fully inside, he twisted it back and forth, making me buck wildly off the bed and scream out my release.

"Oh, my God!" I sobbed as he continued to press the vibrator into me as the rhythmic pulsing of my climax blazed through me.

It was almost too much, but it felt so good. Fire raced up my spine as I felt a sharp pinch on my nipple, and the toy started oscillating inside me. He ratcheted the speed up another notch, and I felt myself skyrocketing toward an even more intense release. I screamed as I thrashed against his touch and the vibrator, an unexpected gush of wetness accompanying my release.

"Too much. Too much," I moaned, my voice hoarse and weak from screaming through the force of both orgasms. I'd had multiples during sex before, but not back-to-back like that.

The vibrations stopped with a click, and I sighed heavily—a bit overwhelmed as he pulled the toy from me. The bed shifted, and I heard a quiet thud from my nightstand.

The bed dipped as Evan sat back down and gently pulled the blindfold off. Tears ran down my cheeks that he wiped gently with his fingertips as he gazed at me with raw desire in his eyes. I'd never seen him look this aroused.

He slowly traced a finger over my peaked nipple with an almost feral smile before he pinched it, eliciting a sharp gasp from me.

"You ready for more?" he asked as he stood from the bed, and I saw his hard cock throbbing, his balls encased by the vibrating ring.

Holy shit.

TWENTY-TWO

EVAN

Boston

CHASE TIED TO THE bed, completely vulnerable, but entrusting me with this side of her was the hottest fucking thing I'd ever seen. She looked completely sated after the orgasms I'd coaxed out of her with the rabbit.

I'd never played with toys before—obviously, my history was completely vanilla compared to now—but I could see why people liked them. It was hot to be able to manipulate your partner's enjoyment. And the fact that she trusted me enough to play like this cracked open some hidden part of my heart that no woman had ever been able to find.

"Holy shit," she exclaimed quietly as she stared at my aroused cock with wide eyes.

It'd been a little challenging to get the cock ring maneuvered into place with a semi, but I knew as soon as I put that vibrator anywhere near her I'd be harder than steel. The little pieces of silicone were doing their job as I was throbbing and hard as granite.

"Is that a no?" I asked, already knowing her answer to my previous question about being ready for more.

"Are you kidding me?" Her eye roll was almost adorable, contrasted by the mascara running down her cheeks.

Climbing between her legs, I slowly kneaded my hands up the long expanse of her shins and paused at the tops of her thighs. Her muscles were still tense from being immobile, but she seemed alright. "Do I need to untie you? We can take a break to relax for a few minutes if this is too much for you."

She lifted her head slightly, giving me a disbelieving look.

"No, God no," she urged. "I can't relax right now. You need to get in there. Don't tease me like this because I can promise you, I'll return the favor once you take these cuffs off if you do."

I chuckled at her frustrated pout, and her hips lifted from the bed as she tried to shimmy closer to where I was kneeling.

"Are you sure you don't want me to undo the cuffs?" I asked again.

"Are you serious right now? If you uncuff me, I'm using the whip in the other room on you," she threatened.

"So impatient," I scolded. "Maybe I should make you sweat a little." Reaching to grab the feather tickler off the corner of the bed, I had trouble containing my smile.

Chase threw her hips upward, trying fruitlessly to line herself up as my cock brushed against her sex.

"Hmmm. Where should I use this first?" I mused as I slowly lowered the feathers to the side of her neck. "Are you sensitive here?"

My hand tilted the handle slightly and gently ran the very tip of one feather over her collarbone. She sighed softly, her arm jerking slightly against the cuff.

"Or how about here?" I traced a path toward her shoulder and then down her side, barely grazing the side of her breast.

"Ahh," she hissed as her body twitched to the side. Obviously, that spot was a little ticklish.

I reversed the direction and traced it back up, and she twitched again, glaring at me as I continued to trace slow patterns across her skin. The fire in her eyes shifted as I ran concentric circles slowly around the skin of her breast. When I reached her nipple, she was arching off the bed and moaning softly.

"Hm, so we know you like this," I teased as I slowly trailed it down her abdomen, setting it down for a moment as I looked down at her covered sex, her wet panties not disguising her desire.

"I'll buy you a new pair." Giving a firm yank, I tore the lace on one side, repeating the same action on the other side and tossing the scrap of lace to the floor.

"Wonder if you like it here?" The tickler slowly trailed across her heated skin. I used my thumb to part her and looked down at the little pink swollen bud.

"Right here," I murmured as I very gently teased her clit with the feather.

"Oh, my God. I hate you," she half moaned, half sighed as her hips shifted from side to side.

"I know, baby. But I think you secretly like it," I teased. Her eyes narrowed at my wink, and I knew I was in trouble once she was finally released from the restraints. "What do you want?"

She huffed and rolled her eyes, her neck arching backward as I teased her with the feather-light touches.

"Use your words," I coached.

"Cocksucker," she growled as I tried not to laugh at her petulance.

"We both know you're the cocksucker in this relationship," I laughed. "Is that what you want?"

She frowned at me.

"Do you want to suck it?" Raising to my knees, I stroked my hard cock a few times—her eyes tracking the movements of my hand. The restraints pulled taut as she huffed and tugged at her bound wrists lightly. She really wanted to touch me, and knowing I was the object of her desire—and frustration, was heady. "If you want me in your mouth, you have to ask nicely. Be a good girl and use your words."

"Fine!" Her voice was strained as she continued to stare at the slow motion of my wrist.

"Fine, what? Use your words, and watch your tone. Nice girls get what they ask for."

"Fine. Stick it in my mouth," she hissed, licking her lips before taking several deep breaths.

"I told you to ask nicely, and you're being a bit of a brat. Maybe I should continue doing this..." Grasping my dick firmly, I sped up the pace. I couldn't help moaning as I shifted my hips into the momentum of my hand as the blood pooled in the shaft from the cock ring. Each stroke was more intense than the last.

"Stop!" she whined as she shifted her hips back and forth again. She still couldn't quite get her legs to touch, but I knew she was trying to rub her legs together.

Dirty girl. She liked watching me touch myself.

"And what should I do instead?" I shifted forward, tilted my cock toward her pussy, and slowly dipped the head inside. "Should I put it in here?"

"Yes!" She pushed into my slight movements and moaned as I slipped deeper. She was so warm and still drenched from before. I didn't remember ever feeling this turned on, this enchanted with a woman, or this desperate to get closer to someone. Especially since I was usually running in the opposite direction or just avoiding them in general.

"Hmmm, I don't know," I teased as I pulled my hips back. "Maybe you'd like for it to go in here?" I placed my thumb on her bottom lip, pressing down lightly. Her pupils dilated, and before I could react, she nipped at my finger, a sharp sensation radiating through my hand.

"Bad girls have to watch," I chastised as I sat back on my heels and grabbed hold of myself again, firmly stroking.

"I think I should see how this feels," I mused as I pressed the button on the end of the vibrating ring, and it began to hum on the base of my shaft. The gentle buzz coursed through me, and I finally understood why sex toys appealed to so many people—men included.

"You're a dick," she growled as I leisurely stroked up and slowly back down, sending pleasurable sensations down my spine.

"Yes. Yes, he is," I laughed, nodding down at my hand.

Chase groaned as she was held captive, completely transfixed by the movements of my hand.

My gaze roamed her gorgeous naked body, watching intently how her tits jiggled as her chest heaved. Her torso was mottled pink, and her nipples were rosy red. I wanted so badly to latch onto one of them, my mouth watering at the thought, but she was being a little mouthy now. She could wait until I was ready to touch her.

"Please," she whimpered as she watched me with rapt interest.

"Hmmm?" I moaned as I began to pulse my hips up as I stroked down. My movements weren't strong enough to get me close, but it felt really, really good.

"Please, Evan?" she begged.

"I'm sorry, what?" I teased as I tried to avoid eye contact.

"I'll be good." She pouted as she tried to convince me to do something––to touch or plunge into somewhere.

"Where do you want me?" I asked as I rose onto my knees again.

She eyed my dick hungrily, staring at me with an intensity that empowered me to keep going.

"In here." She licked her lips again. "Put your cock in my mouth."

I arched an eyebrow. Having this kind of control over another person's pleasure was addictive, and I easily dropped into a dominant role.

"Please?" Her voice was a breathy whisper.

How could I resist that?

I clicked the end of the bullet, and the vibrations stopped.

Carefully raising my knees over her outstretched legs, I straddled her torso and shifted my knees until my cock was poised out of reach of her mouth.

"You want it here?" I asked as I pressed on her lower lip with my thumb.

"Yes," she sighed, and I felt her breasts brush against the insides of my thighs.

"You sure?" I confirmed, knowing her answer but enjoying prolonging her seduction.

"Please stop teasing me," she whispered as she raised her head, her lips barely grazing the head.

I shifted forward a little more and eased my way inside.

"Since you asked so nicely..."

Her hot mouth enveloped the head of my cock, and she hollowed out her cheeks, sucking lightly.

"Fuck," I cursed as I grabbed the headboard with one hand, my hips slowly rocking into her mouth. My sexy, greedy girl tried to lift her head to take me further, but I was completely in charge of the depth and speed.

"Mmmm," she moaned, making it extremely hard to maintain my cool as I made shallow thrusts, watching closely to ensure she could breathe. Choking my writing partner would make it difficult to continue our research.

"Shit," I groaned, finding myself getting over-excited with every hum of her mouth against my overheated skin. The ring amplified the sensations, making everything more intense. Chase's eyes fluttered as I stroked her cheek, and she suckled the head when I started to pull out. "You're going to make me come."

"Mmmm," she moaned as she lightly scraped her teeth against me. She would never make things easy on me, and I loved it.

"Bad girl," I scolded as I pulled out and leaned back, reaching down to pinch her nipple.

"Fuck me," she moaned. Her lips were swollen and pink, moisture glistening on the bottom one. The sight of it made me pause momentarily, transfixed by how stunning she was, but I quickly centered myself in the cradle of her thighs, lifted her hips, and slipped my knees under the backs of her thighs.

She was literally dripping. I'd never seen her this wet. I'd never seen any woman quite this undone and full of desire because of me.

"You ready?" I asked as I traced the head of my cock through her wetness, waiting for her answer.

"This again?" she groaned playfully as she wiggled as much as her bound position on my lap allowed.

"Be nice, or I'll make you watch as I cum all over your pretty tits." I held my dick and slowly stroked it up and down. She groaned as I pressed the tip down on her clit and tapped it firmly a few times, making her throw her head back and moan. It was fucking hot to make her frustrated like this. I was going to have to hide the wooden spoon.

"Can you be nice?"

"Yes," she huffed. I smacked her clit again. "Damn you."

My fingers searched for the button on the side of the vibrator, and it hummed to life with a press, sending subtle vibrations down the length of me.

"Oh my God," she moaned as I pushed the head onto her clit and slid against her slowly.

Her hips pulsed up with my movements, and I couldn't hold back anymore, no matter how much I was enjoying this. Tilting slightly, I drew back before plunging inside of her in one smooth thrust.

"Fuck!" she exclaimed loudly as her head pressed into the pillow, her neck arching enticingly.

Burying myself as far as I could inside her, pausing as the sensations rolled through us from being this deeply connected. She moaned as the vibrator pressed into her clit, and her eyes rolled back before she closed them.

She cried out, moaning as I pulled out and snapped my hips forward again, rotating them as I bottomed out.

"God, you're so fucking hot. My wrecked little toy." Her chest and neck flushed an enticing shade of pink, her cries indicating she was close. I was desperate to get her there so that I could watch her fall apart again. Giving her orgasms was addictive, and I never wanted to recover.

One of my fingers traced the soft folds of her pussy as I disappeared inside, and I pressed her clit lightly, drawing slow circles as I continued to thrust into her.

Chase was babbling as she cried out, her hips flexing on my lap as I felt her start to pulse. She was so far gone she couldn't help but vocalize her pleasure, and I became more enamored with her wanton inhibition every time she did. A sense of masculine pride ran through me, knowing I was the one causing it.

"Fuck," I groaned as I sped up, her cries increasing as the vibrator continued to stimulate her through her orgasm. Her muscles clenched even tighter, and I couldn't hold back, coming inside her in several long streams.

My heart pounded in my chest as my thumb clicked the vibrator off. Looking down at where she was lying limp against the bed, her arms still outstretched, I sighed at how utterly spent she was.

"That's enough. I'm sorry," I panted as I leaned forward to unhook one wrist cuff and then the other. My cock slipped from her as I leaned back to unhook her ankles. She sagged against the bed, staring at me with a dazed look.

Her eyes fluttered closed again as I massaged one wrist, rubbing lightly before slowly moving my way up her forearm and toward her shoulder. She sighed quietly as I massaged the tightness in her joints and muscles. I switched sides, and then my hands traveled to her thighs, digging my fingers into her muscles to ease the discomfort she probably felt.

"Come here," I whispered, gripping her hand and tugging.

"Hmm." The sated look in her eyes and happy sighs helped to ease my worries that I'd taken things too far, but I knew I needed to take special care of her in this state.

"I'll help you." Gripping her waist, I lifted her toward me, pressing our chests together. She placed her arms around my neck and hugged me to her as I drew my hands softly over the sweaty skin of her back.

"That was..." she sighed. I was worried that maybe it'd been too much. I didn't even know what possessed me to do half that shit. "That was the hottest thing I've ever done," she whispered into my skin.

"Oh, thank God," I sighed as I tucked her face into my neck.

We sat quietly before Chase shifted and groaned from her perch on my lap.

"Want me to draw you a bath?" I asked quietly.

"That would be amazing." She kissed the side of my neck and leaned back, her fingers scratching my neck. "You going to join me?"

Smiling, I leaned forward and kissed her gently. "I may be able to be persuaded."

I gently laid her back against the sheets and kissed her forehead as I climbed off the bed, grabbing the rabbit and the Wartenberg wheel as I went.

Once in the bathroom, I carefully maneuvered myself out of the cock ring. My skin was sensitive from being restricted for so long, but it was worth every bit of discomfort. Using the toy wash, I washed it with the wheel and the rabbit and left them on a towel to dry before I started the water flow to the bathtub.

There was a canister of bath salts under the sink, and I figured it couldn't hurt, so I sprinkled some into the warm water. The aromatic vapors filled the bathroom as the salts dissolved into the steamy water.

When I returned to the bedroom, Chase was curled up in the sheets, her eyes closed.

"Let's go, sleepy," I coaxed a soft smile out of her as I lifted her shoulders and helped her sit up. She clung to my arm as we walked to the bathroom, and I helped her into the tub. She scooted forward, and I climbed behind her, drawing her back into my arms.

"How're you feeling?" My voice was low in the quiet of the room.

"Mmmm. I was a little sore, you know, down there...but this is helping."

"I would say I was sorry, but..." I trailed off.

"We both know you're not," she laughed quietly.

"Nope. Not even a little. That was explosive. And even that word doesn't seem to grasp what just happened in there. It almost felt like an out-of-body experience."

"Well, you may have been out of your body, but you were very much in mine," she laughed before she asked me a question, sounding amused and a little curious. "Are you sure you've never played with toys before?"

"Pretty sure." I nodded against the side of her head. Knowing sex toys existed didn't mean I'd ever seen one outside of something on the incognito tabs on my tablet.

"That was some expert-level shit in there. You were a very quick study."

"Thanks, I'm self-taught." She bounced lightly against my chest as we laughed quietly. I'd had no fucking clue what I was doing. At all. "Glad you enjoyed it."

"We're keeping everything in those bags," she giggled as she turned slightly and ran her hand behind my head, scratching the hair at the back. "Every single thing. And don't think you can get out of trying them all with me."

"Mmmm. I agree. We still have much more research to conduct." I kissed the top of her shoulder. "So...much...research..."

My hands came up to her breasts, cupping them lightly and coaxing the nipples into points with my fingers.

"Ahh. Be gentle," she hissed, and I decreased the pressure.

"Maybe we need to take another little break," I told her. I didn't want to hurt her by pushing it too much. This wasn't just about the sex with me. I enjoyed her company outside of all the things we'd done together.

"We can work on clothed research. You'd better practice your knots, or Emory will punish your ass tomorrow," she teased. "And I'm talking in the literal sense."

I shuddered at her thinly veiled threat on his behalf, knowing there was an element of truth to it.

"Thank you for trusting me enough to get you into all this," she whispered.

"Why are you thanking me? Of course, I trust you...I..."

Love you.

"You?" she asked softly.

"I care so deeply about you," I whispered into her hair. I was afraid to tell her how I really felt. There was no way I'd recover if she wasn't ready for me to say it yet or didn't feel the same way. If I mistook our physical closeness for something else, it'd devastate me.

Her breath caught, and she turned in my arms, water sloshing out the side of the tub as she turned to straddle me. Chase's hands framed the sides of my face, her thumbs stroking across my cheekbones.

"I care deeply for you, too," she whispered as she leaned forward, kissing me firmly. It was wet and slightly frantic, and I couldn't remember ever kissing anyone but her——ever. And I never wanted it to be anyone but her, ever again.

TWENTY-THREE

CHASE

BOSTON

"WAIT! I THOUGHT I got to tie him up!" The glare I aimed at Emory barely fazed him. This was some bullshit.

The smug little smirk on his face was clearly intentional as he lifted an eyebrow at my tone. "Excuse me?"

"Why does he get to be the one to use the whip?"

"You're pouting like a child," Emory scolded as he stood with his arms crossing his broad chest. "I taught you better than this, Chase. In this playroom, we respect the wishes of our mentor."

Evan stood to the side, his head darting between us as we faced off.

"I'm serious," I insisted. "I'm writing the Dominatrix. Why does he get to whip me first?"

Questions you don't expect to be asking your Dom for $100, Alex.

"You know how this works," Emory responded evenly. "You have to be willing to be on the receiving end before you do it yourself."

"But I already know how to use it." I flicked my wrist as he taught me, and the end of the flicker whip cracked softly in the air.

"Very impressive, Chase. I'm sure your Dominatrix will be quite intimidating," Emory sighed and rolled his eyes. "He's still going first."

I narrowed my eyes. He was such a dick sometimes.

"Bra on or off. Your choice," Emory nodded as he looked at my chest.

"On!" Evan practically yelled. He was still worried about Em seeing me unclothed, as if he didn't see models half-naked daily. Em seeing my breasts—at least in Evan's mind—was obviously going to turn him into a wild animal. Not that my brain didn't enjoy letting that little fantasy reel play. But ew, no. The only person I wanted going feral over my tits was Evan.

"Standing or kneeling, Chase?" Emory asked expectantly. "I'll let you pick the position."

"Kneeling," I sighed.

"Grab the rope, Evan." Emory nodded over at the tightly coiled rope he'd laid on the edge of the large leather bed that dominated the main space in Emory's playroom. "Let's see if you did your homework."

We'd spent a few hours curled up on the couch after our bath, watching TV and talking. It wasn't about anything of substance, but I felt like we weren't dancing around the subject of being together anymore. We were together, and I was sure we were on the same page...at least, I hoped we were. There hadn't been any grand declarations yet, but I could tell how strongly he felt for me. It was returned with equal vigor. Especially if he handled this whip as well as he'd dealt with the restraints we'd played with. Nothing said love like tying up your girlfriend and whipping her.

Evan had laughed when I ordered Chinese food, and the delivery driver expressed concern that I hadn't been home the week before for my usual order.

After dinner, we'd sat down facing each other, practicing basic knot-tying skills. Evan practiced on me until he felt like he got it right. If we hadn't been taking a break from strenuous activities, I would have mounted him right then and there at his adorable look of accomplishment when he successfully recreated the knots I'd demonstrated.

"Alright. What would you like me to do, Sir?" Evan asked quietly as he glanced over at Emory.

Emory pointed at the large leather bed in the center of the room. He motioned me over, and I knelt on a small pad he'd put on the floor in front of the edge.

"We want her arms up out of the way and a nice stretch on her back," Em instructed as he raised my arms in front of me and rested them near one of the leather straps running down the surface. "Bind her wrists and tie her into the strapping. We want her to be outstretched but with a little wiggle room."

"Yes, Sir." Evan sat on the edge facing me and picked up one of my wrists, running his thumb over the underside. "Chase, can you hold them six inches apart?"

I nodded and shifted into position as he took the nylon rope from Em and began looping it around my wrists. After making five even loops, he crossed the rope ends over each other and wrapped the space between my wrists. He crossed the rope ends again and then carefully stretched my arms over one of the straps, fastening me to the leather strap with neat knots.

"Very nice. He's a quick study, Chase. Better than your first attempt to tie me up," Emory complimented while simultaneously taking a jab at me.

Evan's eyes searched mine before they flashed over to Emory. I knew he had trust issues, but it truly was platonic between Emory and me, and it always would be.

"Don't worry," Emory assured. "It was for practice. Talia was enjoying seeing me bound and on my knees. Doesn't happen very often."

"You hate giving up control," I nodded. Emory's submission was a rare sight.

"You should feel accomplished knowing that you're one of the very few I trusted enough to do it," Emory stated. "That's what this entire lifestyle is about. Not control, not dominance. It's about trust. Trusting your partner enough to give them the control to make your desires come true. In a truly balanced dynamic, both partners trust each other to do what the other needs. A true power exchange can never happen without trust."

Evan's eyes locked with mine as Emory talked, and I knew that I completely trusted him with all of me. My heart. My mind. My body. I knew he'd keep me safe and care for me.

"Now select your equipment. I think she'd look particularly nice with an array of pink splashed across her pale skin from that flogger," Emory told him as he stepped closer to the wall holding all the whipping and paddling instruments.

Evan stood and stepped out of my line of sight. Their voices mixed with the gentle clanking of the metal brackets as things were moved around while they talked.

My heartbeat started to pick back up as the soft pat of bare feet sounded on the floor behind me.

Closing my eyes, I leaned my forehead against the leather, trying to straighten my back and remain balanced on my knees. I knew posture affected how the hits impacted your skin, so I tried to be the model sub while Evan was learning. My trust in him was solid, but he was new at this, and I wanted to set him up as best as I could. He'd be upset if he hurt me.

"Chase, you ready?" Emory asked quietly.

I nodded. "Yes, Sir."

"Evan, feet shoulder-width apart. Strike from the shoulder, not the wrist. It should be a fluid movement, not a snap."

A shaky breath escaped me as I heard the telltale whoosh of leather cutting the tension in the air. The tail lashed across my back, and I tried not to jolt at the impact. It wasn't hard enough to hurt me, but I still felt the sting from my blood rushing to the surface of my skin. As Emory continued to coach Evan behind me, endorphins surged as I anticipated his next move.

"Not bad," Em appraised. "Try to follow the whole motion through this time, don't hesitate at the end. It'll distribute the impact evenly across the skin."

There was little you could do to prepare yourself for the strike of an impact implement adequately, but I took a few shallow breaths anyway. I could keep still as it hit this time, my adrenaline spiking as the mild pain rushed through my body. It didn't really hurt, but it made me acutely aware of all the nerve endings in my skin. I could see why this excited certain people.

"Chase, are you still okay?" Evan's voice was uncertain behind me.

"I'm good," I nodded. "Keep going."

Em whispered some corrections to Evan's stance, and I braced myself.

A loud moan escaped as he landed two strikes going in opposite directions across my lower back.

"Chase?" Emory questioned with concern.

"All good, Sir," I sighed, trying to keep myself calm. The endorphin release from the pain fading was causing more arousal than I expected.

Before, when I'd been on the receiving end of Emory's hits, I'd felt the rush, but it was not as intense as the thrill that I experienced when I knew it was Evan working me over.

"Just a few more swings. Try to evenly distribute them so you don't hit the same place twice," Emory instructed. "That's how you get bruising or skin damage. The goal is a warm, even pink across the surface."

My loud moans were involuntary with the next set. My nipples were painfully hard, and I could now see why Em had joked about a bed in the back. If Evan weren't up for it, I'd steal one of Talia's toys and finish myself off in front of them both at this rate.

"Alright. I think you've got the hang of it," Emory told Evan. "Go ahead and release her."

Evan sat down in my line of sight to my side and ran his hand gently down my hair. I gazed up at him, a little drunk on the hormones coursing through my bloodstream.

"Are you okay?" he asked quietly.

"I'm great," I whispered as I heard the door to the studio click closed.

Evan quickly untied the fastenings and uncoiled the rope from around my wrists. He massaged the discomfort I had and moved onto my shoulders before lightly running his fingers down my back, admiring his work.

"I can see why you enjoyed the wooden spoon. That was a rush."

His dopey smile looked proud, and I loved how self-assured he was with this. It was a nice change from the timid man he'd been even days prior.

"It's different being the giver, isn't it?" I asked.

He leaned down and brushed his lips on my ear. "I'm so fucking hard right now. Those little noises you couldn't hold in didn't help either. Every time your mouth opened, and another sound escaped, fuck. You don't even know how hard it was to listen to his instructions."

My breath caught in my throat as I raised my head to look at him. His pupils were dilated, and he was staring at me with intense naked desire in his eyes. "He left to go get Talia. Told me he locked the door, and we've got an hour. If you're still sore, I can..."

"Then what are you waiting for?" I rose to my knees, interrupting him as I eagerly grasped his hips—turning him in front of me. I tugged on the waistband of his shorts, impatient to get him naked.

"Shit," he moaned, lying back as he raised enough to slide them down his thighs along with his briefs.

My God was he hard, almost as hard as he'd been with the ring on. I licked my lips and glanced up at him as my mouth hovered above his erection. I'd never wanted to throat a dick so badly in my life.

"You don't have to do... ahh!" he moaned as I engulfed him in my mouth and sucked hard before relaxing my jaw and taking him all the way down, gagging myself a little, but it didn't stop me.

"Fuck!" he yelled as he gathered my hair and held it out of my face. Evan's other hand pulled the band on my bra, freeing my breasts.

His long fingers rolled my nipple slowly, adding more pressure as he went, making me moan around his length. His hips pulsed upward as I took him in, building a quick rhythm.

"I'm gonna come, baby. Stop," he panted as he cupped my jaw and lifted me off him. He patted his lap as he sat on the edge of the bed. "Get up here. Straddle my lap."

"Yes, Sir," I winked as I took his hand and stood up. He grabbed my hips and turned me so I was facing away from him. He pushed down my shorts and panties, helping me step out of them.

"Put your legs up here." He ran a palm across the leather, and I carefully straddled him on my knees backward as his large hands supported my stomach.

Once I was steady, he grasped the base of his erection as I eased myself onto him. I emitted an embarrassingly loud moan as my thighs settled against his lap. "Oh God, you feel so good. The way you handled that whip made me so wet."

"Fuck, watching you squirm while I did it about ended me." He gripped my waist and slowly raised and lowered me onto his lap, pushing up into me at the end of each downward stroke. My head fell back onto his shoulder as his hands moved to cup my breasts, and he rolled my nipples between his fingers.

"Ride me, baby, take that dick like you own it," he groaned as I sped up the rhythm of my hips, grinding into his lap and rotating as he bottomed out. One of his hands traced down my stomach and gently pinched my clit between the pads of his fingers. At this point, I frantically rocked onto him as his fingers vigorously slipped through my wetness.

"Fuck, Evan, I don't know if I can hold off..."

"Keep riding me. Fuck me hard. I wanna feel you come," he groaned into my shoulder. My hips faltered as I started to feel myself falling over the edge, but his strong hands helped me keep up the frantic pace.

"Evan!" I moaned loudly as he pushed me onto him while bucking up from the bed. My orgasm crashed over me, and he groaned into my neck as I felt him pulse inside me.

"Oh...my...fuck," I panted as I tried to catch my breath.

Evan kissed along my shoulder blades as his palms caressed my breasts while we came down together. "That was fucking hot. Reverse cowgirl is definitely on the list of new positions I approve of. I think your nipples agreed."

I giggled as I kissed the side of his face and dragged my fingers through his sweaty hair. "You're wearing me out, stud."

He chuckled, and the vibrations shook me right along with him. "We can soak in the tub again when we get home."

I loved how he didn't even hesitate to call us going back to my condo home. His place...my place...as long as he was there, it was home.

Groaning as I pulled myself up from his lap, I climbed off the bed. My arms and legs—among other things—were sore, but I couldn't help myself around him. "We should probably clean this place up. I don't want to get punished and miss out on beating that fine ass of yours."

"Going straight to spanking, huh?"

"You've got a date with a leather paddle later, mister," I winked as I walked over to Em's toy chest of drawers and took out a few wet wipes. I cleaned myself up and quickly redressed, throwing Evan his underwear and then walking back over to push him off the edge of the leather bed. "Get your cute little butt dressed and help me clean that whip."

"You think my butt is cute?" he teased as he shook his underwear-clad ass at me.

"Quit it, you dork," I laughed, spraying some leather cleaner on a cloth and throwing it at his face. "If you weren't convinced I liked your butt from what happened, I can't help you. Playtime is later. We need to be respectful of Em's space."

"Yes, Ma'am." I raised my eyebrow at him and smiled. He cleared his throat, and his Adam's apple bobbed as he swallowed.

"Mistress," he whispered, and his head dropped as he gently ran the cleaning cloth over the handle and the tail of the whip he'd used on me.

He would probably benefit from a conversation with Nathan. Evan seemed able to switch between Dominant and submissive with a few words or commands. Maybe we could work that into the storyline somehow.

With all the playtime-induced chemicals streaming through my blood, I already felt the need to write.

Frances—Fanny—had already booted Kallie out, and her story was starting to work through my brain. I needed to remember to bring a notebook to our next session. Evan had distracted me this morning, and I was off my game.

"Where'd you go?" His fingers gently tilting my chin upward startled me.

"Hmm. Oh. I'm starting to get the itch to write again," I told him absently as I recoiled the rope we'd used.

"I love that you get it." He pecked my lips, slowly caressing them with his. "Writing is ingrained in us. Once the words start building, keeping them in is hard."

"You say that now, but on day four of being under the influence of the imaginary people in my brain, you'll be questioning my sanity."

"Only then?" he asked, his face completely blank.

Narrowing my eyes, I pinched his nipple. "You know what I mean. When the muse strikes, you get lost in it. I don't want you to be disappointed if I sit with the laptop on my lap for hours at a time, ignoring you."

"I'll be right there with you," he assured. "Except for the ignoring part. I'll probably be interspersing writing with thinking about you naked. And wet... And moaning around my..."

"We can be crazy together," I interrupted, smiling as I looked into his eyes and wrapped my arms around him.

"I like to call it creative," he smirked.

It was hard to hold in a laugh as I squeezed him and leaned back. We stepped apart as the lock on the door clicked and slowly swung open.

"Did you miss me?" Tal asked as she stepped inside and took in how closely we were standing next to each other.

"Of course!" I told her enthusiastically. I always loved the energy Talia brought to any room.

"Who's ready to get spanked?" she laughed as she crossed the room and tapped her hand on my butt.

"It's not my turn." I shook my head.

"Ohh. Can I watch?" she asked as she ran her eyes down the length of Evan's form. I would have been worried if I didn't know she was completely committed to Em. She was a bit of a voyeur.

"Up to him," I shrugged as I looked at Evan. His eyes searched mine, and I gave a subtle nod. I didn't mind if she watched. I planned to cuff him to the wall if Em let me choose his position.

"Uh...I...uh," Evan stuttered.

"You're so adorable," she cooed as she squeezed his shoulder.

"Thanks?" He looked at her like she was a little batty and then at me with wide eyes.

This should be fun.

TWENTY-FOUR

EVAN

BOSTON

AT FIRST, I'D BEEN almost paralyzed with nerves for Talia to sit in the room while Em taught us about erotic spankings.

Watching the demonstrations at the showcase as an outsider was an experience totally removed from being put into the position of submission. The only thing that kept me from working myself into a full-blown panic attack was how Emory calmly explained everything as Chase provided silent support by holding my hand. It was startling how much the touch of someone you trusted could keep you centered.

The room was warm, but I was exposed—clad in only the leather jockstrap. I felt a little cold and a lot vulnerable as I stood with my leather-bound wrists hooked onto the wall frame. My almost nudity didn't bother anyone but me, but I didn't care once Chase brought the paddle down for the first strike. She worked my cheeks evenly until my skin burned and my cock throbbed underneath its scant cover. She'd described how the pain would infiltrate your body and somehow morph into ecstasy like she'd described it in her book, but as the endorphins flowed, I felt all my anxiety fade away.

Once we'd finished the lesson, Emory walked us through more aftercare options, and then he and Talia left so we could get changed into our street clothes. But not before Chase eagerly stroked away the tension, falling to her knees and catching the mess on her tongue.

"You ready to do this?" she asked as we left through the gallery doors, walking hand in hand back to the car.

"So ready. I can already hear their voices forming." I knew we were both dying to write. The endorphins flowing through my bloodstream were inspiring scenes I'd never have imagined myself writing even a month ago.

"You hungry?" Chase asked as we sat down at the kitchen island once we'd arrived back at her place.

"I could eat," I shrugged. We'd probably burned a fair number of calories today. If we stayed in Boston longer, I'd need to figure out a running schedule. It helped clear all the clutter in my brain so I could focus on writing. Though banging out plot points with Chase seemed to have the same effect. Maybe what I needed all along was a sexy, curvy muse without a verbal filter.

She nodded and pulled a stack of takeout menus from a drawer in her kitchen island. "What are you in the mood for?"

"Surprise me? I'll take a page from your book and tell you I'd put just about anything in my mouth right now." Her teeth dug into her bottom lip as she fought the urge to deliver a dirty comeback. She leafed through the stack and pulled out a menu for a Thai place. I hadn't been in a city with accessible takeout in so long, and I wasn't even sure where to start, so I was glad she took the choice out of my hands.

"I'm gonna go shower," I told her as I stripped off my shirt. I always did my best plotting under the warm spray of the showerhead.

She bit her lip and ran a finger across my abdomen. "I'll order this and come join you."

I wasn't sure how sore she was from the last few days, so I planned to let her rest, knowing how hard she'd ridden me earlier. But I needed to relieve some tension desperately.

My clothing hit the floor next to my bag in moments, and I stroked my semi-erect cock on the way to the bathroom as if it were second nature. Setting the water to warm, I stepped into the spray and ran my hands through my hair a few times.

Bracing my forearm on the tile, I hung my head as I fondled myself with the other hand. This afternoon had me worked up. Emory being in the room had been the only thing that had kept me from coming all over that flimsy jockstrap. And the one release Chase had coaxed out of me was barely enough to take the edge off.

Groaning as I worked my hand, twisting at the head before rapidly traveling back down to the base, I tried to pinpoint when the stigma of being a sexually driven person fell away. All the insecurities I'd held for so many years, ingrained in me from previous partners, didn't seem to matter any longer. Chase had opened my eyes and taught me things about myself in the past few weeks that I would never have discovered on my own.

She was bound to join me soon, but the thought of getting caught jacking off in her shower only made me harder. Something that would have crippled me with anxiety before her.

"That's so fucking hot," she whispered as she slid the door the rest of the way open and stepped in behind me. Her hands ran down my back and cupped my hips before she molded herself to my back. Peeking around my side, she eyed where my hand had never faltered, stroking the hard flesh I was no longer ashamed of pleasuring.

"Keep going," she urged in a sultry voice.

"Ahh, fuck, baby," I hissed as she slowly skated her fingertips along the ridge at my side, letting them follow the path to where my hand was currently preoccupied.

"Make yourself feel good," she whispered. My hand resumed a slow circuit of up and down as I felt her lips travel down my side, one of her hands reaching down to roll my sac in her fingers. "Imagine all the filthy things you want to do to me while you touch yourself. How much I know you enjoyed aiming your cum at my tongue earlier. How you watched as I swallowed it all, knowing you greedily wanted more."

"Fuck," I groaned as my legs started to shake a little. The skin on my backside was a little sore, but I didn't even care, with the naked woman wrapped around my back, whispering dirty encouragements.

"That's it. I can tell you're close. Don't slow down. I know you want it." The combination of her touch, her soft voice, and the sensual kisses on my back pushed me rapidly toward the edge.

As her hand ran over the tip of my shaft and slightly overlapped with my own, I groaned into the steam of the shower. She squeezed the head as our hands worked me over, my hips starting to rut into the motion.

"Come for me, baby," she whispered into my neck as she rubbed her tits against my back. Chase was breathing almost as hard as I was. "I want to feel it cover my hand and drip through my fingers."

"Fuck, yes," I groaned as I pulsed and painted the shower wall and her fingers with my cum.

"You feel better?" She sounded amused as she placed a few more kisses on my back. I nodded, catching my breath. Chase straightened, pulling away from me.

A few moments later, her fingers performed their magic on my scalp, working the shampoo into my hair. I'd had more Chase-induced orgasms in the last two weeks than in the previous two years by anyone else, including myself. Other than when I was reading her books, I hadn't felt inspired to touch myself regularly.

"I needed to clear my head," I confessed. She hadn't seemed to have a problem with me pleasuring myself, but I felt a little self-conscious. I normally was not this sexually pent up.

"I get it. Sometimes we all need a little self-love to focus," she told me quietly. "Food should be here in about fifteen minutes."

She kissed my shoulder and stepped back into the spray, quickly washing and handing me the bottle of body wash. I lathered up and rinsed off before she turned off the water and leaned out the door, returning with towels. We were quiet as we dried ourselves, but my brain was not. Different scenarios were running through my mind, and I had a good idea of where I wanted the story to go.

"You ready?" she asked, pushing the door open and stepping onto the floor mat.

"As ready as I'll ever be."

We dressed quickly, and the delivery guy showed up shortly after we walked into the living room.

"Netflix?" she asked as we settled into the couch. Neither of us seemed to want silence right now. After eating, Chase tucked herself under my arm and laid her head against my chest as we watched whatever mindless show she'd put on. I was having a hard time focusing on anything but her right now.

"You're not expecting some *chill time* right now, are you?" I whispered as my fingers twined in her hair, and I ghosted my lips over the shell of her ear.

"I think you're gonna break me if I don't take a breather," she laughed as she looked up.

"Fair enough. I probably shouldn't be distracting you with that anyway. We need to start making some writing progress," I agreed. "Adrian and Isobel will get suspicious with too much radio silence."

"Is told me I had until Friday to send her some pages." It was Wednesday.

"For the book you were working on before you came to Connecticut?"

"Yeah. It's kind of stalled. I've been a little distracted," she told me with a guilty smile.

"I would say sorry, but..."

"You're so not," she laughed. "And we both know I'm not either. If I wanted to prioritize writing right now, I would have."

"Not even a little sorry. This has been the craziest past few weeks," I told her. "But I wouldn't trade any of it, even if my ass is sore."

"You'll live," she rolled her eyes at me. "You weren't on the receiving end of a whip."

"I'll live as long as I don't piss you off."

"Damn straight. I'll beat that ass," she cackled.

"I know you will." I wasn't joking; if I fucked up, I knew she'd lay me out.

"But seriously. We need to start working tomorrow, although this has been nice." Her shy smile made my heartbeat pick up.

"It has," I wholeheartedly agreed, "but it's back to the grind."

She smirked as she looked up at me, clearly holding in a dirty retort.

"Not that kind of grind. You're being awfully suggestive for someone who needs a breather," I teased. It was second nature now. If it were anyone else, I'd be overanalyzing every word I said, but conversation and teasing flowed naturally with her. I'd always thought the idea of people being obsessed with each other was a little unhealthy, but it was hard to avoid when you were in that kind of relationship with someone. "Not that I'd expect anything less."

"You know I'm a giant perv. That's why you love me."

The way she said it, I knew she didn't register what she'd said, but I did. She glanced up at me with wide eyes when it finally connected. "Oh. I didn't mean like that. You know I don't have a filter."

I pulled her upright next to me, my throat dry as I whispered two words with my heart in my throat. "I do."

"You do...?" Her cheeks turned pink as she stared at me, looking as vulnerable as I felt.

"I know you don't have a filter," I whispered, and her shoulders slumped slightly. Clearing my throat, I pushed through the nerves and confessed. "But I do. I love you."

My heart was hammering in my chest as I waited for her to register my words and formulate a response. I'd mistakenly said those words in the past, but the genuine feeling of completion with her cemented that it was what I was feeling. It was likely too soon, and I was probably setting myself up for heartbreak, but I wasn't sorry I said them.

"I uh..." Her eyes scanned my face, and my stomach dropped. I knew I'd taken a chance, but I didn't want to hold back how I felt any longer. Saying the words to her was simultaneously freeing and terrifying.

"I do, too," she whispered, and my pulse skipped. I wished she'd use another three words, but maybe she wasn't ready. I opened my mouth to speak again, and she pressed her palm against my lips.

"You think I'd be better with words," she laughed as a shy smile pulled at her lips. "I love you, Evan. I know that sounds crazy, but I've never felt like this before. I've written about it a thousand times, but I've never craved time with another person like I have with you. I'd even love you if you keep your pants on, but I kind of like it when you don't. Especially when you let me play with your butt."

Laughing, I cupped the sides of her face and rubbed my thumbs along her cheekbones. She was stunning, even with her hair half wet, a messy bun on her head, and zero makeup.

"Will you come back home with me? So we can start writing in the quiet. It's not that your place isn't nice, but being in the city makes me anxious. Especially if we're at risk of running into people we know. But if you don't..."

"Breathe." Chase smiled indulgently, pressing her cheek into my hand as I finally stopped rambling. "I'd go anywhere with you. You're kind of stuck with me now. You don't need to worry about telling me what you need. If you need to be home, let's go home."

My lips found hers as I pulled her toward me, quickly closing the distance. I tugged on her bottom lip and suckled it with my tongue, appreciating that she understood me enough to be patient when I started to spiral. She climbed into my lap, and we continued kissing, simply enjoying being close to each other.

She'd agreed to come back with me without any hesitation. I'd been worried that she didn't feel this pull between us this whole time, but she was right there with me.

"Hey," I smiled at Chase as she stirred on her pillow. I'd been up with the sun around 5:00 am. First, I'd made coffee, run a quick mile on the quiet streets before the morning rush, and then I returned to her apartment, pulling out my laptop.

"Mmmm. How long have you been awake?" Her sleepy smile was adorable.

"A few hours." It was almost 9:00 am, I'd thought about waking her earlier, but I knew our sleep schedule would be thrown off as we started to write—she might as well have some rest now.

"What are you working on?" she asked curiously.

I had about ten pages in front of me filled with a detailed outline of the story we'd plotted out. I'd also started a glossary of characters with mini-bios and where they appeared in the plot. Even though it was nowhere close to being related to the content I normally wrote... it seemed to flow easily.

Frances was a Dominatrix who worked training other Doms and subs. Her regular sub, Dominic, had been in a non-exclusive dynamic with her for about a decade. People within their circle started going missing and turning up dead. When Dominic suddenly disappears, she doesn't know who to trust and fears he might be involved. She never anticipated being targeted by a serial killer, and it may not be who she thinks...

"What did you do?" Chase asked warily as I failed to contain my grin. She would likely think I was even nerdier than she already did when she saw all the background work I did in the plotting stages. I knew from how she talked about her writing; she just jumped right into it and let the story develop as she wrote. Part of me was jealous that she possessed that kind of creativity, but not knowing if I would write myself into a corner would be too much for my nerves to handle. If Adrian thought it was bad when I wrote mediocre sex scenes, he'd be dealing with daily panic attacks if I wrote without an outline.

"Sit up." She pushed herself up, settled against the headboard, and held out her hands. Placing the laptop onto her legs, she began to read.

"Oh, my gahhh-shh," she yawned. "You take type A to a whole new level."

I shrugged as I smiled at her. I liked having a plan. "What do you think?"

"I think this is fucking amazing. Can I hire you to write with me full-time? I need an Evan to make sense of the mess in my head."

I leaned over and kissed her head, slipping my arm around her lower back. "You don't need to hire me. I'd be happy to help you. I have this outline I use to make series bibles."

"You're too adorable this morning." She reached up and ruffled my hair. "Do you have any of the dialogue started, or did you only work on the outline?"

I used the tip of my finger to tap the screen to switch to another tab.

"Someone has been productive this morning."

"I have," I told her as I looked into her eyes and ran my finger down the side of her face. "Something has me feeling extra inspired lately. And as long as we keep up with the detailed research, I should be able to handle this jump into a new genre."

"Love looks good on you," she sighed happily. Her soft lips caressed mine as she ran her fingers into my hair.

"Is that what this is?" I teased. "I thought I looked this good all the time."

"And you've got jokes, too," she giggled. "You don't need me to inflate your ego. If you actually tried, I doubt you'd have any problem with the opposite sex."

"Except for the fact I haven't been able to handle a normal conversation with one in years. You saw how I behaved when we first met. Think that times 100. Only your pervy brain seems to bring out this side of me." I kissed her softly and took the laptop back, saving the various open documents and closing the lid. "Do you want me to make you breakfast?"

"Have you eaten?"

I shook my head. "Not really, only some coffee and a piece of toast."

"Do you want to go out to breakfast somewhere?"

My pulse raced at her question. It was innocent enough—and would be nice—but being back in the city still made me nervous. The familiar panic I felt when surrounded by this many people started to build.

"We don't have to," she backtracked, and I immediately felt guilty, diffusing my chaotic feelings. If I could convince myself that it wasn't terrifying, maybe I could manage to let Chase distract me long enough to get through it. Simone always thought it was obnoxious that I was such an introvert, but she later realized it made it easier for her to control me—and my career.

"No, it's okay," I assured her, determined to leave my comfort zone. I couldn't hide away from the world with Chase by my side. "Let's do it. Want to take a shower with me?"

"Do you really have to ask that question? I'm always up for ogling you naked," she laughed.

"Ah, so that's why you keep me around. We both know it's not my sparkling personality," I rolled my eyes dramatically.

"Hey, I happen to love your personality. And your dick. But mostly how you don't realize what a catch you are."

"I'm glad someone sees more than my awkward staring," I teased. "Let's get ready."

Chase and I showered quickly, surprisingly keeping our hands mostly to ourselves. We took an Uber across town because neither of us felt like dealing with traffic. She gave the address to the driver and cuddled silently against my side in the back seat until he pulled up at the curb.

"Okay, so this place looks like a college hipster spot, but they have amazing breakfast sandwiches," she explained as we opened the door to the nondescript restaurant.

"Do we need to stop at a thrift store for some ironic fake glasses or a fedora?"

"It's not that bad," she sighed.

"I'm out of touch with the youth of today."

"Alright, Grandpa. You make it sound like you're eighty."

"I wasn't known for my ability to be trendy in college," I confessed. I was just as awkward back then but hadn't taken up hiding from it yet.

"I'm sure you broke all kinds of hearts, Mr. Soccer Star," she cooed as she batted her eyelashes at me.

"Hardly," I scoffed. "You know Raj from Big Bang Theory?"

"Yes?"

"That was my nickname," I confessed. It'd been accurate in comparison as well.

"Big Bang? Damn, should I be worried? Have you been holding back?" She giggled as she sat at a table near the back and picked up her menu, hiding behind it.

I pushed it down with my finger and rolled my eyes at her. "No, smartass. My nickname was Raj because I never talked to girls." Except alcohol didn't magically make me talkative as it did with Raj. "I even stopped going to parties because the girls called me the 'creepy hot guy.'"

"At least they thought you were hot..." Chase shrugged her shoulders, and I rolled my eyes, flicking her menu as I released it.

"Do you two know what you want?" the waitress interrupted, looking expectantly at Chase. I could see what she meant by hipster. The waitress had gray-dyed hair pulled up into some kind of twist and a bandana tied over it. Her denim overalls and plaid shirt reminded me of what you'd see in nineties music videos.

"I'll take the fried rice."

The waitress looked over at me after jotting Chase's order and winked. "And you, sugar?"

My eyes widened, and I stuttered out my answer as Chase snickered at me. "Uh...breakfast burger?"

"See. Women can't help themselves around you," Chase teased as she grabbed my hand across the table.

"Well, you don't need to be worried. You're the only woman I seem to be able to articulate a coherent sentence around."

A college-aged guy dropped off our food a few minutes later, and we dug in.

"Oh, my guh... this sooo goo—" I mumbled through bites of the amazingly flavorful sandwich.

"I'm assuming that was English?" she smiled indulgently.

I swallowed and stuck my tongue out at her. "You're right. This place is good."

"Of course, it is—I'm always right..." She trailed off as her eyes widened.

"Oh shit! Incoming." Chase put her hand next to her face and looked toward the wall. I turned toward the door and saw a statuesque brunette determinedly approaching our table.

"Who is that?" I asked as I leaned across the table toward her.

"Shit, shit, shit," she muttered as the woman stopped beside our table. "Kristine! How are you?"

"Chase..." the woman sighed her name in a way that made me feel chastised. "So, you are alive. I was beginning to wonder."

"Yup, still here," Chase nodded. "What are you doing here?"

"Picking up an order for dickhead. He claimed he had a craving, and his intern was 'busy,'" she said in a mocking voice doing air quotes.

"Is actually let him send you on an errand?"

"Those two are being weird. She's super distracted lately, and, to be completely frank, she's pissed off at you."

"Crap." Chase cringed as she looked at me.

"So, are you the reason that Chase isn't meeting her deadlines?" the intimidating woman asked, aiming an arched eyebrow at me.

"Kristine, be nice," Chase warned.

"It was just a question, Chase. He's a big boy. He can answer questions."

"Uh..." Shit. She was staring at me. I was afraid of this girl. She couldn't have been older than her early twenties, but she was obviously skilled at intimidating men.

"Okay, so maybe he can't." She squinted at me and gave me a look. "I know you."

I shook my head and tried to make my mouth move. "I... uh. I've never met you."

"No—your face is familiar. Where do I know you from?"

"Kristine, seriously. Leave the guy alone."

She turned her intense gaze back on Chase. "Fine. Maybe I'm mistaken, but I doubt it."

"Anyway," she sighed. "You better come up with something, or she's gonna take it out on me."

We heard a phone buzzing, and Kristine reached into her pocket.

"Damn. I'm being summoned. Good to see you, Chase. I'm sure I'll see you around." She quickly tapped onto her screen and then walked to the counter.

The cashier handed her a large paper bag, and she took off out the door with a salute in our direction.

"Who was that?" I breathed, my heart still racing a little.

"Kristine," Chase sighed as she poked at her bowl. Most of the rice was gone by now.

"I got that much."

"She's one of Isobel's interns. She does copy editing," she explained.

So that's why she was so insistent she knew me.

"She seems a little..."

"Intense. Yeah," she agreed. "She's a force to be reckoned with, but she's good at her job. And 'dickhead' is Adrian. She never calls him by his real name."

"Well, he is kind of a dick. Makes perfect sense."

She laughed as she poked at my half-eaten burger with her fork. "Finish up. We've got work to do."

"Yes, Mistress."

TWENTY-FIVE

CHASE

BOSTON

> *Isobel: Seriously, Chase, I need pages, or you have to apply for a submission extension.*

SHIT. I GUESS I couldn't ignore Is anymore. I had three chapters done, but I was completely absorbed in writing with Evan. I'd never flaked out on submissions before. I'd been writing up to the very last minute sometimes, but I'd never outright ignored and dismissed an agreed-upon deadline.

> *Chase: I'm sending you what I've got so far but get me the extension paperwork.*

Fuck—now she was calling me.

"Yes," I answered cautiously. I had a feeling she was about to give me an earful.

"What the hell, Chase?" She did not sound happy with me. "You have nothing to say for yourself?"

"I'm stuck," I whispered. Lying to her wasn't something I was proud of, but I couldn't draw focus from our project when we were making consistent progress.

"You seemed to be fine until I had to farm you out. What the hell is going on?"

I wasn't sure if I wanted to come out to her yet. She was bound to tell Adrian, and I couldn't volunteer info if I hadn't cleared it with Evan.

"I need another two months, and then I promise I will get back to this..." I begged. Evan and I should have a rough draft proofed by then, and I could devote whatever I needed to my draft once this set of characters was out of my head. Writing a romantic comedy when I was elbows deep in dead bodies, and bondage was the last thing on my mind.

"Two more months!" she shrieked, and I shied away from the phone, holding it away from my ear. "You were supposed to have this manuscript done and submitted in two months!"

"I know..."

"You know?" she continued yelling. "Are you freaking kidding me? Legal could cite breach of contract on this, Chase."

"They won't. I promise."

"Look, I know you've always delivered before, but I'm worried about you." Her voice was much quieter. Concern etched in her tone.

I looked over to my kitchen table where Evan was sitting—earbuds in, crazy bedhead, shirtless—wearing only pajama pants. He was completely focused on typing on the laptop in front of him.

"I've honestly never been better, Is." My confession was completely, one hundred percent honest. This felt right to be working with him. I'd never done a full collaboration before, but with us, it was seamless.

"Are you still in the city? Did something happen?"

I looked over to make sure his earbuds were still in. Evan was in the zone.

"Only until tomorrow. I met someone," I whispered quickly. Partial truths might get her to back off a little.

"Like you met someone and you're having a hot passionate fling to gain inspiration, or you met someone and..." she trailed off.

"I met someone, and I'm fairly sure he's the real deal," I admitted. Imagining my future with anyone but Evan wasn't a reality for me anymore. "No. I know he's the real deal. He's all I can focus on right now."

The phone line was quiet for a few minutes. "Is he there? I'm coming over."

"No!" I shouted, and Evan startled across the room, pulling a bud out of his ear.

"You okay?" he asked quietly, a small frown on his face. "What's wrong?"

I nodded as I pointed to my phone. "I'm fine." I mouthed and growled silently at Isobel.

"No," I repeated more firmly. Evan was finally relaxed enough around me that he was making solid progress with everything. Isobel showing up could spook him, and I wasn't willing to risk it. "I promise I'll come to see you later next month. Right now, I need you to give me space to see this through."

"You can't break up with your editor, Chase," she scolded. "I know you have a personal life, but please keep me in the loop. It's not like you to go off the rails."

"I'm not going off the rails, Is. Please stop being dramatic. I'm working on a project and need to finish it before I can focus on something else."

"Project? Like a writing project?" Her voice sounded a little frantic and a lot excited.

"Kinda." Shit. I hadn't meant to tell her. She was way too good at weaseling information out of me. "It's really kind of a passion project, and I'm not ready to share any..."

"Send me what you've got!" she interrupted. "We can pitch it to Sloane and..."

"Is, calm down. You're going to have to wait for this. It's not mine to share. I'll send you a draft once it's done. This project is a secret right now. If you tell anyone, I'll pitch it elsewhere."

"Not yours to share? What does that even mean?" she asked skeptically.

I sat there and tapped my pen nervously on my thigh. Evan had resumed his frantic typing at the table.

"Chase?" she questioned again, sounding a little irritated.

"I'm writing something with someone."

"Like a book? You're writing a manuscript with someone and won't give your editor details?" Her voice still had an edge to it that I didn't like.

"Yes..." I answered warily.

"Who? Is it someone who even knows what they are doing? I don't want someone to take advantage of you and jeopardize your career. This isn't like you."

I laughed, only focusing on her second question. Evan certainly knew how to do all kinds of things now. "He definitely knows what he's doing."

"He?" Now she sounded angry. "Is this guy you're seeing trying to use you to get his book published? I thought you were smarter than this..."

"Oh, thanks for having faith in me," I scoffed. "Trust me, Is. He needs no help from me to get published."

Silence filled the line before she gasped loud enough Evan likely heard it despite his firmly fixed earbuds.

"Holy shit, Chase! Really?"

"What?" My heart started beating faster as I waited for her to respond.

"Is it Evan? Are you sleeping with Evan?"

Fuck. She really did have me all figured out. "Um..."

"Adrian has been making my life hell since his golden boy dropped off the grid. The two of you aren't very good at the cloak and dagger routine."

I'm sure he's been giving you a really hard time. Emphasis on the hard...

"It's the only thing that makes sense," she insisted. "You're being secretive while Evan's gone radio silent."

"I'll call you later, Is. Something has come up! Bye!" Panicking, I hung up on her and turned off my phone, throwing it on the coffee table. My heart pounded as I leaned forward on the couch cushion with my head in my hands. I took several deep breaths to calm myself down, but it didn't help. This project was messing with me. I wasn't ashamed of it nor afraid of Is finding out the truth, but I'd become consumed. Maybe she was right that this would implode my career.

"Hey. You alright?" Evan sat on the couch beside me and pulled me into his arms. "Who was on the phone?"

"Isobel."

"About your deadline?" he asked as he ran his hand down my back, combing through the loose hair. "Authors miss deadlines all the time. She needs to give you some slack."

"Yes," I whispered into his neck. "And no."

"If you need me to take point on this and write the first draft, I can," he offered as he hugged me to his chest a little tighter. "The outline is solid and we can always change things during editing if you aren't happy with it."

"No—no," I immediately disagreed. "I want to be doing this with you. I'm just overwhelmed." As my chest tightened with every breath, I could empathize with Evan regularly dealing with this kind of anxiety.

He nodded and squeezed me closer, his lips on my temple.

"She knows we're sleeping together," I whispered, waiting for him to inevitably freak out.

"Oh." He tensed up, holding me tighter. Was this the moment he finally ran?

"I didn't tell her," I insisted. "She guessed. I've never been able to keep secrets from her. She's like an FBI profiler, she's always two steps ahead of me."

"It's okay," he assured quietly. "I'm not mad, don't worry about me. I don't want to jeopardize your career because I'm interfering with your working relationship with your editor."

"I just panicked when she figured it out and I hung up on her and turned off my phone." Nodding to the offending piece of technology I'd abandoned on the coffee table, the tightness in my chest started to ease.

He laughed and kissed the side of my head. "She was going to find out we're together eventually. I don't plan on going anywhere."

"I know. I wasn't hiding it, but I don't like letting her down. I feel like I'm disappointing her by not fulfilling my obligations."

"Baby," he sighed, pulling me up to look into my eyes. "I'm sure you're not letting her down. She deals with writers all the time. She knows the words don't always come according to some contract."

"I know, but..." Panic was building inside me as I thought about what this meant for my career. This was the first time I would miss a contract deadline. I felt like a failure. In the last few years, I'd finally felt like my career was finding its footing. Evan didn't understand what it was like to fight for every reader.

"Just relax, take deep breaths, focus on my voice," he encouraged, and I gave him a shaky nod. "What can I do to help?"

"Take me home?" My voice was quiet and vulnerable, but for once, I didn't feel safe staying in the city. I needed him to take me back home.

He kissed me gently and leaned back into me, rubbing his hand down the back of my head and tucking my face into his neck. "Right now?"

I nodded as I took a deep breath and inhaled.

"Did you just sniff me?" he laughed.

"Maybe..." I admitted as I picked at a frayed thread along the piping on the couch cushion under my legs.

"Let's go pack. If we leave soon, we can make it there in enough time to get groceries for dinner."

"Oh take out. I will miss you so," I sighed dramatically.

"You're so weird," he laughed as he hugged me tighter. "I'm not sure if I should be offended by your attachment to take out meals."

"Pretty sure you're stuck with me and my crappy taste in food," I giggled as I leaned into his embrace.

"I'm okay with that." His voice was amused, but I could tell he was quite happy with that fact. I was as well, despite my earlier freak-out. "You know I'm happy to take care of you. I can even attempt to recreate some of your take out favorites."

"Does this mean I get more naked chef time?"

He sighed and shook his head. "You've got a one-track mind."

"You didn't answer my question."

"You have to start running with me at least three times a week," he bargained.

"Three?" I looked at him; my face scrunched in distaste. "Two?"

He shrugged as he shook his head. "Then I get to keep my briefs on."

"Dammit." I pretended to think about it.

"Fine. No running—then shorts stay on too."

"You suck," I groaned as I pretended to be put out.

"Pretty sure that's you who does the sucking." He bit his lip to keep back laughter.

"Not if you make me go running all the time. I'll be too tired," I insisted.

He rolled his eyes. "Your mouth won't be the thing running. Although, on second thought..."

Part of me tried to be annoyed with him, but the teasing meant he was finally comfortable enough to stand up to my dramatics. I was also relieved that he hadn't been upset by my editor sussing out our new collaboration. She didn't have the details of the actual book, but we were on her radar.

"Are we doing this?" he asked as we sat upright.

"Yeah," I nodded as I looked at the front door. "I'm half terrified Isobel will show up here any second. Or send Kristine in her place."

"Adrian keeps texting me, but I sent him an 'out of office' text," he confessed.

"You don't even have an office," I giggled. Clever, clever man.

"I know, but it pisses him off. I have it saved in the notes on my phone, so I copy and paste it every time he texts or emails me."

"You're an evil genius, Evan Stineman."

"I try." The slight blush on his cheeks made me love him even more. His personality was not all that different from mine when we were alone. It was in social interactions where we differed. I wished l he'd show this part of himself to the world, but I was perfectly happy keeping him all to myself.

"Make sure you don't forget the apron." I winked as I stood up from the couch and held my hand out. He pushed himself up and followed me into the bedroom, lightly bumping into me from behind.

"Maybe I should order you an apron, too," Evan whispered as he let go of my hand and slipped his hands around my waist. "You could burn water in it, and I'd bring my big hose to extinguish the fire."

"Maybe I don't need an apron." His arms tightened around me, and I could feel his warm breath wash over the side of my neck. "Your hose is welcome to douse my fire whenever it likes."

He groaned as he kissed my nape. "You'd never get to eat if you prance around my kitchen naked all the time."

"What about yo—oh!" I laughed as I got his double meaning. *I'd* never get to eat, but apparently, he'd be eating something. "You're bad."

"You seemed to enjoy it the other day. But maybe I need to put you back on the kitchen island and remind you what it felt like to have my tongue buried in your..."

"Okay, hands off mister." Pulling his arms from around me, I darted to my closet before he disintegrated my panties with his dirty whispers. "We need to get packed."

"Are we driving separately, or...?"

"Do you want me to drive myself?" I pulled down my bag and peeked out the closet door. His face was drawn as he nervously shifted from side to side.

"No." His voice was soft as he finally looked up. "I don't want to spend another car ride without your creative renditions of pop songs."

"Okay. I'll ride with you." I nodded and placed my bag down on the corner of the bed. "I wouldn't want to deprive you of my musical stylings."

"I'll bring you back whenever you want, but..."

"But...?" I asked curiously.

"You're welcome to stay as long as you'd like." He mumbled something I couldn't hear under his breath, but I let it go.

I'd been serious when I told Isobel I needed two months. Leaving my condo behind for a few weeks or even months to write this book with him was okay with me. If I was completely honest with myself, I'd probably be content not coming back and staying with Evan indefinitely.

"You'll get tired of me eventually."

He crossed the room and pulled me into his arms, kissing me softly as he held me. When he pulled back, his eyes were no longer guarded as he shook his head. "I don't see that happening any time soon."

DESPITE MY INITIAL URGENCY to leave, we slept at my condo for the night. There weren't any unexpected visitors, but Evan had distracted me enough to keep my mind off my paranoid worries. The next morning, we woke up early to prepare for the long drive back to Connecticut, heading out after breakfast. I missed staying in bed and snuggling with him, but we could catch up with that later.

"Are you alright with stopping for groceries somewhere along the highway?" he asked as he turned down the music from the car speakers.

Evan had been quiet so far on the trip back to his house, but I was equally zoned out with my laptop open on my knees.

"Looking for something you can't find in Ashford?"

"Not really. I don't want to have to go into town when we get back. I like the anonymity of Walmart rather than the Ashford market. No one stares at me there. I still don't see the appeal of being curious about my boring life buried in a laptop, but I've found residents of small towns are a bit nosy."

"They're gonna stare at you everywhere, but I see what you're saying." I reached over and squeezed his hand.

"It's these shorts, isn't it?" he laughed, pulling awkwardly at the hem of his very short white athletic shorts. The other pairs in his bag had been dirty, and we hadn't had time to wait for the laundry.

"Well, they're not helping," I giggled. "But why the hat?"

"I didn't feel like styling my hair," he shrugged.

"And the hat was a better alternative?" I giggled as I reached over to flick the underside of the brim. After rummaging in his trunk, he'd put on a trucker hat that was taller than a standard one. It looked awkward as it stood up from his head.

"Oh, now that we're official, you've got a free pass to tease me?" He smiled. I knew he wasn't entirely serious.

After another twenty minutes on the highway, he pulled off toward a Walmart right off the exit.

"Ready to go get stared at?"

"Pfft. I make this look good," he laughed as he took off the hat and threw it in the back seat before he got out of the car.

"So that's why you took it off?" I giggled as I took in the bedhead he was hiding underneath.

"Happy now?" he sighed loudly.

"Still better than the hat," I laughed as he made a face at me over the car's roof. "Oh, poor baby, I'm making you go out in public without your hair done," I teased. My own messy bun was probably chaotic. I was sure pretty much any Walmart had seen much worse than our unkempt appearances.

"You're mean," he pouted.

I rushed around to his side of the car and pinched his butt. "That's why you like me."

I took off half-jogging across the parking lot, and he chased after me, landing a hard smack to my right butt cheek as he caught up with me. "Alright, feisty. ..behave. We're in public."

"Since when has that stopped me?"

"Let's get what we need so we can get home." We were both tired, but at least we had each other to stay entertained on the car ride.

"Yeah, yeah." I followed him along as he pushed the cart through the produce section, filling it with various fruits and vegetables.

"What kind of meat do you want?"

I grinned as I eyed his shorts and wiggled my eyebrows.

"Okay, nympho, focus. Pork?"

"Oh my God," I giggled as I leaned against his shoulder.

"Can you pull your head out of the gutter and tell me what you want?" he sighed loudly.

"I could..." I shrugged, "But I won't."

"Sausage?" My giggles returned, and he rolled his eyes. "Obviously, I'll be grocery shopping alone from now on."

"Fine. Fine, I'll be good," I told him as I tried to quit laughing.

"I doubt that. But I'll still feed you my meat anyway."

I kept the suggestive comments to myself for the rest of the trip through the store—aside from my commentary about the slightly curved zucchini he put in the cart. Most of the things in the cart were healthy, and I realized that my usual writing snacks were missing.

"I'll be right back." I wandered toward the aisle with the chips on one side and the candy on the other. I grabbed my usuals, returned to the cart, and dumped the packages inside.

"You can't be serious." He looked down at my additions with wide eyes and a disbelieving look.

"Hey, I can't be held responsible if Fanny goes a little crazy because I don't have my Twizzlers."

"I'm sure you'll be fine without them," he insisted as he picked up the package and stepped away from the cart.

"Put down the snacks," I warned. You do not come between a girl and her candy stash. That was just not okay.

"But these are garbage."

"Don't care. They're mine," I shook my head as I reached for the packages.

"You're impossible," he sighed as he shook his head.

"You mean impossibly awesome. Now step away from the snacks. I don't judge your phallic snacks. You leave mine alone."

"Phallic snacks?" he laughed. "They're carrot sticks."

"If you want to put tiny orange dicks in your mouth, then you can't judge my Twizzlers."

"Fine. Keep your junk food," he conceded. "Now you're definitely going running with me."

"As long as you're the one in the lead," I teased as I pinched his ass.

"You're incorrigible."

"But I'm yours." Flashing him a bright smile, I gave him a cheeky wink.

"Yes, yes you are." He put his hands on my waist and pulled me toward his chest, kissing me softly. "And I'll keep you around despite your need to make everything sound dirty."

"It's one of my best qualities."

EVAN

CONNECTICUT

"COME ON, BABY," I coaxed as I tried to pry the blanket out of Chase's hands. "You promised."

"But wouldn't you rather stay in bed with me?" Her pout was almost my undoing.

We'd been back in Connecticut for almost a month, and this was the first time she'd refused to get out of bed for a run with me. "I thought we were making progress. You said you didn't hate it last time."

"I didn't say I liked it either. We can always go later. I think you should get back into bed. It's warm under these covers."

I was having a hard time denying her. She was playing dirty this morning.

"Please? I miss having your big, strong body wrapped around me."

Blowing out a heavy breath, I sat down next to her.

"I promise you'll still break a sweat," she teased as she rolled to her side. Her partially covered body caused a stirring in my shorts as she started to caress her bare breasts, rolling her nipples and moaning softly.

"You play dirty."

I watched with rapt attention as one hand traveled down her chest, dipping beneath the sheets. I grabbed the covers and pulled them back as I watched her hand cover her mound.

"Help me?" she sighed as she reached for my hand and brought it down with hers, slowly parting her folds.

"Fuck, you're so wet," I groaned as I dipped two fingers inside her opening. "You're making this really hard to resist. You know I love it when you're all cuddly and horny in the morning."

"I hope you can't resist," she cooed as her hand reached inside the bottom of my shorts, gripping my stiffening length through my boxer briefs. "I want you."

"Fuck," I moaned as her fingers parted the flap and encircled my shaft. Working me up and down, her thumb spread pre-cum around the tip. She knew exactly how to get me going. "You don't play fair. You've completely destroyed my routine as it is."

Not that I was truly complaining. Her being here was an adjustment, but the pros outweighed the cons.

After we started writing and returned to Connecticut, I thought our sex life would wane, but we still couldn't keep our hands off each other. We'd tried out a few more things from Talia's bag of toys, role-playing certain scenes as we wrote.

We'd even experimented with a few new things I didn't think I'd be into. Chase made me try the leather cock cage while I watched her play with herself. It was by far the most erotic thing I'd ever seen. I'd exploded the second she released me from it and took me in her mouth afterward to kiss it better. I hadn't realized exactly how powerful edging could be. The delayed gratification made the intense release that followed worth it.

"Take off your clothes," she panted as I continued to slowly fuck her with my fingers, my thumb rubbing firmly on her clit.

"Shit," I hissed as I pulled her hand out of my shorts and stood beside the bed. "You're a bad influence."

Chase sat up and kissed along the muscle on my pelvis as I slowly lowered my shorts. My cock sprung free, and she grabbed it with one hand, flicking the head with her tongue. "But you like it. You love it when I can't keep my hands off you."

"Mmmm," she hummed, taking me further into her mouth.

Pulling my T-shirt over my head, I tried to toe off my shoes as she started a slow rhythm with her mouth.

"Get up on the pillows," I rasped out once I wrestled free from my clothes.

She released me and scooted backward on the bed, her naked body splayed against the sheets. I finished pulling off my socks and shoved my shorts the rest of the way off as I climbed onto the bed. Her fingers played with her clit as I made my way on top of her.

"Keep touching yourself," I whispered as I cupped her breasts and teased her nipples with my tongue. My finger pinched one lightly as I bit down on the tip of the other, and she arched off the bed, moaning my name. "It's so fucking hot how you aren't afraid to pleasure yourself in front of me."

"Oh fuck, Evan."

"Just keep fucking yourself, baby," I urged as I moved one hand to her hips and tilted her pelvis. Scooting myself over, I lined my cock up with her entrance, slowly slipping the head inside her lips as she continued working her clit.

"More," she begged as she tilted her hips further, her legs wrapping around my sides and pulling me toward her warmth. Sitting back on my knees, I pulled her toward me, grasping her thighs and supporting them against my chest.

"You're in so deep," she moaned as I thrust inside her. Grasping the back of her knees, I pushed them toward her chest as I sped up the movements of my hips.

Chase moaned loudly as her fingers continued rubbing. "Harder. I need it harder."

As she pushed herself over the edge, I was transfixed, watching myself slide in and out of her. I continued to fuck her roughly, pushing her knees out and spreading her legs.

Moaning babbles escaped her lips as she gripped the sheets on either side of her hips, pressing into my movements.

"Fuck, Chase. I'm gonna come," I warned as I thrust into her repeatedly. Feeling her tightening on my shaft again, I fought to push her into a second release before I finally let go.

Loosening my hold on one knee, I wrapped her leg around my hip, licking my fingers and pressing on her clit. She whimpered as I rubbed harder, her moans increasing in volume. The headboard smacked rhythmically against the wall as I teetered on the edge of exploding inside her.

"Come on, baby. Give it to me," I urged as my hips faltered. "Give me one more. Want to watch you fall apart again. You're so pretty when you come."

"I'm so close..." she moaned, pressing her hips into my motions.

Roaring as I felt her clamp down on me again, I couldn't hold back—snapping my hips twice and gripping her leg tightly as I came inside her. I was sure my fingers would leave marks, but she confessed she liked it when I was rough and couldn't control my passion with her.

My heart was beating frantically as I tried to come down. Chase's arms were thrown haphazardly to her sides, one leg still wrapped around my hip and the other grasped firmly to my chest. She hissed as I slipped out and my cock dragged against her ass.

"Oh..." she jerked as the tip slid against her other hole.

"Have you ever...?" My voice was cautious, but I was curious about her experience. She seemed so adventurous in bed, but I was discovering there were some things she'd only done in her imagination while writing about her characters.

Her head shook against the pillows as she bit her lip. "No."

I hadn't either, but the thought made me stir again.

"Do you want to?" she asked quietly, looking up at me. I had to admit I was intrigued. The bitch who shall not be named was only into traditional missionary, so I had no experience whatsoever.

"Uh..." My brain had stopped working. I was trying to work out the logistics in my head.

Chase propped herself on her elbows, bringing her hand down to experimentally run down my shaft.

"Do you?" I asked with a loud moan as she started to jerk me. I wasn't fully hard yet, but if she kept going, I'd get there.

"I trust you."

Holy shit. I hadn't expected this when I woke up this morning.

"And you want to right now?"

"You have somewhere else to be?" she smirked as her hand tightened.

"No...but--"

"Do you want to try?" She reached up to poke me in the chin so my jaw wouldn't hang open.

What did I do to deserve this girl?

"But I don't know what I'm doing." My heart beat harder at the thought of going through with this. I didn't want to hurt her, but I also really wanted to try it.

"Then I guess it's a good thing I don't know either. We can learn together," she giggled.

My hand rubbed up and down her thigh, as she continued to get me hard. "Shouldn't we research this before we..."

"No, Evan...geez," she laughed at my need to be fully prepared for something new. "Do you have lube?"

I nodded and reached over to the nightstand, pulling out a small bottle of lubricant.

"Go ahead. I've heard lube is your friend if you're planning on me enjoying this." She nodded at the bottle. I flipped open the cap and squirted some on myself, her hand sliding easier with the added moisture. I coated the tips of my pointer and middle fingers before I dropped the bottle.

She moved her leg from my chest and loosely wrapped it around my hip as I reached full mast. I scooted back and tilted her hips up with my free hand. My breathing picked up as she licked her lips, nodding at me.

Chase moaned lowly as I lightly ran my fingers along her skin. "It's okay. This is going to be different for both of us. I'll tell you if you need to stop."

I pushed the tip of one finger into her ass, and she flinched a little, closing her eyes. My finger retreated, and I waited until her eyes opened again to try again.

"I'm fine. Keep going." She grabbed my wrist and pulled my hand back toward her. My finger slipped further, and I slowly twisted it as I pulled back. "It's just...a lot."

"Are you okay?"

Chase held her breath every time I pushed inside, but I couldn't tell from the look of concentration on her face if she was enjoying it.

"I'm... I'm good," she panted as she shifted her hips from side to side.

Her muscles relaxed slightly as I continued to open her up. It was definitely a different sensation. More concentrated pressure where she constricted my finger. Going slow seemed to be helping her relax, her hips shifting into my movements as the minutes ticked by.

"Are you ready?" she whispered as I pulled my fingers out. Nodding, I watched as she opened the lube again, squirting some on my fully engorged head. "Just go slow."

"I should be asking you if you're ready. It's pretty obvious when I'm ready to go. But I don't want to hurt you."

She gave a jerky nod in response, and I grasped my cock in one hand, guiding the tip against her. She gasped as I pressed it into her tight hole and shifted into my movement. Her hips jumped as the head started to disappear inside.

"Fuck," I panted as I stilled and let both of us adjust to the sensation. It was tighter. Much, much tighter. I couldn't imagine what it felt like for her. Maybe we should have done something more to prepare her for this.

"Keep going," she encouraged.

I exhaled a few shaky breaths as I pushed further, feeling the resistance of her tense muscles.

"Touch yourself," I moaned as I tried not to lose it; she was so tight.

She nodded and licked her fingers, bringing them down to her clit and starting to circle slowly. After a few moments, I felt her relax, and I slipped in a little further. As I pulled back out slightly, she hissed.

"Go. Just keep going." She wiggled her hips, and I slid back inside her ass. "It's not bad, it's just—"

She squealed and pushed one hand against my chest as I did what I was told. I tried to retreat, but her eyes locked with mine. "Just go slow. I'll adjust."

I nodded and gripped her hips, slowly thrusting with shallow movements.

"Shit," I groaned as I watched the speed of her fingers increase, her neck flushing as I watched her pleasure start to crest.

Chase moaned again as I continued to keep my motions shallow, speeding slightly as I felt her relax.

"I'm gonna come." Her fingers pressed hard on her clit as she rubbed faster. Her breasts were flushed red, and I was in awe as I watched myself slide in and out of her. I could feel her muscles clench as my heart practically beat out of my chest.

"Fuck, baby. That's so hot," I groaned as her hips stiffened, and I watched her pussy pulse rhythmically. Once she started to let go, I couldn't hold on anymore and slipped out, cumming all over the sheets as she arched against them, moaning.

Resting my forehead on the arm braced against the headboard, I panted as I looked down at her. "You alright? That was fucking intense." And I wanted to try it again when we'd had more practice.

"Fuck," she groaned as her head rolled to the side. She was panting as much as I was.

"I'm gonna feel that later," she giggled as she ran a hand along my abs.

"I'm sor——"

"No, it was good. I obviously enjoyed myself once I relaxed enough."

Letting out a breathy chuckle, I carefully collapsed to her side on the bed.

She had a satisfied smile as she looked over at me. "Well, that was new."

Reaching over, I pulled her against my chest, kissing the side of her head as she snuggled into me. "I love you."

"Mmm. I'm sure you do now. I've heard the way to a man's heart is good anal."

Laughing at her sarcasm, I pinched her side.

"I love you too." Her voice was tired, and her eyelids started to droop. "Nap time?"

I was quite sure I'd had more of a workout than running would have given me this morning.

"Go to sleep, baby."

She sighed and burrowed into her pillow as I reached down to pull the covers back over us. My thoughts drifted to the almost complete manuscript sitting in Google docs. Another week or so, and it'd be ready to send to Is and Adrian.

I closed my eyes and pulled Chase tighter, trying to shut off my brain and live in the moment.

"Are we really doing this?" We worked on the book all day and were almost ready to submit the manuscript.

"Yeah, I think we are," she nodded as she smiled at me. "It feels ready. I'm sure Kristine will decorate it with her red pen, but the storyline is solid."

"They're going to freak out."

"Probably," she shrugged, "but how else are we supposed to do it?"

"You set it to locked, right? Only they have access, but no edits, right?" I was always overly cautious with document settings before sending them. You never knew when an email would fall into the wrong hands.

"Yes. I'm not an amateur," she said, rolling her eyes at me. We sat on the couch with the laptop propped on our legs as we finished getting the completed manuscript ready to submit to Isobel and Adrian.

"Should we turn our phones off?" Adrian would be on the phone as soon as he realized what we were sending him. I was almost afraid of his reaction; he was unpredictable sometimes.

"No, as much as I'd like to, Isobel would make Adrian drive her out here."

"She probably would," I agreed. "We definitely don't want that. One of them would be bad enough. I don't want both of them teaming up to come after us."

"You ready?"

"No," I groaned as I looked over at her.

"Do you want to delay sending it to them?" Her voice was filled with concern. I knew she would wait if I asked her to, but that wasn't fair considering all the work we'd put in.

I growled as my finger hovered over the send button. "No. We need to submit it, but I don't know if they will go crazy. What if the house won't publish it? We're both locked into other contracts. What if we wrote a book no one will ever read?"

"They'll publish it, trust me," she assured. "They fast-tracked my last book. It's trendy, and people are curious about it. I think we put a new spin on the subject that'll sell. Crossing over genres will bring new eyes to both of us. That means more sales for them."

Her hand came up to caress the side of my face. "It's good, Evan. If I thought it wasn't ready, you know I wouldn't turn it in.""

"I know, but what if my readers all flame it?" Her audience obviously liked sexual content, but mine would not expect it in my current book, much less another one with much more racy content.

"The buzz from your new book has been positive, right?"

I nodded as I looked at her. My book had been released the previous week. Some more conservative critics didn't endorse it, but I hadn't expected them to. Adrian kept sending me all the comments from my fan site. I didn't even have login info, so I avoided it. For the most part, my readers loved the spiced-up version of my book, and I'd gained a bit of a female following on Facebook. I thought it would make Chase uncomfortable, it would've angered Simone, but she thought it was hilarious her thirsty readers were lusting after her boyfriend.

"Yeah, it's more than I expected. I was expecting pitchforks and book bans, but I know it really wasn't that spicy in comparison to other books."

"Then this will be fine. If they're not running away from prostitutes, a fairly tame Dominatrix should be okay too." Her warm hand cupped my jaw as she tried to talk some sense into me.

"Tame Dominatrix," I laughed. "Little bit of an oxymoron."

"Would you rather have modeled Fanny after someone like Grace?"

I shook my head. "Nope. Not even a little."

Emory had texted Chase to let her know Grace had been asking about us. Apparently, she'd wanted to volunteer her consulting services. Our answer had been a resounding 'hell no!'. Neither of us wanted to kink shame, but sadistic humiliation didn't appeal to either of us.

"Ready now?"

I nodded nervously and pressed my finger to the touchpad. The little dialogue box popped up as 'document shared,' and I looked over at Chase with wide eyes.

"Hold me?" I whimpered as she laughed and picked up the laptop, placing it on the coffee table. She leaned back and opened her arms. I laid my head on her chest, and she ran her fingers through my hair.

My eyes closed, and I relaxed into her touch while we waited. Almost on cue, our cell phones started vibrating across the coffee table.

"That didn't take long," she giggled as she reached for hers and tossed mine into my lap. Adrian's name flashed across the screen, and I knew it was time to face the dickhead.

"Let's do this."

I sat up in the corner of the sofa opposite Chase, and we both accepted our calls at the same time.

"Yes?"

"You dirty dog. I didn't know you had it in you." His voice sounded half amused and half proud as he praised me over the line.

Chase rolled her eyes as she talked quietly to Isobel.

"That's all you have to say?" I asked. I was expecting feedback, not some macho congratulations.

"This is gold, Evan. Obviously, I still need to read through the whole thing and send it to Sam, but I expect a contract on this by the beginning of next week."

I could hear a female voice in the background, and Adrian covered his speaker before answering her quietly.

"I gotta go. I'll call you later," he said quickly before he hung up.

"So?" I asked as Chase finished her call only moments later.

"She hung up on me."

Isobel must have been the female voice I heard in the background. "They're so doing it."

"Yup," she giggled, climbing across the couch and into my lap. "You'd think they could at least send us a thank you note."

That had gone better than we expected.

Chapter

TWENTY-SEVEN

CHASE

Boston

"Are you kidding me, Is? I can't make him do that."

"Well, if you two don't want another ten percent of sales taken off the top of your royalties, you'll convince him." She was perched against the edge of her desk in front of me.

Kristine was sitting in a chair in the corner of Isobel's office, typing away. Her top lip kept twitching, so despite the earbuds in her ears, I knew she was eavesdropping. That girl knew everything that happened in and out of this office.

"He's gonna tell me no." Not to mention I'd never want him to question my motives if he felt like I was coercing him into doing something he specifically told me he didn't want to do. I knew it wasn't my place to be sharing more information about his anxiety, but maybe Isobel would understand if she knew what boundaries he set to protect himself. But it wasn't my conversation to have with her.

"You'd be surprised what a whipped man will do," Isobel replied with a wink. She would probably know all about whipped men. Adrian may wear pants, but Isobel was wearing the pants in that relationship for sure. He may have liked to look like an Alpha male, but I wasn't sure he had the personality to back it up past his dickish façade.

"Is, seriously. You need to have Adrian ask if you guys are forcing this."

"Evan already told him no," she sighed.

"Then what are you expecting from me?" Evan was free to make up his mind. I was not going to force or coerce him into anything. Knowing his name was attached to this was already taking a big leap for him; if he didn't want to do this, I would not lean on him for our editors.

"I don't know, Chase. Cut him off or something. The legal department has told me that your royalties will be cut if there isn't at least a six-city book tour with this one."

"It's not like I'm struggling, Is."

"That's not the point. This could affect your next contract," she sighed. "They want to cash in on this one, and you with Evan as the face of this book, is their way to do it. You both add a bit of sex appeal to the equation—but together, I can see real potential if we market it right."

"So, you're pimping us out." The nerve of both her and Adrian. I'm sure they would also get a hefty bonus if they convinced us to do this. While Isobel wasn't the type to take advantage of her authors, she also wasn't the type to risk the forward motion of her career to placate people.

Isobel shrugged casually, and Kristine snickered from the corner. Isobel's fingers snapped toward her, and Kristine pulled out an earbud. "Can I help you?"

"Quit spying," Isobel chided. "You better not be sharing this information with Sam."

"Why would I be telling him about this? That cock monkey isn't exactly discreet."

I bit my lip to keep from laughing at the hostility in her voice. Kristine didn't always play well with others.

"This conversation is fence-posted." Isobel shot Kristine what was supposed to be an intimidating look, but the younger woman rolled her eyes.

"What the hell is that?"

"It's between you, Chase, me, and the fence post."

"Is's office is like Vegas," I nodded.

"That phrase never made sense to me. It stays in Vegas as long as you don't pick up an STI," Kristine scoffed as her mouth pinched up in disgust. "Then it's the poor vacation decision that follows you home."

"Well, let's pretend you're wearing a condom," Isobel rolled her eyes. "This doesn't leave these walls."

"Yes, Ma'am." She saluted, and I started laughing.

"Something funny, Mistress?" Kristine winked at me, and I lost it, giggling even though I was mad at Isobel for trying to manipulate me for the profit of the publishing house. She'd never leaned on me with my previous releases, but I'd never had a writing partner.

"Hey!" Isobel yelled as she pinned Kristine and me with an admonishing look. "Chase. Seriously? I'm trying to cover your ass here. Sloane wants to market this as a hot romantic thriller with two authors who may or may not be sleeping with each other. She thinks amping up the relationship beyond the page will drive sales. While I'm not suggesting you two start making out at book signings, I think a sexy book release needs some sexual tension."

Kristine snickered as she slumped in her chair, the laptop on her knees hiding her face. "I think she has Evan around for covering her ass."

"Alright, children," Is rolled her eyes.

"The best I can do is ask him. If he says no, I'm not riding his ass about this."

Kristine started laughing again at my choice of words, and even Isobel cracked a smile.

"Perverts," I sighed in exasperation. Coercing Evan to help our careers was the last thing I wanted to do. But I also knew the head of publishing wouldn't accept no for an answer. If she wanted us to flirt with each other while we traveled to promote the book, both our careers depended on Evan agreeing to do a book tour.

"Is this something you want?" Evan had come with me to meet with our publisher, despite his reluctance to set foot in Boston this soon after our research endeavor.

I wasn't sure what to tell him. Honestly, despite the long hours and travel, I liked book tours. "I'm not going to force you. This is entirely up to you. Your contract is ironclad, so Sloane can't make you do this if you don't want to."

"That's not what I asked. Do you want to go on the tour?" he asked again. I tried to read his facial cues, but he wasn't giving anything away. Part of me was expecting the panic to set in any moment like it had when we were submitting the manuscript, but he seemed to be clear-headed right now. Irritated but not panicked. Yet.

"I don't mind them. I like interacting with readers and meeting interesting people. And it makes sense that they'd want to present the 'are they or aren't they' marketing approach. Look at how many shows get huge followings when the lead characters build up the unresolved sexual tension."

"But our sexual tension is resolved." He sighed as he settled into my couch cushions. We were staying in Boston while we were in contract negations. My lawyer had already reviewed the contract and submitted a few revisions. Evan was the only thing we were waiting for. I wasn't going to pressure him into going on tour with me. I'd offered to go on a regional tour by myself, but legal said marketing wanted both of us or neither.

"Do I have to speak?" He wasn't saying no, but he also didn't sound enthusiastic about it, either.

"Well, you, as a mute sub, could be kinda hot. Slap a collar on you and some leather pants. I'm sure Kristine would like to see me lead you around on a leash."

Expecting at least a smile from my joke, I cringed when his face remained solemn.

"Chase," he sighed as he leaned forward, and his head fell heavily into his hands. "I don't know if I can do this. Panic attacks and awkward staring aren't sexy. They want something from me I don't know I can deliver."

"I'll be there," I pointed out. "Not sure if it's helpful, but Adrian will be there. Usually, they send someone from PR. But you know all this—you used to do book tours back in the day, before..." Knowing he wouldn't respond well to the mention of Simone, my voice trailed off.

Trying to pull him out of this self-loathing funk, I rubbed my hand up and down his back, slipping it under the hem of his shirt and scratching his bare skin. "I can take care of any requested readings, and I'll be at the table next to you for signings. You won't be alone. Just think of all the motivational blowjobs I can give you to ward off nerves. You can't have a panic attack if you're a walking—not talking—hard on."

Evan completely ignored my ridiculous line of commentary, his fingers clenching in his hair.

"What cities do they want?"

"Bare minimum—Boston, New York, Chicago, Denver, Seattle, LA," I replied. Isobel had been specific about those cities. We could add on if we wanted, but those were locked.

"Shit..."

"What?" I asked quietly, continuing to rub his back.

"My family will want to come if we go to Chicago."

Mine would probably drive in from Minneapolis if we were there too. "And is that a bad thing? They only want to support you."

"Or my sister wants more ammo to embarrass me publicly," he groaned, his voice hoarse, but at least he was still talking. I could tell he was on the verge of totally losing it, but if I could keep him distracted, maybe he could work through the nerves. I was only partially joking about motivational blowjobs. I'd invest in knee pads if getting on my knees kept him coherent enough to salvage our careers.

"I'm sure it's not that bad." My brothers could be shits when they wanted to, but they never tried to diminish my writing. Having an annoyingly supportive family was kind of amazing as long as none of them asked me about research or where I got my story ideas. There were certain things you never wanted to talk to your mother about—research methods for a scene involving being tied up and spanked were pretty close to the top of that list.

"You'll see. It's Kelly's goal in life to humiliate me as many times as possible."

"My brothers like to embarrass me too."

"They're probably amateurs compared to her," he huffed.

"I didn't date most of high school because they had the entire baseball team convinced that I was really their little brother," I told him with a pointed look.

"They told them you were a guy?"

"Bad haircuts in middle school provided their photographic evidence," I nodded. Those two assholes better not still have access to those photos.

"Oh my God," he chuckled a little. "That's mean."

"Add in that everyone called me Chase, and I was assigned a locker in the girls' locker room away from everyone else." High school was one big awkward suck for me. "Pretty sure half of them thought I had a dick. The boys in my class used to aim for my crotch during dodgeball in PE."

"I would have pegged you as having been popular in high school," he confessed as he looked at me.

I laughed a little too loud at that comment. "Nope, not even a little. I was the dorky girl in the school newspaper with giant glasses who no one talked to. Add in my brother's mission to keep boys from me, and I was a mess."

"I probably still would have thought you were cute."

"And I love that you think that, but let's be honest. You would have been out of my league."

"I was shy, too," he insisted.

"For me, shy was code for a loser. For you, shy was code for mysterious and quiet," I rolled my eyes. "So, what exactly did Kelly do to you?"

He grimaced as he looked over at me. "The question is, what didn't she do? She plastered nude baby pictures of me to my locker on the first day of high school, she used to make me get out of the car two blocks from school so people wouldn't realize we were related, and she told my first girlfriend I had eyesight problems because I beat off too much. She convinced her that it really does make you go blind."

"She sounds like a real keeper if she believed that," I snickered.

"She was the only girl who would talk to me. She wasn't the smartest."

"Then why did you date her?"

His cheeks turned pink, and a guilty smile followed. "She had big boobs."

"Oh, my God. Even teenage Evan was a little pervert."

"Teenage Evan had an overactive imagination, and his sister bought him a bottle of lube for his fifteenth birthday," he laughed. "And she gave it to me in front of my parents."

I couldn't hold back the laughter with that information. "What did they say?"

"My dad gave me a package of condoms, and my mom told me if I was going to 'engage in fornication' that she wasn't raising any more children and I should 'wrap it up.'"

My entire body was shaking as I tried to hold back more laughter. His family sounded amazing. He was trying not to laugh, but it wasn't working.

"They'll love you." He took my hand and kissed the back of it.

"So, you'll go?" I hedged, hoping that he was open to the possibility.

"I really, really don't want to," he shook his head, "but I'm not jeopardizing either of our careers because I'm afraid. Do I really have to wear leather pants?"

I laughed and climbed into his lap, grabbing his cheeks and laying one on him. "Hell yes, you do. Just don't forget that ass is mine."

"Never." He put his hand on the back of my neck and brought our lips together, slipping his tongue into my mouth. I loved this man fiercely, and I was so proud of him.

"ANY OTHER QUESTIONS?" ISOBEL asked as she finished explaining our contractual obligations.

"Just one...?" Evan asked quietly.

Kristine laughed softly from behind us. "This should be good."

"Can we set the order of cities?"

"Dates haven't been booked yet," she told us, "so I'm sure we can work with the PR office on this."

"I still think you should do Vegas. That'd be awesome," Adrian chimed in, and I managed to keep in a snarky remark.

"Ad, we talked about this," Isobel sighed as her lip curled toward him in annoyance. He was eating it up. He'd been staring at her cleavage for half the meeting. It might have turned my stomach if I wasn't worried about Evan's state of mind. "We're starting with the release and doing a limited twenty-day tour with six cities. Anything other than that is up to Chase and Evan."

"You people suck," he pouted, much like the child he was. "but Vegas is awesome."

"Can't you put a leash on him?" Kristine sighed loudly. She and Sam were seated behind us, kicking each other in the feet and trading smartass remarks low enough that their bosses couldn't hear them.

"I have no control of that overgrown frat boy," Sam scoffed.

"You speak his language. Seriously. It's painful to watch him try to be professional."

"How do you think I feel on a daily basis?" I bit my lip to keep from laughing. Adrian's own copy intern couldn't stand him from the sound of it.

"Isobel needs a shock collar for him." Biting down harder to hold in the laughter, I hoped I wouldn't draw blood. That'd be hilarious. Maybe we needed to introduce Adrian to Grace. I was sure she'd love to employ her humiliation tactics on his overinflated ego.

"Do you really think they're...you know..." I could see Sam make a lewd hand gesture out of the corner of my eye.

"He must be huge. That's the only explanation that makes any sense."

"Pfft. Nope," he shook his head.

"Chase?" Isobel asked loudly, drawing my attention away from the pair behind me.

"Hm?"

"Chase!" My head snapped toward Isobel's voice. Her features were drawn in irritation. She could tell I hadn't been paying attention to what she'd discussed with Evan.

"Yes?"

"Nice of you to join us." I cringed a little at her tone.

"Busted," Sam said under his breath to Kristine.

"Any issues with booking travel for Chicago the day after the release party in Boston?"

"No. Why aren't we doing Boston first?" It would make more sense to do the book signings here if we had the release party in Boston.

"We'll do New York and Boston last," she explained.

"I'm okay with whatever Evan wants."

"I thought maybe it would be good to be near family for the first leg," he explained, looking at me.

"If that's what you want."

He nodded and picked up my hand, interlacing our fingers.

"Let me double-check with travel and PR. We can get a sample schedule worked up and send it through for your approval," Isobel offered.

"Sounds good," Evan nodded, and I did as well. I was following his lead on this one.

We all started packing up our things to leave. Kristine and Sam went first, and I swore I saw him smack her butt with a notepad right outside the door.

"Chase. A word?" Isobel requested as she perched at the edge of her desk with her arms crossed.

"Come hang out in my office, man," Adrian told Evan as he patted his arm.

Evan leaned in, whispering in my ear. "Come rescue me when you're done. Love you."

He left a lingering kiss on the corner of my mouth and followed Adrian out of the room.

"I've got news." Isobel's face didn't give away anything.

"Good news?" I asked hopefully.

"Maybe..."

The cryptic one-word answer didn't foster any hope for positive news. "What now?"

"Good news is, they granted you a contract extension." I nodded and motioned for her to go on. "Bad news is, they want a finished manuscript going to final proof in three months max."

"Shit, seriously?" That was a narrow timeline if we would start a book tour soon.

"I know. I tried to go to bat for you, but they said you can cancel your contract without penalties or fulfill the obligation."

"Three months? They realize I'll be on tour or doing promotional work for half of that, right?"

"They are aware, but I couldn't get them to budge." Her sympathetic smile was supposed to make me feel better, but it wasn't working. This was going to be a hard deadline to meet.

"What happens if I opt to cancel?"

She shook her head and leaned toward me. "You don't want to do that, Chase."

"Three months?" I asked, my neck sweating from the thought of how much work I still needed to complete. "I don't know if I can do it."

"At least take the weekend. Go talk to Evan. I know it seems impossible, but you've pulled through on tighter deadlines."

I nodded and exhaled slowly. My mind was still focused on the project we'd finished. There was no way I could switch gears to romantic comedy and put out a quality product that quickly.

"I'll check in on Monday, and don't even think of ghosting me like you two did before." She pointed at me and squinted. "I will hunt you down."

As unease started to build, I empathized with Evan's anxiety.

"Don't pretend like you weren't sneaking around. Taking a staycation, my ass," she continued with a scoff. "Next time, don't hide in plain sight. You're lucky I couldn't figure out where I'd seen your boy."

"Obviously, I was being productive." She'd gotten a damn book out of it.

"Not the point," she said, pinning me with an unamused smirk.

"Fine. I'll let you know on Monday."

Nodding, she sat at her desk, pulling open the cover of her laptop.

Apparently, I was dismissed.

I was a little flustered as I walked down the hallway, through the open office area in the middle of the floor, and across to the hallway where Adrian's office was located. Hopefully, Evan had fared a little better in his conversation.

Evan's voice was raised as I got closer. Clearly, he and Adrian were having a heated discussion as I got to the corner near his office. I wasn't sure if this was something I should interrupt, so I leaned against the wall and listened to what they were saying.

"I'm telling you, man. I never expected something like this out of you." Adrian's cocky voice almost seemed a little proudly smug.

"Because I'm boring?" Evan's on the other hand, seemed annoyed.

"No, because you've always been so concerned with brand integrity."

"I still am concerned with that," Evan insisted.

"So, you're not worried that getting into this kinky shit will damage your credibility as a writer?"

"No, Adrian, I'm not. Chase and I worked hard on this book and have put a lot of time and research into it," he told him, raising his voice as he spoke. "It's not sensationalized, and it's not an attention grab. This was a well-planned plot that I feel is different from everything else out there. Aren't you always the one telling me I need to research market trends?"

I silently cheered at how passionately Evan defended us and our work from my hidden location.

"I know it's been a while for you, and Simone mind-fucked you into seclusion, but you need to protect yourself."

"Excuse me?" The growly quality of Evan's voice would have been a bit of a turn-on if I didn't want to rush in there to save him from his jackass editor.

"Chase, deep down, is a good girl, but she's still capable of using sex to manipulate you. I don't want to see her turn you into something you're not and then bail."

"Alright, Adrian. I know this is your misguided attempt to protect me, but I'm a big boy," Evan's voice rose again, and I looked around to make sure no one saw that I was eavesdropping. "I can handle myself. If you've got some childish grudge against my girlfriend, that's your problem. Because if you had read the manuscript entirely, instead of farming out your workload, you'd see that my voice is in those characters as much as hers. And if you can't respect the entire body of my work, knowing that sometimes authors want to write something different, then I don't know how to change that for you."

Evan's voice got more pinched as he talked. My eyes widened, and my pulse raced as he delivered his final blow. "But I'm fully intending to marry that woman, so if you don't back off, I can always find another editor."

"Fair enough," Adrian conceded quickly. "I wanted to make sure you were prepared to follow through with this whole thing. You may get pushback from some industry professionals, and you need to be able to stand up for yourself like you just did to me."

"God, you're a dick," Evan sighed, and I took a deep breath.

He wanted to marry me?

"What are you doing?"

"Shit." I jumped as I turned around to face Kristine.

"Are you spying on your man?"

"No—maybe... I was coming to get him and didn't want to interrupt," I mumbled.

She rolled her eyes, shifting her weight to lean against the wall across from me. "Sounds like he handled himself pretty well."

"So, you were spying too."

She shrugged her shoulders with a grin. "I've got to be fully informed if I want to keep these clowns on their toes."

"You're sneaky," I smiled. She really enjoyed knowing all the dirty details around here.

"A girl has got to have talents," she proudly proclaimed as she nodded toward the door. "Is Sam in there?"

"I'm not sure. I haven't heard him speak," I told her. "What's going on there?"

Despite her exaggerated eye roll, her pink cheeks gave her away. "I tolerate him. We were forced to 'play nice' for your little collaborations. And since we have another book to finish editing now, I still have to work with him."

"Mmm-hmm. Looks exactly like 'tolerance' to me," I laughed as she tried to look annoyed.

The rumored relationship between Is and Adrian might not be the only forbidden office romance brewing.

EVAN

CONNECTICUT

"YOU NEED TO EAT, baby." I pulled the headphones from Chase's head and talked quietly in her ear.

"I will. Give me a minute."

"Chase, I'm beginning to feel like your parent."

She sighed and closed the laptop lid, placing it on the table in front of her. "I'm sorry."

Hugging her shoulders from behind, I pulled her back toward me. "You don't need to be sorry, but you do need to eat something today. And you probably need to shower."

She didn't really smell per se, but she needed to recharge. She'd been pushing herself to meet this ridiculous deadline before we needed to leave for the book tour. I'd flat out told her we were leaving Boston if she was going to write. With fewer distractions, it'd be easier to clear her head. And we wouldn't have to dodge running into people we knew.

Isobel had kept Adrian away from me and given us space. It would have been ideal for us to get some alone time, but she'd been absorbed in her work. I knew I was the same way when I was actively writing, but I'd never been on the other side of it. And living by yourself in the middle of nowhere meant no one cared if you stayed up until the middle of the night writing until you passed out on your keyboard. Not that I'd done that—much. "How's the manuscript coming along?"

"I think I need a few more days. I might have the first draft done when we return to the city."

"Are you ready for anyone to read it?" I was secretly dying to get my hands on another one of her books. A few months ago, I would've never admitted to reading smutty books in a single sitting, but Chase's writing had hooked me from the beginning.

"I just want to get the first draft off to Is. She's good at helping me focus and restructure my writing as needed."

Disappointment over her dismissal bothered me momentarily before I nodded my head. Despite being a gigantic ass sometimes, Adrian was good at giving me constructive feedback. And she'd been working with Isobel for years, so waiting to read it wouldn't kill me. "Is there anything I can do to help you relax?"

"Hmmm, pulling me out of my head is nice," she sighed as she leaned back into my embrace.

"Can I run you a bath?"

"Only if you join me." She smiled as she pushed her hand into my hair, scratching my scalp lightly.

"You naked...wet...covered in bubbles..." I kissed along the side of her neck and nibbled on her ear. "Sounds like a good writing break to me."

"Mmm," she moaned quietly as her hand tightened in my hair.

"Finish what you were working on and come to the bedroom."

"Yes, Sir."

I laughed and released her. While I knew it riled her up a little for me to tease her by calling her Mistress, 'Sir' didn't have the same effect on me. It was all role-playing, and controlling Chase would never be my goal. I loved how unpredictable she could be.

She opened the laptop and started saving documents. I knew it'd probably take her a few minutes, so I went straight to my linen closet and dug out a housewarming gift from my parents.

My mother had insisted that my house needed battery-operated LED flickering candles. I hadn't been convinced but took them out when she visited and put them in visible places.

I was a single man living by myself in the woods at that point. What mood did I need to set?

Carrying the box into the bathroom, I turned on the tap of the bathtub before I went in search of something else under my sink.

My sister had given me masculine-smelling bath products for Christmas the previous year, and there was a small bottle of bubble bath in the set. It'd make Chase smell like me, but the caveman part of me was fine with that. I may even have to dig out an old soccer jersey and strategically leave it in one of the drawers I'd cleaned out for her to use.

After I placed the candles around the room, I stripped down and pulled my nicer towels from the bottom shelf of the linen closet.

"Now that's a view."

I smiled as I straightened back up. "That was quicker than I expected."

She smirked and bit her lip.

Something naughty was happening in her brain, and I wasn't sure I wanted to know. Who was I kidding? I always wanted to know what dirty thoughts formed in her mind.

"What?"

"I was going to say 'that's what she said', but let's hope not," she giggled as her hand slowly traced up my spine. Her body pressed into me from behind, and all I felt was soft, bare skin on mine. "You gave me an incentive to hurry."

"Then let's get you relaxed," I sighed as her hand traced along my side to cover my heart. I placed mine on top of hers and squeezed as it soared. "I love you."

"I love you too." She punctuated her declaration with a kiss on my shoulder blade, lying her cheek against my back.

Even though she'd been in my house for the last few weeks, I still missed her. Chase was physically here, but besides brief conversations about meals, we sometimes went all day without talking. She seemed to be making solid progress on the manuscript, and I was proud that she buckled down to make it happen. It was sometimes hard to write when you knew there were expectations attached to it.

"I'm sorry if I've been distant."

"Hey, you don't need to apologize." I shook my head and pulled her around my side, caging her between my arms against the bathroom counter. "Baby, I am amazed at what you have been able to create in the last few weeks. If Adrian gave me a deadline like that I would have crumbled under the pressure."

She pushed to her tiptoes and placed a soft kiss on my mouth. "Thank you for being supportive. I do miss working together. That's been the hardest part. I want to ask you for input, but we're not writing this one together. And I can't rely on you to fulfill my selfish need for praise."

"Baby, I'm in this. I want you to know I will always support you," I told her seriously. "If you want me to read something, let me know. I would happily lend a second set of eyes to your book." As her number-one fanboy, I would fawn all over her characters.

She nodded and smiled shyly, but I could tell she still had difficulty believing I was as big a fan of her work as I was. To her, it didn't make sense for another author from a different genre to truly enjoy her writing. Chase could write an advertisement for hemorrhoid cream, and I'd rush out to buy it.

"You ready?" She tugged at the waistband of my boxer briefs as she gave me a playful smile.

"To get naked with you, absolutely." I ran my hands over her bare shoulders and down her arms as she slowly lowered my briefs, my cock springing loose. She looked at me under her lashes, and I knew this would not be an innocent bath-time interaction.

"I'm glad you're happy to see me," she cooed as she pushed them to the floor. Chase licked her lips and ran one palm over the muscles of my abdomen as she knelt and brought her tongue out to flick the crown of my cock.

As she licked around the head and eased me into her mouth, I tried to think unsexy thoughts to calm myself down. While she'd never been critical of my stamina, I didn't want to embarrass myself too quickly.

Chase bobbed her head a few times before she pulled back, placing a kiss on the tip of my cock before she stood up, sliding her arms over my shoulders. "I've missed this. Just touching your skin and focusing on you instead of character arcs and plot holes."

I knew if she were in my position, she would have made a crass joke about holes, but her soft, warm skin made it hard to think about anything but being inside her. My hands traced up her back and played with the ends of her hair as I kissed her again. The pleasure of holding her against me and sliding my tongue into her mouth would never get old.

The more time we spent together, the more my passion toward Chase grew. I knew it was too soon, but I meant what I'd said to Adrian. I fully intended to marry Chase someday if she'd have me.

"Should we get into the tub?" I whispered my question against her cheek as we both tried to catch our breath.

Her eager nod was all the confirmation I needed as I leaned down to check the water. It was nice and warm, a thin layer of bubbles skimming the surface. She held my hand as she climbed into the tub, and I slipped in behind her. Pulling her against me, I placed sensual open-mouthed kisses along the skin below her ear and along her jaw. I could feel her heart hammering beneath her skin as I cupped her full breasts in my palms.

"Mmm. That feels good," she hummed as my lips explored as much skin as I could reach.

"Just lie back and relax, baby. Let me do all the work." My hand traveled down the smooth skin of her abdomen, her breath faltering as it dipped lower, my fingers sliding against her clit.

"Oh God, yes," she sighed as I began a slow slippery tour of her hot sex with the tips of my fingers.

"You're so sexy," I murmured in her ear as she arched against me, pushing her head back into my shoulder and rubbing herself against my erection. My cock was throbbing as she writhed against me, moaning softly. "Love feeling how wet you get for me. How greedy you are for my touch. When you moan like that, I want to fuck you harder, so you moan even louder."

"It feels so good." Chase was gripping my thighs under the water as her hips undulated with the movements of my hand. "Fuck. I dreamt about riding you in this tub last night. When I woke up, I was disappointed it wasn't real."

"We can make it real, baby. Do you feel how hard I am against you?" The skin on her shoulder erupted in goosebumps at my words as I slipped two fingers inside her. "You like that, baby? When I tell you how much you turn me on?"

"Mmmm." Her hips surged into the motion of my fingers. "I like hearing your voice in my ear."

"That's it, ride my fingers." I wanted to be inside her, but waiting meant I could use my cock to make her fall apart all over again. "Be a good girl and show me how you like it."

"Oh God," she whimpered as she began to shake in my lap.

"I wanna fuck you so bad." My cock was pressed tightly against her back, hard as a rock. "Feel you quiver around me as your moans fill this bathroom. Flood the floors because you ride my cock so hard we make a mess."

A chorus of yesses echoed against the tile as she clenched my fingers, coming apart in my arms.

After the pulses subsided, she raised onto her knees, grabbed my cock, and sank onto me. Fire raced through my veins as she started to rock in my lap, my hips bucking into her fluid movements.

"Ride that dick, baby. Fuck me like you want to. Use me to make yourself come again."

"Fuck, you're so hard," she moaned, her fingers tightly gripping the sides of the tub as the water sloshed with the rhythm of our movements.

The bubbles on the surface concealed half her body from me, but I was mesmerized by the sway of her hair in front of me. She was so unbelievably beautiful. I was still in shock sometimes that she was mine.

A few months ago, I never would have imagined that Chase was what was in store for my future. Had we not met the way we did, I wouldn't have had the courage to talk to her.

"I'm so close," she panted as her head fell backward, the damp ends of her hair sticking to my chest.

"Just let go, baby. Come on me," I groaned as I pulled her tightly against my chest. One hand slid into the water, pressing against where we were joined, while the other firmly grasped one breast in my palm.

Chase used the friction of my dick to push herself closer and closer to release, rapidly flexing her hips. I tried to push mine up to meet her in the confined space, but she didn't need my help to get off.

Her movements faltered as her head fell to my shoulder, and she cried out with her release.

Groaning into her hair as I came right after her, I fought to slow my breathing.

After a few moments, she sighed as she adjusted her legs to stretch out and settle back into my chest.

"Feel better now?" I asked quietly in her ear.

"Much. I needed that. I've been a little on edge trying to ignore you and was starting to feel guilty." She had been ignoring me, but coming from the perspective of someone who did the same thing when he was in the zone, it didn't bother me.

"Maybe if you would've let me relax you a few days ago, you wouldn't have gotten so tense." I knew her guilt would flare as I teased her, but I'd been trying to get her to take a break for days now.

"At least you're here now. I kind of like having my own stress relief on call."

"Is that all I am to you?" I smiled against the skin of her shoulder. "Stress relief?"

Chase shook her head and pulled my arms around her. "No, that's just one of the perks." She sighed as she turned to the side to look up at me. "You...you're." It wasn't like her to be short on words, but I let her formulate her thoughts unhindered. "You're everything."

My heart swelled at her words. She was my everything too. Kissing the side of her head, I tightened my hold on her. "I love you, too. So much."

We sat quietly in the bath until the water started to cool. Chase got dressed and returned to her laptop as I started dinner. Our cohabitation was something I was still getting used to, but I wanted to wake up with her every morning and go to sleep with her every night.

We'd already informed Is and Adrian that we'd only need one room for each stop on the book tour. We weren't hiding our relationship from anyone, and I think the publishing house liked that we seemed to be a united front on this one.

"Any preference on meat?" I called out to her from the fridge.

"Your meat never fails to please," she snickered, looking over the back of the couch.

"That's for after dinner..."

She gave a dramatic sigh. "Oh, alright. I guess I'll have to settle for putting another kind of meat in my mouth."

"Dirty girl," I teased. She couldn't resist the naughty flirtatious banter.

"That's how you like it." She was right.

"Do you have everything you need to go back?" I was sitting on the edge of the bed, waiting for Chase to finish packing her bag.

We were headed back to Boston. The official launch party for our book was in two days, and we needed to head into the office to go over the final schedule details with the promotional marketing team.

We'd be spending tonight at Chase's condo, but the publishing house had agreed to put us up in a suite at the hotel where the party was being held for the next two nights.

"Can I leave some of these clothes here?" she asked over her shoulder while she stood at the dresser. Her open suitcase was sitting beside me on the bed, but it was empty.

"You can keep whatever you want here. I'm hoping after the tour is over, I can convince you to come back here with me."

"You won't be sick of me by then?" Her smile was warm. She already knew my answer to that question.

"If I was going to get sick of you, I'm pretty sure it would have happened already over the last five months."

"Has it been that long?" she winked at me with a smirk.

"Not that I've been counting or anything," I shrugged. I totally had.

"Sure, mmhmm."

"Fine. Stay behind in your lonely condo. I don't mind going back to being allowed to use my covers."

"I'm not the one who steals covers!" she yelled as she spun back in my direction.

"Tell that to my frost-bitten parts."

"Pretty sure I keep your parts plenty warm." She grabbed one shirt from the stack in front of her before putting the rest back into the drawer and shutting it. I wanted to ask her to move in with me permanently, but after the last time I lived with a woman, I was a little gun-shy. Chase was nothing like Simone—although she'd been different, too, before we lived together.

"Can I leave my toothbrush here?"

Following her into the bathroom, I pulled her back into my chest and rested my chin on her shoulder. "You can leave whatever you'd like here. As long as you come back with me, I want this to feel like home to you."

We shared a meaningful look in the mirror, and I knew my strong feelings for her were reciprocated. "Wherever I go, it feels like home as long as I'm with you."

Smiling, I squeezed her tighter, placing a lingering kiss in the crook of her neck. "You should write that one down."

"Life imitates art." She smiled. "Maybe I already did."

"Are you quoting your new book at me?"

"No," she said, "but I can see where it'd work into the storyline nicely."

"I'm glad I can provide quality source material for you."

"You're the best research assistant ever," she snickered, probably remembering all the research we'd been doing for months.

"Happy to be of service."

"It sure makes Isobel happy."

"She liked the manuscript?" I asked curiously. Chase would let me read it eventually, but I was having a hard time letting her go through the process her own way.

"She said that it was very romantic."

My heart swelled as I recalled the time we'd spent together. "So, was it inspired by us?"

"Nope." Chase shook her head, dramatically rolling her eyes.

"Brat," I growled.

"I left out all the spanking. But the love interest is pretty much a giant dork. So I guess in a way it's about you..." she trailed off as she looked back, amusement clear on her features.

"Well, I am packing some pretty impressive equipment."

"I said dork, not dick," she laughed.

"Did you know in the nineteen fifties that dork was another word for penis?"

"Wow. Have you been reading the dictionary again?" she responded dryly.

I laughed as she looked over her shoulder in disbelief at me. She knew dirty things, but etymology was my forte.

"You're jealous you don't have the same grasp on the English language."

"The words I use are all the important ones," she shrugged.

"Is that so? I never realized *cock*, *pussy*, *fuck*, and *harder* were so important."

"You can use as many big SAT words as you want, but you're lost if you don't know how to really use them to portray a picture." Damn. Remind me never to piss her off or goad her into an argument.

"Are you saying I'm a hack?" I asked in mock disbelief.

"No. I'm simply saying it's important to know how to use what you're working with." She winked and wiggled her eyebrows.

Letting out an exaggerated sigh, I squeezed her sides. "Is everything dirty to you?"

"Was that a real question?"

I shook my head and smiled at her in the mirror. "What am I going to do with you?"

"Whatever you want, big boy. As long as it involves cock, pussy, fuck, and harder."

Chapter

TWENTY-NINE

CHASE

Boston

"Come on. It's not going to be that bad. I've met Di before. She's the sweetest."

"Why do we need public relations coaching?" Evan grumbled. The closer we got to the book tour starting, the more anxious he became.

"They want us to have a game plan in place for promotion. I've had to do this every time I have any kind of press coverage."

"I'm kind of wishing I could crawl back into my hole now," he sighed dramatically. His custom house on the lake was hardly a hole.

I laughed as I stepped forward and straightened the lapels of his suit jacket. We were already dressed for tonight's party because our day would be too busy to have time later.

We met with Is and Adrian this morning. They'd be with us tonight but wouldn't be on location again until we returned to the East Coast. They both had too many projects to spare three weeks out of the office. Their dedicated interns had been voluntold that they were coming with us.

"You do not. I know it's making you uncomfortable, but I think it will be good for you to interact with your readers more. You've gotten too used to being 'Mr. Famous Recluse'—time to get back on the book-tour horse."

"If you weren't here with me, I would have fled to Connecticut by now." The sad thing was that I knew he wasn't joking. I felt guilty for putting him through this, but he was committed.

"Then I guess it's a good thing I'm here." I leaned up and kissed him softly. He gripped my hips and pulled me closer as he deepened it and took possession of my bottom lip.

I was having a hard time concentrating today. With the excitement of the book launch and Evan wearing his fuck-hot glasses, I was in cerebral overload.

"You two ready to stop making out in public places and get this over with?" Kristine sighed with exaggerated annoyance.

Sam frowned down at her and then smiled back over at us. "Kris, leave them alone."

"Oh, I'm sorry. If you'd like me to pop some popcorn so you can watch, I'll be right back," she snarked as she elbowed him in the arm.

I smiled against Evan's lips and leaned back slightly. He looked a little mortified but also turned on. Apparently, getting caught was something that excited him. Never would have pegged him for a secret exhibitionist. He continued to surprise me.

"Let's go in with Di, and they can join us when they're ready." Sam nodded toward the conference room where our meeting was being held.

"We're good. He's a little nervous, and I was talking him through it," I assured as I flashed them a bright smile.

"Sure. Talking...right. You were trying to swallow each other's fricking tongues in a hallway, and it's talking..."

"Leave them alone." Sam rolled his eyes, pushing Kristine toward the open door with his hand on her back. "Come on."

"Quit tugging on me, Spammy. They're adults. They can take a little bit of teasing."

"I told you to stop calling me that," Sam said in a low voice, clearly full of irritation.

"Well, I would. But I know it irritates you, so I won't," Kristine replied smugly.

"Do we really have to spend the next three weeks with them?" Evan whispered in my ear.

I looked over his shoulder at Kristine and Sam standing together on the other side of the hallway. They were facing each other, and her hips tilted slightly toward him. There was some unresolved sexual tension going on between those two.

"Want to bet how many signings we can get through before we catch them making out in a hallway?" I whispered back, so the two potential love birds couldn't hear me.

"I'm thinking LA," Evan nodded.

"I'm betting on the first day in Denver. They're about to jump each other right now."

"You're on," Evan told me with a decisive nod.

"What do I get if I win?"

"A kiss," he shrugged.

"Pfft. I don't have to win a bet to get those." He shook his head at my naughty smile while I eyed his full lips.

"Maybe you need to be cut off." He smirked as he ran his thumb along my hip, covered only by the thin material of my dress.

"You wouldn't even last to the party." He huffed at my eye roll, but I knew I was right. Evan had turned out to be a very affectionate partner.

"Hmm. The winner gets to pick the subject of our next book." I let out a heavy breath, and he looked down at me with concern. "You okay?"

"We're going to write another one?" I had a hard time keeping the excitement out of my voice.

"I mean, it's fine if you don't want to, but I really liked wor—" His words cut off when I gripped the sides of his face and planted one on him.

"And they're making out again. I think we're gonna need a hose." I could practically hear Kristine's eyes rolling back in her head.

"I think it's great," Sam whispered.

"Of course you do. You're probably hoping for live-action porn."

"Oh, stop it. I've never seen him like this." Sam's voice held a little bit of awe. Apparently, everyone else could see the changes in Evan as well.

"Are you going soft on me? Watching too many Lifetime movies?"

"Since when has anything on me ever been soft?" Sam's voice had a bit of a seductive edge, but Kristine shot right back in her usual unaffected sarcasm.

"You think quite highly of yourself, don't you?"

"You didn't seem to mind me taking my shirt off at the gym the other day. I saw you watching," Sam taunted.

Evan broke the kiss and silently laughed against my lips. The next few weeks were certainly going to be entertaining.

"Should we interrupt them?" I asked as I looked up into his much more relaxed eyes.

"I think Kristine's head will explode if we don't go in there." He nodded at the door.

"I guess we should go act like professionals."

"Do we have to?" he whined.

"Put on your big boy panties, and let's do this."

I stepped around him and crossed toward the open conference room door. He gripped my hips and pulled me back into his chest, pressing himself into the back of my dress.

"Who said I'm wearing any? These pants are very snug." Wow. I'd clearly created a monster...or maybe that was only what was in his pants. Evan's game had upped significantly in the past few weeks. I felt like a proud mentor that he was such a quick study in innuendo.

"I'll have to inspect that situation later. Let's do this." I reached behind me and grasped his hand, tugging him after me into the conference room where the public relations representative going with us on tour was waiting.

"Hello all," Diana, our new public relations specialist, chirped from the front of the room. I loved working with her. She was unflappable. Always polite and classy.

When things went wrong or off schedule, she firmly handled business and got you back on track. It was impressive to watch her maneuver in a room full of the press without being pushy or rude.

"Let's ensure we're keeping to the itineraries in your daily briefing packets." She'd compiled folders detailing everything we'd be doing over the next several weeks. From hotel reservations to scheduled breaks, it was all in there.

"See. I told you she's keeping us on a tight leash," Kristine told Sam quietly as they leaned toward each other in the seats to our right.

"She's keeping them on the leashes," Sam whispered, nodding in our direction.

"Pretty sure they keep each other on leashes," she muttered.

I bit my lip to keep from laughing at her snarky comments.

"We could probably go MIA for an afternoon, and they wouldn't notice," he coaxed.

"And why would I want to run off somewhere with you?"

"I'm sure I could convince you to let your hair down a little," he shrugged.

"My hair already is down, ya doofus."

He sighed loudly and crossed his arms on his chest. "God, you're impossible."

"Yet you still keep following me around."

She'd obviously upset him with all the brushoffs. His voice was cold as he responded. "We work in the same office."

"So that's why you're always conveniently within earshot." Kristine shot back with a sardonic laugh.

"Yeah. They won't even last to Denver at this rate," Evan whispered, his warm breath tickling my neck.

"I thought we liked to banter as foreplay," I giggled as I watched Sam and Kristine square off. It was like they couldn't help themselves.

"They take their whole love/hate relationship very seriously." He nodded as he looked around me toward the two of them.

"If she hated him, she'd ignore him. I think she likes him riling her up," I told him quietly.

"I know you like it when I rile you up," he teased as his hand covered my knee underneath the table.

"What can I say? I'm a sucker for a mouthy guy." I could see his chest shaking from the corner of my eye.

"And we both know I like having my mouth all over you."

Diana was still talking to us, but I don't think any of us were paying attention. "Okay, I think that covers about everything. Does anyone have any questions?"

All four of us slowly shook our heads as she smiled from the front of the room.

"Don't worry. I know you weren't paying attention to me. All the information I went over is in the front of the folders for Chicago," Diana laughed as she held up a folder. "I'm old school and would rather have everything in writing, printed out, than rely on you to pay attention to emails."

"But you're still sending us a digital copy, right?" Kristine asked anxiously. She was permanently attached to her phone, so I couldn't see her getting on board with something as archaic as a paper-filled folder.

"Yes, Kristine. I understand I'm a dinosaur. You'll get PDFs the night before with the next day's information," Diana sighed. "I'm sure I'll see all of you tonight. Congratulations, Chase and Evan."

"Thank you," I smiled and then apologized. "Sorry, we're a bit distracted."

"Not a problem. I'm used to much worse," she smiled widely.

"Thank you, Diana. It was nice to meet you." Evan was talking to someone voluntarily; that spoke volumes about how approachable she was.

"Likewise," she nodded and was out the door, meaning we had an hour left to kill before we had to return to the hotel for our stylists.

"Nice job, Kristine. Diana is already annoyed with us." I pinned her down with a scathing look. Diana could make the next few weeks easy or hard, and I wouldn't risk Evan's first book tour in years for a moody intern.

"Hey, why is this my fault?" Kristine protested. "You two weren't exactly concentrating on what she was saying either." She pointed at Sam with her thumb. "And he has a mouth too."

"That I do." Sam rolled his eyes.

"Smartass." She rolled her eyes back and gathered her laptop and bag. "I'm going to do my job before I'm forced to babysit you for the next three weeks. See you tonight."

She stopped on her way out the door and pointed straight at Evan and me. "You better not get distracted and show up late tonight. I'd like to actually enjoy myself at one of these things and not get stuck being Is' errand girl."

"Got it," I confirmed with a nod. "Don't worry. The alarm is set on my phone."

"Uh, good to see you guys. Guess I should check in with Adrian. I'm not sure he can survive three weeks on his own." Sam smiled as he gathered his things and stood up from the table.

"Probably not," I laughed, and Evan's hand tightened on my knee as he chuckled too.

"Back to the hotel?" He asked with an arched eyebrow, and heat pooled between my legs. I knew exactly what his intentions were.

"Don't get any ideas, mister."

"I didn't say anything." He held up his free hand and turned on the faux innocence.

"Mmhmm. Could you keep it in your pants? We have enough time to grab food and get back to the room to get all dolled up, and that's all."

"You mean to get you all dolled up," he clarified.

"Nope. They'll attack you too." He was about to be styled to within an inch of his life. I was willing to bet he'd never had his face lightly contoured or his nails manicured.

"Really?"

"Yup. They'll send a whole team. The talent has to look flawless to work the room at the party," I winked. "Romance is a whole different ballgame. We're selling an image. And you know Sloane wants us to keep it sexy."

"I look fine," he pouted.

"You look amazing, baby, but you're gonna have to sit back and let them do their thing." He looked mighty fine, but if photographers were going to be there tonight, he needed to look polished *and* fine. "With the press being invited to the party, they want us to look good for pictures."

"Fine, take me to my torture."

We took his car back to the hotel, parking in the garage before we grabbed some food in the restaurant to take back to the suite rather than risk the delay waiting on room service.

"Are you sure we can't...?" he asked as he tilted his head toward the bedroom.

"Save it for after. We've only got fifteen minutes," I smiled. Knowing he was constantly thinking about sex now was hilarious compared to the shy man I met a few months ago who could barely look me in the eye the first day.

"I can work with that." I knew he could, but then I'd need to shower again, and I'd be getting cursed out by the stylist for having wet hair.

"Oh, baby." I rolled my eyes. "Just eat your food already."

"Fine," he snarked. "Suit yourself. Don't come begging to me later when you're desperate for my dick."

"I'm sure I can control myself for a few hours." Little did I know it'd be for more than just a few hours.

CHASE

BOSTON

EVAN WAS VERY CHARMING with the team of stylists. He had all of them eating up every word he said. The stuttering, awkward man I met several months ago had come out of his shell.

"Am I pretty enough for you?" he asked, pulling me back into his chest while we rode the elevator down to the ballroom.

"You're always pretty, baby." I looked back at him over my shoulder and winked.

"I can't wait to peel this dress off you later," he whispered directly into my ear, his voice low.

I closed my eyes and relaxed into his embrace. I couldn't wait for the end of the night either. "Promises, promises."

"If there weren't cameras in here." He punctuated his suggestive remark by pressing his pelvis into me. He wasn't hard, but I was sure he could get there quickly with a little coaxing. It was tempting, but our editors would murder us.

"You've gotten brave," I giggled as his hand rubbed the material of my dress right below my breasts.

"You make me brave," he whispered into my hair. "Are you sure I can do this?" I could hear the nerves appearing in his voice as we watched the elevator numbers count down as it neared the ground floor.

"You've come so far in the last few months. And you had those ladies and one very smitten gay man eating out of your hands earlier."

"He was gay?" Evan asked with a surprised smile.

"He kept making excuses to restyle your hair and called you handsome about forty times. Pretty sure," I nodded.

"Please stay with me." His other hand gripped mine and interlaced our fingers.

"I'll try." I nodded. "But Is wants us both to work the room and talk to the press. The buzz is already starting to grow about the book. And remember, this isn't your first book launch. You were also rusty at other things and look at you now. You've got this."

"I don't want to talk to the press by myself. What if I say something embarrassing?" Evan was falling into his old habits of expecting himself to fail. I wanted to find the person who made him doubt himself and punch them square in the face.

"You'll be great. Just stick to the information Adrian and Diana gave you. Do that whole quiet, mysterious thing, and they'll eat it up."

"Are you sure we can't go hide in the room?" I could hear him swallow hard as his body tensed behind me.

"Baby, it'll be okay. Everything after this will be busy but low-key. I'll be by your side for everything else if we can make it through tonight."

I could feel his chest press against my back as he took several deep breaths. His heart was still racing, but I knew he could do this.

The elevator pinged as we reached our destination, and I stepped forward with my hand outstretched behind me. Evan sighed loudly and took my hand as I led him out the doors and down the hallway.

Soft music floated out the partially open doors as we approached, and I hoped the room hadn't filled up yet. Evan could use a few minutes to ease himself into it before the hordes descended.

"I'm fine. Let's go." He walked around me and held the door open wide, motioning for me to proceed.

"I'm really proud of you," I whispered as I passed him, leaning up to kiss his cheek. "I know this is out of your comfort zone, but you're doing it anyway."

"Let's hope you're still proud after tonight." His hand found the bare skin on my back, and he guided me to the other side of the room where Is and Adrian were stationed by a small stage with a raised podium.

"Right on time!" Isobel smiled as she hugged me and then briefly squeezed Evan's arm.

"At least you two don't look like you've been screwing in the supply closet," Adrian laughed.

"Oh my God, Adrian. Just don't talk anymore," Isobel scowled in his direction.

"It was a joke. It was supposed to be funny."

"No. Just no." I shook my head as I pinned him with a scathing look.

"You put your foot in it again, Dickhead?" Kristine laughed as she joined us, seeing everyone scowling at a contrite Adrian.

"Sounds like he put his whole body in it." Sam was right behind her, looking at his boss with amusement.

"Hey, I thought you were supposed to be on my side. Traitor!" Adrian scowled at his intern.

"What sides?" Kristine asked. "Seems like only one person is making an ass out of themselves right now."

"I was trying to be funny. How come that one can make remarks, and I get jumped on?" Adrian asked while he pointed at Kristine.

I cringed as I saw her face completely change to a blank stare.

"When you get your dog to quit peeing on the floor, let me know where you want me for the night," Kristine said to Isobel, completely ignoring Adrian's presence. She walked off toward a table where there was a poster stand with the book cover on it.

The table was stacked with promotional materials and copies of the book. Most of the press invited had been mailed advanced copies, but it wasn't uncommon to provide them to anyone who might post positive reviews online.

"I'm gonna..." Sam pointed over his shoulder before he followed Kristine. It was probably a good thing Adrian wouldn't be with us for the next few weeks. His brain-to-mouth filter had degraded considerably.

"So, anyway. I will be giving a brief introduction in about fifteen minutes, and then we'll start the party," Isobel told us. "All the invited press was notified that this is a social function and that they are welcome to attend any of the events when you return to Boston to ask questions."

"Did you get a response from the people I asked you to invite?" Evan looked at me with confusion as I put the question to Isobel.

"I thought we weren't inviting family to this since we're flying out tomorrow?" he asked quietly.

"We're not." I turned to face him, saw a few people enter the ballroom, and got my answer. "I wanted to make sure they were invited."

He turned, and his mouth stretched into a smile as we watched Emory and Talia cross toward us, holding hands. Nathan was a few steps behind them.

"I thought they wanted to remain anonymous?"

I nodded, "They do, in respect of what they do behind closed doors. They're here as friends tonight."

"Thanks for inviting us," Emory greeted as he slipped an arm behind my back and kissed my cheek. Talia elbowed him out of the way and hugged me while Nathan shook Evan's hand.

"You know I'll never turn down a party," Talia smiled before she turned to Evan and hugged him as well.

"It's kind of refreshing to go to one where everyone keeps their clothes on," Nathan said quietly as he scanned the room.

Adrian's eyes went wide as the pieces connected in his head. Luckily, Isobel whispered something in his ear before he said something inappropriate.

"I'm so glad you all could make it. It'll be nice having some friendly faces in the crowd tonight," I told our friends. They'd helped us get here, and they deserved to enjoy their part in it as well.

The room had started filling in, and I recognized quite a few prominent people in the local press and blogging communities.

"I'll need to steal these two for a little while," Isobel told our three friends as she nodded at Evan and me.

"No problem. I'm sure we can entertain ourselves while they're on duty," Emory assured her.

"I can always entertain myself with an open bar," Talia said, eyeing the well-stocked bar at the back of the room.

"I think I'll manage," Nathan nodded, staring toward a group of female bloggers who'd congregated near the bar.

"You two ready?" Isobel asked as the other three headed off.

"I don't have to speak, right?" Evan confirmed.

"No," she laughed as she nodded toward the stage. "I'll take care of it, but Di might ask you to once you're in a smaller venue."

"You're fine. Just take a deep breath and pretend I'm in my underwear," I whispered in his ear as we turned to follow Is to the stage.

He laughed and tugged me toward him, leaning down to whisper back. "I don't think you want me to give the room a show."

I giggled as he took my hand and helped me up the stairs. As he reached the top, he ran his hand down my back and casually grazed my ass.

"Hey, behave." I shook my head at him, and he returned it with a nervous smile.

I tried to pay attention to Isobel as she spoke, but I had to admit I was a little nervous too. I hated the first days after a release where you're waiting for the critics and reviewers to respond.

"And thank you all for coming tonight to celebrate two of my favorite authors who have created something really special." Isobel finished speaking, and Adrian stepped in front of the mic.

"Let's give them a round of applause." He'd surprisingly kept his bad jokes to himself. It probably didn't hurt that Is was hovering next to the microphone like an overprotective parent.

Evan plastered on an almost believable smile and reached over to interlock his fingers with mine. I had difficulty taking my eyes off him to face the crowd.

"They'll be here all night," Isobel smiled over at the two of us. "Enjoy the spread, and we hope you enjoy the book if you haven't read it yet. Hopefully, you won't be too hungover to read it tomorrow."

Is ushered us off the stage and made straight for some of the execs from the publishing house. They did the usual patting themselves on the back for associating themselves with 'such quality talent'. Evan was quiet but respectful. He commented, smiled, and nodded when needed, but I could tell he was distracted.

"You okay?" I asked as we stepped to the side and took a moment to ourselves.

"I'm a little out of it. I forgot how overstimulated you could get at these." His eyes nervously scanned the crowd as I held his clammy hand.

"I'm sorry if we pressured you into this."

He took a deep breath and gave me a small smile. "It's alright. I just need a minute. I think I'm gonna step out for some air."

"I can come with you," I offered, but he was already shaking his head.

"Nathan looks like he's trying to get your attention. Spend some time with your friends. I'll be right back." He kissed me on the cheek and snuck out the side door, his hand running roughly through his hair as it closed.

I felt bad he was having trouble, but I knew he was insistent on doing this. He needed some space to work through the anxiety.

"Hey," Nathan greeted as he came up behind me and placed his hand on the back of my arm. "Someone wants to meet you, and I said I could arrange an introduction. Can you spare a few minutes?"

"Sure, yeah. No problem," I said distractedly as I looked toward the door Evan had left through.

"She told me she's a blogger, but she's been out of the literary fiction rotation for a while," he explained as I turned away from where Evan had escaped.

"Is she someone that Is invited?"

"Not sure," Nathan shrugged. "I think she may have heard about it through the grapevine. She wasn't wearing an ID badge."

As we crossed the room, I saw a tall, slender, dark-haired woman send Nathan a calculated look. She would look harmless to a casual observer, but something about how she glanced at me sent alarms off in my head. "What did you say her name was?"

"I didn't. We didn't get that far. She only asked if I knew you personally."

I nodded and sent her a tight smile as I approached her and raised my hand. "Chastity Rose."

She nodded and sent me a predatory smile. "Oh, you don't need to hide behind silly pen names with me, Chase."

"Do I know you?"

"Not exactly," she flashed that smug smile again, "but I know all about you."

"I'm sorry, I'm at a loss here. Did Isobel invite you?" I'd never seen this woman before in my life. Was she some gossip rag columnist?

"She invited someone from my office, but I told her I'd be happy to take her place tonight," she smiled as she waved her hand, looking around the room. "I was hoping to catch up with an old friend."

"Oh, is there someone here you know?" I'd almost forgotten that Nathan was still standing there as he placed his hand on my back and stepped closer to me as we faced this woman. I think he could also tell there was something off about her behavior.

"You could say that, but I'm sure Chase thinks she knows him better. He's certainly different than he was when I last saw him." Her voice was light but full of sarcasm and condescension. "Apparently, drawing him down to your level lightened him up a little."

"What is that supposed to mean?" Nathan asked as he stepped forward, his body acting as a defensive barrier beside me.

"Oh, nothing, just that introducing him to all your kinky friends has finally made him interesting." She rolled her eyes and waved her hand.

"Excuse me?" *Who did this bitch think she was?*

"I'm well aware of your little *research quest* for this book. People in this industry talk, and I'm unfortunately aware of your last book as well," she said lowly as she flashed me a dirty look and turned her nose up at Nathan.

"Okay, I don't think you realize who you're talking to, but take the condescending attitude elsewhere." Nathan's voice had a dangerous edge; I could see his Dom side starting to creep out. "People who follow my lifestyle don't take highly to ignorant comments like the ones you're making."

"Nathan, it's fine. I can handle this." I placed my hand on his shoulder and tried to ease him back.

"Oh, I'm sure you can. Is Nathan here one of your 'boyfriends' too?" The woman rolled her eyes and looked at my hand on his arm in disgust.

"Not that it's any of your business," I laughed dryly as I took a step toward her with my own fake smile. "But Nathan is a friend, and my boyfriend is obviously someone you think you know."

"Oh, honey. I know him so much better than you ever will. Your precious Evan can't even carry on a conversation in public, much less an interesting one."

My eyes widened as she said his name in an entirely too familiar way. "Who are you?"

She smirked as she leaned down toward me.

"If you're not here to support the book, why are you wasting my time?" I growled.

"You're going to realize how much time you've wasted soon enough," she laughed, but it sounded forced.

"Quit with the cryptic bullshit," I snapped as I straightened my back and looked directly into her dead eyes.

"My name is Simone Woods." She put one hand on her hip and looked down at me like she was something to be respected. I knew exactly who this bitch was, and she was evil trash.

"I think it's time you left," I told her as I glanced toward the hotel security in the corner.

"Oh, I got what I came here for," she said as she pulled a small recorder from the pocket of her dress.

Nathan quickly grabbed her wrist and flipped the small device down into his other hand. She looked at him with mild panic, but he simply shrugged as he pocketed the device and gave her a challenging look.

"I don't know what you think you've accomplished tonight, but you need to leave before Evan realizes you're here," I told her quickly.

"Protecting your precious pet?"

"I don't need to protect him, he's a grown man, but I'm not subjecting him to your little mind games," I scoffed as I narrowed my eyes at her. He still hadn't told me everything about their past, but she clearly manipulated him and destroyed his self-esteem.

"You're a little late. I think we've been spotted." She laughed as she looked toward one of the doors entering the ballroom.

"Nathan, can you make sure security escorts her out?" I asked as I watched the door close with a shell-shocked Evan standing on the other side of it.

"I'd be happy to," he responded flatly as he nodded toward a security guard who had stepped closer to where we were standing. He'd obviously sensed we'd encountered someone here to cause trouble.

"Oh, don't worry, I'll leave. I only wanted to see the tramp who managed to get Evan to grow a pair."

I didn't even think about my actions until I was left shaking my hand after my fist landed squarely in the center of her perfectly made-up face.

"Ahh! I think you broke it," Simone shrieked as she held onto her nose, a trickle of blood spilling down her lips.

A small crowd had turned to look toward us, Simone held securely by one of the security guards while another looked at my hand.

Held firmly by her upper arm, Simone was escorted out a side door while Isobel talked to the DJ. Not everyone in the room had seen my fisticuffs routine, and apparently, loud music was her method of distraction.

"Holy shit, Chase! I knew taking you to kickboxing was a good idea," Kristine cheered as she stepped close to my side. The security guard returned my hand but advised me to put some ice on it to prevent swelling.

"I've never hit anyone before." I blinked over at her, still a little in shock.

"Well, you got the job done with that one," she told me with comically wide eyes. I scanned the room, hoping to see Evan return—I knew I needed to find him. Kristine was talking, but I didn't really hear what she was saying.

Looking back toward the exit several minutes later, I saw a disappointed Sam walking toward us.

"Where's Evan?" I asked as he stepped up next to Kristine and me.

"Um..." Sam scratched at the back of his neck nervously.

"Shit, Spamela, I gave you one job," Kristine sighed.

"I tried, but he's fast," he looked over at her and then turned his wary eyes to me.

"Who's fast?" My heart beat erratically in my chest as I looked between them.

"Evan. He took off in a cab."

"What do you mean he took off in a cab?" My voice was a little bit frantic at this point. Evan saw me talking to his bitchy ex, and now he was gone. I couldn't even imagine what was running through his head.

"Call him!"

My phone was back in the hotel suite; I hadn't thought I'd need it tonight and had no pockets in my dress.

"About that..." Sam held up a familiar iPhone and cringed. "Adrian asked me to hold this for Evan until the end of the night."

"Frick me!" We both looked over at Kristine's outburst, and she shot us a death glare that warned us not to say anything.

"So, he's gone?" Panic started to swell in my system. Evan was gone, and we had no way to find him. He had a history of major anxiety issues and sometimes even panic attacks. I hadn't seen him have a bad one, but he was alone. What if something happened to him?

"I'm sure he'll come back once he's calmed down," Kristine assured, but she had no idea. Evan retreated into himself if he felt any sort of stress.

As I looked toward the doors he'd fled through, wondering what was going through his head, I wasn't so sure it'd be that simple.

THIRTY-ONE

EVAN

Boston

I PACED THE HALLWAY outside the ballroom, taking deep breaths and trying to calm myself. I hated that I still got like this when I was forced to interact with people I didn't know. Chase, our friends, and even Adrian and Sam didn't freak me out. I knew them, they knew my limits, and they respected me.

The press and the execs had no idea I had issues with anxiety. I preferred to keep them in the dark and let them assume that my seclusion was simply part of my artistic mystique rather than I was prone to having panic attacks in large groups and generally had trouble looking people in the eye. I'd always hated crowds.

When I was sixteen, Kelly teased me relentlessly when I didn't want to go to Disney World. My dad had understood, though, and he had taken me to a therapist to get some anxiety meds. We also researched the weeks when the parks were least crowded and went then.

It still made me nervous, but I'd been able to push through because my family was supportive. Even Kelly stopped teasing me once my parents had explained the situation to her.

Chase understood my need to walk away sometimes and wasn't upset. Being with her the last few months had been simultaneously the most stressful and easiest thing in the world. She pushed me to want to step outside my boundaries, but she understood when I told her no. Not that it'd happened often.

I'd never had anyone who got me as she did.

"Shit. Get a hold of yourself," I muttered as I shook out my arms and took a few deep breaths, letting them out slowly. Counting my breaths always seemed to help calm me, so I started slowly and gradually got myself under control enough to go back inside.

"Hey man, you doing okay?" Sam asked as he approached me from the doors to the ballroom.

Sam was a good guy. He connected with Adrian on all the fitness stuff, and initially, it made me think he was a younger model. I'd come to learn he was an intelligent and thoughtful guy. He'd been working with me on minor editing before Chase, and now Sam and Kristine were in regular contact with both of us.

"I think I'm alright. I've definitely felt better, but I'll manage." My chest didn't feel quite as tight now that I was out of that crowded room.

"My sister has some anxiety issues. Take your time. I can run interference with Adrian."

"Thanks," I told him sincerely. I appreciated people who supported you and didn't try to jump in to fix things.

He headed toward the doors and gave me a quick nod before returning inside.

Take a deep breath in, deep breath out. In... out...

"You can do this."

Once I felt calm, I walked slowly toward the door and opened it, scanning the room as I stood there. To the left, beside the bar, stood Adrian, talking to his boss, Sloane. He made eye contact and subtly signaled to me with his hand. I nodded and swung my gaze to the other side of the room.

Chase was standing with Nathan beside her. I took a moment to admire the expanse of exposed skin across her back. Her dress dipped down to her lower back, and I ached to touch her skin when we were finally allowed to leave. I'd been sneaking in subtle touches all night, and the feel of her skin on my palm had helped me stay calm.

She shifted her weight, and her posture changed, becoming more defensive, and from what I could see on his face, Nathan looked upset. I tried to see who they were talking to, and then Chase moved over a step, and she came into view.

"Fuck."

Simone stood opposite Chase, looking every bit the polished, entitled, condescending bitch she'd been when I last saw her two years ago.

My heartbeat picked up, and I felt my palms break out in a cold sweat as she looked up with a sly smile, making eye contact with me. She said something, and Chase laughed. It didn't look particularly humorous, but it threw me, nonetheless.

I started to back out of the doorway, my breathing already ragged and my clothes feeling too tight. Seeing Simone was about to send me into a full-blown panic attack.

Right as I let go of the door, Chase turned fully toward me with a look of shock on her face, probably pretty similar to mine.

"Fuck, fuck, fuck."

I stumbled a little as I hurried down a hallway, through the lobby, and out the front entrance.

My pulse was racing, and I felt my neck tightening—seeing floaters in my line of sight. I could hear the rasp in my breathing start, a tingling sensation creeping along my jaw. Pacing back and forth outside the door, struggling to pull in full breaths, my worst nightmare came walking toward me.

"I wondered where you ran off to." Her voice was sugary sweet, totally at odds with the blood crusted in one nostril and the start of some severe bruises underneath her eyes. She looked like she'd been in a fight. Her dress was a little wrinkled, and droplets of blood were visible on one of her straps.

"Go away."

"Oh, come on, baby, don't be like that," she cooed as she stepped closer.

"Don't-d-don't call me that," I stuttered as she stepped closer to me once more.

"Still have that nervous stutter around me, I see." She pressed herself along my side, and I started gasping for air. She really couldn't take a hint.

"Cause looking in the face of e-evil...freaks me out."

"You used to not be able to keep your hands off me," she said suggestively as she ran her hand down my front and stopped at my belt. "We could go upstairs, and you can teach me your new tricks."

I pushed her away and looked back toward the hotel. Sam was coming around the corner, headed straight for us. My mind raced through my options as I tried to distance myself from Simone.

I knew I needed to talk to Chase but also to calm myself down. There was no way I could do that with Simone harassing me.

"L-le-leave me th-the f-uck a-alone," I growled and gesticulated wildly as she tried to come near me again.

My whole face tingled, and now I was finding it increasingly difficult to breathe as I tried to wave her off. Sam came through the door at the same time a cab pulled up on the curb, and I made a split-second decision.

Stumbling across the sidewalk, I made a break for the cab and wrenched the door open, jumping inside and slamming the door.

"G-go...please..." I panted as the driver hesitated and looked at me like I was crazy through the rearview mirror. My voice was pinched, and I was wheezing as I put my head down and tried to take deep breaths.

He pulled away from the curb, and I could see the little meter start on the computer screen in the back.

"You gonna tell me where we're goin' or do I gotta guess?" he sniped. He had a very pronounced South Boston accent and looked like he didn't put up with anybody's shit.

"Uh..." I was still having trouble drawing a full breath, and I couldn't get my eyes to focus.

"Come on, man," he groaned. "If you're on something, I don't need to get mixed up in that shit. No junkie is gonna OD in my car, nice suit or not."

I tried to calm my breathing enough to talk, but my throat was dry, and I felt a little lightheaded. "I-I-I'm..."

"What the hell you on? You can't even fuckin talk."

"No-noth-nothing..." I gasped.

"Yeah, right, and I'm a priest. Come on. I don't need this bullshit. I'm dropping you off atta urgent care center."

I shook my head back and forth, but he'd already turned into a parking lot, the red lights of the "EMERGENCY" sign blurring in my vision. He parked at the curb and got out, crossing over to my door and opening it, pulling me out by the arm, and guiding me to a bench beside the clinic entrance.

"I'm not even gonna charge ya. Get some fuckin help before you kill ya self."

My throat was tight as I leaned forward and put my head in my hands, desperately trying to slow my breathing. Several people passed through the doors to my side as I sat there trying to calm down.

A figure approached in my peripheral vision, and I glanced up at a concerned-looking woman wearing scrubs.

"Are you alright, Sir?"

I sat up a little and tried to respond, but my words were caught in my throat.

"Are you asthmatic? Are you injured?"

She sat beside me on the bench and touched my shoulder. She pursed her lips as I shook my head, and she watched me trying to force air into my lungs.

"Do you have panic attacks frequently?" she asked, guessing what was wrong with me.

I shrugged as I felt like my chest was easing up slightly. It was still hard to breathe deeply, but the numbness was starting to fade from my jaw.

My lips quivered as I responded. "Some...times...I...used to..."

She nodded and placed a stethoscope on my back. "I think you're okay, but can you walk? Would you like to come inside with me?"

I nodded and stood up slowly, black spots appearing in the corners of my vision.

"Just take it easy. We'll get you checked in." She led me through automatic doors and to a reception desk.

"I'm going to go ahead and take him back since we're slow." She told the woman at the front desk. "Can you send someone back to get him registered?"

"Of course. I'll start a chart for him."

The woman, whose name badge indicated she was a physician's assistant, led me through a door and down a hallway, sitting me in a chair in an exam room. She took my vitals, and by then, my breathing had eased enough I wasn't wheezing.

"You seem alright, but I'd still like to let you calm down a little back here." She nodded after she listened to my chest.

"Th-thank you."

"Do you have someone to talk to about these episodes?" she asked as she put down her stethoscope.

"Not recently," I shook my head. "I used to have a psychiatrist, but I haven't had a full-blown panic attack in t-two years."

"And something triggered one tonight?" She guessed.

I nodded as I drew in a shuddering breath.

"I won't make you go into it. But I want to give you something tonight to help relax you."

The receptionist came back then and got me registered. I had my wallet with my identification, but it didn't occur to me that I'd given Sam my phone until I tried to give her emergency contact information.

"I'm gonna get a doctor's permission to put you on a low dose of Klonopin," the PA told me as she took my information sheet and scanned over it. "Do you have any allergies, or have you had any adverse reactions to anxiety medications?"

"No."

She left the room and returned a few minutes later, verifying my birth-date and last name before handing me a few little white tablets to swallow with water. "These should help relax you enough to get through this episode, but I'd recommend following up with your psychiatrist if you'll be exposed to your source of stress regularly."

"Hopefully, that won't be a problem." I nodded but would try to check in with Dr. Singh if I had time while we were on the road.

"If you start to feel any tightness in your chest, abnormal swelling, or difficulty breathing, you need to come back in." She finished her discharge instructions and then walked me back to the lobby.

I wasn't entirely sure where I was, and I wasn't sure how I would get back to the hotel without my phone.

There was a microbrewery across the street from the urgent care, and I found myself walking across the road before I thought about it.

"Hey man, what can I get you?" the bartender asked as I sat across from him, avoiding the other patrons sitting at one end of the long bar top.

"Can I get some water, please?"

"Sure thing. You look a little weary. Want to talk about it?" He picked up a glass from a nearby rack and dried it. I think he could tell that I was not doing so well.

"Just been a long night. Do you have a phone I could use?"

He walked down to the other end of the bar and picked up a cordless phone, sliding it toward me. "No long distance, but you're welcome to make a local call."

I dialed the first three numbers and then realized I wasn't 100% sure of the last four digits of Chase's phone number. Smartphones made it so easy to be reliant on not remembering phone numbers.

I was also starting to feel a little lightheaded.

Laying the phone down, I drank some more water and wished I'd bought the Apple Watch with cell service. The Wi-Fi one wouldn't do me any good without my phone.

The bartender refilled my glass several times, and I realized I absentmindedly kept drinking it.

"You doing alright?" he asked, and I noticed for the first time that several groups had cleared out of the bar.

"I-I think so?" I knew time had passed, but I couldn't tell how much. The windows to the street showed it was darker than I remembered.

"Don't worry. You've got about an hour before I need to start cleaning up. Feel free to hang out as long as you need to."

"Thanks." My voice slurred a little as I swayed on my stool. I wasn't sure how much more time had passed, but I was slightly startled as my wrist started buzzing. A Find my iPhone alert was flashing across the screen.

"What's wrong with you?" I asked, tapping the little square watch face. "My phone isn't lost. It's in Sam's pocket."

Alerts for missed calls and texts started flashing across my wrist. I squinted as I tried to keep up with them but couldn't focus on the letters.

"You're drunk, Apple Watch." I tapped at the screen to dismiss all the alerts, the screen finally clearing.

"You need a refill?" asked the bartender, looking down at me with an amused smile.

"Whoa—where did you come from?" I chuckled as I tried to focus on his face. Bright colors surrounded his hair, and I wondered what lightbulbs they used here.

"Been here the whole time," he frowned. "Need me to call ya a cab?"

"No, no more cabs. They don't like me." I shook my head, but it threw me off balance, and I had to grab the edge of the bar to stop sliding off my stool.

"You sure you're okay?" he asked skeptically. Mr. Bartender did not look amused.

"Peachy," I smiled, at least I think it was a smile. My face felt funny.

He squinted his eyes at me and looked at my glass. "Why don't I get you some fresh water."

He sighed as the door to the bar opened, and I saw two blurry figures walk in, my wrist buzzing again.

"Leave me alone, stupid watch."

I laid my head down on the bar in front of me as the room started to sway.

"Is he drunk?" I heard a familiar voice and tried to lift my head again, but the room continued moving.

Or maybe it was me moving.

Either way, it was making me dizzy.

I wanted to go to sleep.

"Nah, I've only been serving him water since he came in here a few hours ago."

Had I been here for hours?

"You're sure you didn't give him any alcohol?" That was Emory. He didn't sound happy.

"Yup, just good old-fashioned tap."

"What the hell is wrong with him?" Nathan asked. I think it was Nathan, but I couldn't lift my head.

"You don't even want to know." My voice sounded funny again.

"What's on his wrist?" Emory asked as I felt my hand move.

"Is that a hospital bracelet?"

Emory appeared right in front of my face, and my eyes widened. "Evan, can we try to sit you up?"

"No..." I groaned as I closed my eyes again.

I felt someone move my arm, but I couldn't find the energy to pull it back.

"It's from the urgent care across the street."

"What happened to you?" Nathan asked. When I squinted my eyes open, it looked like his head was floating in the air behind Emory.

"Tha birch attacked me." Why did my voice sound like that?

"A tree attacked you?" Nathan laughed.

"No...no...no. Moan. Tha birch."

"Simone?" Emory guessed. It sounded like he was trying not to laugh. Asshole.

"Yup."

"That bitch attacked you? Is that what you're trying to say?" Nathan asked again.

I nodded my head slowly. "Couldn't breathe."

"Is that why you were at the urgent care?" Emory was talking again. "You couldn't breathe?"

"Uh-huh." Why were they asking me so many questions? I only wanted to sleep.

"You guys are fine for now, but I need to start closing up. Can I get ya anything before I close down the taps?" the bartender asked quietly. I could still hear him.

"I think we'll gather up our friend and get out of your way. Thanks for taking care of him." Emory was a nice guy. Well, unless he was teaching your girlfriend how to whip you... with an actual whip.

"No problem. Quietest non-drunk drunk I've had in a while." The bartender laughed. I think they were talking about me.

"Okay...up you go." I think his name was Nathan...told me as he put an arm behind my back and slowly sat me upright.

"Evan? You still with us?" Emory asked as I closed my eyes again.

"Do you think we should take him back to the urgent care center?" Nathan sounded worried, but I was fine.

"I don't think so."

"Evan? Can you breathe okay now?" Emory's fingers snapped in front of my face, and I felt myself falling backward.

"Nope, I got you," Nathan laughed as he propped me back up. "Evan? You need to see the doctor again?"

"Nooo... No doctor. Just nurse." I shook my head. "She gave me little white pills."

"The nurse gave you something?" Emory asked too many questions.

I tipped forward on my stool as I tried to nod. "For my anxiety..."

Why was I giggling? Was I giggling?

"For your anxiety?" Nathan asked. That was what I said. Why wasn't he listening?

"Hold up there, big guy." I felt Emory's hands grab my shoulder and pull me back upright.

"The little whiiiite pills make me feel weeeiiiird." I blinked heavily as their faces swayed, getting bigger and then smaaaaller...

"Evan, we're gonna take you to my studio to sleep this off," Emory told me as he snapped his fingers in front of my face again. "Okay?"

"Mmmhmmm..." I blinked heavily and closed my eyes.

"You've still got his phone?" Emory asked. I don't think he was talking to me.

"Yeah, in my pocket," Nathan answered him.

"You support one side, I got the other."

I felt myself moving and cracked open one eye, watching the bar pass by as they got me closer to the door. The colors that moved on the walls were freaking me out. I needed to get out of here and snuggle up with...

Chase!

Fuck. She was gonna be mad at me.

The door swung outward into the sidewalk, and I stumbled a little as we crossed the threshold.

"Wait...way...wait... I gotta call Chaser...now," I slurred.

"I texted her that we found you," Nathan said loudly. Why was he right next to my ear? Personal space, dude.

"No, no, no. Need to talk to her now," I slurred as I shook my head. It only made the colors move faster.

"Evan, you're a little out of it right now. Let's get you lying down to rest, and we'll call Chase." Emory was way too close to my other side. Geez.

"No...now." I shook my head again but couldn't hold it up anymore.

"Man, I'm glad I never want kids." Nathan laughed.

"Did he just stomp his foot?" Emory tried to hold in his laughter.

"Now, dammit!" I yelled but then cringed at how loud my voice was.

"Okay, calm down. I'll dial it for you." Nathan told me as he pulled my phone out of his pocket and typed in my passcode.

How did he know my passcode?

"Don't steal...my...shit." I narrowed my eyes at him, but he laughed.

"Fine. Take it. Just press call."

"I know how to use a−−oh shit..." As I tried to press the button to call Chase, I felt my knees give out, and the phone started to slide out of my hand.

I watched as it fell in slow motion onto the sidewalk and bounced off the curb. There was a hollow clank noise as it hit, and I heard Emory curse as he let go of me.

"Shit." Nathan pulled me into his side as I watched Emory approach the curb and look down.

He scratched the back of his neck as he turned back to me. "Well, you're going to need a new phone."

"Damn. Did the screen crack?" Nathan asked.

"Not exactly," Emory shook his head. "There's a grate here. It's about six feet under us right now."

"No! I needed that..." I whined as I clung to Nathan.

"It's gone. We'll have to worry about it tomorrow," Em told me sympathetically, but I could tell he was trying not to laugh.

Emory came back and grabbed my other side, helping lift me back in between them again. They loaded me into the back of a black SUV, and I laid down with my cheek touching the cool leather seats. I could hear them talking as they climbed into the front seats, but I couldn't focus on what they were saying. I heard a clunk, and the vehicle started moving.

My mind drifted back to Chase. I hoped she wasn't too mad at me. This wasn't how I planned on this night going. Then the thought scattered...

"Let's go, lover boy!" Em pulled me upright in my seat, helping me to climb down from the SUV. He and Nathan guided me through the gallery and into the studio. Emory stopped to unlock the playroom door.

"The king-sized bed in the back room?" Nathan asked as we entered the playroom. They led me past the play space into a dimly lit alcove at the back, a large bed covered with dark bedding dominating the room.

"Yeah. It's already made. We should be able to lay him down. Hopefully, he'll sleep off whatever reaction he's having."

"I'm fine...it's fine, fine, fine..." I couldn't stop saying fine. It made my mouth feel funny.

"You doing alright?" Nathan asked with concern in his voice. "Em, his color doesn't look good."

"Hold on." Emory walked away and came back with a small plastic trash can. "Just in case you need to be sick."

"I don't need to..." He thrust the can into my face, and it appeared just in time. The huge amount of water made a sour splash against the can.

Ugh...

"You feel better?" Nathan asked as I peeked over the side of the trashcan. I shook my head, and Emory took the trash can to a sink in the corner and rinsed it out.

"Do you want me to stay with him?" Nathan offered. Were we going to spoon?

"You don't have to do that," Emory shook his head.

"I know," Nathan sighed. "But I feel like I owe it to Chase."

"You can sleep on the leather bed out there," Emory told him as he gestured back to the playroom. "I can grab you some blankets."

"Thanks."

I slowly felt the world sway back and forth and wanted to lie down.

"Evan. You doing okay?" Nathan asked as he helped me sit on the edge of the bed.

"I don't feel so good," I mumbled as he pushed the trash can into my lap again.

"Why don't we try to get you to lie down? You might feel better if you get some sleep."

My head nodded, and I could feel my whole body get heavy. Nathan brought me to the pillow, and I sighed as I felt the covers settle over my body. "Just a little sleep."

My eyes were firmly closed, but I still felt like I was moving.

"I'll put the can here in case you need it," Nathan whispered.

"M'kay."

Sleep came easily, but I didn't know how long I slept before I felt my stomach revolt again. I was able to grab the can and throw up into it before I collapsed back into the bed and drifted off to sleep once again.

THIRTY-TWO

CHASE

BOSTON

THE NEXT MORNING, I woke up with a headache and a dead phone battery. Pounding on the suite door woke me, and I saw the time. I had fifteen minutes until I needed to be packed to meet the car service.

"Shit." I had no idea if they'd found Evan, but he obviously wasn't there. The pounding started again, and I dragged myself out of the bed.

"I'm coming. Calm down," I groaned as I pulled the door open.

Kristine was standing there looking relaxed for travel. She held a drink carrier with insulated cups in one hand and her suitcase handle in the other. "Oh, come on. Get your ass dressed, and I'll pack up your suitcase. Isobel is on the war path because we're running late."

"Did they find Evan?"

She bit her lip and shook her head slightly. "I have no idea. Emory's phone keeps going to voicemail, and I don't know how to contact Nathan. All I know is that he's not here."

I swallowed hard and tried to keep the tears building in my eyes from falling. Worried didn't even begin to describe what I was feeling for Evan. I hoped he was alright. It wasn't like him to fall off the grid, but with a dead phone battery, I had no idea who may have tried to contact me.

"Which one is mine?" I asked as I surveyed the cups. If I was even going to attempt to adult today, especially leaving my boyfriend behind missing in the city, I needed caffeine.

"The one in the front. Caramel macchiato with two extra shots of espresso."

"At least something is going my way this morning." I sipped the coffee, stepped back into the room, and headed for my suitcase. Comfort was my motivation for my travel wardrobe. The press event wasn't until 4:00 pm, and we'd be getting into Chicago around 10:00 am local time. I didn't even want to go but I knew Is would murder me, and it'd probably screw over Evan's and my career, if I missed it.

What I really wanted to do was punch that bitch Simone in the face again. Talia had told me about Simone confronting Evan in front of the hotel and then him fleeing. He had to be so traumatized by the whole thing. He never told me everything, but she seemed a toxic part of his past.

Evan had moved to a different state and secluded himself because the thought of running into her gave him crippling anxiety. Then she had to go and show up unannounced somewhere that he was already on edge.

"Plotting ways to kill the she-bitch?" Kristine asked, startling me out of my racing thoughts.

"How did you know?" I laughed as I put my toiletries back into the suitcase and zipped it up.

"Cause I've been plotting revenge since I woke up this morning. She crossed way too many lines. Cunt-muffin isn't getting off easy with this one."

Kristine eyed the second suitcase sitting next to the bed. "What are we doing with that?"

"I don't know," I shook my head as my eyes started to burn again. "I need to check out. Do you think they'd keep it at the desk? I don't want to take it with us. He may have something in there he needs."

I sat down heavily on the end of the bed and wiped at the few tears that slipped out.

"I think Mr. Blithe will do anything we ask him to."

"Who is Mr. Blithe?" I asked curiously. I didn't remember meeting anyone yesterday with that name, not that I was paying attention.

"The general manager. We're tight. I might have threatened to sic the press on him if he didn't cooperate with us last night."

"They've still got Evan's phone?" I didn't see it anywhere around the room this morning.

"Nathan took it," Kristine reminded me.

"Can you try calling it?"

She tapped on her screen a few times and then held it to her ear. A frown appeared as she pulled it away and shook her head.

Kristine looked thoughtful for a moment and sent off a text. "I texted Sam. He's pretty tech-savvy. He may be able to send him a push alert that'll come up once he turns it back on."

"Can't you call him?" she asked as she nodded at my phone on the bed.

"Dead battery." I held up the blank screen, and she nodded.

"Let's get you packed up and stop at the desk. Maybe there's a portable charger we can buy at the gift shop. If not here, I'm sure the airport would have something."

"I forgot all mine at home." Normally they were my lifeline, but I'd been so distracted with keeping Evan calm that I hadn't thought to pack them.

As I pulled both suitcases off the bed, a card slid down from the end of the sheets to the floor.

Kristine knelt to pick it up, and her eyes widened. "Damn, he's really got game," she laughed, thrusting it into my waiting hand.

> *'There's no one I'd rather go through life's adventures with than you. You've made a permanent mark on my heart in the past four months. Thank you for supporting me unconditionally. Love, Evan'*

Fuck.

Three sentences, and he'd managed to shatter me completely. Nathan had better have found him. I pinched my nose as I closed my eyes, but the tears still leaked through.

"Hey, I'm sure he's fine." Kristine awkwardly patted my shoulder and my back before she stepped away. I knew we needed to get out of here before I lost it.

"Got everything?" she asked as I blew out a shaky breath and pulled out the handles on the suitcases.

"No..." I sighed as I followed her out the door and to the elevator, dragging two suitcases behind me with each of our carry-ons over an arm.

Evan needed to be here. He deserved to be here celebrating his successes too. Not lost in the city, with no way for me to contact him.

Damn Simone. Damn social anxiety. Damn contracts and bureaucratic bull-shit.

"So...uh—Diana sent over the itinerary this morning," Kristine awkwardly tried to change the subject once we were in the elevator.

"And?"

"You going to be okay handling the press solo?" she asked, giving me a tight smile.

Shit. I didn't want to do any of this right now. "Don't really have a choice."

"She said there'd be some people from the Tribune," Kristine explained. Great—largest distribution in Chicago, and I would be completely distracted. "If you want to push it to later, you're in Chicago for four days."

"Wait, I thought Chicago was for three days?" The original itinerary was for three days.

"Oh, uh. Day four only has one signing in the morning. Evan asked for the schedule to be clear for the rest of the day."

"Why?" He hadn't said a word to me. It wasn't like him to start hiding things.

"No clue, but Is was all smiley after talking to him on the phone. I'm assuming it's a surprise," she shrugged.

"Shit." I knew the bookstore we were going to last was near where he grew up; maybe he was planning to meet up with his family.

When the elevator got to the ground floor, a little crowd was waiting for us off to the side of the lobby.

"Hey," Sam greeted us cautiously and shot Kristine a disarming smile.

"Hi." It must be hot in here because I saw some pink appear on her cheeks. Kristine was not the type to blush.

"Sup?" Adrian gave me the male head jerk.

"Really? Get out of my way." Isobel elbowed Adrian to the side and pulled me into a hug. "How're you holding up?"

I shook my head and felt my eyes tear up again.

"He'll be alright. The second anyone hears anything. You'll be the first to know. I'm sure they've found him," she assured. I hoped they did, but the radio silence was scaring me.

"Do we really have to do this?" Leaving town was the last thing I wanted to do right now. That troll had shown up at the worst time possible.

"As your friend. I say fuck it," Isobel shrugged. "But as your boss, you have to get on that plane. If you don't, I can't salvage this."

"It'll be fine. He's disappeared before and he's always been fine," Adrian tried to console, but it fell a little flat.

"You're not helping," Is growled as she looked down at the two suitcases by my side. "Just shut your mouth and try not to get in the way."

She nodded toward the one with the blue luggage tag that belonged to Evan. "Do you want us to take that one?"

"No. I'm not sure what to do. I don't want to take it if he needs something." I shook my head as I felt myself getting choked up again. "God, this fucking sucks."

"I can take it," Adrian offered.

"No, I'm going to see if the desk can hold it." He would have to come back here eventually, right?

"Let's go visit my friend Mr. Blithe." Kristine smiled as she grabbed the suitcase handle and led me toward the reception desk.

"DID YOU FIND A charger?" Kristine asked as she stood next to me in the convenience store near our gate at the airport. We'd made it through security alright, but we only had a few minutes before we needed to be at the gate for boarding.

"I'm not sure which to get," I told her as I looked at the phone and laptop accessories wall.

"We don't have time for this. Just pick a fricking charger and let's go," she sighed impatiently. She did not like being thrown off her schedule.

"Geez, control freak. Just go to the gate, and we'll meet you there," Sam elbowed her out of the way and stepped in next to me.

Kristine did not like people making her late. We still had a few minutes, but I knew time was tight.

Before I paid, I grabbed water, a bag of Twizzlers, and the portable charger, buying them quickly before hurrying to the gate as they announced to start boarding.

Evan and I were booked in the extra legroom business class. Sam and Kristine were in the row behind us. Diana had used her travel miles to upgrade to first class.

"Have you ever been to Chicago before?" Sam asked as we settled into our seats outside the gate.

"Several times," I nodded. "Minneapolis is only six hours away. My parents brought us for summer road trips."

"How about you, Kris?" I raised my eyebrow at the nickname. Usually, no one could call her anything but her full name. Another intern had called her Krissy once, and no one ever saw him again.

"Nope. My parents thought the Hamptons were the only appropriate place to spend summers," she rolled her eyes. "Not that they were ever there to know."

"Okay, then." Sam looked over at me nervously as he sat next to Kristine.

"Have you, Sam?" I asked as I glanced over at him.

"Yeah, once or twice a year. It's a cool city. Lots of museums and things to do," he nodded.

"Oh, look. They called our group number, so we can stop the painfully awkward small talk." Kristine perked up as she stood and grabbed her bag. I was ready to get on this damn plane. She led us toward the gate agent and scanned our digital boarding passes before we walked down the jet bridge to the aircraft.

Diana smiled as we passed her, and we quickly sat down in our rows on the other side of the little curtain.

I opened the packaging for the battery-charging pack and plugged in my phone. Needing a distraction to get through this flight, I pulled a paperback book out of my bag and the water bottle.

Sam and Kristine sat quietly behind me, but I could tell he was whispering things to her. I saw her mouth twitch through the crack between the seats. She was trying to act unaffected by him.

The seat beside me stayed empty as the plane filled. I was half relieved I didn't have to sit next to a stranger and half depressed the owner of the seat was still missing. This was going to be a long-ass day.

While the flight attendant went through the safety spiel, my heart started racing as the little Apple icon lit up on my phone.

One missed call.

I opened the menu and saw an alert that I'd received a call from Evan's phone number hours ago.

My phone only had one bar, something interfering with the reception, but I tried to call Evan's number back anyway. I knew I needed to hurry. They were already closing the boarding door and getting ready for takeoff.

"Come on." It rang once, then let out several beeps and showed the call was dropped. I tried again, and it started ringing this time. It rang through, and then his voicemail picked up. "Oh, come on. Answer your phone!"

"Ma'am," the female flight attendant stood beside the empty aisle seat, giving me an impatient look. "I'm going to have to ask you to hang up the phone. You must put your digital device in airplane mode as the cabin door has been closed for departure."

"Just give me a second," I begged, hating myself for being *that* person who didn't obey the rules.

"I'm sorry. You'll need to make your call after we land." Her defensive posture as I looked down at my phone was a little intimidating, but this was time sensitive.

I pressed the call icon again, and it rang through to voicemail...again.

"Please hang up and put it in airplane mode." Her voice took on a no-nonsense quality, and I knew I'd pushed my luck far enough.

"Okay, okay." Swiping down, I pressed the little airplane icon and locked my phone screen.

"Thank you," she replied, nodding before she resumed her path down the aisle.

Unlocking the screen as soon as she was out of sight, I pressed the little airplane again and scrolled through the text messages. There were several from Isobel. A few from Talia, checking in. Some from my brothers. My sister-in-law, Elle. But the one that stood out was from Nathan.

"You're such a rule breaker," Kristine teased as she stuck her face to the space between the seats.

"Nathan texted six hours ago and then again twenty minutes ago."

"What do they say?" she asked eagerly in a quiet voice, trying not to attract the flight attendant's attention again.

"I haven't opened them." My heart would be crushed if there still wasn't any news.

"Better hurry before the phone police comes back," she urged as she glanced over her shoulder.

I opened the menu, and the first made me sigh in relief.

> *Nathan: Found him.*

But the second one made me worry.

> *Nathan: He finally stopped puking around 4 am. I'll get him headed in your direction after he wakes up.*

Shit. What the hell happened to him?

"Is that in airplane mode, ma'am?" She was back.

Turning my phone screen away from her, I swiped to pull down the control panel and selected the plane icon.

"It is now." She gave me a curt nod as I flashed the screen at her with a guilty smile.

I hoped Evan would be awake by the time I got to Chicago. I fully planned on calling Nathan for some answers.

I REACHED FOR MY phone when we arrived at O'Hare International Airport.

"Come on." Groaning as I took my phone out of airplane mode, I saw I only had 3G coverage.

I pulled up Nathan's number and hit the call button. It rang twice and then the call failed. Evan's number now went straight to voicemail.

"No luck?" Kristine asked as she peeked over the top of the seat.

"Maybe you'll have better reception once we get into the airport," Sam suggested apologetically.

We waited for the plane to arrive at the gate and the attendants to announce that we could deplane. I was exhausted, still had a headache, and my phone was being difficult. Diana was waiting for us in the gate area and waved us over as we came out the door.

"We need to get down to baggage claim, and then there is a car service waiting," she told us quickly as she started walking toward the center of the terminal. "I confirmed our hotel early check-in, and the venue is expecting us around 2 pm."

I tried to text Adrian, Emory, and Nathan the entire walk to the baggage claim escalators. No one was responding, and I hadn't gotten any more messages.

"Stupid fucking phone," I growled, feeling frustrated that I still didn't have any answers.

"Let me try Talia again," Kristine held her phone up to her ear and rolled her eyes as she waited for it to ring.

"Hey!" She held a thumbs up as we stood there and waited for our bags to arrive at the baggage carousel.

"Yeah, we just landed."

"Uh-huh. Oh shit! Really?"

What was going on?

"What?" I mouthed, and she waved me off.

"Okay. I'll tell her. Guess we owe Nathan."

"Tell me what?" I asked impatiently as she hung up the phone and tucked it into her pocket.

"Evan's on the move. Nathan dropped him off at the hotel," she smiled.

"That's it? Is he at the hotel? Why isn't he answering his damn phone?" My voice was a little high-pitched, but I didn't care. I wanted answers.

"About that..." she cringed.

"What now?" I asked with an exhausted sigh. My poor heart and brain couldn't handle any more stress.

"He tripped and fell on the curb outside where they found him, and his phone ended up in a sewer grate."

"Oh, shit." Sam's eyes widened comically.

That was the cherry on top, as if yesterday couldn't have already sucked enough. "So, I have no way of contacting him?"

She shook her head, and then we were interrupted by the alarm going off and the sound of luggage being thrown onto the belt.

"Let's get to the hotel, you can re-group, and we'll figure it out from there," Diana suggested as we stood waiting for our bags to appear.

THIRTY-THREE

CHASE

CHICAGO

I SPENT HALF THE ride to the hotel hopelessly staring at my phone. Even though I knew Evan was at the hotel and was theoretically alright, I still worried about him. Was he even coming to Chicago?

"You gonna be okay?" Kristine asked as we headed toward the elevators after Diana checked us all in. She had a small room that adjoined Sam's on a lower floor, down the hall from Diana. Evan and I were in a one-bedroom suite again, except I wasn't excited about this one. I had no clue if he'd even be showing up to share it with me.

"Meet us in the lobby at 1:45 and the car service will pick us up again," Diana told us as the elevator stopped on their floor. "Please try to relax."

"I will. Not sure how successful I'll be, but I'll try," I nodded.

Kristine and Sam sent me sympathetic looks as they exited the elevator and left me alone for the rest of the ride.

I felt the exhaustion hit me as soon as I reached the end of the hallway where the room was located. I had two hours to figure out what to do with myself.

A frustrated groan poured out of me as I saw the bottle of champagne with two flutes on the desk and the basket of gourmet snacks next to it. The card was from Isobel and Adrian, congratulating us on the book's release and our successful collaboration.

Hot tears streamed down my cheeks, and I felt terribly guilty for talking Evan into doing this tour. If we'd returned to Connecticut, none of this would have happened. We could have continued to hide in our bubble and escape this bullshit.

My suitcase felt like it weighed a thousand pounds as I hoisted it up onto the luggage rack in the closet. Normally, I'd have at least tried to unpack, but at this point, I didn't really care.

Pushing the sheets down on the neatly made bed, I kicked off my shoes and unzipped my jeans, leaving them in a pile next to the bed. I climbed in and curled around a pillow, letting the remnants of my tears soak into the soft fabric.

"Oh, Evan. When are you going to get here?"

THE ALARM ON MY phone woke me from a restless sleep, and I quickly poked at the screen, trying to silence it. Still no messages. The screen only had a calendar alert for the appearances I would have to fake my way through for the rest of the day.

While I would have liked to slip on a pair of sweats and eat my way through the basket of goodies on the desk while watching sad movies, I knew I needed to get ready.

"Fake it till you make it," I grumbled as I went into the bathroom with my cosmetics bag in an attempt to tame my hair and put on my face.

Twenty minutes later, I looked refreshed but didn't feel it. The ride down the elevator in silence helped me get into the right headspace. I'd done press appearances before. I'd done book signings and readings before. If I could make it through this, I could climb back into that empty bed in a few hours and go back to sleep.

"Well, you look human. Did you hear anything?" Kristine greeted me as I joined the others in the hotel lobby.

I shook my head as the four of us headed out to the car service. I knew if I started talking about Evan, the sadness would creep back in again.

"Alright, crew. Let's focus. I know this won't be exactly to the original plan, but we can still pull this off." Diana was in full PR mode, always trying to spin things positively.

"What should I tell the press if they ask about Evan?" Surely, they'd notice his absence when it was billed as a joint book tour.

"Obviously not that he's MIA," Kristine said sarcastically.

"Yeah, I figured that much," I replied with an equal amount of sarcasm. I was sad and worried, not an idiot.

"We can stick to a simple, semi-truthful statement," Diana explained. "Evan was feeling under the weather and unable to join us for the first day in Chicago. We're hopeful he'll recover soon and be able to join us further during the tour. What's working in our favor is that today is only print media. You don't have to perform for a live camera or do any in-depth interviews."

"It's a simple Q and A," she reminded me with an encouraging smile. "You've been briefed on our public message about the book, so stick to the script, and we'll be fine."

I hoped we—I—didn't get any nosy press members inquiring about my personal relationship with Evan. As long as it was about the book, I could handle it.

"Let's do this." Kristine rubbed her hands together as she scooted toward the car door.

Sam slipped out first and helped each of the ladies out, his hand hovering near Kristine's back as I followed the three of them into the venue for the meet and greet.

"We'll be over there with Diana." Sam nodded toward a side table where promotional items related to the book were already set up. Another table beside it was piled high with a stack of books.

At least we didn't need to go anywhere after this; the first book signing was directly after in the same location.

Deep breaths. I could do this.

"YOU DID GREAT," DIANA praised after I finished the first part of our obligations. "If I weren't aware of the last twenty-four hours, it would never have occurred to me that something was off with you."

"Real subtle, Di," Kristine snickered from her place with Sam near the promotional table.

Ignoring Kristine, Diana continued talking to me as we moved away from the crowd. "Just get a drink. There are some snacks over there off to the side. We have another ten minutes until we can expect people to start showing up for the reading."

I absentmindedly snacked on a cookie and drank some coffee as I tried to run the passage I was reading through my head again. Public speaking made me nervous, but I never had a problem once I started talking.

Reading my work to a crowd who was a captive audience used to be one of my favorite things about promotional tours. Something about sharing your characters with your readers for the first time made all the sleepless hours and weird schedules worth it.

It didn't feel quite the same this time. These weren't only my characters. Evan was just as much responsible for the development of Frances' character as I was.

"You ready?" Sam broke me out of my contemplative state, and I realized that the room had started to fill up.

The room was filled with a pretty diverse crowd. I wondered who was here because of me, and which were Evan's readers.

"Diana is going to introduce you, and then you'll start the reading," he said quietly as he steered me toward the small podium.

I nodded, got into place off to the side, and waited for my cue.

"Now, one of the authors of this amazing book will be reading an excerpt to you. We'll open it up to questions at the end." Diana finished and held her hand out in my direction. It was showtime.

I wiped my hands off on my pants and took the marked copy of the book from Kristine as I walked to the podium.

"You got this," she whispered as I passed.

"Thank you for joining me here today and for your support of this collaboration with another amazing author who could not join us today," I started, my voice shaky. "I know that Stone and I appreciate every reader who has supported our separate works and now this joint endeavor."

As I looked out at the crowd, I felt a sense of calm wash over me, and I knew that while I desperately missed Evan, I could do this.

"Let me take you on a journey with our female lead. For those of you who have read the book, this scene is pivotal. It shows our main character, Frances, learning to step up and become completely self-reliant."

"Her partner had become such an integral part of her life that when he wasn't there, she had to find her inner strength to push through a difficult situation."

"'Frances realized that while Dominic's role in her life was that of a submissive, she wasn't in control. His influence had seeped into every part of her being, and having him abruptly taken away was leaving her questioning her sense of self...'"

My brain read through the passage we'd picked to share on autopilot. Loud applause jolted me back to reality after I finished reading the last sentence aloud.

"Let's open the floor to some questions," Diana announced from my side.

"I've got a question." Kristine raised her hand from the side of the room, and I braced myself for it, hoping it'd be an easy starter to settle me down.

"Go ahead," I nodded.

"When developing a book like this, a certain amount of research goes into making sure things seem believable." She paused, her eyes glancing toward the other side of the room, then quickly returning to me.

"Go on..." I prompted, curious as to where she was going with her question.

"How into character did you and your writing partner get while researching?" Of course, Kristine would delve into a semi-difficult—and potentially inappropriate—question first.

"As with my previous book, I used a consultant who practices the lifestyle. He helped us develop and simulate scenes within the book," I explained as I looked out to the crowd.

Kristine's eyes drifted to the other side of the room, which was blocked from my view by a set of bookcases.

My curiosity about what she looked at almost outweighed my irritation that she asked a question and wasn't paying attention to the answer.

"As with people who practice BDSM, we both got a chance to learn how to use the tools of the trade in a controlled environment from both sides. It helped put us into our character's heads and feel the sensations they may have felt in certain scenes."

"Thanks," Kristine said as she glanced pointedly at the other side of the room. After smiling at Sam, she handed the microphone back to Diana.

A hand shot up from the other side of the room, but their face was partially obscured by the person in front of them.

"I've got a question for you." My eyes widened as I recognized the familiar voice.

THIRTY-FOUR

EVAN

BOSTON

MY EYELIDS FELT LIKE they weighed a thousand pounds, and the top of my mouth felt fuzzy. As I woke up, the smell of food turned my empty stomach, and I heard low voices, but I was too disoriented to distinguish anything around me.

"Is he doing alright?" a feminine voice asked quietly, sounding like Talia.

"He's fine. Probably had an adverse reaction to the anti-anxiety meds they gave him. Maybe the dosage was off, or he took too much," Nathan told her in a barely audible whisper.

"Should we wake him up?" Emory's voice was louder, and I cringed as my head ached.

"Did you text Chase to tell her he's alive but sick?" Talia asked.

"Yeah, a while ago, but she never responded," Nathan confirmed.

"Their plane has already left. Adrian is trying to get Evan a seat on a later flight," Emory told her.

"Let's hope he can get there. It was strange seeing Chase so depressed. I don't think she laughed for the rest of the night."

"I'm such a fucking idiot," Nathan sighed. I didn't understand why he thought this was his fault. Simone didn't come with him. They didn't know my history.

"Hey, I talked to that crazy witch too. She flipped a switch on a dime. There was no way for you to know who she was," Emory assured.

"First Grace, now Simone, am I a psycho chick magnet?" Nathan growled in a low voice.

I could hear all three of them laughing.

"You knew Grace was like that before you ever stuck your dick in her," Talia taunted.

"It never went *in* her. Just near her," Nathan grumbled.

"So scary..." I mumbled, rolling toward them and trying to open my eyes.

"He lives!" Talia cheered, and I cringed at her volume.

"Even Evan knows to stay away from Grace," Emory teased as he pushed against Nathan's shoulder.

"Yeah, yeah." He smiled wryly.

"How are you feeling?" Emory asked quietly. I think he could tell the loud noises were jarring.

"Like I got run over by a car, and then they backed up," I replied hoarsely.

"Here." Nathan held out his hand with two tablets and an uncapped water bottle in his other hand.

"What are these?"

"Just Tylenol. Nothing like the little white pills the nurse gave you," he laughed.

"Oh, my God. I will never be going near Klonopin again. Last night was scary," I cringed.

"I'm glad it was us who found you." Emory's mouth twisted. Yeah, that could have been bad.

"Me too," I nodded.

"Let's get you showered so you can catch up with your girl." Talia gave me a sympathetic smile as I gingerly pushed myself to sit up on the edge of the bed.

"Fuck. I really screwed up."

"Oh honey, no, you didn't. She's worried, but you can't feel bad about a crazy ex making you have a panic attack." Talia's voice was trying to be soothing, but I still felt like shit, both physically and emotionally.

"I'm sorry," Nathan apologized again. "I didn't know who she was."

"None of you did. Chase barely even knows about her. I wish I could have left her buried in the past," I sighed. With an actual shovel.

"We've all got skeletons," Emory grinned. "Some are kinkier than others."

"Yeah, Simone is the opposite of kinky." I laughed, glad they weren't judging me for my horrible taste in women in the past.

"You seem to have caught on fine. Mr. Pink Vibrator," Talia giggled.

I furrowed my brow as I looked at her. She gave us the vibrator, why was she... oh!

"Where is my suitcase?"

"Still at the hotel," she smiled. "They left it at the reception desk. But I should warn you that Kristine was the one who found it in there last night while we put Chase to bed."

"Oh geez."

Cause that's not awkward.

"If you throw these on, I'll drive you over there and then take you to the airport if you want," Nathan offered as he gestured at a pile of clothes beside me.

"Thanks. Although I'm sure at this rate, I'll miss everything scheduled for today." Even if we left soon, it'd still take a while to get to the airport, and even if my flight were on time, it'd cut it close.

"I'm sure Chase can handle it," Talia assured.

It wasn't that I didn't think she could. "I feel horrible that she has to."

"Get dressed, stud," she nodded at the clothes. "There's a shower in the bathroom over there. If you don't get out of here, you'll miss your next flight too."

The three of them left, crossing through the playroom and shutting the door to the main studio behind them.

My head still hurt, but at least I wasn't seeing double anymore. The shower helped clear my head, but when I put on the clothes, I knew they were trying to mess with me. Under a clean pair of black socks and boxers were a pair of leather pants and a mesh shirt.

Rather than going shirtless, I nutted up and put on the clothes. Afterward, I slipped on my black dress shoes and folded up my wrinkled clothes from the previous night. I was sure they smelled horrible.

"Told you he'd put it on. Nice pecs, Evan," Talia whistled as I entered the photography studio.

"You guys are dicks." I could feel my lip twitch as I tried not to laugh.

"Oh, it was just for a little fun. Here." Nathan tossed me a black T-shirt, and I pulled the mesh one off to catcalls from Talia.

"There's an Apple store on the way to the hotel. Let's go." Nathan gestured toward the door as he stuffed my soiled clothes into a bag.

Forty-five minutes later, I had purchased a new phone and retrieved my luggage from the hotel.

"Thanks for doing this. I'd much rather it be you than Adrian." Nathan really was a nice guy. I wasn't sure what I was expecting, but you'd never be able to guess his proclivities by hanging out with him.

"I feel bad that I took Chase to your ex, and she said those nasty things to her." His still feeling guilty showed me that he was a good person, and Emory was right. We all had skeletons.

"I can't believe she showed up. How did she even know about it?" I hadn't talked to her since I got my new phone number upon moving to Connecticut.

"Stole her employer's pass," Nathan said dryly. I didn't even know who she worked for anymore.

"I haven't talked to her in two years," I sighed. I wished that were still true.

"She must have heard you'd moved on. She came at Chase pretty hard. Your girl sure does have a nice right hook," he praised.

"Chase hit her? Holy shit!" No wonder I thought Simone looked like she'd been in a fight when she accosted me outside the hotel. When I'd seen them together in the ballroom, Chase was laughing at something Simone had said. I'd obviously missed a lot after that.

He nodded with a proud smile. "She's probably sporting double black eyes right about now."

"Can't say that I care," I shrugged. "Have you heard from Chase?"

"A few missed calls and texts, but I haven't talked to her." He shook his head. "She wasn't answering her phone, so I texted her. They were on the plane before you woke up."

"I hope she's not mad at me," I sighed heavily. If she was, I probably deserved it. It would be an understatement to say that last night had been less than ideal. It was such a fucking shit-show.

"She's not. Just worried," he assured, pulling up to the terminal at the airport and popping his trunk.

"Thanks again. You guys saved my ass by coming to find me. Lord knows where I would have ended up after that bar closed."

"You'd save my ass if I needed it. Now, go get your girl," he laughed. I closed the door, pulled my suitcase out of the trunk, and went to check in for my flight. I'd be getting into O'Hare around 2:00 pm and hoped I'd make it to the book reading and signing before it was over.

When I reached Boston Logan International Airport and finally got through security and to my gate, I had twenty minutes until boarding.

"Let's see if I can get you to work." I unwrapped my new phone and took it out of the package. Plugging the power cord into a charging tower beside my seat, I tried to power it up. The guy at the phone store had activated the SIM card and my phone number, but I still had to sync it with the data in the Cloud.

Following the prompts, I finally got it to start syncing information and waited impatiently. I didn't memorize many phone numbers, but I knew my sister's. I would have to beg for Kelly's help to get to the bookstore on time.

She answered on the first ring. "Do you need bail money?"

"I don't even get a hello?" I laughed.

"You never call me during the day, so I'm guessing you need something," she deduced. My sister may have been a pain in the ass, but she was a smart one.

"I need a ride from the airport," I sighed. Arranging a car would take longer than I had, and who knew how long I'd have to wait for a cab.

"Wait. I thought you were already in the city. Didn't your flight get in at 10:00?"

I let out a long sigh.

"What did you do?" she asked. She always knew when I'd fucked things up.

"It's a long story..." A long, weird, messy story.

"I've got time. Do I need to make myself some popcorn?" she laughed. Of course, she'd want the dirt before she agreed to help me.

"You're the worst."

"So, you don't need my help anymore? Gonna catch an Uber?" she teased.

"An Uber driver probably wouldn't give me as much shit as you, but I haven't had the best of luck with hired transport lately," I laughed. That cab driver was not amused. I still can't believe he thought I was on drugs.

"What exactly did you do? Expose yourself in a cab or something?" she laughed loudly in my ear.

"No, but I did basically get dumped in a parking lot by one." And roughly manhandled by a beefy cab driver.

"What the hell happened?"

"I had a panic attack, and he thought I was on drugs." Might as well rip off the damn Band-Aid and let her make fun of me now.

"Were you?"

I laughed at her blunt question. "Not until later."

"Anything good?" she laughed.

"Apparently Klonopin makes me act like a drunk person," I confessed. And throw up profusely.

"Oh, my God! I would have paid good money to see that." I cringed at the loud laughter coming through the phone, but I was sure I'd find it funny someday.

"It also makes me drop my phone in a sewer grate and get violently ill. Fun times," I said dryly. Yesterday truly was a clusterfuck.

"Oh man, wait till Mom hears this one."

"No! Please don't. You know she'll tell the book club." I shuddered. Those ladies were brutal. I couldn't even imagine the social media messages they'd send to make fun of me. Not that I'd know how to check them.

"Speaking of, they got T-shirts made," she laughed. Great.

"Kill me now."

"Oh, come on. They're harmless...mostly. Mrs. Elkins apparently signed up for Tinder."

I cringed as I thought about my mother's over-sixty-year-old friends on Tinder. "That's just wrong."

"She's gone on dates, too," Kelly giggled. "Horny old cougar."

"Please make it stop."

"Fine," she sighed. "What time does your flight get in?"

I gave her my details, and then we hung up because they'd started boarding. In a few hours, I'd hopefully be able to redeem myself. I missed the banter and teasing from Chase. She'd become such a fixture in my life that I missed her terribly after less than 24 hours apart.

I ARRIVED IN CHICAGO a few hours later. Kelly was waiting for me near the baggage claim. Holding a sign that said 'Stoner.'

"Haha. You're so funny," I rolled my eyes.

"Hey, I could have put 'Rock Hard' on it," she shrugged. I wouldn't put it past her to do it. Nothing embarrassed her.

"Why did I call you again?"

"Because you looove me." She reached up to pinch my cheek and threw her arms around me. "How did you get so tall?"

"I've been taller than you since I was twelve," I laughed as I hugged her back. It was good to be home.

"You're still my wittle baby brudder," she cooed in that ridiculous baby voice.

"No more cheek-pinching," I leaned back as she came at me again.

"Alright. Let's get out of here. Does this mean I get to meet Chase?" she asked eagerly. My family was excited that I'd finally found someone.

"I obviously didn't think this part through," I cringed, and she smacked me in the shoulder.

"We all would have met her in three days anyway. Mom is gonna be so jealous," she laughed, clearly happy she could rub meeting Chase sooner in Mom's face. "Loved the book, by the way. I read the pre-release copy Adrian sent me. Damn, you guys are hot!"

"I'm not talking to you about this." I shook my head. It was already weird for her to have read my last book; this was mortifying. And that is exactly why I had a pen name.

After my suitcase came through, we got in the elevator to the parking garage.

"So, how many sex toys do you own now?" she asked with an entirely straight face as she popped her trunk.

"I'm gonna go walk into traffic," I sighed as I pulled the handle on my suitcase back out and pretended to walk away.

"Ain't no shame in the game," she laughed, pulling me back by my shirt.

Once my luggage was loaded, I decided to turn the tables on her. "So, have you met any nice guys lately?"

"Touché," she laughed. "I'll stop teasing. For now."

She told me all about her new position at her company on the way downtown. By the time we reached the parking structure down the street from the venue, I was nervous.

"You're gonna be fine. Just stop sweating. You don't want to be like Ross in *Friends* with those leather pants," she laughed.

"I was hoping you didn't notice them," I told her as I pulled at the leather covering my thighs.

"Oh, I already snapped a pic of you in them to send to Mrs. Elkins."

"I hate you."

"Come on," she bounced in her seat as she turned off the car. "I want to see this hot girlfriend of yours."

We walked quickly down the sidewalk and quietly snuck in behind the crowd while Chase was reading up at the podium. I sat behind a broad man wearing a baseball cap in the back corner. A few quiet murmurs started as people looked over and recognized me.

"She's killing it," Kelly whispered into my ear. "I like her. Your girlfriend is a fox."

"Shhh," I scolded, wiping my sweaty palms on my shirt.

As Diana opened the floor to questions, I caught Sam doing a double take as he saw me. Kristine's question was good, but I was dying to ask Chase one or two of my own. My hand shot up when they moved on, and Diana pointed at me, smiling from ear to ear.

"I've got a question for you."

Chase's eyes widened when she heard my voice. I saw her hand tighten on the sheet of paper she was holding on the podium.

"Go ahead," she nodded as I stood up from my seat and came into her line of sight.

"I've heard that while writing this book, you spent a lot of time with your writing partner."

She nodded, and a smile pulled at her amazingly sexy lips. "I did."

"Was that something you'd like to repeat with another collaboration? Maybe on a more permanent basis?" I asked, willing my voice not to crack.

"With him or...?" she teased.

My pulse was racing as I could see most of the room looking back and forth between the two of us.

"With me. Would you like to live with me in a more permanent arrangement?" *And marry me and have my babies.*

"Hmmm. I'm not sure," she teased as she laughed and stepped down from the podium.

"Go get her, stud," my sister laughed as she stood and pushed me forward.

I walked quickly behind the crowd, and Chase appeared at the top of the aisle of chairs as I rounded the end of them. Two quick steps and I wrapped my hand around the back of her neck. Her arms encircled my waist, and we took possession of each other's mouths in a crowded room full of people.

The noise of my sister whistling and Kristine telling us to get a room was lost as I finally had Chase back in my arms.

We separated, and I leaned my forehead down to hers as she framed my face with her hands.

"I missed you," she whispered, tears forming at the corners of her eyes.

"Does that mean yes?" I smiled.

"Hmm. What's in it for me?" Her eyes narrowed, and I pulled her closer to me.

"Just me," I assured her quietly. "You'll get me."

"Sold. You're all I need."

THIRTY-FIVE

CHASE

Chicago

"When did you get here?" I whispered as I cuddled into his side. I hadn't realized how much comfort his physical presence gave me.

After the spectacle of our reunion, the two of us returned to the podium to answer more questions. I couldn't believe he'd shown up—and in leather pants, no less.

We were currently sitting on a couch toward the back of the bookstore. Diana had given us ten minutes to take a breather before we needed to return for the book signing. I felt bad that we'd made the readers wait, but I wasn't sorry for the time alone with Evan.

"My flight arrived at 2:00. My sister drove me straight here."

"Kelly's here?" I was nervous about meeting her, but she sounded hilarious from the stories he'd told me.

"Yeah, she's dying to meet you, but I think she's hanging out with Kristine and Sam right now," he smiled.

"Oh man, they'll all gang up on us," I laughed as I thought about Kelly and Kristine teaming up their powers.

"We can take 'em," Evan grinned.

"Were you serious? You want to live together?" I was afraid that now we didn't have a room full of people staring at us, he'd rescind the offer.

"We already have been living together," he smiled.

"But permanently? How are you going to escape from me?" I laughed.

"I don't want to escape from you. That's the point," he rolled his eyes as he squeezed me tighter, kissing the side of my head.

"What are we going to do with my condo?"

He smiled as he leaned forward so he could look at me. "You own it, right?"

"Yeah, but it's not as big as your house. Living together would be cramped, and I thought you hated being in the city."

"Why don't we keep it for now," he smiled.

"As a safety net?"

He shook his head. "No. So, we have somewhere to stay when we're in the city. Chances are we'll need to make trips in, and why spend money on a hotel."

"Are you sure you're okay moving into the middle of the woods?" he asked quietly.

"I love your house. There's plenty of stuff to do around there," I smiled. "You know I'm going to make you actually leave the house now and again, though—and not only to go running."

"I know." He held my hands and kissed my fingers. "As long as you're with me, I'll manage."

"We'll probably need more than a few minutes, but what happened?" There was half a day while he was missing that I needed to be filled in.

He took a deep breath and pulled my legs over his lap, leaning his head against mine. "I had a panic attack."

"Oh, my God. Why didn't you come to get help?"

"Wasn't really thinking rationally. I went outside to get some air, and she was there," he shook his head as he closed his eyes.

A rumbling growl formed in my throat as I thought about his nasty ex-girlfriend.

"I heard you punched her in the face," he told me, sounding amused.

"I should have punched her in the throat...and some other places," I growled again.

His deep laugh filled the air, and I smiled as he kissed the side of my head, running his fingers through my hair. "She'll probably leave us alone now that you've stood up to her."

"She better." I nodded with a steely edge to my voice.

"So, go on," I coaxed as I tried to return to our original subject with the limited time we had left.

"Abridged version—hopped in a cab, cab driver kicked me out at an urgent care center, a nurse gave me some anxiety meds that made me feel woozy, Emory and Nathan found me, I got sick and passed out, woke up this morning and had already missed you guys leaving, Nathan took me to the airport, Kelly picked me up, and then I was here."

"Wow. I don't even know what to say," I told him with eyes wide at the truncated version of an exceptionally long night...and morning.

"It's okay. I know it was a little unexpected. I felt horrible I wasn't there this morning." Worry lines appeared on his forehead, and I reached to smooth them out.

"I wasn't worried about that. I was worried about you. When I couldn't get a hold of you, it freaked me out. Kristine told me you dropped your phone down a sewer?"

"I'm here now. And I bought a new phone. So, it's all good." He put his fingers on my jaw and turned my face toward him, leaning in and slowly caressing my lips with his. My face flushed as I felt the familiar surge of energy I got every time he touched me. His touch was never going to fail to turn me on.

His other hand slowly slipped around my waist, running the tips of his fingers up my spine. I moaned a little against his mouth, and he pulled me closer, biting at my bottom lip and then soothing it with firm strokes of his tongue.

"Do you have a spray bottle?" Kristine asked loudly. "They're eating each other again."

"Guys. It's time," Sam laughed, and we broke apart. Panting and staring at each other.

"Do we have to? Think we can sneak out of here?" I whispered as I leaned close to his ear.

He chuckled and leaned in close to mine. "I came all this way to help you do this. Shouldn't we go ahead since we're here?"

"Hmmm..."

His lips caressed the edge of my earlobe. "I promise I'll make it up to you tonight. I packed something fun in my suitcase."

I pulled back and bit my lip while I stared into his eyes. "I did too."

"Come on," Kristine sighed. "You two can eye-fuck each other later."

Sam leaned over and whispered something in her ear, and her cheeks turned pink. "We'll see you up there in a few. I can't promise this one won't return with reinforcements if you try to run off."

"I'm willing to bet those reinforcements will be your sister," I laughed as Evan looked over wide-eyed.

"They totally will be. She's relentless," he confirmed.

"But she brought you back to me." I kissed his cheek and stood up, straightening my dress and running a hand through my hair.

"You look beautiful," he said, smiling softly, and I blushed under his affectionate gaze.

"Hopefully I don't look like I've been fooling around in the back of a bookstore," I laughed as I ran one hand down the side of his head and flattened out where I'd messed up his hair.

"The whole room saw us making out less than fifteen minutes ago. Fairly sure our cover is blown."

We held hands as we walked through the aisles of shelving, finally appearing behind the table where Diana awaited us.

"So, they did find you," she teased as she gestured for us to sit down.

A tall, curvy brunette stood on the other side of the room, talking to Kristine. She looked over at us and waved as she saw us. That must be Kelly. I was a little scared of what those two would come up with together.

"I'll go make the announcement. You two get your signing arms stretched and ready to go." Diana walked to the podium, announcing we were ready to start signing books.

The small line that was already formed started to move up, and others from around the room joined it. Evan nervously bounced his leg next to me, and I put my hand on his thigh to try to calm him.

"You okay?"

He nodded, his eyes wide. "Yeah, I'm out of practice."

"You'll do great," I winked. "Just fake it till you make it, baby."

"I'll try." He blew out a breath and nodded, picking up his pen.

The first person in line was one of Evan's die-hard fans. He'd read all his work.

"Stone, it's such an honor to meet you. I've read every book you've ever written," he told Evan enthusiastically.

"Oh wow. Thank you for being so supportive."

"Man, between you and me..." He leaned over the table as Evan wrote a message on the book cover. "I've been writing online under an alias for a while now, and I finally had the guts to start writing some sexier content when you branched out."

Evan's cheeks turned a little pink, and he brought his hand to rub the back of his neck. This was making him nervous.

"That's great!" I chimed in as Evan's cheeks continued to redden.

"And I can totally see where his inspiration came from. If I had a hot writing partner like you--damn!" The guy leaned in toward me and wiggled his eyebrows.

"What do you do? I'm sorry, I didn't get your name...?" I asked.

"I'm a baker, and it's David. Can you sign it too?" He pushed the book toward me.

"Of course," I nodded.

He leaned down over the table again. "I've read a couple of yours, too."

I smiled up at him, and I could see his eyes dilate. "What did you think?"

"That I wouldn't mind you tying me up." He grabbed his book, tucked it under his arm, and winked in my direction as he held his hand out for Evan to fist bump.

"What did he say to you?" Evan asked as he leaned close to my ear after David walked away.

I bit my lip and tried to hold in the laugh that wanted to burst out of me. "That he wanted me to tie him up."

He laughed out loud and leaned in even closer, his lips touching my ear. "You can do that to me later."

My eyes widened as my head turned in his direction. "Seriously?"

"Why not? It's my turn," he shrugged. Our stare-off was interrupted by the next person in line. We talked to our readers for the next hour and signed their book copies.

No one else offered to let me tie them up, but we did get some comments about how cute we were together.

"How long do you think before Isobel gets wind of us being outed?"

He pulled out his phone and opened the texts.

> *Adrian: I thought the plan was to keep your relationship on the DL?*

"So, they already know," I laughed as Evan shrugged. Neither of us cared, but with the sex appeal of the book, they'd wanted us to appear as unattached but flirtatious.

"Can't say I care. I get to shack up with the hottest woman in the room. I'm not hiding that," he told me proudly.

"How did they find out?"

His phone buzzed again, and he held it up.

> *Adrian: Only ten pictures I can find on Instagram. A few are showing tongues on Twitter. You two better start taking selfies. Make them steamy.*

"Is he trying to get us to take pictures of ourselves making out?" I laughed.

"I'm game if you are..." Evan raised his eyebrows and bit his lip. God, he was adorable.

He held his phone out and pulled me to his side, hovering over my lips before he kissed me softly.

"Some of us are trying to enjoy a party here. Quit making me want to throw up." A feminine voice laughed as she flicked Evan on the forehead. The dark-haired woman I assumed was his sister, was standing beside the table.

"Let's see if that gives them something to talk about," he laughed as he cropped the photo and texted it to Adrian. I found it humorous that Evan still didn't know how to log in to his social media.

"You ready to finish up and get back to the hotel?" I asked quietly. I was still exhausted.

"Yes, please, but we have to ditch Kelly first." He whispered the last part.

"I heard that, you douche canoe," his sister laughed.

"Maybe you were supposed to." I watched as Evan devolved back into a teenager, giving his sibling a hard time. Their back and forth was adorable.

"I like this girl." Kristine smiled as she pointed her finger at Kelly.

"Of course you do," Evan laughed.

"Excuse me?" Oh shit. Kristine was giving him the bitch face. "I'm just kidding. I think I'm gonna kidnap her and take her back home with us."

"That's not a bad idea. She could stay in my condo." My mind started planning a visit with Kelly back in Boston. I wanted to get to know Evan's family better.

"Yes!" Kristine agreed.

"Maybe we should sell the condo." Evan shot me a wry smile as he reached behind me to pull me into him. I laid my head on his shoulder, and we watched Kelly and Kristine banter back and forth while Sam looked on with a smile.

"That bet still going?" Evan whispered into my hair.

"Why don't we see how things play out."

I could tell that Sam was enjoying watching Kristine bond with someone. Usually, she was a little more sarcastic and snarkier around new people. It seemed that she and Kelly were kindred spirits.

"Think we can sneak out the back?" Evan's lips were tracing along the side of my neck, the exposed skin on my shoulders breaking out in goosebumps.

"Seriously? You can't keep your hands off each other for three whole minutes," Kristine accused, rolling her eyes at us.

"Just ignore her," he whispered in my ear, placing a heated kiss behind the lobe.

"Who knew my brother had game?" Kelly laughed as she looked at him proudly.

"I sure as hell didn't," Kristine laughed.

"I'm over here taking notes," Sam laughed as he mimed writing things down on his hand.

"Oh my God, Sam. No." Kristine rolled her eyes as she bumped her hip into his.

He put his arm behind her back to steady them both, and I saw something spark in the look they gave each other. It was only a matter of time.

"Why don't we ditch these losers and go get a drink? I know a great place down the street from here," Kelly suggested as she waved her hand at Evan and me.

"That sounds amazing. I need a drink after the fuckery of the last twenty-four hours," Kristine sighed loudly. "Speaking of—how's your hand, Rocky?"

I looked down at my right hand and flexed it, feeling a tightness in my knuckles that was a remnant of last night. There was slight bruising along a few of my fingers, but it wasn't really all that painful. It was worth it to knock that bitch down a peg.

"What did you do to your hand, Chase?" Kelly asked curiously as she glanced around at all of us.

"Knocked out some bitches," Kristine laughed under her breath.

"I didn't knock her out, but I might have punched someone..." I shrugged, blushing a little, "...in the face."

"Damn, girl. Who pissed you off?" Kelly laughed.

I looked at Evan, and he nodded as I saw his jaw clench.

"Simone."

"Simone who—oh! Are you kidding me? Where did you see that nasty piece of work?" Kelly asked as she narrowed her eyes at her brother. Obviously, she felt the same way as the rest of us about her brother's ex.

Kristine and Sam started laughing off to the side.

"She was there last night," I told Kelly quietly, glancing at Evan to look for signs of his previous anxiety returning.

"Is that why you had the panic attack?" Kelly asked Evan, sisterly concern written all over her face. She knew his history with that twatapotamus.

"Yeah," he sighed as he rubbed the back of his neck.

"Well, at least your girl was there to lay a bitch out. I can't believe she'd go near you after the last time," Kelly growled.

"N-neither could I."

Looking over at Evan, I frowned. He'd withdrawn into himself as soon as she was mentioned. I could tell it made him intensely uncomfortable.

"Okay." I yawned, my eyes watering a little. "I think we're ready to get to bed. I'm exhausted."

"Yeah, whatever. Hope you put in fresh batteries before you guys left, Evan," Kristine teased with a pointed look at Evan.

He coughed and looked at Kristine like she'd lost her damn mind.

"Batteries for what?" Sam asked curiously.

"La la la. I don't want to know. Let's get our drink on. Later lame brother." Kelly blew kisses at Evan and ushered Kristine and Sam out the door.

"You two get some rest," Diana instructed as she approached the table. "I need you both rested and focused for the next two days."

"Of course," I nodded, smiling.

"I mean it. No more disappearing acts, and please be on time."

We both nodded, then Diana shooed us out of the bookstore side entrance and into an Uber she'd ordered to take us back to the hotel.

"Would you mind terribly if we took a nap before..." Evan asked quietly as he traced a pattern on the exposed skin of my knee.

"Or I could help relax you to sleep and then after..." I raised my eyebrows at him.

"Fuck, I missed you," he whispered, cupping my jaw with his warm hand and drawing me toward him. We exchanged soft closed-mouthed kisses until a sharp clearing of a throat pulled us apart.

"Sorry, man." He apologized to the driver, who was eyeing us through the rearview mirror. He didn't say anything, but the kissing made him uncomfortable.

Once we arrived, Evan slid out of the car, holding his hand to help me onto the curb outside our hotel. I was hungry but wanted to curl up with him in the big bed in our suite more.

"Do you think we can find someone who will bring us a pizza?" I asked curiously as we stood on the sidewalk.

He laughed as he pulled me into his side. "I'm sure we could ask, baby. I love how your mind works. Offering sexual favors one minute...asking about pizza the next."

"You're so hot," he breathed into my ear.

"Oh, you stop it." His stomach growled. And I laughed as I put my hand on it. "See! You're hungry too."

"Let's go. We can stop at the desk. Maybe we can bribe someone to bring up some Giordano's," he conceded.

Twenty minutes later, Evan and I were moaning uncontrollably on the couch back in our suite.

Pants had been unbuttoned.

My bra had been removed.

And I was mid-foodgasm as he fed me his deep...

Dish pizza.

"Oh...muh...gah..." I moaned as I took another bite. I missed pizza in the Midwest. The thin stuff on the East Coast couldn't compare.

"So good. This is what I think of when I imagine home," he sighed as he eyed the pizza adoringly.

I giggled, readjusting my legs across his lap and leaning my head on his shoulder. "Not your family? Just pizza?"

"You've met Kelly," he laughed.

"She's awesome. I always wanted a sister," I sighed. Two older brothers were a lot to grow up with.

"You can have mine," he offered.

"Maybe we can share."

He took our plates, put them on the table in front of him, lifted me by the waist, and turned me to straddle him.

"You know I love you." He swallowed hard before he licked his lips and sighed.

"I do," I nodded. "You alright?"

"I might have done something." I raised an eyebrow at him. He looked a little guilty.

"Which was?"

"On the last day in Chicago..."

I nodded. "The day where we have mysterious plans?"

He nodded as he rubbed his thumbs along the waistband of my panties. "I invited our families to come to see us."

I wasn't expecting that. My brothers and their partners had full-time jobs, and my dad still worked. They'd all implied on the phone that they wouldn't have time to visit while I was close to home.

"Really?"

"You're not mad?" he asked nervously.

I shook my head as a wide smile spread across my face. My hands cupped his jaw, and I leaned forward to kiss his lips softly. "Of course not. I have no idea how you managed to do it, but I'll take it."

"I knew you missed seeing them halfway across the country," he said quietly.

"You're amazing," I sighed as I cupped his jaw and looked into his eyes.

"We'll see if you're still saying that when you're trying to escape my parent's house full of people," he laughed.

"As long as my niece is there, I won't even notice," I smiled.

"Just your niece? No one else can hold your attention?" he teased.

I hummed as I pretended to think about it. His hands pulled my hips flush with his, and he flexed up into me. "No one else is coming to mind."

"Hmm," he hummed. "Maybe I need to remind you who else will be there..."

I arched my back, and my head fell backward as he nuzzled into my neck, running his nose and lips slowly up the underside of my jaw.

"Mmm. Miguel isn't into girls," I sighed with a little moan at the end. While one of my favorite people in the world, my brother's husband was sickeningly into him.

Evan ghosted his lips along the soft skin at the front of my throat, earning himself another moan. "Oh God."

"Hmmm...he won't be there either..." he whispered as he sucked on the skin where my collarbones met.

"Fuck, Evan," I panted as he traced his palms up my sides, cupping my breasts through the material of my dress.

"So, you do remember who I am," he chuckled, bunching the fabric at my waist and slipping his hands underneath.

As he grazed his thumbs over my nipples, my hips rocked against him, the soft slide of the leather of his pants a contrast to the zipper dragging along the center of my panties. I was hyper-aware of the rough scratch of it through the thin satiny material covering my pussy. I could vaguely feel the hardness he was hiding beneath, but I ached to feel him fully against me.

"Pants—off..." I moaned as he leaned forward, capturing one of my nipples between his teeth through the thin material.

"Just wait a minute," he whispered, using his teeth to tug on it. "Let me enjoy these."

I was writhing on his lap, the bite of the zipper almost unbearable as he continued to tease me. The wetness between my legs had seeped through the material, and I could feel it sliding against the leather.

As he pinched, bit, and sucked, I moaned, his touch sending shockwaves through my body.

"Let's get this out of the way," he murmured as he pulled my dress away from my chest, carelessly tossing it behind me.

"God, yes," he groaned as he cupped my tits in his large hands, caressing them, licking his lips before he dove back in.

Desperately wanting him inside of me, I squirmed in his lap, unable to control the movements of my hips.

"Pants—off... Now." My command was half moaned, half growled, as he bucked up into me.

I rose to my knees and tugged at his waistband, sliding his pants partially down his hips. He released my chest and lifted his hips, helping me work the material down, his solid erection jutting out of his boxer briefs into the space between us.

"I can't wait," I moaned as I gripped him with one hand and pulled my panties aside with the other.

"Yes." I cried out as I slowly eased myself onto him, the sensation of being stretched by him causing both of us to moan loudly.

His deep groan resonated as I slowly lowered my hips, rocking them in slow, steady motions until he was able to slide inside, his cock completely encased in me.

My forehead dropped forward to rest on his as I gripped the back of the couch with one hand and the side of his neck with the other.

Our panted breaths mingled between us as I rotated my hips and began to rock in his lap. He was so impossibly hard inside of me, pulsing and throbbing as I began to pick up speed.

"Fuck me faster," he breathed into the curtain of my hair as I pushed us closer to the brink.

His large hands gripped my hips, and he clutched the side of my panties in one hand as the other encouraged me to pick up the pace. My moans echoed in the air around us as I felt myself start to pulse around him.

He growled curses as he flexed his hips into my movements, causing him to hit even deeper inside me.

I couldn't stop thinking about how we looked as I stared down with hooded eyes at where we were joined. Each movement drove us closer and closer to experiencing the bliss of release.

"I'm... I'm..." I moaned loudly, barely able to formulate words.

"Come on, baby. Come on me. I want to feel you," he encouraged. "Use me. Fuck me until you come."

My hips frantically slid back and forth, his hard cock sliding into me with a bruising force.

I was so close. As I tilted my hips, he started sliding along the perfect place to press on my clit, and my eyes clamped shut. I concentrated on the feeling as he tightened his hold on the material partially covering me. Stars appeared behind my eyelids as I started to pulse on him, my hips jerking as my orgasm rushed through me.

"God, yes," he moaned, using his hands to force me down onto his cock repeatedly.

I felt him pulse inside of me, and he groaned loudly. The movements of our hips slowed as we heaved in quick breaths, sweat building on our brows.

"I love you," I whispered, lowering my forehead to his shoulder and hugging his neck.

"That was—fuck—I love you so much," he panted, wrapping his arms around my back and holding me tightly. His shirt was warm and slightly sweaty as I cuddled up to his chest, inhaling his masculine scent.

My eyes closed, and I felt my body relax as our heartbeats slowed back to normal. I could feel his pulse point on my lips as I cuddled into him, and it was a steady cadence that matched mine.

We didn't need toys or surprises to reconnect with one another. Those could wait until another night—when I didn't need him so desperately.

Chapter
THIRTY-SIX

EVAN

CHICAGO

THE LAST TWO DAYS had been surprisingly enjoyable. Chase and I slept soundly after we'd reconnected. We'd awoken later in the night, and I'd handcuffed her and fucked her hard in that amazing hotel bed. The next morning, we met up with Diana bright and early for another bookstore appearance and signing.

There'd been a little buzz in the local literary circle with the pictures that'd surfaced from the other night. It'd all been positive, and I loved that Chase was finally getting the recognition she deserved. She'd always had positive press before but had been written off as only a romance writer. Having her name tied to mine had also awoken the critics to her ability to tell a suspenseful story.

It'd also been humbling to have a few of my readers tell me they'd been impressed that my writing had grown. I hadn't even realized that my last few books had lacked a depth of emotion until Chase came along and shook up my world.

This morning we were driving to a bookstore near my parent's house on the north side of Chicago.

"You doing okay?"

I glanced over at her out of the corner of my eye. We were flying solo this morning. Sam and Kristine had stayed downtown to sightsee. Diana had conference calls all morning, so she briefed us on the store we'd be at and sent us on our way.

"Yeah," I sighed as I tried to loosen my grip on the steering wheel. We'd rented a car for the day, so we didn't have to rely on hiring a ride-share.

Kelly had already headed to my parent's house to cook for the crowd we'd expect this afternoon when Chase's family drove in.

"Just thinking about this afternoon. I hope your brothers don't try to murder me."

Her rich laugh filled the car, and I smiled despite my nerves. "They're not going to kill you."

"You know they've read the book?" I pointed out, worried they'd think I was taking advantage of their baby sister. She'd told me how protective they were.

"Oh, they definitely have," she nodded with a smirk. "I got some interesting text messages from Drew and Miguel the day after they got their copy."

"Shit. They're not mad, are they?" I asked anxiously. She started laughing hysterically, and my palms began to sweat, slipping on the leather of the steering wheel.

"No! Calm down. They were sending me links to leather Dominatrix outfits," she giggled.

I took a deep breath and let out a nervous laugh. "Did you order any?"

"No, you nut. But I may have packed some lacy things inside the secret compartment in my suitcase," she shrugged.

My eyes widened, and I gripped the steering wheel as I felt a twitch in my pants. I'd seen her in sexy underwear and no underwear but not dressed in lingerie.

"You're going to make me hard," I groaned as I tried to think of anything but Chase in barely-there lacy lingerie.

"And what did Ethan think of the book?" He was the one I was worried about. Ethan was the oldest and, from what Chase had told me, the most resistant to her dating when she was younger. I could only imagine what he thought of me.

"Oh, you don't have to worry about him. He's already one of your loyal fanboys. He probably thinks I corrupted your art," she said in an annoyed tone and rolled her eyes dramatically as I glanced over at her.

I wasn't sure how to respond to that. I'd never expected her family to be fans of my work. "So, how big of a fan are we talking?"

"Well, Elle may have teased him before they found out about you, that you were on his freebie list."

"His what?" I had no idea what list she was talking about.

"You know how sometimes couples joke that if they ever meet a celebrity, they'll give their partner a free pass..." she trailed off.

"Wait. I thought Drew was the gay brother?"

"He is." She smiled, trying to hold in her laughter.

"I'm not even sure how to respond," I told her honestly. I'd never been told I was on anyone's sex list before, much less the straight brother of the woman I was dating.

"Just be prepared for Elle to roast him. She's the sweetest person, but she loves to give my brother a hard time," Chase told me in an amused tone.

"No wonder the two of you get along so well," I smiled at her.

"You know you love it when I taunt you." She grinned back.

Six months ago, my life was devoid of any affection other than my immediate family, and even that was at a calculated distance. I'd resigned myself to a life of solitude in the woods with my words. Those same words that could craft a story read by millions couldn't come close to describing the way Chase made me feel. "I only know that I love you, and I'm grateful for you being in my life."

She reached over, clasped my closest hand, and interlaced our fingers. I knew that she felt the same way. She'd always been much more social than me, but sometimes despite being surrounded by people, you can still feel alone.

When I was with Chase, I never felt alone.

"Are you sure you're not a romance writer?" she teased as she ran her thumb over my knuckles.

"Pretty sure," I laughed. "If it weren't for you, I'd still be putting tab A into slot B. B being my hand."

Her laughter filled the car, and she leaned against my shoulder. "You can put your tab into my slot any day."

"Are you sure you're ready to meet my mother's friends? I can take you back to the hotel," I asked warily.

"Not a chance." She shook her head as she bounced in her seat excitedly. "I can't wait to meet them."

"They're...a little much," I told her hesitantly. That might be an understatement, but they loved my mother fiercely.

"They want to support you."

"Um, I'm pretty sure Mrs. Elkins is a cougar," I laughed.

"So, she probably wants to be your Mrs. Robinson. I don't blame her. You're hot," Chase laughed.

A shudder ran through me at that thought. Mrs. Elkins was very pretty when I was younger, but she was probably over 70. For my part, that was a hard pass.

"I'd rather my older women be in their thirties."

Chase grinned over at me, shaking her head. "Sweet talker."

"You can be my Mrs. Robinson."

She pinched my armpit, and I jerked away from her touch. "I was in preschool when you were born, not college, you perv."

She snuggled back into my arm, and we sat quietly listening to music for the rest of the drive to the bookstore. It was in Germantown, on the north side of the city. My parents' house was only about fifteen minutes away.

I was able to find street parking nearby. After I parked the car and killed the ignition, I took a few deep breaths before I moved to open the door.

"It'll be fine," Chase assured me, knowing my nerves threatened to get the best of me. "No crazy old ladies are going to scare me off. If I survived your bitchtastic ex-girlfriend, I could survive them."

"You say that now," I warned. She hadn't met them yet.

"Bitches better back off my man," she teased as she squeezed my hand.

I knew she could handle herself, but it still made me uncomfortable that my mom's friends read all my books. I'd hoped that having a pen name would give me some anonymity, but my mom couldn't help telling all of them.

Now with the last two books, I was terrified of their reactions. I knew they sometimes liked to read racy books, but looking them in the eye would still be hard. I'd known most of them since I was a little kid, and a few had kids my age.

"Okay, now or never. I'll chicken out if we don't go inside."

My palms were sweating as I followed Chase into the store. I'd been inside frequently when I'd been home before, but it was weird knowing I was here for people to see me.

"Great, you two are here," the shopkeeper greeted us as we walked inside. "We've been looking forward to this."

She looked vaguely familiar; I was certain I'd seen her before. "Evan, it's good to see you again. You may not remember me; it's been about a decade since I saw you last."

She laughed as I squinted at her. "I'm Dorothy—Dottie for short. I helped teach part of your AP English class. Mrs. Farmer is a friend of mine."

I'd been in all Advanced Placement classes my senior year; our teacher had contracted pneumonia, leaving us with a sub for most of the last part of the first semester.

"Wow, that's been a long time," I told her with an impressed nod. I couldn't believe she remembered me being in that class.

"It has," she laughed. "I'm glad you retained some of what I taught you over the years. Folks around here are pretty proud of what you've made of yourself." She squeezed my shoulder and then beamed at Chase. "Don't tell this one's mother, but I'm so happy you pulled him out of his comfort zone. He's grown as a writer with those last two books."

"Your secret is safe with me. He's also helped my writing," Chase told her with a proud smile.

"Do you have another book coming out soon?" Dottie asked with curiosity.

"I do," Chase nodded. "My editor is working on editing the complete manuscript right now. Should be out in a few months."

"She wrote the whole book in six weeks. It was amazing to watch," I gushed as I looked at my phenomenal girlfriend.

"I remember being amazed by watching a very determined young man sit with his laptop for hours in that corner over there." Dottie nodded toward my favorite corner of the shop. I had spent quite a bit of time when I was writing one of my earlier books in Chicago. It'd been before I officially made the move to Boston. Before I'd met Simone.

I shook off the bad memories she conjured and turned my attention back to Dottie.

"I'm sure your fan club will be here soon. Why don't you two get the table situated where you'd like? My assistant set up the promotional materials Diana sent."

Dottie excused herself to talk to the few customers milling around, and Chase came with me over to where we'd be doing the book signing. The store wasn't overly large, but it was packed with books.

"So much for being anonymous," I sighed once Chase and I were alone.

"You can only hide it so much when your picture is inside the back cover. I know I can't hide when I'm back home either," she laughed.

"I'm sorry in advance for whatever they say to you." It seemed like everyone supportive in my life enjoyed embarrassing the crap out of me.

"I'm hoping they tell me a few embarrassing Evan stories." Chase rubbed her hands together and shot me a mischievous smirk. She did love having dirt on people.

"Kill me now," I sighed.

"Oh, come on, I'm sure you were adorable. I'm counting on Kelly to pull out all the naked baby pictures later," she giggled.

"Don't think I won't enlist Elle to do the same for you," I threatened.

"Girl has got my back. She'll never tell," she grinned.

As the time got closer to when the reading was supposed to start, the shop began to fill up. I saw a few familiar faces in the crowd and realized that, in isolating myself, I'd neglected the people I knew who supported me.

Old friends from high school, neighbors who watched me grow up, and family friends. I saw all of them among the people milling about. It simultaneously made me feel warm inside and terrified. My last two books had some borderline taboo things, and I would have difficulty making eye contact with some of them.

"Alright, ladies and gentlemen, let's settle down and let these two get started." My pulse raced as Dottie herded everyone to the front of the shop and handed Chase the microphone.

"Thank you all for joining us today. I, for one, am excited to be in Stone's hometown. I'm sure some of you knew him before he was this ridiculously successful, handsome, professional..."

I heard laughter filter through the crowd, and someone coughed, "Evan is a dork." I was sure it was one of the guys I used to play soccer with.

"But I am honored to call him both my writing partner and now my life partner."

The ladies toward the back all *awww'd* at her words. I knew I felt a rush at her publicly claiming me.

"The last several months have been a whirlwind, but I know he has improved my writing. He's made me push myself and try to grow as a writer."

I grabbed the mic from her impulsively and swallowed hard before speaking. "And we all know she's made my writing better."

More laughter filtered through the crowd, and I smiled as I returned the microphone to Chase.

"That's probably enough of us gushing over each other," Chase laughed as she grabbed my hand and winked at me. "Let's talk about this book and our female protagonist Frances."

Chase read a passage like the one we'd used before, her voice calm and strong, the whole room captivated by her.

"That was wonderful, Chastity. Let's open it up to some questions." Dottie smiled as she borrowed the microphone from Chase.

"I've got one." A tall, slender figure stepped forward from the back of the room, and I immediately recognized Dorrie Elkins, one of my mother's best friends. "This is for Chase, I mean, Chastity."

Chase smiled as she shook her head. "That's okay. I think our cover is a little blown around here."

The crowd chuckled.

"So, we know that you've been working with erotic fiction for several years, and quite fantastically, I might add," Mrs. Elkins complimented. "But my question is, how does a collaboration work with two authors from such different genres? Do you each write certain parts and try to combine them? Or do you write it all together?"

"Well, for this book, we developed a structured story outline first, mapping out the scenes we wanted to include, and then we decided which of us felt comfortable writing a draft of that scene," Chase explained.

"Then we read the scene together and edited as we needed to. Luckily, our styles seemed to fit together well," I added as I leaned close to Chase.

"Seems that's not the only thing that fits well together with you two," Mrs. Elkins laughed, and I felt my cheeks warm at her insinuation.

"I've got one too," said Sharon, another of my mother's old friends, excitedly as she pulled Dorrie's arm in her direction. "What kind of research went into this book?"

I knew that one of them was going to ask this question. I felt my throat tightening and knew I couldn't answer this one.

"I have a consultant I've worked with before that helped teach Evan about the BDSM lifestyle," Chase explained calmly. "He worked with us to develop Frances' inner dialogue and some of the scenes we included."

"Was there any first-hand experience you two drew from in the book?" Sharon asked with an innocent smile on her face.

I coughed and rubbed the back of my neck, my eyes dropping to the floor. I could hear low laughter from the third woman standing in the back, my neighbor Hazel, with her hand covering her mouth.

"We did have to learn quite a bit to get into her head, but I'd rather not reveal any trade secrets on this one," Chase winked, successfully deflecting their inquiry about our sex life, but I knew it'd take a while to calm my flaming cheeks.

The rest of the questions were tame, but Chase still fielded most of them. She was so much better with the crowd than I was.

"You've got five minutes to regroup, and then we'll get started with signing," Dottie told us once the questions were done. "I'll have them start coming to the register to purchase their copies."

Chase pulled me down a quiet aisle and pushed me up against a shelf in the back corner of the store. She cupped my cheeks and forced me to look into her eyes. "You did great. I know you're not used to those questions, but don't be embarrassed. People are simply curious by nature."

"I don't want my mother's friends speculating on my sex life. It's kind of weird."

"Honey, your sister has said they're a little raunchy in that group. I wasn't surprised by some of the questions, to be honest," she smiled.

"It's still embarrassing," I insisted, a little shudder running through me. They did not need to know those kinds of personal details about me.

"No. What'd be embarrassing is..." Chase started, but a masculine voice interrupted.

Chapter
THIRTY-SEVEN

EVAN

CHICAGO

"WHAT'D BE EMBARRASSING IS your older brother reading a book you wrote with your boyfriend he didn't know about, whose main character is a badass Dominatrix?"

Chase spun around as two men, probably a little older than she was, walked down the aisle toward us.

"Oh, my God. When did you two get here?"

The one who'd spoken was slightly taller than Chase and shared a few of the same traits. He had bronzy reddish hair and more freckles than she did, but it was obvious by his face shape and nose that they were related.

This must be her middle brother, Drew, based on the matching wedding band of the handsome guy he was with. His husband had dark features and chocolatey brown eyes, his hair a rich shade of brown.

"Are you two gonna gossip all day, or do we get to meet your man?" Drew asked impatiently. "We rode six hours in a minivan to see you."

"Where's my baby?" Chase asked excitedly.

The darker-haired man, who I assumed was Miguel, put his hands on his hips and raised an eyebrow at Chase. "You better be talking about me."

"Oh, you are too, but I was talking about the smaller ginger-haired one who has all of you wrapped around her finger," she laughed.

"She's back at the hotel with Elle and Ethan. We stole their ride to come surprise you," Chase's brother explained, and I saw her mouth form a little pout.

"Surprise!" Miguel cheered and held out his arms. "Now give me a hug."

Chase stepped away from me and opened her arms, drawing her brother and Miguel into a three-way hug.

Miguel kissed her on the cheek and then leaned back to say something. "You too, lover boy. Get in here."

Chase held out her hand toward me, and I grasped it. "Evan, this is my brother Drew and his husband, Miguel."

"I...uh, I'm glad—it's nice to meet you." I fought the urge to facepalm. Apparently, I'd forgotten how to speak.

"Oh, the pleasure is all ours. Chase has finally met her match," Drew laughed.

"I don't know about that," I told him quietly. I wasn't sure I'd ever been her match, but I was in this as long as she wanted me.

"We do. She won't tell us any gossip. That means she must like you," Miguel grinned as he shook Chase a little in his arms.

"And I'm not going to." She stuck her tongue out at them and put her arm around my waist.

"Put that away, girl. I don't need to know what freaky stuff you get up to with your little writing partner," Miguel laughed as he made a disgusted face.

"Oh, he's not little," she winked, and Miguel's eyes widened.

"Really don't need to know that," Drew laughed and cringed as he looked at me. "You're nice to look at, but I don't need details about who Chase plays hide the sausage with."

"Are you two ready to get started?" Dottie interrupted our little reunion as she peeked her head around the corner.

"Of course. Sorry for holding you up." I smiled at her and looked over to Chase, who nodded. Dottie headed back toward the front, and Miguel started laughing.

"What's so funny?" Drew asked his husband.

"Better watch out for the cougars, Chase. They're eyeing your man," he laughed.

"Speaking of cougars," Chase giggled.

"Don't remind me," I groaned. My mother's friends were still roaming free in the bookstore.

"We'll wander around. Go do your thing," Miguel insisted.

"You ready?" Chase asked as she turned to face me. I felt like she always asked me that, and my answer was always the same.

"No."

"Well, too bad. This is the only thing keeping me from squishing some cute ginger baby cheeks, so let's go," she told me, grabbing my hand and tugging me toward the front of the shop.

"You better listen to her, or she's gonna start asking for her own ginger babies," Miguel laughed. And I wanted to give them to her one day, but I needed to get her to agree to marry me first.

"Don't scare the guy," Drew laughed as he pulled Miguel into his side.

We hadn't discussed children, but the prospect didn't scare me. I didn't want to share Chase yet. Maybe someday.

"It'll take much more than babies to scare me away from Chase."

"Damn, he's smooth," Miguel cooed.

"You two try not to get kicked out, and we'll see you in a little while," Chase warned them.

"I make no promises," her brother laughed as he put his arms around Miguel's waist and nuzzled his neck.

"Let's get up there before your fan club starts a riot," Chase urged as we resumed our path back toward the front.

The line for the signing table was wrapped around the small cafe and down one of the aisles of shelving. The first dozen people who came through were nice and supportive of Evan. He talked and kept engaged with people, but as the book club ladies started to creep up in the line, he began to stammer more.

"And finally, it's our turn," Dorrie smiled widely as she stopped before us.

"We've been waiting for this day since your mom said you'd be coming to town," Hazel nodded. "We may have called your publisher to suggest this shop."

"They said they'd love to have Evan return to his roots," Sharron added.

"Not that we wouldn't have come to find you in the city, but we've been buying your books from Dottie for years," Dorrie explained as my head bounced between the three of them.

"So, are you planning on introducing us to your gorgeous lady friend?" Sharon asked, wiggling her eyebrows.

"From those pictures I saw on Instagram, I think they're a little more than friends," Hazel laughed.

"You don't write smut like this if you haven't been *doing some research*," Dorrie winked, and I wanted to disappear underneath the table.

I sat there and watched them as they kept talking over each other. I wasn't sure how to even get a word in edgewise.

"Sign me up for that research," Hazel laughed loudly.

"My husband looked at me like I was crazy when I bought him handcuffs for his birthday," Sharon told us. "We can't all have young bucks like Dorrie."

My eyes widened as they kept going. Chase had the biggest smile as she kept glancing from them to my continuously reddening cheeks.

"I told you Tinder would be worth my time, Hazel, but no, you refused to believe me," Dorrie taunted.

"I don't think any of us expected a swipe-right connection with that fine specimen," Hazel whispered, nodding toward the door to the shop. A blond man with some gray creeping into his hair was staring in our direction. He was tall and fit; I was impressed that Dorrie hadn't found a creepy one.

"Wow. He is very handsome. Nice catch," Chase laughed as she introduced herself and started signing their stack of books.

"He's French. I knew I had to keep him after the first date. The things that man can do with his tongue," Dorrie told her as she leaned in.

I coughed as they all looked in my direction, and they broke into raucous laughter.

"Wonder what he thinks of our shirts," Hazel mused as she straightened out the plain gray long-sleeved blouse.

"I don't care what my husband thinks of the shirt. He said I could get my motor going however I'd like to as long as I come home to him to get my tune-ups," Sharon laughed.

"I'm sure he's ready to check your oil with his dipstick," Hazel giggled. "Especially with that new prescription, he came home with."

"Oh, my God. You, ladies, are amazing," Chase laughed. I was at a total loss for words.

"We can get you an extra shirt if you'd like," Dorrie offered, laughing as they all looked at each other.

"Should we show him?" Hazel smiled as she looked over at me.

"Of course," Sharon laughed loudly and then winked at me.

"You ready for it?" Dorrie asked with a hint of mischief in her voice.

"Yes!" Chase agreed and sat up a little straighter in her chair.

The three of them turned around simultaneously, and I barked out a laugh. The backs of their shirts read, 'Stone's Snow Leopards' in a bright pink script, surrounded by black leopard spots.

"You're not quite old enough to be a snow leopard, Chase, but we'll still make you an honorary member," Hazel told her.

"Snow leopard?" I had no idea what she was talking about.

"Snow leopard, silver fox—we know we've still got it," Dorrie laughed as she turned and fluttered her fingers at her Tinder boyfriend on the other side of the room. He blew a kiss back, and Hazel giggled. Oh my God. Kelly was right. Dirty old cougars!

"We would've liked to have a longer visit with you both, but we don't want to hold up the line. Don't be a stranger, Evan. We'd love to have you and Chase as guest speakers at our book club sometime," Dorrie told us, picking up her stack of books.

"Consider it done," Chase readily agreed. "We'll have to catch up with you in a few months after my next book is out."

They all waved and blew kisses, and then the mortification was done.

Miguel and Drew came to find us after the crowd thinned out, and I was already exhausted.

"We're going to swing by the hotel to pick up the others, and then we'll meet you at the Stineman's," Drew told us as they stepped in next to Chase.

"Sounds like a plan. We'll see you there," she nodded.

They left the shop hand in hand, climbed into a red minivan parked at the curb, and took off.

"Thanks so much, you two. Would you mind signing this pile of books before you go?" Dottie asked as she tapped a small stack of hardback copies of our book.

"No problem, Dottie. We'd be happy to. Let us know if you need anything else from us," I nodded.

She smiled and walked back over to the register to take care of customers, and I sighed as I sat down and cracked open the first book.

"You know we can't stall all day. There's a house full of people you invited who are waiting for us," Chase teased.

"But I can try," I smirked back.

She leaned over and kissed me softly. I was terrified to meet the rest of her family, but I knew that I needed to take care of some arrangements with a few important members of our families before we left town.

THIRTY-EIGHT

CHASE

CHICAGO

"COME TO AUNTIE CHASE," I cooed as I held my hands out to my sister-in-law, Elle.

"She just woke up, so she might be a little surly," she laughed.

"Oh, she'll be fine. She loves Auntie Chase. Yes, you do, Princess." I did not even care that I probably sounded like an idiot. My little, almost-bald niece was adorable.

Evan was still inside, with both our moms, getting food prepared. We'd been at his parent's house for about an hour after we left the bookstore when my brothers showed up. I was out in the backyard with my older brother Ethan, his wife Elle, Kelly, and Miguel.

"I see how it is. We don't see you for months, and the baby is all you care about," Ethan teased with an exaggerated eye roll.

"I'm glad you're not jealous," I smiled over at him.

"I've gotten used to being ignored by now. Although most people assume I'm the nanny, not the mom, since she got the red hair," Elle laughed.

"I love her ginger hair, but I wish she had more." I ran my hand over the downy layer of red hair on my little niece's head.

"So does mom. She keeps buying her these hair clips. How are we supposed to put hair clips on a kid with no hair?" Ethan laughed.

"It'll come in eventually. She's gorgeous," Kelly said as she walked up beside us and rested her hand on the back of Sadie's head.

"I can't wait till I have nieces or nephews," she told me as she looked at me out of the corner of her eye.

"Don't look at me," I laughed.

"It's only a matter of time," she teased, looking back toward the house.

"We've barely even decided to move in together. Marriage and babies aren't happening yet," I shook my head. I hoped they would in the future, but I wasn't in a hurry.

"That keyword is yet," Kelly teased.

"I'd like some nieces and nephews, too," Elle smiled, and I narrowed my eyes at her.

"Traitor." She laughed at me and shrugged her shoulders. "You already have a niece."

"Miguel and Drew's dog doesn't count," Elle rolled her eyes.

"Hey," Miguel said quickly, holding his hand over his heart. "My dog is an adorable niece, thank you very much."

"Got any pictures? I wanna see." Kelly sat beside him in the grass and leaned in as he held up his phone.

"This was when we first got her. She's a Frenchie." The grin on his face was priceless. He adored that chubby little dog.

"She's so cute!" Kelly told him as she fawned over more pictures.

"Speaking of adorable. Is something going on with your interns?" Kelly suddenly asked, swiveling her head in my direction. I laughed at the abrupt subject change.

"I'm not sure," I shrugged. "One minute they're fighting, the next they're making FMEs at each other."

"FME?" Kelly asked with a frown.

I reached down and covered Sadie's ears with my palms, which made her giggle. "Fuck me eyes."

"You mean how Evan keeps looking at you out the kitchen window?" Elle nodded toward the picture window in the kitchen nook. Evan was staring intently in our direction with a small smile.

Both of our fathers were sitting across the table from him. He looked back after a few seconds, and they continued their conversation.

"You don't think our dad is giving him a hard time, do you, Ethan?" I worried. Sometimes, my father could be a little strict, and I wanted him to accept Evan. He was important.

"Nah. He asked to talk to them both earlier," Ethan shook his head.

"Evan did?" He hadn't told me he had plans to talk to our dads. That was weird.

"Yeah. It's why I joined you lovely ladies out here," Ethan nodded.

"I'm not a lady," Miguel smirked as he looked at his brother-in-law.

"But you gossip like one," Ethan shot back.

"You're just mad I introduced your thirsty wife to the male models on Instagram," Miguel sassed, and we all laughed.

"You can hook me up with some hot male models on Instagram," Kelly laughed and reached for a high five.

"Here, give me your number and I'll text you some links," Miguel laughed as he handed Kelly his phone.

"Does Drew know you're drooling over random guys on your phone?" I teased.

"He knows," Miguel nodded proudly. "Who do you think sends me new guys to follow?"

Kelly started laughing, and I couldn't help joining in. Sadie clapped, laughing along with us. I'm sure she'd follow some Insta hotties once she was old enough too.

"I don't even think Evan knows he has an Instagram," Kelly laughed at her social media inept brother.

"He does. He doesn't know the password. Adrian manages it for him," I told her.

"That's frightening," she shuddered. "He still hitting on random interns?"

"Actually, we think he's hooking up with my editor," I whispered as I leaned toward her.

"Wow. You and Evan are bringing all sorts of people together." She laughed loudly. "Does Adrian have any other hot interns since it looks like Sam is spoken for?"

I laughed. I couldn't imagine that Kelly was struggling for male attention, but I did know a certain handsome single guy she might get along with. It was too bad she lived 1,000 miles away. "Not that I know of, but what are your thoughts on tall men with dark hair? And leather pants? Any hesitations about rope?"

"I'm thinking I need to come to visit more," she smiled widely.

"Me too!" Elle agreed.

"If Elle is coming, so am I," Miguel nodded.

I laughed as Sadie started clapping again.

"Why don't you guys let us get through this book tour, and then we can talk about visitors."

"You're going to need to build a guest house on all that land you've got," Kelly told me. It wasn't a bad idea.

"I can draw up some plans if you think Evan would be interested," Ethan offered.

"Why don't you people let me get moved in before you start planning expansions," I shook my head. Although someday, I'd love to have them all come to visit.

"I can design a kitchen for the guest house," Elle smiled widely. She was a kitchen design consultant for my brother's architecture firm. They'd had a naughty little coworker affair once upon a time as well.

"Whose guest house?" Evan sat on the ground behind me and reached around me to tickle Sadie's foot.

She giggled at him and reached out her chubby hands toward him. "Up...up..."

"Yours," Miguel told him. "We're all coming to visit."

I turned and lifted Sadie around to Evan, and he settled her on his lap. "Hey, pretty girl."

"Da!" Sadie exclaimed, clapping her hands.

"What about me? Am I not your Da anymore?" Ethan pouted as he made a sad face at his daughter.

"Oh, quit being jealous. She calls the guy who delivers the Amazon packages Da, too," Elle teased.

"Because he's at my house more than I am." Ethan gave her a knowing look.

"Since when are we building a guest house?" Evan laughed as Sadie leaned in and gave him slobbery kisses on his cheek. The girl had good taste.

"Since our pushy siblings insisted they needed to come and visit," I shrugged.

"We're going to need somewhere to stay once the baby comes. Your house is too small," Kelly told him with a straight face.

"Baby..." Evan coughed as he looked between his sister and me with wide eyes.

"She's kidding. There is no baby," I shook my head.

"Yet," Miguel laughed.

"You stop it, or I'm gonna tell Mom you want to adopt," I pointed at him and dared him to challenge me.

"Ew." He made a face, and Elle smacked him on the shoulder.

"Hey!"

"You know I love little bug, but nope. Not gonna happen," he shook his head.

"Sorry, Sadie, you're going to have to wait to get some cousins," Evan told her in his version of the baby voice. It was pretty damn adorable.

"What were you talking to our parents about in the house?" I asked curiously as I leaned in toward Evan.

Shortly after Evan had joined us outside, our parents filled the table on the back patio with a huge spread of food. Everyone had filled up their plates and spread out across the seating available in the backyard.

Evan and I were sitting on a blanket in the middle of the yard, Elle and Ethan a few yards away, trying to keep Sadie from crawling over to us.

My niece seemingly had a crush on Evan, climbing into his lap at every opportunity. I couldn't blame the girl; if it were socially acceptable, I'd be in his lap all the time too.

"They were asking how the book tour had started, and if we had anything planned in the cities we're stopping in," he answered quickly. He refused to look me in the eye, picking at a piece of grass past the edge of the blanket. I felt like he was hiding something, but I couldn't quite put my finger on it.

"And what did you tell them?"

He shrugged as he smiled over at me. "Just that I'd worked with Diana to figure out some things we could do in our downtime. No use in wasting our travels spending it all between bookstores and the hotels."

"Do I get to know any of these plans?" Evan was all kinds of sneaky on this trip. I was kind of impressed with his planning.

"Can't you let a guy have some surprises?" He laughed as he leaned over and kissed my shoulder.

"You better not have us doing anything crazy," I warned, but we both knew I'd do it anyway.

"You think I'm going to plan something crazy? I have difficulty getting up the nerve to talk into a microphone in front of a crowd. Since when do I do *adventurous?*"

I raised my eyebrows at him and bit my lip. "I can think of some pretty adventurous things you've done recently." His eyes widened as I leaned in to whisper in his ear. "Don't you remember the other night?" I drew my finger down the skin exposed by his unbuttoned neckline. "Or the time with the wooden spoon?"

He shifted around on the blanket, pulling down on one of his pant legs. "You're going to embarrass me in front of our families."

"Still not going to share what our plans are?" I asked as I bit my lip, looking at him from underneath my lashes.

He laughed as he traced the bare skin on my knee with one of his fingertips. "You're going to have to be patient. I promise it's worth the wait."

OUR NEXT STOP—DENVER—WAS A whirlwind. Diana had us booked for back-to-back appearances, and we barely had time to breathe before she dragged us to the next venue.

"You guys ready?" Sam asked as we waited in the hotel lobby for the app alert that our car was here.

"Tell me again why I agreed to this?" Kristine sighed and looked around, an irritated look on her face.

"Because we're awesome, you would have just spent the day inside your room, and we get to drink beer paid for by the publishing house," I shrugged.

"Sounds like a win to me. Come on, Kris, live a little." Sam winked at Kristine, and she rolled her eyes at him. Obviously, they hadn't declared their undying love for each other yet.

"I'm looking forward to a little bit of a break," Evan agreed, his thumb stroking my fingers lightly as he held my hand.

"But we have to get on a plane at the ass crack of dawn tomorrow," Kristine whined.

"Since when have you gone to bed before midnight?" Sam asked with a raised eyebrow.

"Have you been monitoring my sleeping habits?" She narrowed her eyes at Sam. I knew they'd shared a mini suite in Boston, but there had been a mix-up when we arrived in Denver, and they were put into a room with two queen beds instead of two queen rooms. Sam had offered to find another hotel, but Kristine had relented and said they were adults and could figure it out since there weren't any available nearby.

So far, Evan and I hadn't seen any additional action from those two, so the bet looked like it wouldn't end up in either of our favor. I wasn't holding out hope the situation would improve over the next few weeks.

"I am sleeping five feet away from you, and the glow of your phone makes it hard to sleep," he rolled his eyes.

"Oh waaah, go buy a sleep mask." She crossed her arms over her chest as she stared him down.

"God, I hope the hotel in Seattle doesn't fuck up the reservations," he sighed, obviously wanting his own space.

"Oh, 'cause it's so impossible to spend time with me," Kristine rolled her eyes as she looked away from him.

"Because I'd like to be able to go to sleep without worrying that I'm going to get glared at for every move I make," he growled at her.

Evan mouthed 'wow' at me, and I giggled as I nodded. They were in rare form today.

"They really should screw each other and get it over with," I breathed into Evan's ear as I clung to his arm. Who needed telenovelas when you had Sam and Kristine to keep you entertained?

"Maybe we should sneak upstairs while they're going at it," Evan suggested. I doubt they'd notice if we left. They'd drifted closer, and Kristine was poking him in the chest as he smiled at her. It appeared to me that Sam was enjoying her ire.

"Alright, kids, break it up. Our ride is here. Get your asses out that door," I said, gesturing to the hotel lobby doors leading to the street.

We all climbed into the Uber, and Evan laughed quietly as Kristine made it a point to sit up front with the driver instead of next to Sam.

"Going down to Lodo?" he asked as he looked into the rearview mirror. Lodo was the lower downtown area and the location of the historic Union Station, Coors Field, where the Colorado Rockies played, the Pepsi Center, where the Denver Nuggets and Colorado Avalanche played, and various businesses and breweries.

"Yeah. We're taking a walking tour and then checking out some of the breweries," Evan nodded.

"Make sure you check out The Oxford. They do tours sometimes. It's a really neat building. One of the oldest in Denver, the oldest hotel in that area," he suggested.

"Thanks. We'll have to check it out," Sam smiled at him.

The rest of the ride from our hotel, Kristina sat in the front typing into her phone, and Sam casually talked with us.

"So, you've got four sisters?" Evan asked him.

"Yeah, I'm the baby. They're all older and married now," he nodded. He seemed a little more sensitive than I expected, so it made sense that he had four sisters.

"I bet you've got a herd of nieces and nephews," I smiled.

"Actually, just nephews. My dad eats it up. By the time I came along, he was so excited to have a son to do manly things with, "Sam laughed. "He'd take me camping all the time and encouraged me to play a ton of sports."

"Evan here was a star soccer player," I teased as I squeezed Evan's arm and smiled at his blushing face.

"I don't know about being a star, but it did help me pay for college," he chuckled nervously.

"That's cool. I played lacrosse," Sam nodded.

"Of course you did," Kristine snorted from the front seat.

I could see Sam visibly tense. He was irritated that she seemed so hostile today, but I figured it was pent-up sexual tension between them.

"Oh, look! We're here," I announced cheerfully, attempting to defuse the tense atmosphere.

We thanked the driver and piled onto the sidewalk, finding our tour guide outside the first brewery. He took us on an hour-long tour of the area, walking through it until we could see Union Station and Coors Field in the distance. Afterward, he took us to another brewery, and Kristine had loosened up with a few drinks in her.

"Oh, come on, you're telling me you'd never used sex toys until you met Chase? I find that hard to believe," she laughed as she looked at Evan curiously.

"Why is that hard to believe? You've met me. Do I strike you as the adventurous type?" he laughed, seeming a little less tense with the alcohol we'd all consumed.

"It's always the quiet ones that are really freaks behind closed doors," Sam laughed.

"You speak from experience, Spammy?" Kristine teased him, and I saw his cheeks turn a little pink.

"Wouldn't you like to know?" he asked as he leaned across the table toward her and licked his lips. From where I was sitting, I could see her eyes dilate as she met him halfway, their faces only inches apart.

"In your dreams, pretty boy," Kristine told him, but it didn't sound all that convincing.

Evan and I exchanged a smile, and he squeezed my thigh. This was getting interesting. Maybe I would be winning the bet after all. By the time we finished our tester flight set of beers, we were all feeling a little happier.

"We gonna try to see if we can get in a tour of the Oxford?" I asked as I glanced at the time on my phone.

"I'm up for it. We've got time," Evan nodded.

"Ugh. Actually, Is just filled my inbox with pages to proof. I can't. I'll head back to the hotel and just see you guys tomorrow," Kristine sighed loudly as she angrily tapped at the screen of her work phone. Isobel was notorious for sending emails at the most inconvenient times. She never worked normal hours, often sending back annotated pages in the middle of the night.

"Want some help? Two sets of eyes might help you get through it faster," Sam offered as he placed his hand on Kristine's back. She didn't flinch away or step out of his touch. Obviously, she'd gotten over her animosity toward him from earlier.

"Just us, baby?" Evan asked me as I wrapped myself around his arm, nuzzling his shoulder.

"Sounds perfect," I nodded, my voice muffled by the fabric of his shirt. It was nice to spend time with him doing things typical couples would do. He hadn't even shown any signs of his anxiety cropping up. He was almost a different person than when we ventured out to the farmer's market months ago.

"We'll see you two nauseating lovebirds later," Kristine sighed as she tucked her phone away and stood from the table.

EVAN

DENVER

SAM AND KRISTINE RETURNED to the hotel in an Uber after we said our goodbyes at the brewery. Chase and I headed out on foot in the other direction—to the Oxford Hotel. A tour was just about to start when we arrived, but I was awed by the architecture and restorations they'd done to the building.

"Oh wow, look at her," Chase sighed, and I followed her eyes. There was a couple getting wedding photos taken in the lobby.

"There is a wedding today, so we'll have to sneak into the ballroom quickly, but we can get started," the tour guide explained as he ushered us toward a set of double doors.

Chase had a hard time taking her eyes off the gorgeous couple getting their pictures taken, seemingly fascinated by how they interacted with each other.

"This place is so romantic..." she sighed as we stood along the edge of the ballroom, watching the staff get everything for the reception into place.

Despite our packed schedule, my romantic plans for Chase were coming together, Adrian surprisingly working behind the scenes to get things set up for me once we headed back to the East Coast.

The ring my father gave me in Chicago was always tucked into the breast pocket of my blazer in a little pouch next to my heart. I couldn't risk Chase finding it before I was ready, so I'd left the box with him for safekeeping.

A few times over the last few days, I'd had to halt and divert wandering hands as Chase hugged or touched me, but I don't think she had any idea that a proposal was coming.

I had a hard time paying attention to the tour guide as he told us the history of the building and the several renovations it'd undergone in the last twenty years. My hand kept drifting to my pocket, fingering the ring inside.

The dreamy look in Chase's eyes made me second-guess my plans for New York. I was ready to throw it out of the window and get down on one knee now.

But I had a goal and couldn't wait to see it through. We just had to get through the next stop on the tour—Seattle—first.

"WAIT, WHERE ARE WE going today? I thought we were going to a bookstore," I asked nervously. We had arrived in Seattle, and this unexpected, last-minute surprise was unsettling. My ability to cope with the demands being put upon me had been tested, but this was not something I agreed to when we reviewed the schedules.

"Change of plans," Diana shrugged. "Adrian set this one up, and I've got to say... with the subject of the book, it makes sense. He even sent a package to Sam with outfits for the both of you."

Kristine stifled a laugh as she looked over at Sam, and I was deeply worried by the shit-eating grins on their faces.

An hour later, the five of us exited the hired car in front of our next venue. From the outside, it looked pretty tame.

I was pulling at the seams on the sides of my newest pair of leather pants. Kelly would have a field day if she knew I now owned four pairs of leather pants.

"I feel like a naughty librarian," Chase laughed as she pulled at the hem of her mid-thigh, flared leather skirt.

"You look..." I blew out a breath and took a good look at her outfit. She wore a fitted white T-shirt tucked into the skirt, her hair curled in loose waves, sky-high black ankle boots, equally bright red lipstick, and a pair of red glasses perched on her nose. I was afraid these tight pants weren't going to contain my reaction.

"Like a hot fucking badass author with a sexy boy toy," Kristine laughed as she smacked me on the ass. I glared at her, not wanting anyone but Chase's hand to be doing the spanking, but she was unfazed.

"Alright. I can't do this," I groaned, holding up the remnants of the get-up Adrian had sent for me. "No more gloves, and what the hell are these necklaces?" He apparently thought I needed some leather gloves with the fingertips cut off and several long chains. I guess he forgot our book was about BDSM and not about bikers.

Kristine hadn't stopped laughing but shoved the gloves and necklaces into Sam's messenger bag as he took them from me.

"I think you need to wear leather pants every day," Chase told me in a low, sultry voice. She grabbed the sides of my unzipped leather jacket and pulled me toward her, slowly kissing me and licking my bottom lip.

"We'll be fine. Two hours and you can take me back to the hotel, lift this skirt, and—" she whispered into my ear, and my heart started racing.

"Stop it," I begged. "I won't be able to walk in these if you keep talking."

Diana opened the door to Gallery Erato, and we followed her inside. I wasn't sure what to expect, but it looked like a cool, restored building venue with an art gallery attached. Upon closer examination, you could see the various images lining the gallery walls were all different kinds of kink and erotic photography.

"Damn, it's too bad we won't be here tomorrow. They're having a class on squirting," Kristine laughed, but she didn't sound like she was joking.

I looked over to Sam, his cheeks had turned pink as he stared at Kristine with wild eyes, and his mouth dropped open. I had to admit the concept of getting a woman to squirt also intrigued me. Maybe some research was in order when we got back home. Chase had almost done it when I tied her to the bed, but I was sure I could do better with practice.

"Let's get set up. You're scheduled to start in a half-hour," Diana told us as she led us further inside.

"Want to go take a look around?" I heard Kristine ask Sam as she nodded back to the gallery walls. His head nodded rapidly, and I heard him clear his throat before he responded.

"Absolutely. Lead the way." He gestured for her to walk in front of him, and I laughed as his hand took up residence low on her back as they disappeared around the closest wall.

"You think they've given in yet?" I asked curiously.

Chase laughed as she leaned around me to look at them. "Nope. Still UST city over there."

I took one last look in their direction, and they looked cozy. Sam was standing with Kristine in front of him. They were facing a piece of artwork I couldn't see, but he kept leaning down to whisper in her ear, and his hand rested on her hip. There was no space between their bodies. Chase was right. You could cut the unresolved sexual tension with a knife.

THREE HOURS LATER, I was still amped up as I stood behind Chase while she swiped the key card to our room across the lock. The book reading had gone well, and I was pleasantly surprised by how full the venue had been, even if it made me break into a nervous sweat under my leather pants.

Chase had been sexy as hell as she read aloud a scene in the book where Fanny and Dominic finally decide to shed their labels and fulfill his fantasy of tying her up. I had to try to keep myself from getting aroused while she read the part where he fucked her as she was cuffed backward to a Saint Andrew's cross. While Emory hadn't sent us home with a portable cross, he had taken turns strapping us to one so we could get the full effect.

"Stupid card," she giggled, the light blinking red as she swiped it again.

I reached around her and took it, flattening myself against her back and turning the card around. I slowly inserted the card and pulled it out, the little green indicator lighting up and the lock clicking open.

"You have to be gentle and slide it in there. You can't jam it in and hope it releases," I whispered against the skin on her neck.

"Oh, is that how it works?" Chase whispered as one of her hands reached between us, squeezing my already hard cock.

With how form-fitting my pants were, I knew that it'd be hard to conceal the engagement ring, so it was zipped inside the interior pocket of my leather jacket.

The lights were off when we opened the door, and you could see the city all lit up beyond the curtains leading out to the private balcony of our suite.

"Care to join me outside?" I whispered as I placed my hands on Chase's hips and urged her to walk toward the doors that led to the exterior.

"I thought you were going to bend me over something and hike up this skirt when we got back here," she teased as she swayed her hips.

I stepped closer as she paused, and I kissed along the side of her neck and sucked at the edge of her jaw, eliciting a breathy moan.

"Oh..."

"That's still the plan," I whispered suggestively, pressing myself against her.

The balcony of our executive suite had a metal railing at waist height that overlooked downtown Seattle. There was another balcony above it and solid walls on either side, so it was secluded enough but still a little risky for what I had planned.

"Do you trust me?" I asked as I fingered the clasp of her necklace and ran it along the soft skin at the back of her neck.

"Yes," she moaned as my other hand came up to cup one of her breasts through the thin cotton of her shirt.

"Can I take this off?"

I took her nod as an answer and unclasped her necklace, gently placing it on the coffee table.

Chase started to reach down to unzip her heeled ankle boots, but I stilled her hand before she could. "Keep them on," I instructed in a low but firm voice.

They'd help even out our height difference, and her legs looked amazing. "Walk toward the door. There's something we haven't tried yet."

Chase hesitated once we got to the balcony doors, and I kissed her shoulder softly.

"What if someone sees?" she whispered, her hand settling on the door handle.

"We're pretty high up. Chances are no one can see us," I tried to reassure her. "If you can keep quiet, no one will know what I'm doing to you."

"Are you sure?"

"Positive," I nodded as I stepped closer and whispered directly into her ear. "Look out there. It's gorgeous tonight. Don't you want to enjoy the scenery while I make you come on my cock?"

In one direction, we could see the Space Needle. In the other, Mount Rainier.

"Isn't it going to be cold this high up?"

"Did I finally find something my fearless girl won't try?" I teased, kissing along the exposed skin of her shoulder. Typically I was the one hesitant to try something, but it seemed the thought of a little exhibitionism had turned the tables.

"Is that a challenge?" she laughed.

"Maybe. Did it work?"

She reached up, slipped a hand behind my neck, and scratched the hair at the nape.

"Just give me a few minutes," she requested quietly.

I nodded against her shoulder and started kissing her neck and shoulder softly. When my hand grazed a nipple through the soft lace of her bra, it was already hardened into a firm peak.

"Does the thought of someone seeing you being pleasured turn you on?" I whispered into her soft skin. It was obvious she was turned on, but I knew this was something we'd never tried that required trust. I was sure Emory and Talia would have indulged this particular kink if we'd asked for it, but the thought of someone we didn't know seeing or hearing us was enticing.

"Maybe," she panted as I pinched and plucked at her chest through the t-shirt and lace.

"You turn me on so much. I want to bunch up the back of this skirt and slip inside you," I told her, my voice much lower than normal. "Thrust into you so hard that your grip on the railings turns your knuckles white."

She let out a little whine and pushed her ass back into my groin.

"I want to whisper things into your ear until you can't stand it anymore, and you come all over me, biting your lip to keep quiet."

Her breaths were coming in shallow pants as she wiggled against me. I was rock hard, my cock pressed tightly against my briefs inside the tight leather of my pants.

"But we both know you won't be quiet. And someone down on that sidewalk will watch how beautifully you come all over me. They'll go home and think of you while they touch themselves. But we both know your pretty moans will be only for me."

"Let's go," Chase said in a breathy voice, pushing the handle to the balcony door and swinging it open.

The sounds of the city traffic and laughter from the hotel restaurant many floors down filtered through the air.

It was slightly windy but not as cold as I thought it'd feel. Chase shivered as we walked forward to the railing of the balcony, and I helped her gently place her hands on the black metal bar.

"You alright?" I asked as I ran a hand between her thighs and palmed her underneath the leather of her skirt. "If you don't want this, we can go back inside. It's entirely up to you. I just want you coming on my cock tonight."

"I want you," she moaned as I slipped a finger under the lace and found her drenched for me. Apparently, exhibitionism was exciting for her. I had to admit it had me throbbing in my pants. "Pull them down," she whispered, and I hooked the bottom of her panties with my finger, slowly drawing them down her legs.

Her hands remained locked around the black iron bar of the balcony railing as I pulled her sopping panties down her thighs. Not wanting to waste any time, I quickly unbuckled my belt. It took a few tugs to get my pants pulled down to my thighs, but I gave up working them lower as she leaned back into me.

My hard cock sprung free as I lowered my boxer briefs, the head already weeping at the thought of what lay under Chase's skirt. She startled as I pressed against her, slowly running one of my hands across her abdomen.

"I love you," I whispered into her hair, pushing the loose curls to the side and nuzzling her ear with my nose. "You're so incredibly sexy. Just holding on like a good girl, waiting for my cock."

Her head pressed back into my shoulder. She sighed as my other hand smoothed over the leather on the back of her skirt. My fingers gripped the edge of it and slowly started to draw the material upward.

"Love you, too," she moaned as my hand gripped her firm ass cheek once the leather was up and out of the way.

"Hold on," I groaned in her ear as I grasped my shaft firmly in one hand and pressed it between her legs. Her heat contrasted with the cool night air, heating my blood. While I knew it was possible someone below could see what we were doing, I didn't give a fuck anymore. I was too desperate to feel her fall apart on me.

"Mmmm," she hummed as I stopped caressing her stomach and used my hand to tilt her hips back.

"Fuck," I growled into the skin of her neck, the head of my cock sliding through her wet folds. One firm thrust, and I was seated fully inside her, the muscles of her pussy clenching me tightly. "You're so tight like this, baby."

"Oh God, it feels so big," she whispered as I held onto the side of her hip and slowly began to rotate my hips against her ass.

The lights of the city blurred as I began to thrust firmly against her. Slowly drawing my cock out and then pushing forward, driving her thighs into the metal railing.

"Harder," Chase moaned quietly, the muscles in her forearms straining to maintain their grip as I started to kiss and suck along the side of her throat.

"Your pussy is so tight," I groaned into her skin as I picked up the pace a little. She widened her legs, and I slipped in further with each thrust, hitting deep inside her. "You're so warm. I love how you grip my cock. So. Fucking. Tight."

She released a series of low moans as I talked, and my hips picked up the pace. My free hand found a place next to hers on the railing, and I anchored her to me with a firm press against the front of her pelvis over the skirt.

"I want to feel you clench that tight cunt around me."

"Oh," she moaned loudly as I punctuated my whisper with a particularly hard thrust against her.

"Shh, someone might hear you," I moaned into her ear as my lips brushed against the lobe. "Or is that what you want?"

I rotated my hips, pulling out and thrusting all the way in. "Do you want someone to hear you?"

She clenched on me again, making stars dance across my vision. "Does it make you want to come knowing someone can hear me fucking you? That they can tell how desperate you are for my cock?"

"Oh...God...yes..." She wasn't even attempting to keep her moans quiet anymore.

That was so fucking hot.

I looked around quickly before I brought my free hand underneath the bunched-up skirt and found her throbbing clit. Her moans increased in volume again as I pressed firmly against it and began to run my finger in tight circles against the wet flesh.

"Oh, fuck me," she cried out as I pounded into her and felt her start to clench.

"That's it, baby," I coaxed with a gruff moan as I kept moving my hips.

Her neck arched as I felt her muscles clamp down on me, and her hands gripped the railing harder. Through the haze of pleasure, I looked down and saw the skin around her knuckles turn white as she leaned forward, forcing her hips back into my thrusts.

"Fuck yes. Come on me, baby," I moaned as I moved both hands to her hips and began to ram inside her forcefully.

"Oh God, I'm coming," she whined, cursing as I felt her muscles pulse against my shaft. The adrenaline of what we were doing and the high of being with her amplified the experience, driving the pleasure higher.

My guttural groan was long and loud as I chased my high, pushing into her with a force that made her bounce against me as she came.

"Oh fuck, Evan, it feels so good."

A few firm thrusts later, I emptied my load into her, the city lights blurring and then snapping back into focus as I gripped her tightly. The muscles in her legs were shaking as I drew her back into me, softly cupping her throat as we both panted, coming down from our highs.

"You're incredible," I whispered into her sweaty temple, holding her. "Absolutely fucking incredible. Let's go to bed, baby."

She nodded, and I brought my hands down to unclamp hers from the railing, slowly massaging out her tight joints.

"I don't know if I can walk," she giggled as she trembled against me with shaky legs.

I pulled out of her, watching my cum trickle down her leg as I bent and scooped her into my arms.

"Be careful," she laughed as she clung to my neck, tucking her face into the side as I cradled her in my arms and turned toward the balcony doors. "We don't need to explain this to any emergency workers if you drop me or fall."

I kissed the side of her head as I awkwardly walked toward the bed, my pants still hitched around my thighs.

"I'm fine," I laughed as I walked around the large king-sized bed and gently laid her on the covers. "No ambulance horror stories about broken dicks for us."

Chase looked up at me in the dimly lit room with a drowsy smile. The city lights were the only thing illuminating her as her wild hair spread out across the pillow.

My mind drifted to the ring tightly concealed in my jacket, and I didn't know if I could wait another eight days to ask her to be my wife.

"I love you so much," I whispered as I leaned down to help her undress, gently lifting her shirt and then peeling the lace from her skin. My fingers found the zipper on her skirt next, slowly lowering it and helping her pull it off, as well as her lacy underwear.

She lay there gloriously naked against the white sheets, and I found my finger gently tracing the curve of one breast as her eyes fluttered closed. I stepped back and unzipped her boots, dropping them to the floor with a thunk.

She sighed contentedly, blinking drowsily up at me.

I unlaced my boots before I pulled them off; my shirt, pants, briefs, and socks quickly shed before I returned to Chase and tugged the comforter from under her dozing form.

Walking around to the other side of the bed, I slipped in next to her, gently pulling her to my chest. Her leg nestled over my thigh as she curled around me as I lightly stroked her hair until her breathing evened out.

It took a little while to calm myself down enough to sleep, but as I drifted off, I marveled at how lucky I was to find her, and how I would never let her go.

Chapter

FORTY

Los Angeles to New York

"I'M SO FRICKING TIRED. Whose great idea was it to go out last night?" Kristine sighed as she settled into her airplane seat.

"Yours," Sam shot back as he tried to hold in laughter.

"Shut it, you dipstick."

I looked through the seats and saw Kristine smack Sam in the chest before laying her head on his shoulder.

Yet again, we were on the move about to take off from LAX. We'd spent the week bouncing between signings and spending some time in Anaheim to visit Disneyland with Kristine and Sam before we traveled back to Los Angeles for promotional events.

The four of us had gone to a club last night and gotten entirely too drunk. Chase was feeling hungover in her baggy sweats and sunglasses.

LA was intense. Everyone was gorgeous. Everyone was oversexed, and the alcohol and drugs flowed freely in the VIP lounge we'd managed to get into, thanks to an avid reader of mine.

The four of us hadn't indulged in the heavier stuff, but we had drunk a shit ton of alcohol. Brilliant when you had a cross-country flight at 7:00 in the morning.

"You feeling okay, baby?" I asked in a whisper as I pulled back the side of Chase's hood. She'd been trying to hide inside her sweatshirt from the small amount of light filtering through the cabin.

"No. Need sleep," she grumbled as she pulled her hood back into place and snuggled into my arm.

"You've got six hours. Get some rest," I assured her.

It seemed neither of us had won the bet, but Kristine definitely had a soft spot for Sam. Last night they'd been joined at the hips or, at times, the groin. I was

both a little shocked and impressed at the dance moves those two pro-
duced when they loosened up a little.

Chase had been endlessly amused by the frustrated look Sam had worn
all night as Kristine rubbed up against him. It was probably similar to the
one on my face as Chase sat on my lap half the night in a super short
dress—the wiggling about killed me.

If I weren't so tired, I'd probably be getting aroused recalling the hot,
drunken shower sex we'd had when we returned to the hotel. I'm sure it
was the only reason I wasn't throwing up right now; the endorphins flushed
the alcohol out of my system.

As I sat there staring at the clouds, my brain started formulating a plot.
With all our commitments over the last few weeks, writing had been the
last thing on my mind, but I was ready.

"WHAT TIME IS IT?" Chase's sleepy voice carried softly as she rubbed her face
against my shirt sleeve.

"Our time or LA time?"

She shook her head and groaned. "I don't even know what time zone
we're in."

"You've been asleep for about three hours, so sometime around 1:00 pm
Eastern," I told her quietly.

"How much longer do we have?" she whispered and then let out an
impressive yawn.

I pulled up the flight on the interactive screen on the back of the seat,
and it said 2 hours, 49 minutes left in the flight time.

"We'll get there around 4:00," I responded.

"Have you been awake this whole time?" she asked, sounding a fraction
more alert but still exhausted.

"Yeah. I got an idea, and it wouldn't go away until I got it written out," I
nodded. And the quiet mixed with Chase's warm presence at my side was
the perfect environment to let out all the ideas in my head.

"You gonna let me see it?" she asked as she peeked around the corner
of the laptop screen.

"Let me finish this bit, and then you can let me know what you think," I
nodded as I flexed my fingers over the keyboard of my laptop.

"Is this for our project or something else?" she whispered, her curiosity getting the better of her. I closed the laptop to foil her attempts to sneak a peek.

As I glanced behind us, I noticed that Kristine and Sam were both passed out cold, her nose pressed into his neck and his arm behind her back as she snuggled against his chest.

"We're not in New York yet. Does that mean I won?" I jerked my head behind us, and Chase peeked through the seats, then leaned back with a smile on her face.

"Close enough," she laughed quietly, a bright smile pulled across her lips.

My arm slipped around her shoulders, and I kissed the top of her head. "I promise it's good."

"You know I'm impatient when I have to wait for surprises," she smiled up at me from under my arm. I knew she wanted to know, but she could wait a bit.

"I promise you'll like what's in store for us in New York."

She settled her head back into my shoulder, and I opened the laptop back up when she dozed off again. This was a new genre, but I felt confident I could tell our story.

I WAS JOLTED OUT of a deep sleep when the wheels met the runway at the airport in New York. Hopefully, Chase would agree to be my wife one more day and a few hours later.

I wasn't nervous about her answer anymore, but I wanted this to be special. Maybe all her romantic notions had rubbed off on me. I never thought I'd want to go to these lengths for anyone, but she deserved a little bit of a grand gesture for showing me that the world was something I could handle.

"Are we here?" Chase stirred against my shoulder and blinked up at me sleepily.

I'd finished the outline about an hour before we were supposed to land, put away my laptop, and dozed off with her for a little while.

I could hear laughing coming from behind us, so obviously, Kristine and Sam hadn't decided to kill each other again.

"Yeah. We just landed, baby."

"I'm still so tired. Please say we don't have to do anything tonight," she whined with a little pout on her lips.

"We can get to the hotel and relax. Adrian and Diana have us booked for a press event in the morning and then a reading," I told her. I was glad that today was only for travel. The time away from home was starting to add up, making us all a little weary.

"Is that all we have tomorrow?"

I shook my head, trying not to give anything away. "Not exactly."

"As long as it doesn't involve a sex shop, I'm in," I laughed because Adrian had mentioned us doing a reading at a BDSM sex shop in Brooklyn, but Diana shut it down quickly.

We were so close to being done with this tour. I was fine with the erotic gallery reading, but we didn't need to delve too deeply into the scene because we already had some positive press.

"But we could always go to a sex shop anyway. Just for research purposes, of course," I suggested.

She smiled up at me and cupped the back of my neck, pulling my face toward hers. "That's what we have Talia for. She's like a sex toy guru."

"Amen." Kristine agreed as she poked her face in between the seats. "Girl knows her shit. I won't buy anything she hasn't tested."

"Do tell," Sam laughed as he pulled her back and tucked her back into his side.

"Well, you already know about the one..." she whispered, but we heard her anyway.

Oh, really? Maybe they'd done more than we thought.

"Maybe it was a draw after all," Chase laughed. "Did you finish what you were working on?"

"I did," I nodded but didn't give her any additional information.

"Still not going to tell me?"

"I will." I shrugged.

"Just not right now..." she sighed.

"Nope, but soon," I promised.

When we got to the hotel, Chase and I grabbed a quick bite to eat before we went to our room. Luckily, we didn't have to go to anything tonight. We were all too tired. It'd been a long few weeks.

"Do you want to stay in tonight?" I asked her as I looked around our spacious suite. The perks of being the talent.

"You complaining?" Chase asked.

I shook my head and laughed at her unamused look at the thought of going out into the city. "No, only trying to stay on the same page."

"My page will include that big bed and my pajamas." She nodded toward the large king bed framed by windows that looked out at the urban landscape.

"It could include that big bed and no pajamas," I told her suggestively. I would fully be on board with that option. I always felt invigorated after I'd gotten some solid work done. The flight out here had been more productive than I'd anticipated.

"Hmmm, that sounds promising." Chase dropped her carry-on bag beside the bed and wheeled her suitcase to the closet. "What else might this plan without clothes include?"

"It might involve a mandatory nudity policy for all participants and a full body massage," I shrugged.

"Massage for who?" she asked as she tilted her head, giving me an appraising look.

"The first person who can get naked."

I didn't intend to win, so I took my time unbuttoning my shirt as Chase peeled off her sweats and threw them at me. I slipped my pants down my legs as she pulled off her last remaining piece of clothing, her panties, and threw them at my face.

"Someone really wants to win," I laughed as she climbed onto the bed and spread herself face down on the comforter.

"Get the hell up here, loser, and rub me," she laughed as she hooked a finger in my direction and then pointed at my crotch. "But lose the shorts first."

"Yes, ma'am." My briefs hit the floor with the rest of our clothes, and I climbed up on the bed, kneeling next to Chase's lower back.

I gently ran a finger down the back of her neck, tracing her spine all the way down. She shifted against the sheets as I lightly ran it back and forth across her lower back.

"You said you would massage me, not tickle me." She continued to squirm against the comforter at my barely-there touches.

"Don't be hating on my appreciation of your lovely curves," I scolded her, and she turned to look at me.

"My lovely curves are sore, start rubbing, dude," she mumbled as her loose hair spread around her. She'd taken out her messy bun after she'd stripped down.

I laughed as I scooted down and straddled her lower legs, my hard cock brushing against her upper thigh.

She groaned as I kneaded her lower back with my thumbs, using long sweeping strokes against her soft skin. I could feel her muscles loosen up as she lay with her head turned to the side.

"That feels good," she sighed as she shifted against the sheets, and the soft skin of her ass cheeks rubbed against the skin of my shaft. Each sigh and moan she made was making me harder and harder.

I was weeping and painfully hard when I got to her shoulders, leaning forward to reach without trying to poke her. Not that she seemed to mind when I poked her. Often repeatedly. But this was about comfort, not sex. Even if her little sighs were driving me insane.

"Did that help?" I whispered in her ear as I pushed the hair off her neck and gently rotated my thumbs against her soft skin.

"Mmmm... maybe you need to do the front," she smiled against the soft cotton underneath her.

I stroked my finger along the side of her breast, and she let out a breathy moan. "So, you need a little attention right here?"

"A little further over," she sighed as I felt goosebumps break out across her skin.

"What about here?" I asked as I scooted back slightly and gently eased my hand between her legs.

"Oh..." Her breathy moan was enough encouragement, and I slipped my hand in further, two fingers sliding inside her.

"I love how wet you get for me," I groaned as she shifted her hips, and my fingers started to thrust lightly in and out of her. The wetter she got, the harder I became, my cock begging to get inside her. "You make me so hard. Can't you feel what you're doing to me with those sexy moans?"

She moaned as I leaned down and thrust my hard cock against the soft skin of her thigh.

"Fuck me." Her quiet exclamation into the soft sheets was my breaking point. "I want you inside me. Now."

I leaned forward, covering her body with my own as I placed my arms on either side of her. I shifted so our hips lined up and pressed my dick between her legs. She was wet and ready for me as the head slipped inside, and I moaned into her shoulder. "Fuck, I love you."

"Me too," she moaned as I thrust forward into her, setting a rhythm of rocking into her that had her grasping the sheets above her head.

The angle created the right amount of friction to make my blood pump and my heart race as I slid in and out of Chase. I reached down and slipped my hand under her, finding her engorged clit and pressing on it firmly until her hips were bucking back into mine.

"Fuck, I'm close," I whispered into her ear as I rested my forehead on her shoulder.

With a few more thrusts of my hips, she was moaning loudly against the sheets, her eyes clamped shut as she clenched around me.

At her loud cries of satisfaction, I couldn't hold back anymore as I wildly pushed my hips into hers, triggering an intense orgasm.

My heart pounded against her back as I kissed the side of her neck and shoulder as we came down from our highs. Gently pulling out of her, I settled beside Chase on the bed, gently pushing the hair from her face and tucking it behind her ear.

She smiled at me drowsily, and I knew that I'd made the right decision waiting until tomorrow to propose to her. She may not say it, but I knew she was a romantic and wanted the hearts and flowers.

I hoped she wasn't disappointed if I said something embarrassing while trying to be romantic.

Chapter
FORTY-ONE

EVAN

NEW YORK

ISOBEL HAD MANAGED TO distract Chase for a few hours after our book reading with edits on her newly completed manuscript. It gave me the perfect opportunity to head to the airport to pick up my family. Chase's brothers, their spouses, and her parents had gotten into town while we were at our morning press event.

They were staying at a hotel a few blocks from ours. Far enough away that it couldn't spoil the surprise but close enough that we could spend time with them for the next few days. If we decided to emerge from our hotel suite.

"Hey, you!" My sister exclaimed as she ran across the baggage claim area and jumped into my arms. She laid a sloppy kiss on my cheek, and I cringed as she dropped back to the floor and pinched it. "I can't believe you're going to get hitched!"

"Shhh..." I scolded her, looking around. I knew there was no way that Chase knew where I was, but I still didn't need my sister announcing things into the airport.

"She hasn't said yes, yet," I laughed as I smiled at my parents, who were approaching us.

"Be nice to your brother, Kelly. You know he doesn't like people staring at him," my mother scolded, smiling.

"Well, he better get used to an audience because there's no way I'm missing the big moment tonight," Kelly laughed.

"I'm sure he'd probably like some privacy while he asks such an important question," my dad told her, pinning her down with a knowing look.

"Thanks, Dad," I laughed as I hugged him and then my mom, kissing her on the cheek.

"Oh, hell no, I'm watching it whether he likes it or not. I'll climb the damn roof that overlooks that garden if I have to," Kelly insisted.

"Don't worry, I'll let you watch," I rolled my eyes at my sister threatening to go all ninja.

"Just the part with the ring, though. I don't need to see you two mauling each other afterward," she rolled her eyes and gagged.

"Whatever, dork, you're just jealous."

SEVERAL HOURS LATER, I was in an Uber with Chase headed toward the river. The Met Cloisters were located north of Manhattan in Fort Tryon Park alongside the Hudson River. They used a rebuilt monastery to house some of their Medieval art collection.

Adrian booked us the courtyard surrounding one of the cloister gardens for a little "business dinner".

"Where are we going?" she asked as she looked out the window and saw the buildings make way for the trees and walking trails of the surrounding parks.

I smiled at her and took her hand, intertwining our fingers.

"Let me guess, it's a secret," she rolled her eyes.

I shrugged my shoulders and blew her a kiss as we pulled into the parking lot next to the building. It'd closed to the public a little while ago, but I'd gotten a text that all our surprise guests were waiting inside.

"Thanks, man," I told the Uber driver as we climbed out, and I led Chase to the door they'd told me to enter the building by.

I led her up the staircase into the main lobby and around the corner into the hallway to the Cuxa cloister garden. Our friends and family were already seated at the long tables, the wine flowing with the loud laughter we could hear as we turned the corner.

Chase squealed as she saw the table come into view, most of our family members cheering as we walked up to the table. "I can't believe you guys are all here! Is told me this was a business dinner."

"And according to my expense report, it is," Isobel laughed from her seat next to Adrian at the foot of the table.

"Gotta love having a corporate credit card," he smiled with a nod.

"Did you know they were inviting everyone?" Chase whispered as she tugged on my arm and turned to face me.

"I may have had an inkling."

"Alright. Let's get this party started. I'll notify the catering crew we're ready." Adrian leaned over and kissed Isobel on the cheek, his hand dragging across her back as he turned and strode toward an open doorway in the courtyard. Guess they weren't hiding anymore, either.

Sam had Kristine tucked underneath his arm, chatting with Nathan at the far end of the table.

Our families hugged us before we took our seats and started dinner. Kelly was oblivious to the looks our parents kept giving her as she laughed loudly at what Nathan said.

"I knew he'd be into her," Chase whispered as she watched my sister and her friend get acquainted.

"You called it. Although I'm not sure he quite knows what he's getting himself into," I laughed. My sister could be a handful, and I didn't see her as the type to take commands.

"Be nice. He deserves someone normal for once," Chase elbowed me and settled against my arm. She looked happy. I was so glad I could pull something like this off for her.

"I'm not even going to comment on that one," I laughed as I watched my sister run her hand down Nathan's arm. He was grinning at her with a huge smile. It was too bad they lived a thousand miles apart.

"Elle, where's my baby?" Chase asked as she pinned her sister-in-law down with a knowing look,

"She's back in Minneapolis with my parents. Probably getting the shit spoiled out of her," Elle shrugged as she gave Chase a guilty smile.

"I don't care," Ethan laughed loudly. "We have a few days in a hotel without a tiny cockblocker."

I laughed as Elle swatted at his arm, pretending to be offended. I had a feeling another grandchild might not be too far away.

We spent the next half hour talking to our family, drinking wine, and enjoying the food. After the sun set, the candles on the table and the dim outdoor lighting made the perfect setting for this get-together.

"I love this place. I can't believe that Adrian would find somewhere so romantic for a business dinner," Chase sighed, laying her head against my shoulder.

"He didn't."

She turned toward me with a little frown.

"I did." My voice was a tad shaky, but the look she gave me made it all worth it. She loved this place, and I did as well.

"I always knew you were a softy," she teased.

"Well. Not all the time, I hope," I smirked, and she started laughing. I loved listening to her sound so carefree and content.

"Go for a walk with me?" I asked quietly, looking toward the open courtyard.

"Do you think they'll mind if we escape?" she whispered, nodding at the table full of our families and our work family.

"I think they'd insist," I told her as I nuzzled her cheek.

"Alright. Lead the way," she whispered with a little nod, smiling at me as I kissed her temple.

I grasped her hand, glancing back at my father, who gave me a little wink and nodded his head.

It was showtime.

Chase and I walked quietly along the stone path of the cloister garden outside the hallway with the arches where our dinner was held and toward the side of the building.

She started to turn in one direction, but I quickly tugged her the other way. "Why don't we start over here? I didn't get a chance to check out the Gothic architecture of the other courtyard when we came in."

"Alright," she laughed, "I didn't realize you were such a big fan of architecture."

My arm encircled her waist, and I steered her around the corner of the building and out of sight. I knew people would follow us, but I wanted a head start. "Maybe I want to get you alone in a dimly lit courtyard."

"Oh, do tell. And what will we be doing there?" she asked as she ran her fingers down the buttons on my shirt and let them linger on the one closest to my belt.

"Maybe it's a surprise."

"You and the surprises today," she laughed as she leaned in and gently placed her lips against mine. "I'm going to think you're a closet romantic or something."

"Maybe you've rubbed off on me," I told her, closing the distance between us and kissing her softly.

When we separated, I pulled open the door that led into the Gothic chapel, and Chase tugged on my arm. "Are we supposed to go in there? Isn't the building closed?"

"I know a guy." I winked and interlaced her fingers with mine, leading her down the steps.

"It's so quiet in here. I love the stained glass," she whispered as I led her toward the door outside to one of the lower cloister gardens.

"Come on, let's check out the other cloister." I nodded toward the door, anxious to keep moving.

"What's the hurry?" she asked with an amused smile.

"There's no hurry, but it's a nice night," I insisted, my nerves kicking in.

"Alright, if you're in such a rush to look at some plants," she laughed as she followed me toward the stairs that led to the lower level.

I slowed down as we reached the door that led outside. My heart was racing as I turned toward her and gently cupped her face.

"I love you," I whispered before I gave her a gentle kiss, slowly caressing her lips with mine.

"Mmm," she hummed into my mouth as she slipped her hands inside my suit jacket and wrapped her arms around me. She laid her head against my chest, over my heart, as she hugged me.

"Your heart is racing," she whispered, and my arms tightened around her.

"That's what you do to me," I whispered as I took a deep breath and leaned back from her. "Outside?"

She nodded. "Let's go."

I interlaced our fingers and opened the door for her, letting her pass through the threshold before I followed behind her.

She looked amazing in a floaty light gray dress with her hair loose. I was one lucky bastard.

The quiet gasp she let out as the gardens came into view was worth every hour of getting this plan into place. "What is this? Is there something else going on tonight?"

"Why don't you have a look around," I suggested, my voice a little tight.

She looked up at my face and searched my eyes before she nodded and let go of my hand. I followed behind as she walked slowly along the red brick path and through the nearest archway leading to the garden.

The trees and bushes had all been covered with twinkle lights. It'd taken Adrian and Sam a few hours with Chase's brothers this afternoon to get it all done in time.

I could tell when she saw the roses and her steps faltered. The path was lined with white and red rose petals. In the center of the cloister was a stone pedestal with a single red rose lying on top of a copy of our book. It was open to the passage I'd written when I realized I wanted forever with her.

She looked back at me, and I nodded, urging her to look. I'd highlighted the line that described how I felt about her.

"I'd die for you if it meant you got to live, but I'd happily live forever with you if we get the chance..."

She picked up the rose from the pedestal and turned away. I glanced back and saw our family crowded against the wall, out of sight, waiting for me.

"Evan... I..." I could hear her start to talk, still facing away from me. She brought her hand to her cheek, wiping something away, and I felt a tear run down my own.

It was now or never.

Trying not to make any noise, I pulled the ring out of my pocket and lowered myself to one knee.

"Chase..." I started, and she turned around, her hand covering her mouth.

"I...uh..." My throat felt tight as she stared at me, and I knew I needed to push through the nerves.

The chance of a lifetime with her was worth more than a few minutes when it felt like I was going to have a heart attack.

"I know we've barely decided to move in together, but I want you in my home, our home, as more than simply my lover."

She smiled and let out a little laugh.

"When I asked you, I knew that I wanted to marry you but was afraid that it would be too big of a step for us at the time."

"After spending the last three weeks traveling the country with you, I know it's a step I want now. I don't want to wait."

I took a deep breath, and she nodded, encouraging me to continue.

"Chastity Rose—and yes—a little gay birdie told me that's not only a pen name."

She laughed and looked over my shoulder to where our families stood.

"Screw you, Miguel." She scowled and pointed in his direction.

I laughed as I looked over my shoulder, and he was blowing her a kiss.

"Anyway..." I cleared my throat.

She giggled and stepped toward me with the rose still in her hand.

"I knew that you would be important when I saw your picture for the first time. I knew I loved you when you relentlessly teased me about my inability to write anything resembling a sex scene. And I knew that I wanted you forever when I wrote that line in the book."

I took a deep breath and looked up at the woman I was determined to have in all my future plans.

"Will you please put me out of my awkward misery and say you'll marry me? Will you be my wife?"

Full tears streamed down her cheeks as she stepped forward again and dropped to her knees before me.

"Yes!" she cried, falling into my arms and tucking her face into my neck.

I closed my eyes and hugged her tightly to my chest as tears pooled in my eyes. She'd allowed me to grow and flourish as a person, and I couldn't wait to start our journey together with her as my wife.

"Give her the ring, doofus!" Kristine called out from the stone pathway, and I shook my head with a laugh.

Chase chuckled into my neck and leaned back, cupping my face with her hands and wiping the moisture with her thumbs.

I brought my hand up, the ring lying flat in my palm.

"Wow..." she whispered as she picked it up with her right hand and looked closely at it in the dim light—the stone sparkling from the lights in the trees.

I took it back from her and grabbed her left hand, slowly sliding it into place.

"It's gorgeous," she whispered, looking up at me and then back to her hand.

"Just like you," I whispered back.

"Flattery will get you everywhere," she laughed as she leaned forward and kissed me slowly before grabbing my face and slipping her tongue into my mouth.

Applause started from the crowd behind us.

"Get a room, you freaks!" Miguel yelled as we continued to kiss passionately.

Chase laughed against my lips and pulled back, flipping him off over my shoulder.

"Do we have to invite them to the wedding?" she whispered in my ear.

"I'm afraid they're all part of the package," I sighed with a laugh as I heard Kelly start whistling and catcalling us.

"As long as you're by my side..." she smiled as she looked into my eyes.

"I wouldn't dream of being anywhere else."

CHASE

CONNECTICUT

AS THE MOVING TRUCK visibly dipped with every bump in the road in front of us, I gripped Evan's hand tightly.

I'd never lived with a guy before.

Well, that wasn't entirely true. I'd lived with my brothers before they left for college. But I'd never lived with a guy I wanted to strip down and do naughty things to.

Moving in together had been more of a challenge than either of us had anticipated. Evan was used to living in orderly solitude, and I...was not. There wasn't one thing that was orderly about sorting through the stuff in my condo.

You don't really think you're a hoarder until you have to evaluate the contents of your living space. Writing had taken up so much of my time in the last several years that I didn't even know when the last time I'd sorted through any of my belongings was.

Evan had cleaned out a substantial amount of room in the walk-in closet in his bedroom, but when I started packing, I knew there wouldn't be enough space.

My sister-in-law, Elle, had flown in without Sadie and had attempted to help with the great purge, but when my brother started calling her ten times a day because he couldn't handle one tiny, ginger terrorist toddler, I'd sent her home to Minneapolis early.

To say that Ethan was on my shit list might have been an understatement. He owed me big. Maybe I would be soliciting his architectural services to design a guest house. But I also sent his wife home with a new toy stash—courtesy of Talia—in her suitcase. She could use them to replace him or teach him new tricks. I really didn't want to know which.

"Are you sure we can fit all this in the house?" I asked as Evan expertly navigated the tree-lined road that led to his—our—house.

"You sorted out a lot, Chase. I'm not really worried about it. There's always the closet in the spare bedroom for you to take over."

"Are you sure you don't mind me being in your office space?"

Evan sighed as he squeezed my palm. He'd been surprisingly chill about me moving into his house. We'd started working on another erotic thriller after I'd finished my romantic comedy series, so it wasn't like I'd spent much time in Boston as it was. And technically, we'd kept the condo and not sold it, deciding it made sense to have somewhere to stay when we needed to go into the city for meetings at Vivid.

I'd floated the idea of turning it into an Airbnb, but with the royalty checks that'd started pouring in after Fanny went viral, we weren't hurting for cash. I was far from earning what Evan did, but my books had gained a new market when Evan's readers had their kinky awakening.

While Adrian was skeptical that the older demographic would be into all the bondage and floggers, there were a surprising number of kinky cougars out there who liked to read traditional thrillers and those with a much spicier storyline.

"Your new desk is already set up, and I got the model of the walking treadmill pad you showed me. If I didn't want you here, I wouldn't have shown up in leather pants begging you to move in with me."

And what an entrance he'd made. But I digress.

"But living with a girl didn't turn out so well for you last time, and I don't want you to hate me, so I might be freaking out a little." More than a little, but we only needed one person in our relationship to have a panic attack at a time.

"Breathe, baby." His thumb traced over my engagement ring, wiggling the center stone as he glanced at me before turning his eyes back to the road. "This wouldn't be on your finger if I doubted your intentions."

"But we've only known each other for like eight months, and is that really long enough to make sure you aren't secretly dating a narcissistic psychopath?"

He chuckled as he navigated the small moving truck into his driveway, parking it beside his car outside his detached garage. We'd decided the moving boxes would live there until I had time to sort through them all. Having the living space filled with boxes would surely drive Evan's orderly brain nuts, and I'd spare him from my haphazard organization skills.

His next manuscript was due to Adrian in six weeks, so I'd blocked that time out on my schedule to unpack while he was distracted. Hopefully, that gave me enough time to have the house in order by the time he didn't have his writing blinders on. Because if it wasn't, it was probably a good thing I hadn't sold the condo. Because he would throw my disorganized ass out.

"Pretty sure your crazy would have shown by now."

"Um. Have you not been paying attention to me lately?" I laughed.

Evan parked the truck and turned toward me, grasping both my hands in his. "You need to relax. There's only room for one anxious person in this relationship, and I'm claiming seniority on that one." He had started seeing a counselor again, deciding to start taking a low dose of an anxiety medication once we returned from the book tour.

He hadn't wanted to 'raw dog it'—Adrian's words—and risk a relapse since he was planning to go on a limited engagement tour with his next release. He'd managed to survive the rough start to ours, but I could understand his apprehension.

"And if I didn't want you to live here, I wouldn't have asked you in the first place. You know I'm ready for this. Are you?"

My mouth opened and then closed, my words suddenly drying up in my throat.

Evan had been a live-in boyfriend before. While his ex had turned out to be a spectacular thundercunt, he had experience with cohabitation.

The last bathroom I'd shared was with my college roommate, who had questionable hygiene practices and ran an underground, illegal prescription drug ring out of her Hyundai. She was now a successful corporate lawyer. #irony

"You do want to do this, right? I know things happened quickly, but I thought you were on board with this."

"I do... I mean, I am. Fuck," I sighed, trying to get this conversation back on track. Evan waited patiently, smiling like he was finally the one with his shit together. It made me want to do unspeakable things to him in this tiny moving truck. But there weren't enough Clorox wipes in the world to sanitize the seats.

"Take a deep breath and try again." *Smug bastard.*

Blowing out a raspberry, I closed my eyes and tried to formulate an eloquent response for my charming fiancé.

"I fucking love you." *So much for eloquent.* "And the thought of being unable to smother you with my body while we're sleeping sounds depressing."

"Glad I can be of service," he laughed. "When someone asks about what I'm bringing to the marriage, I'll make sure warming body pillow makes it on the shortlist."

"You can add personal chef to that list too. I mean, if you're making one," I chuckled, knowing he was trying to use sarcasm to relax me. This guy knew it was one of my love languages.

"I'll make sure to show them my apron." He nodded, bringing one of my hands to his mouth for a kiss.

"And the spoon. Can't forget that. It really completes the ensemble."

"Well, we do have a box of them on this truck somewhere, so I can always hand them out as wedding favors. Tell them the bride specially designed it to make our wedding weekend memorable."

During the downtime after my last book was published, I'd developed a bit of a habit of designing swag to give away at book signings. A wooden spoon with the words *Please Spank Responsibly* had been in one of my midnight online orders.

"Yes, I'm sure all your mother's book club ladies would love to own one for themselves."

The Snow Leopards were already on the guest list for the wedding because I knew they'd crash it if we didn't invite them. Several of them had started following me on social media and regularly sent me testimonials about scenes from my books they'd tried in real life. It was humbling knowing your writing was the reason for someone's Viagra prescription.

"Are you ready to get out of this truck yet?" he asked, his nose wrinkling. "I've been trying to breathe through my mouth for the last two hours, but this thing smells."

"You mean dirty freight truck isn't listed on your places to make romantic declarations?"

"Is that what you're doing?" he laughed, reaching over to push his door open. "I thought you were having a freak out over the fact you think I'm not aware you're a bit of a slob."

"I prefer the term Spicy Disaster. Or maybe even Hot Mess. I'm not dirty; I'm just disorganized."

"And if you think I didn't know that before I put a ring on it, you're delusional." Evan hopped down from the truck and walked around to open my door, offering me his hand to climb down. "Let's start getting these boxes into the garage while we still have daylight. I have plans for later."

"What kind of plans?" I asked, following him to the back of the truck. He unlocked the rear sliding door and pushed it up, revealing the dozens of boxes I'd brought. Overall, it wasn't a lot, but as he'd pointed out, my organizational skills were lacking. Maybe we should collaborate on that next.

"Talia sent me a box a few days ago before we left."

"And you hid it from me?" *How dare he.* I thought it was agreed upon prior to our engagement that sex toys were communal property. We'd even written some of them off as business expenses. Research implements were an important part of our writing process.

"She told me it was an early wedding present." He climbed into the back of the truck, carefully releasing the ropes that secured the boxes in place.

"That's all you're going to share?"

Evan grinned as he coiled the rope and tossed it to me where I stood outside the door. "And Emory tucked in some reading material as well. You up for trying out some Shibari?"

Was I ever.

"Fuck the boxes. Let's go research our next book. I have a feeling it will take us a long, long time to master all those knots well enough to describe them."

Evan shook his head as he handed me a box, nodding toward the open garage door. "Help me unload these, and I'll even let you tie me up first."

Fuck me. Living together was going to be fun.

THE END

Also By
E.L. KOSLO

THE DIRTY WORDS SERIES

Foreplay on Words (Amazon)

Book One of The Dirty Words Series
Evan and Chase
Preview of Foreplay on Words: https://BookHip.com/WCJHJGA

Mark my Words (Amazon)

Book Two of The Dirty Words Series
Sam and Kristine
Preview of Mark my Words: https://BookHip.com/QHWGXTZ

Bound by Words (Amazon)

Book Three of The Dirty Words Series
Nathan and Kelly
Preview of Bound by Words: https://BookHip.com/NRRHRBN

More Than Words (Amazon)

Book Four of The Dirty Words Series
Adrian and Isobel
Preview of More Than Words: https://BookHip.com/TARMSTL

MASKED MEN OF SAGE SPRINGS

Accidental Abduction (Amazon)

Book One in the Masked Men of Sage Springs Series
Hudson and Charley
Preview of Accidental Abduction: https://bookhip.com/CDPWXAB
Coming to audio soon!

Illicit Illustration (Amazon)

Book Two in the Masked Men of Sage Springs Series
Reid and Hazel
Preview of Illicit Illustration: https://bookhip.com/CDPWXAB

Smokin' Situation (Amazon)

Book Three in the Masked Men of Sage Springs Series
Annie and Tristan
Preview of Smokin' Situation: https://bookhip.com/FCDAKTZ

STANDALONES

The Midnight Voyeur (Amazon)

Now available in Duet audio featuring Branden Davis-Butler, Cole Eubanks
and Troy Duran: https://books2read.com/themidnightvoyeur
(Wide at all audio retailers)
Spicy, taboo, reverse age-gap, stand-alone – Ginny
Preview The Midnight Voyeur: https://BookHip.com/SZXGKKQ

The Mystery Correspondent (Amazon)

Steamy Christmas novella, stand-alone – Ryder and Stella
Preview of The Mystery Correspondent: https://BookHip.com/XPBVAMB

Meet Him at the Altar

New Adult coming of age, written like a romcom/mystery
Kendall & The Groom
Preview of Meet Him at the Altar available on ELKoslo.com

Website: ELKoslo.com

Instagram: @elkoslo_writes
Threads: @elkoslo_writes
TikTok: @elkoslowrites & @elkosloauthor

Facebook: E.L. Koslo
Page: EL Koslo Romance Writer
Private Reader Group: E.L. Koslo's Dirty Words Brigade

Pinterest: @elkoslo

X: @ELKoslo
BlueSky: https://bsky.app/profile/elkoslowrites.bsky.social

Amazon: amazon.com/author/e.l.koslo

Linktree: linktr.ee.Elkoslo

Newsletter: https://elkoslo.beehiiv.com/

About E.L. KOSLO

FIND THE FUNNY IN YOUR LIFE.

E.L. writes spicy romantic comedies with a variety of cinnamon roll heroes and strong heroines. She grew up in the midwest US, married her college sweetheart, now lives in one of those flyover states with her four spirited children and emotional support/writing companion Bernedoodle, Quinn. Banter and second-hand embarrassment are her jam, so be prepared to laugh with or at her characters.

Her novels combine her love of steamy romance, awkward but loveable leading males, and headstrong heroines with a dash of humor and a little bit of kink.

www.ingramcontent.com/pod-product-compliance
Lightning Source LLC
Chambersburg PA
CBHW021219310726
48971CB00006B/1618